EL BARCO DE VAPOR

Gran-Lobo-Salvaje

René Escudié

www.literaturasm.com

Primera edición: diciembre 1981
Cuadragésima segunda edición: febrero 2012

Dirección editorial: Elsa Aguiar
Ilustraciones: Patrice Douenat
Traducción: Manuel Barbadillo

Título original: *Grand-Loup Sauvage*
© Fernand Nathan, París, 1980
© Ediciones SM, 1981
    Impresores, 2
    Urbanización Prado del Espino
    28660 Boadilla del Monte (Madrid)
    www.grupo-sm.com

ATENCIÓN AL CLIENTE
Tel.: 902 121 323
Fax: 902 241 222
e-mail: clientes@grupo-sm.com

ISBN: 978-84-348-0980-2
Depósito legal: M-42384-2010
Impreso en la UE / *Printed in EU*

Prólogo

¡OH! —se le escapó al niño.

—¿Qué ocurre? —preguntó su padre, echando una mirada por el retrovisor.

—No, nada —respondió el niño.

—¡No me digas que nada! Has dicho «¡Oh!». ¿Qué es lo que pasa?

El niño no respondió.

—¡Te he hecho una pregunta! —gritó el padre.

El niño siguió mudo.

Procuraba mirar a todas partes... menos al retrovisor, pero no había nada que hacer: a cada paso, allá volvía sus ojos y veía a su enfurecido padre.

—Me apuesto cualquier cosa a que se trata del perro —dijo el padre al cabo de un rato—. Me apuesto a que esa porquería de animal se ha hecho pis en mis asientos.

—No son tus asientos —replicó el niño, enfadado—. Son los asientos del coche.

—¡Niño! —dijo la madre, sin volverse.

El coche frenó bruscamente. En el silencio se oía sólo el ruidito del intermitente.

—¡Dame ese perro!

—¡No quiero! —gritó el niño.

El niño apretó contra su pecho aquella bolita de pelos calentitos.

—¡Que me des el perro!

—Obedece a tu padre —dijo la madre, sin volverse.

—¡No!

La bofetada le hizo daño al niño. Tanto, que levantó las dos manos para protegerse de una segunda. Su padre aprovechó aquel momento para agarrar al cachorro por la piel del cuello, y fue y lo dejó sobre la hierba del arcén. Luego, vino y volvió a ponerse al volante.

—¡Ya te lo había advertido! —gritó—. Y deja de llorar que te voy a arrear otra.

Y arrancó.

—Ya sabes de sobra que no podemos tener un perro. Sobre todo en vacaciones. No tenías que haberlo traído ayer de casa de tu amigo. ¡Ya te había dicho que yo no quería perros! ¡Y para de llorar...!

Ya te lo había advertido: a la primera tontería, nos deshacemos de él. ¡Que dejes de llorar!

—Te compraremos un helado —dijo la madre, sin volverse.

1 *Perdido en la autopista*

EL perrillo permaneció un momento sentado al borde de la autopista.

Arrugó su negra naricilla. Aquellos olores no eran demasiado agradables: caucho quemado de los neumáticos y una peste a gasolina y aceite que subía de la carretera con el calor.

Vacilando con sus patitas aún torponas, se fue justo al centro de la carretera.

De repente hubo un enorme ruido, *¡Brrrrrruuuuuummmmmm!*, y luego un tremendo *¡Grrrrrrrriiiiiii!*, y una cosa negra, una sombra enorme, le pasó por encima de la cabeza. Espantado, se había pegado contra el suelo.

El automóvil se detuvo un poco más lejos, balanceándose.

El cachorro dio entonces media vuelta y salió corriendo.

De repente ya no sintió bajo sus patitas el cemento duro y caliente, sino una cosa blanda y fresca que todavía no conocía: la hierba. Detrás de él hubo aún el enorme ruido ¡*Brrrrrruuuuuummmmmm!* de otro coche. El perrillo corrió más aprisa y desapareció bajo unos matorrales, escondiéndose lo más adentro que pudo. Finalmente, unas ramas le impidieron avanzar, y allí se quedó, acurrucado, latiéndole locamente el corazoncillo.

—¡Te digo que estaba por aquí! —dijo una voz no muy lejos.

—¡Y yo te digo que has visto visiones! —dijo otra voz, que parecía cansada.

—¡Que no! Que lo he visto como te estoy viendo a ti. Era un cachorrillo chiquitín, negro del todo. Con unas orejas que le caían.

—De todas formas, aunque lo encontremos... ¿qué quieres que hagamos con él?

—¡Pero es que lo van a aplastar! No lo podemos dejar en medio de la autopista...

—Ya sabes que no podemos tener un perro en casa. No tenemos sitio —dijo la segunda voz.

En ese momento se oyó el ruido de otro

motor, más ligero éste que el de los automóviles. El ruido fue descendiendo y pronto se paró. Luego, unos fuertes pasos hicieron temblar el suelo.

—¿Qué hacen ustedes ahí, señores? —dijo una tercera voz—. ¿Pero es que no saben que está prohibido detenerse en las autopistas, como no sea en las zonas de aparcamiento?

—Sí, señor guardia —respondió la primera voz—, pero es que por poco aplasto a un perrito que estaba en medio de la carretera. Tiene que haberse escondido por aquí.

—¡Esa no es una razón!

—Pero es que puede provocar un accidente.

—Ustedes sí que van a provocar un accidente como no circulen inmediatamente.

—Pero...

—¡Vamos! ¡Que circulen! Si no, les pongo una multa —dijo la tercera voz.

Se oyeron unos pasos que se alejaban, el golpe de unas puertas al cerrarse y un motor que se ponía en marcha.

Hubo un ruido en los matorrales, y la tercera voz llamó: «¡Eh, pequeño, pequeño...!», y el cachorrillo vio unas botas relucientes muy cerca de él. Y se agazapó aún más en su escondrijo.

Por fin se alejaron los pasos y, por un pequeño hueco que había entre las hierbas y las ramas, el perrillo vio cómo el policía se montaba en su moto, daba un gran taconazo en la palanca de arranque y se alejaba con un enorme estruendo.

El perrillo permaneció aún un momento sin moverse.

Todavía no era más que una bolita de pelos cortos y negros. Solamente las puntitas de sus cuatro patas y la extremidad de la nariz, justo antes del morro, eran marrones. También tenía dos mechoncillos de pelo rojizo encima de los ojos, que le daban ese aire de asombrado.

Nunca había abandonado la caja de cartón en la que había nacido. El era el más fuerte y el más despabilado de una camada de seis cachorros. Hacía poco tiempo que había comenzado a escapar al control severo pero cariñoso de su madre, para trepar por encima de los bordes no demasiado altos de la caja y lanzarse a descubrir el ancho mundo.

Y luego, un día, un animal enorme de dos patas lo había agarrado por la piel del cuello y lo había depositado entre las manos de un animal semejante, aunque más pequeño.

Durante algún tiempo había viajado apretado y acurrucado contra el pecho del niño. Luego, habían entrado en una casa desconocida y, por primera vez, el perrillo había podido oír el trueno rugiente de los gritos encolerizados de un hombre.

Al día siguiente, el padre de aquel niño abandonó al cachorrillo en la autopista...

Y ahora, el pobre animalito, con el estómago vacío, buscaba desesperadamente entre las hierbas y los matorrales a su madre, con sus ubres a reventar de leche calentita y dulce, y el suave calorcillo de los cuerpos de sus hermanos y hermanas.

Sin darse cuenta, cruzó por entre las mallas de una gran alambrada.

Y un olor le dio en las narices. Primero débil, luego cada vez más fuerte a medida que avanzaba. Era un olor recio formado por cientos y cientos de efluvios que, demasiado joven e inexperto todavía, él no podía reconocer aún.

Se coló por debajo de unas ramas, se arrastró, quiso ir lo más lejos posible, y no vio el borde de un hoyo que comenzaba justo donde terminaba el matorral. Y rodó como una bola a lo largo de una pendiente muy pronunciada.

Rodó a más y mejor durante unos segundos.

Felizmente para él, su caída terminó en un charco poco profundo de agua y barro. Se sentó en medio del charco, y miró y olfateó a su alrededor.

Era un paisaje muy raro.

Allí había neumáticos negros y usados, montañas de cajas de cartón parecidas a aquélla en la que él había comenzado su existencia, residuos informes de mil colores y chasis de unos aparatos cuyo uso ni conocía ni jamás conocería.

Y por encima de todo aquello flotaba una mezcla de olores que a veces asqueaban a su pequeña naricilla recién estrenada, y otras veces le llenaban de contento. Arrugó su nariz, volvió la cabeza de un lado y del otro. En medio de aquel mar de olores que llegaban hasta él, acababa de distinguir uno que conocía muy bien: el olor de la leche.

Seleccionándolo de entre todos los otros olores, lo siguió. Y dio, por fin, con un montón de cajas de cartón que desprendían, todas, aquel olor tan bueno.

Comenzó a lamer suavemente las aberturas. Luego, furioso al ver que aquello no le alimentaba, se puso a desgarrar las cajas con sus pequeños y afilados dientes.

Actuando así, acabó por encontrar suficiente líquido como para calmar su estómago.

Y, satisfecho, levantó entonces su cabeza.

Frente a él, encaramado en lo alto de una lata oxidada de conserva, vio un extraño animal que antes nunca había visto. Un extraño animal que lo miraba con unos ojillos penetrantes y crueles.

Una rata.

2 Cómo fue bautizado Tritus

ERA una rata enorme, una vieja rata toda llena de cicatrices.

Estaba mirando al cachorro con sus ojillos vivos y sin piedad, y diciéndose que allí tenía un magnífico postre, tan tierno, tan fresco, después de todos los desperdicios con que acababa de alimentarse.

El cachorro, la mar de tranquilo, creyó que la rata sería alguna especie de perro. Por primera vez en su vida, salió de su garganta un pequeño ladrido amistoso.

Pero la vieja rata no era animal que se asustase con los primeros ladridos tímidos de un perrillo, y se acercó, arrastrando por el suelo su larga cola callosa. Entonces, el cachorro ladró otra vez, con voz algo menos tranquila. Y retrocedió un poco.

Sin hacer ruido, sin previo aviso, la rata se le abalanzó y le mordió profundamente en la oreja derecha.

El cachorro lanzó un aullido y echó a correr con toda la rapidez que le permitían sus cortas patas, a lo largo del basurero, con la enorme rata pegada a sus talones.

En un momento dado, al pasar por delante de un montón de apestosas inmundicias, vio con desesperación cómo salían otras ratas que, a su vez, se lanzaban también en su persecución.

Corrió durante un largo rato, como hasta entonces nunca había corrido. Su corazón, chiquitín, martilleaba frenéticamente contra sus costillas.

Sentía que ya no podía más. Entonces vio la boca abierta de una lata grande de conservas, y allá se metió y se echó jadeando.

Las ratas se plantaron en círculo a cierta distancia de la lata de conserva.

La vieja rata se destacó del grupo y se dirigió sin miedo hacia el refugio del cachorro.

Entonces, éste, desesperado, se abalanzó contra la rata con su pequeña boca abierta, como lo hacía cuando jugaba con sus hermanos y hermanas. El sabía que sus dientes minúsculos podían hacer daño, porque, más de una vez, su madre había tenido que regañarle por apretar demasiado fuerte con ellos en las orejas o en las patas de los otros. Pero ahora, ahora quería hacer daño, vengarse del miedo que tenía y de su oreja atravesada.

Los dientecillos penetraron con fuerza en la pata de la rata que, sorprendida ante aquel ataque, pegó un bote como un resorte y, al saltar, se desgarró la piel de la espalda con el borde cortante de la lata de conservas.

Al ver llegar a su jefe sangrando abundantemente, las otras ratas, prudentes, ensancharon el círculo.

El perrito había retrocedido y las ratas no veían más que sus dos ojillos que brillaban en la oscuridad.

Los roedores parecieron deliberar, y después, de repente, pasaron todos al ataque al mismo tiempo.

Pero en aquel instante se oyeron unos ladridos furiosos; un perro saltó en medio del círculo y, con los dientes y con las patas, arremetió contra las ratas.

Estas, llenas de heridas, tomaron las de Villadiego sin decir ni pío.

El perro continuó un momento con el lomo erizado; de su garganta salía un gruñido sordo, y miraba en dirección hacia adonde habían huido las ratas.

Luego, los pelos del lomo volvieron a su posición normal, movió dos o tres veces el rabo como si estuviese contento de sí mismo, se sentó y, con su pata trasera, empezó a buscarse una pulga.

Desde el fondo de su lata, el cachorrillo, lanzó un gemido.

El perro levantó las orejas, atento.

Era un perro de talla media, blanco y canelo, con una cola fina. Su hocico, ligeramente achatado, estaba encuadrado por dos largas, muy largas orejas marrones. Tenía el pelo corto y los flancos delgados. Al descubrir al cachorro, sus morros se levantaron y se arrugaron como si estuviese riéndose, enseñando unos colmillos amarillentos y desgastados. Era un perro viejo, con aire cansado y de mal alimentado.

El cachorrillo gimió más fuerte todavía, avanzando hacia la boca de la lata.

—¿Pero esto qué es? —gruñó el perro viejo acercándose para olerlo—. Así que era contigo con quien se estaban metiendo esas ratas cobardes... ¡Si llego a saberlo, las mato a todas! —y lanzó un sonoro

ladrido en dirección del fondo de aquel basurero.

—A ver, sal, que te vea un poco —dijo luego.

Fiándose de aquel perro que hablaba el lenguaje de su madre, el pequeño se acercó.

—¡Pero si te han herido esos asquerosos! —exclamó el viejo—. Tan cierto como me llamo Pompón que como coja alguna vez a uno de ésos...

No, acabó la amenaza, pero lanzó un nuevo ladrido de desafío.

El perrillo, asustado, retrocedió un poco.

—No tengas miedo —le dijo Pompón.

Y, despacito, se puso a lamer la oreja herida del cachorro.

Cuando la herida dejó de sangrar, el perro viejo se tumbó y el pequeño fue y se acostó entre sus patas delanteras, donde le gustaba echarse, en la caja de cartón donde había nacido, entre las patas de su madre, sitio que disputaba con éxito a sus hermanos y hermanas.

—Y a todo esto... ¿qué hacías tú aquí? ¿No podías haberte quedado junto a las tetillas de tu madre? Sí, ya sé, aún eres demasiado pequeño para saber hablar... En todo caso, no ha sido tu madre la que te ha traído hasta aquí. No, tú hueles a hombre. ¡Como haya sido un hombre el que te ha traído...!

Y una vez más enseñó los dientes y gruñó ferozmente.

—¿O, acaso, has venido solo...? Bueno, da igual, lo que tienes que hacer ahora es volverte a tu casa.

Al oír hablar de su madre, el cachorrillo se había levantado y se había arrimado a la barriga del perro.

—¡Eh, eh! ¿Pero qué estás haciendo...? ¡Que yo no soy tu madre para que mames! Además, soy un perro, no una perra. ¡Chico, para, que me haces cosquillas!

Y riéndose con sus labios contraídos, alejó un poco al perrillo con el hocico.

—¡Hala, vete a tu casa! Me quedaré aquí hasta que te vayas, y mientras yo esté aquí, las ratas no te harán nada.

El perrito le oía, doblada la cabeza con un aire muy cómico.

—¡Hale, largo de aquí, fuera! ¡Vete, vuélvete a casa de tu madre!

Pero como el cachorro no se movía, Pompón sacó su voz gruesa y le ladró.

El perrito, sorprendido, retrocedió al instante, con su pequeño rabo entre las piernas, y se detuvo un poco más lejos.

—¡Que te vayas! —gruñó una vez más el viejo perro.

El cachorro gimió en voz bajita.

Pompón se puso a reflexionar arrugando la frente y rascándosela con una de sus patas traseras.

—Ya... Comprendo —dijo al fin—. Eres un perrillo abandonado. Estás solo. Como yo. Yo te llevaría conmigo, pero es que eres demasiado pequeño. En fin, haremos lo posible por encontrar alguien que se ocupe de ti. ¡Ven!

El cachorro no se movió.

—Te digo que puedes venir conmigo —repitió el viejo perro—. Y antes que nada, ¿cómo te llamas...? Bueno, claro, aún no hablas... Espera... te llamaré... «Cachorrillo-Negro-Encontrado-En-Los-Detritus». Sí señor, ese será tu nombre. Y para que sea más corto, te llamaré «Tritus». ¡Ven acá, Tritus!

Y el viejo perro echó a andar.

Confiado, el cachorro le siguió, pegado a sus talones.

3 *Pompón*

ANDUVIERON largo rato.

Poco a poco el cielo se oscureció y las sombras se hicieron más alargadas. Se levantó viento y el ambiente refrescó algo.

El viejo perro caminaba delante, sin volver la cabeza. A sus espaldas oía el trotecillo ligero del cachorro.

Más tarde, dos o tres veces, le oyó tropezar y caer.

—¿Estás cansado, Tritus? —preguntó deteniéndose—. Sí, ciertamente estás fatigado. Yo, también. Ya no soy joven, ¿sabes?, y mis viejas patas ya no son lo que eran.

Fueron a refugiarse debajo de un matorral. Pompón dio cuatro o cinco vueltas sobre sí mismo antes de acostarse en un lecho de hojas secas, y Tritus le imitó antes de enroscarse como una bola contra el costado de su amigo.

—Aprendes rápido, ¿eh? —le dijo Pompón riendo—. Ahora, descansemos. Mañana, aún tendremos que andar bastante hasta encontrar un sitio donde te adopten.

El cachorrillo lanzó un gemido de satisfacción, sus párpados guiñaron una o dos veces y se durmió al instante.

—¡Juventud, juventud...! —murmuró el viejo Pompón—. ¡Si yo pudiese dormirme así...! Pero hay demasiadas cosas dentro de mi cabeza...

Y con los ojos abiertos en la oscuridad, sintiendo a su lado la respiración tranquila y reposada del perrillo, el viejo Pompón se puso a pensar en su vida.

De nuevo se veía —¡de eso hacía tiempo, tanto tiempo!— como un joven cachorro tímido, igual que el pequeño Tritus. Luego, joven perro lleno de vida que sólo pensaba en juguetear. Veía luego a su amo, que le conducía a su casa atado al extremo de una cuerda, y las buenas raciones de comida que le daba, y las caricias de su mano, suave, sobre su cabeza, y también a su viejo amigo el gato Gruñón, con quien se entendía bien.

Todos esos recuerdos felices le venían a la memoria y, dos o tres veces, no demasiado fuerte para no despertar a Tritus, lanzó unos gemidos suaves al evocarlos.

Pero luego se acababan de golpe los recuerdos felices y acudían a su memoria los malos tiempos. Un día, su amo se acostó y ya no le siguió nunca más, a pesar de que él se le acercaba con la correa en la boca, invitándole a salir de paseo. Su mano era débil, muy débil, cuando la ponía sobre su cabeza.

Y una tarde ya no se movió más. Vinieron hombres vestidos de negro y con un olor muy raro, y metieron a su amo en una caja. Luego, la caja la metieron en un agujero.

Y vino después el nuevo amo, y las patadas, y la comida ruin y escasa, y los gritos continuos.

Y también volvía a ver aquel día en que, medio muerto de hambre, robó de encima de la mesa un trozo de carne; y los ojos asesinos de aquel hombre, y el fusil apuntando hacia él. Y su fuga entonces, adelante, siempre adelante, con toda la rapidez que le permitían sus viejas patas cansadas.

Y su vida errante desde entonces, sin esperanzas, hasta el día en que encontró a Gran-Setter-Marrón.

Gran-Setter-Marrón era un perro que había vivido y viajado mucho. Había vivido con los hombres, pero también había vivido solo. En su cuerpo llevaba cicatrices de palos, cicatrices de golpes con una horca y mordiscos. E incluso, encima del lomo, la larga cicatriz de un disparo que le dieron un día en que se metió demasiado en un coto de caza.

El fue quien le habló de Gran-Lobo-Salvaje.

—Gran-Lobo-Salvaje —le dijo—, es el antepasado de todos nosotros, de todos los perros. Hace tiempo, muchísimo tiempo, todos nosotros éramos lobos, libres, orgullosos. Pero un día nos capturó el hombre y, poco a poco, nos ha ido cambiando para que le sirvamos. Nos ha hecho fieros para que ataquemos a otros hombres. Nos ha hecho cazadores para que le demos de comer. Nos ha hecho guardianes para que cuidemos sus rebaños. Nos ha hecho pequeñitos para que sirvamos de juguete a sus hijos, o de hijos a los hombres y mujeres que no tienen. Pero, en el fondo, todavía somos lobos libres y fieros, y nuestro antepasado es Gran-Lobo-Salvaje.

—¡Gran-Lobo-Salvaje! —había murmurado Pompón—. Es una bonita leyenda.

—A lo mejor es más que una simple leyenda —había contestado Gran-Setter-Marrón—. Yo he oído decir en mis viajes que Gran-Lobo-Salvaje sigue todavía allá arriba, en los negros bosques de la montaña, allá adonde nunca va el hombre. Allí está todavía, aguardándonos siempre.

Gran-Setter-Marrón se había ido igual que había venido, sin decir ni adiós.

Y con la mayor naturalidad del mundo, como si desde siempre hubiese estado aguardando aquel momento, Pompón había vuelto el hocico hacia el norte y se había lanzado a la búsqueda de Gran-Lobo-Salvaje.

Hacía ya varias semanas que había emprendido su viaje, alimentándose en los enormes montones de basura que los hombres dejan por todas partes, durmiendo dentro de los setos, evitando los pueblos y las casas; hacia el norte, siempre hacia el norte.

Volvió la cabeza para mirar a Tritus con ternura y le pasó despacito la lengua por el hocico. Entre sueños, el cachorro dio un gemido de felicidad.

—¿Pero qué voy a hacer yo con éste? —se preguntó Pompón—. Es demasiado pequeño para venir conmigo. Además, no puedo perder mucho tiempo en buscarle un refugio. Me siento viejo, sé que ya no me queda mucho tiempo. Y yo quiero ver a Gran-Lobo-Salvaje antes de morir. ¿Qué haré con este perrillo?

Y con esta pregunta, lanzando un profundo suspiro de cansancio, se hundió por fin en el sueño.

4 *Cómo Pompón y Tritus encontraron a Mally-Pop*

AL día siguiente, al despertarse, Tritus empezó a meter su hociquillo por entre los pelos de la barriga de Pompón.

—¡Eh, eh, alto ahí! —gruñó éste—. Ya te dije que no hay nada que mamar. ¡Que soy un perro, hijo, un perro, no una perra!

Tritus se le quedó mirando debajo de su hocico, la cabeza doblada, con aire de estar diciéndole:

—De acuerdo, lo comprendo, no se puede mamar... pero, a pesar de todo, ¡tengo hambre!

El viejo perro se sacudió, se aseó rápidamente a base de unas rápidas lametadas, imitado punto por punto por el pequeño.

—Tienes razón —dijo finalmente—. Es preciso encontrar algo que comer. Y también tenemos que encontrar un sitio donde dejarte. Compréndelo, lo he pensado bien, realmente no puedes venir conmigo a buscar a Gran-Lobo-Salvaje. Eres demasiado pequeño.

Husmeó el aire, volviendo la cabeza a todos los lados.

—Por allá hay un pueblo —dijo finalmente, señalando en una dirección—. No está del todo en mi itinerario, pero, en fin, quien dice pueblo dice montañas de desperdicios, y cubos de basura, y también gente a quienes les gustan los perrillos.

Así pues, echaron a andar por el carrascal. A su alrededor no había más que hierba pobre, escasa y baja, piedras blancas, olorosas flores, recias matas de tomillo.

Por encima de ellos, el sol iba subiendo a lo largo del cielo azul, calentando más y más.

—El setter me dijo —comentó a media voz el viejo Pompón— que nuestros antepasados los lobos sólo caminaban por la noche, y que durante el día dormían ocultos, igual que todos los demás animales salvajes. Pero que desde que vivimos con los hombres, hacemos igual que ellos. ¡Somos idiotas!

Finalmente divisaron un poblado. Desparramándose por la ladera, un rebaño de techos ocres descendía escalonadamente, hasta llegar al verdor de la llanura.

Encontraron un pequeño ribazo que bajaron con precaución. Las piedras rodaban bajo sus patas. Dos o tres veces, Tritus perdió el equilibrio, rodaba unos cuantos metros y siempre acababa, con cara de asombro, detenido por un matorral.

Pompón lo levantaba dándole un empujón con el morro.

De repente, se acabó la pendiente. Había hierba y, más lejos, el gran lecho seco de un río que sólo llevaba entre las arenas un hilillo de agua que corría perezosamente de charco en charco.

Pompón echó a correr seguido por Tritus y empezó a beber a grandes tragos.

Al oír el chasquear de la lengua, Tritus se dijo que allí había algo bueno y acercó el morro a la superficie del agua. Aquello no olía a nada, no tenía aspecto de nada; sobre todo, no se parecía en nada a la leche, tan buena, de su madre. Aspiró por la nariz y retrocedió.

Pompón comprendió que el cachorro nunca había bebido todavía agua. Entonces le pasó varias veces por el morro su lengua húmeda. El perrillo, extrañado al principio, se lamió finalmente el borde del hocico; sintió que estaba fresco y su cuerpecito sediento se estremeció de placer. Intentó entonces mamar en la superficie líquida, pero el agua le entró por las narices. Estornudó.

Pompón se echó a reír.

—¡Así no, hijo, así no...! Mira, así...

Le enseñó cómo hacerlo y el cachorro le imitó.

Después de beber hasta hartarse, se dirigieron hacia el pueblo, al que rodearon en busca de alimento.

Guiado por su olfato, Pompón se dirigió a una calle desierta de la que aún no habían retirado la basura. Desgraciadamente, los cubos colgaban de unos ganchos, fuera de su alcance.

Finalmente, un poco más lejos, vieron dos o tres cubos sobre la acera. Pero ya otro perro andaba rebuscando por allí: un cocker marrón de pelo largo, que había desparramado el contenido de uno de los cubos y lo estaba revolviendo tan alegremente.

—¡Hola! —dijo el cocker moviendo amistosamente su pequeño trocito de rabo—. Acercaos sin miedo. Donde come uno, comen tres. Además, si estoy revolviendo los cubos de basura no es porque tenga hambre, sino porque me divierte, y porque está prohibido, y porque me gusta mucho hacer lo que está prohibido.

Se retiró un poco, e invitó a Pompón a servirse de un papelón lleno de cortezas de queso, de recortes de carne, de huesos de pollo y mendrugos de pan.

—¡Hale, amigo, cosa fina!

Fue a rebuscar un poco más lejos y volvió haciendo rodar, con su hocico largo y fino, una lata abierta de leche condensada, hasta donde estaba Tritus.

—¡Venga, pequeño, disfruta! Cuando acabes con ésta, hay más latas.

Pompón y Tritus no se lo hicieron repetir dos veces. Arremetieron el uno contra los restos, el otro contra la lata de leche condensada, y pronto quedaron hartos. El cocker jugueteaba junto a ellos, encantado de verlos comer con tanta satisfacción.

Cuando hubieron acabado, se miraron los tres.

Iba Pompón a dar las gracias al cocker

cuando se oyó el ruido de una puerta que se abría:

—¡Mis cubos de basura! —gritó una estridente voz de mujer.

Los tres perros echaron a correr al mismo tiempo, en medio de una nube de polvo.

5 *Cómo Pompón y Mally-Pop abandonaron a Tritus*

SE fueron, corriendo, a la orilla del río.

Empezaron por beber un poco para ayudar a pasar la comida, y luego se instalaron confortablemente a la sombra de un árbol.

—Me llamo Mally-Pop —se presentó el cocker—. Al menos, así es como me llama mi ama. A veces también me llama Pupuche. ¡Pupuche...! ¿Se dan ustedes cuenta? Yo sé muy bien que mi nombre, mi verdadero nombre de perro, es Hermoso-Perro-Marrón-De-Pelo-Largo-Y-De-Largas-Orejas. ¡Pero los hombres son de lo que no hay...!

41

—Es cierto —afirmó Pompón—, unas veces son simpáticos con nosotros, otras veces son malos.

—Pues yo... mi ama es simpática conmigo —dijo Mally-Pop—. Me acaricia y me besa mucho. Aunque hay veces que me irrita... ¡Me pone nervioso! ¿Ustedes no han notado cómo huelo?

—Sí, claro que lo hemos notado, sólo que no me había atrevido a decir nada. Por educación...

—Bueno, pues ya lo ven ustedes —dijo el cocker con un gesto de asco—. Es una cosa muy rara que saca de una botellita y me la echa por todas partes. ¡Cómo apesta! ¡Es horrible! Un perro tiene que tener olor de perro, ¿no? Por eso, en cuanto puedo, me escapo y me revuelco en los desperdicios. ¡Eso sí que huele bien!

—Es cierto —dijo Pompón—, un perro tiene que oler a perro... Y a propósito de desperdicios, gracias por habernos permitido revolver en sus cubos.

—¡Bah!, no las merece. Yo estoy muy bien alimentado, ¿sabe? Tal vez, incluso, hasta un poco demasiado. Soy un glotón y engordo en seguida. ¡Hasta tengo una escudilla con mi nombre! Lo que me da rabia es que mi ama me sujeta las orejas con una pinza de tender la ropa, para que no se me metan en la comida. Y mi comida... ¡de mi comida también habría que hablar! Solamente cosas bien machacaditas que mi ama saca de un bote. Huesos, nunca. ¡Como si eso me fuese a hacer mal! ¡Como si un buen hueso le hubiese sentado alguna vez mal a un perro!

—¿Y por qué no se escapa usted?

—¡Oh...! Bueno, es que esto también tiene sus ventajas, ¿sabe?...

—¿Qué ventajas?

Mally-Pop reflexionó un instante.

—Hombre... de acuerdo que no todo es agradable, sobre todo cuando me pone un lacito en el collar y me saca a pasear con la correa por la calle, con todos mis amigos y amigas riéndose de mí. ¡Me da una vergüenza...! Pero... a pesar de todo, la quiero mucho... Es cariñosa... Sufriría mucho si me escapase... Y no me gusta hacerle sufrir.

Los dos perros permanecieron un rato en silencio. Junto a ellos, Tritus se divertía girando sobre sí mismo, intentando cogerse el rabo. Al final, acababa tumbándose de espaldas en el suelo, agitando sus patitas.

—¡Qué rico es! —dijo Mally-Pop—. ¿Es suyo?

Pompón le contó entonces cómo había recogido a Tritus.

—¡Pobre hijo! —dijo Mally-Pop acercándose a olisquear la oreja de Tritus que ya estaba cicatrizando.

—¡Tengo una idea! —dijo de pronto el viejo Pompón, con un «¡Guau!» de alegría—. Si usted quisiera venirse conmigo, podríamos dejar a Tritus con la dueña de usted y así ya no se quedaría triste. Para este pobre pequeño, el viaje resultaría demasiado largo.

Y se puso a contarle al cocker lo que le había dicho el Gran-Setter-Marrón.

—Ya lo creo que me gustaría ir con usted —dijo Mally-Pop—. Y eso, ¿está muy lejos?

—Allá arriba, hacia el norte, en las montañas.

—Las montañas... —dijo Mally-Pop pensativo—. Una vez fui allí con mi ama. Hacía fresco, hacía buen tiempo, todo estaba lleno de olores fuertes y extraños, y yo podía correr, correr por los bosques... Me gustaría volver otra vez allí...

—Pues véngase conmigo —insistió el perro viejo—. Dejemos a Tritus con su ama.

—No sé... No sé... —repetía Mally-Pop un poco triste.

Entonces, una silueta humana se asomó al ribazo.

—¡Mally-Pop! ¡Maaaaaaaaallyyyyyyyy...! ¡Ven, Pupuche, lindo! —gritó la voz clara de una joven.

Los perros se escondieron aún más en la sombra.

—¡Ven, Pupuche, guapo, ven corriendo! Que te voy a echar tu rico perfume por tus lindas orejitas...

Mally-Pop se aplastó contra el suelo, como si quisiese penetrar en él.

La voz llamó dos o tres veces más, y finalmente se alejó y ya no se oyó más.

—¡Decidido! —dijo bruscamente Mally-Pop—. Me voy con usted. Ya estoy harto de no oler a perro de verdad.

—De acuerdo —dijo Pompón—, dejaremos a Tritus en su lugar.

Y subieron hacia el pueblo.

—Ahí es, en esa casa vivo —dijo Mally-Pop señalando una casa cubierta de hiedra.

—Escucha, Tritus —dijo Pompón lamiendo al perrillo—. Aquí es donde vamos a dejarte. Tendrás una dueña muy simpática, te cuidará mucho, te dará una comida deliciosa...

—Y te echará colonia... —añadió Mally-Pop con un poco de ironía. Luego, en voz baja, añadió:

—Y te hará muchas caricias...

Se le hizo un nudo en la garganta y dos lagrimones le asomaron por el rabillo del ojo. «Los cocker lloran mucho», se dijo Pompón, que ya había conocido unos cuantos a lo largo de su dilatada vida.

—Yo volveré pronto —dijo Mally-Pop—, es sólo unas vacaciones.

El viejo perro blanco y marrón colocó al cachorro delante mismo de la puerta. Con el hocico le hizo sentarse y, en voz baja, le ordenó que se estuviese quieto.

Luego, se alejó un poco. El cachorro estaba echado delante de la puerta, sin moverse, pero tenía sus dos ojos negros clavados en su viejo amigo.

—No te muevas de ahí, Tritus —dijo Pompón, un poco velada la voz—. Estarás muy bien, muy contento, serás feliz... ¡Venga, Mally-Pop, ahora te toca a ti! —dijo bruscamente, dirigiéndose al cocker.

Mally-Pop se acercó a la puerta y ladró dos veces muy fuerte.

46

Se abrió una ventana en el piso de arriba de la casa y una voz humana exclamó:

—¡Ah, por fin, ya estás ahí, vagabundo! ¿Dónde te habías metido? Espera, que ahora bajo a abrirte...

Pero los dos perros no aguardaron. En cuanto oyó la voz, Pompón se alejó a todo correr. Y, tras un breve instante de duda, Mally-Pop lo siguió.

Y el uno detrás del otro, recorrieron las calles del pueblo y fueron a esconderse, jadeando, a orillas del riachuelo.

—Descansemos un poco —dijo Pompón—. Echaremos a andar cuando se haga de noche, y haremos como nuestros antepasados los lobos, como Gran-Lobo-Salvaje: caminaremos bajo las estrellas, cuando los hombres y los otros perros estén durmiendo.

—Y así tendremos menos calor —resopló Mally-Pop sacudiendo su espesa pelambrera dorada.

—¡Cuidado! —dijo Pompón—. He oído un ruido.

Allá arriba, por lo alto del ribazo, se oía el ruido de la hierba al ser pisada y unos pasitos ligeros. Los dos perros se aplastaron contra el suelo, tiesas las orejas, olfateando la brisa con el morro levantado.

Y luego se oyó una vocecilla torpona, mitad ladrido, mitad gemido:

—Pom...pón... Pom...pón...

El viejo perro lanzó un «¡Guau!» de sorpresa, y los gemidos se cambiaron de repente en unos grititos alegres, y una forma oscura bajó rodando el ribazo hasta pararse justo ante sus patas.

—¡Es Tritus! —exclamó Mally-Pop sorprendido—. ¡Nos ha seguido el rastro! ¿Se da usted cuenta?

—Está muy despabilado para su edad —dijo Pompón lamiendo alegremente al cachorro.

6 *Cómo Pompón, Mally-Pop y Tritus se encontraron con Nenúfar*

LOS tres perros caminaron durante varios días. Pompón, a la cabeza del grupo, avanzaba siempre con el mismo paso decidido, el hocico orientado hacia el norte. Después venía Mally-Pop, que se apartaba frecuentemente del camino para ir a olisquear el tronco de un árbol o lanzarse en persecución de las mariposas; por último venía Tritus, que trotaba animosamente.

Los dos mayores se detenían a menudo para que el pequeño pudiese descansar, pero de día en día iba creciendo y se endurecían sus músculos. Ya no era aquel cachorrillo asustado que Pompón había encontrado en un basurero.

Comían lo que podían, por el camino: restos de comida abandonados por excursionistas poco cuidadosos, o cadáveres de conejos aplastados bajo las ruedas de los automóviles.

Mally-Pop ya no olía a perfume; había vuelto a encontrar un verdadero olor a perro, un olor fuerte, áspero, del que estaba muy orgulloso. Su pelo, sedoso antes y bien peinado, se enredaba ahora en mechones llenos de hierbas o de semillas erizadas de pinchos. Había perdido peso y sus formas ya no eran tan redondas. Pero había ganado fuerza y ya no se veía obligado, como al principio, a suplicarle al viejo perro, a cada paso, que le aguardase.

UN DIA, cuando caía la tarde y ellos acababan de meterse por un camino que llevaba hasta unas colinas, Pompón divisó de pronto un perro enorme que parecía estar esperándolos, justo en medio de la carretera.

Pompón se detuvo, olfateó el aire que venía del desconocido y en él notó olores de cólera. Detrás de él, Mally-Pop, que aún no se había dado cuenta de nada, husmeaba en un matorral. Más atrás, Tritus subía aún la cuesta.

La garganta de Pompón dejó escapar un gruñido de advertencia.

Las ramas del arbusto de Mally-Pop dejaron de moverse y apareció la cabeza del cocker.

Inquieto, Tritus fue a pegarse a Pompón, gimiendo.

A pasos cortos, tensas las patas, erizado el lomo, con un gruñido en el fondo de la garganta, tiesa la cola, el perrazo se acercó al viejo Pompón. Dio dos o tres vueltas a su alrededor, lo olió desde todos los ángulos y olió también al aterrorizado cachorro.

Era un perro muy grande, un animal espléndido, lleno de fuerza, aleonado el pelo, el hocico alargado, el pecho poderoso, el lomo fuerte y ancho, la cola peluda, levantada hacia arriba como una trompeta.

—Apártate, viejo —dijo a Pompón que, inmóvil, movía suavemente la cola—. Largo de aquí, abuelo —repitió el perrazo—.

Vete con tu cachorro. Contra vosotros no tengo nada.

Volvió lentamente la cabeza hacia Mally-Pop, que ya había salido completamente del matorral.

—¡Vaya! ¡Pero si es un perro de raza! —dijo irónico—. ¡Un lindo perrito de su mamaíta...! ¿Qué haces tú aquí, engendro?

—¿Y a ti que te importa? —replicó Mally-Pop, que no estaba asustado ni mucho menos. También él estaba tenso y tenía erizados los pelos del lomo.

—¿Que qué me importa? —rugió el otro—. ¡Estás en mi territorio! ¿Es que no has olido mis señales?

—¡Yo no he olido nada! —dijo el cocker.

—Porque ya no tienes ni olfato —dijo despectivo el perrazo rojo—. Te han educado demasiado los hombres. El olfato lo perdiste con tantos olores embotellados como te han echado por la piel. ¡Cómo apestas! ¡Con esos pelos que te cuelgan, pareces un erizo enfermo!

Al oír ese insulto, Mally-Pop se puso tieso —¡odiaba tanto a los erizos!— y, gruñendo, dio un paso adelante.

Eso era lo que estaba esperando el perrazo rojo; saltó contra el cocker.

Pompón hizo un gesto como para acudir en ayuda de su amigo, pero tenía suficiente experiencia de combates como para quedarse al margen. Aquel era un asunto entre el cocker y el desconocido.

Pero Tritus no conocía aún las reglas del juego y se tiró a la pata del perro rojo. Menos mal que Pompón lo agarró al vuelo y lo apartó rápidamente de aquel torbellino.

Durante largo tiempo no se pudo distinguir nada en aquella nube de polvo levantada por los dos combatientes. A veces se veía una pata, el brillar de unos dientes, un trozo de piel. De aquel remolino salía un tumulto de ladridos, de gemidos, de gritos roncos e inarticulados.

Tritus ladraba hasta desgañitarse, con su vocecita. Pompón, tranquilo, observaba la refriega rascándose las orejas con las uñas gastadas de sus patas traseras.

Y de pronto, todo se despejó. Mally-Pop estaba en el suelo, de espaldas, abierta la boca, los colmillos fuera, frente a los colmillos del perrazo rojo, que estaba encima de él, a unos centímetros. Aquel enorme perro tenía al cocker agarrado fuertemente entre sus dos patas delanteras, rígidas.

Dos o tres veces, el perro rojo hizo ademán de atacar al cocker en la garganta y, poco a poco, comprendiendo que el otro era más fuerte que él, Mally-Pop fue ocultando los colmillos, y finalmente se estiró hacia atrás ofreciendo su frágil garganta, reconociendo así la victoria de su adversario. Y, siempre de espaldas como estaba, agitó tímidamente su corto rabillo.

El perrazo rojo permaneció unos instantes inmóvil, rígido, con las patas tiesas. Luego, su pelo dejó de estar erizado, sus colmillos desaparecieron, y acabó por retirarse, moviendo también él la cola.

—¡Bravo! —dijo Pompón—. ¡Qué pelea más bonita! Ya hacía tiempo que no veía una igual. Te has defendido muy bien, Mally-Pop, no hubiese creído yo que te defendieses tan bien —le dijo al cocker que, sentado en el polvo, se lamía el costado.

—Es cierto —reconoció el perrazo—. Se ha batido muy bien.

—No estarás herido, ¿eh, Mally-Pop? —preguntó inquieto Pompón.

—No, no tiene nada —intervino el perro rojo—. Sé batirme correctamente y nunca he herido a un adversario en un duelo leal.

También él se lamió; luego dijo:

—Pero, ¿qué hacéis aquí, en mi territorio? ¿De verdad que no habíais olido mis señales?

—De verdad que no —dijo Mally-Pop—. Seguramente estaríamos distraídos.

—Entonces es que las he hecho mal. O que la lluvia de esta mañana las ha borrado.

Fue entonces a olfatear en dos o tres arbustos, levantó la pata delante de cada uno, olfateó de nuevo.

—Ya está —dijo—, ahora ya huelen.

—Tan sólo íbamos de paso —dijo Pompón—. Nos dirigimos a la montaña, a la búsqueda del antepasado de todos nosotros, Gran-Lobo-Salvaje, que aún vive allá, en los bosques.

—¡Ja, ja, ja! —soltó la carcajada el perrazo rojo—. ¡Esta si que es buena! ¡Menuda historia! ¡Tan cierto como me llamo Nenúfar, que nunca he oído cosa igual!

—¿Perdón? —dijeron a la vez Pompón y Mally-Pop.

—¿Perdón de qué?

—Su nombre... Que cómo se llama usted —dijo Mally-Pop.

—Nenúfar... Sí, ya sé, eso suena a ridículo, pero así me puso mi hombre. O «Nenu», para hacerlo más corto. Pero mi verdadero nombre de perro es Gran-Perro-Rojo-Muy-Fuerte-Y-Muy-Peleón.

—Yo me llamo Pompón.

—Y yo Mally-Pop.

—Y yo soy *Titu* —dijo el cachorro.

Los otros tres acogieron aquella afirmación con unos grandes ladridos de risa. Humillado, el cachorrillo fue a refugiarse entre las patas de Pompón, que lo recibió con un lametazo indulgente.

—Así pues, según me han dicho, van ustedes en busca de Gran-Lobo-Salvaje —dijo Nenúfar—. ¡Esto sí que tiene gracia! Amigos, ustedes no tienen ni idea. ¡Gran-Lobo-Salvaje no existe! El antepasado de todos nosotros, los perros, es Gran-Perro-Amarillo.

7 Cómo Nenúfar y Loa se unieron al grupo

EL antepasado de todos nosotros —repitió Nenúfar —es Gran-Perro-Amarillo.

—¿Y eso, tú cómo lo sabes?

—Porque es lo que siempre he oído decir. Cuando nos dejen en libertad y cuando mezclemos todas las razas que hoy somos y que han sido fabricadas por el hombre, la mezcla de todos nuestros hijos no va a ser el Lobo, sino el Gran-Perro-Amarillo. Como debió de ser nuestro antepasado. Un perro grande, poderoso, con la cola levantada como una trompeta, vivo, inteligente. Algo así como yo. ¡Mirad!

Se irguió todo lo alto que era, y los otros no tuvieron más remedio que admirarlo, aureolado como estaba por el sol poniente.

—Aunque, sin embargo, yo no soy Gran-Perro-Amarillo. No lo soy, no... Todavía no. Pero acaso los hijos de mis hijos lo sean.

—Yo, yo creo en Gran-Lobo-Salvaje y lo encontraré —dijo Pompón.

—¡Que estás chocheando, abuelo, que no sabes lo que dices!

—Sí, lo sé, Gran-Setter-Amarillo me lo dijo. Y él es, por lo menos, tan listo como tú. Tú puedes hacer lo que quieras —le dijo a Mally-Pop—, o quedarte o volverte a tu casa. Yo seguiré mi camino.

Y echó a andar hacia el norte, sin mirar atrás a ver si los otros le seguían.

Tritus corrió tras él.

Mally-Pop estuvo dudando un momento, pero luego le lanzó a Nenúfar un ladrido de despedida y se puso en camino.

—¡No sois más que un atajo de tontos! ¡Los tres! —ladró Nenúfar—. ¡Venid acá, volved! No vais a marcharos así, sin comer. ¡Volved, os invito a comer!

Al oír eso, Mally-Pop volvió la cabeza y regresó agitándose nervioso.

—¡Ven acá, viejo loco! —gritó Nenu a Pompón.

Y como éste no se detuviese, echó a

correr y, con unas cuantas zancadas ágiles y rápidas, le cerró el paso.

—Déjame pasar —gruñó Pompón—. Voy en busca de Gran-Lobo-Salvaje.

—¡Vamo buscá Gan-Obo-Sabaje! —aseguró Tritus.

—Está bien, de acuerdo —dijo Nenu en tono conciliador—. Pero antes de continuar el viaje, venid a descansar un poco y a comer un bocado, os lo ofrezco de todo corazón.

El viejo perro dudó, pero luego, al final, movió la cola en señal de aceptar, siendo imitado inmediatamente por Tritus.

El gran perro rojo los condujo fuera del camino, por un laberinto de maleza espesa y de nudosos troncos de árboles. Al llegar al borde de un pequeño claro, se quedó inmóvil y lanzó dos ladridos cortos.

Del otro lado del claro, una voz le respondió.

—No tengáis miedo —dijo Nenu a sus invitados—. Es Loa, mi esposa. Es una perra joven que recogí hace algún tiempo. Perdió a sus amos por correr detrás de los pájaros. Le encanta perseguir a los pájaros, aunque nunca atrapa ninguno.

Loa vino a su encuentro. Era una perrita fina y viva, de pelo mezclado, a la vez rojo y plateado.

Empezó por olfatear a su compañero, le pasó luego delicadamente la lengua por el morro y terminó por mordisquearle una oreja. Después, saludó debidamente a Pompón, oliéndolo por delante, oliéndolo por detrás, y finalmente miró atentamente a Mally-Pop antes de dirigirse hacia él agitando nerviosa el trasero.

—¡Ojo! —gruñó Nenu dirigiéndose al cocker—. Nada de familiaridades, es mi esposa.

—Ya lo sé —dijo Mally-Pop dirigiendo un saludo lejano y afectado a la perrita.

Esta se detuvo al final delante de Tritus, con cara de asombro.

—¿Qué es esto? —exclamó riéndose.

—«Esto» é *Titu* —ladró el cachorro enfadado.

—¡Qué divertido es! —dijo ella, y se puso a correr a su alrededor a toda velocidad. Luego, dirigiéndose de repente hacia él, de un empujón con el hocico lo hizo rodar por la hierba.

El perrillo comprendió que era un juego y pronto el claro del bosque retumbó con el ruido de sus diversiones.

—Ahí está —dijo Nenu con un movimiento de cabeza de gran señor, señalando hacia el oloroso cadáver de un cordero, ya medio devorado, casi oculto por las ramas bajas de un árbol.

Los otros no se lo hicieron repetir dos veces y se precipitaron hacia la carnaza, seguidos al instante por Tritus que, hambriento, había abandonado el juego, con gran desesperación de Loa.

Después que se hubieron saciado, se tumbaron en círculo alrededor del perrazo rojo. Tritus, con la barriguilla inflada, enseñó sus pequeños colmillos blancos y puntiagudos a la perra, que le molestaba para que siguiesen jugando, y se durmió reclinado en su gran amigo Pompón. Loa fue a tumbarse un poco más lejos, con la cabeza puesta sobre las patas, la mirada brillante, atentas las orejas.

—Respecto a lo de su Gran-Lobo-Salvaje... —dijo Nenu.

—No hablemos más de eso —gruñó Pompón.

—De acuerdo, no hablemos más. Simplemente yo quería decir que me habían entrado ganas de ir con ustedes. No es que yo crea en su historia, sólo que no me gusta quedarme mucho tiempo en el mismo sitio. Y ya llevamos aquí varios días Loa y yo; desde que encontramos este cordero muerto.

—Entonces, ¿no lo mató usted? —preguntó Mally-Pop.

El perrazo se estremeció.

—¡No! —dijo con una voz sorda—. No, ha debido de morirse él solo, o sufriría algún accidente y el pastor no lo encontraría. No, no lo he matado yo. Yo he sido perro pastor y el hombre me prohibía siempre hacerles daño.

—¿Ya no es usted perro pastor?

—No. Un día, fueron unos hombres y se llevaron el rebaño. Mi amo me llevó a otro pastor, pero yo me escapé para buscarle...

Quería mucho a mi amo... Y desde entonces viví solo, hasta que encontré a Loa.

Y dirigió un ladrido cariñoso a su perra. Loa hizo volar las hierbas al agitar el rabo.

—Ustedes deberían descansar algún tiempo —continuó el perrazo—. Aunque sólo fuese el tiempo de acabar este cadáver. Así estarían más en forma para reanudar el viaje.

8 *Vicky*

ALGUNOS días más tarde, después de haber acabado Tritus el último trocito de carne y cuando ya no quedaba de la oveja más que algunos huesos, blancos y bien roídos, esparcidos por el claro, los perros reanudaron el camino.

Un poco adelantado al grupo, Nenúfar abría la marcha. De vez en cuando se detenía para olfatear el viento. En ocasiones, se alejaba algo para hacer un reconocimiento.

Detrás, un poco más lejos, venían Pompón, Tritus y Loa. A veces, la perra intentaba aproximarse a Nenu, pero el perrazo marrón le hacía volverse a su sitio de un gruñido.

Pompón avanzaba siempre al mismo paso, sin mirar a los lados del camino, firme en su decisión de encontrar a Gran-Lobo-Salvaje.

Tritus caminaba junto a las patas del viejo perro, pero a veces, de repente, sin motivo aparente, por jugar, se ponía a correr de un lado a otro del camino.

En retaguardia, convencido de lo importante de su misión, iba Mally-Pop.

Caminaban en silencio y sus raras pausas eran también silenciosas. Entonces, se tumbaban los unos contra los otros.

Un poco separado, con la cabeza erguida, Nenúfar vigilaba los alrededores.

Una noche en que reposaban así, a unos pasos del sendero, antes de reemprender su marcha, Nenúfar levantó de repente las orejas, en actitud de alerta. Los otros se quedaron igualmente inmóviles.

Al acercarse al sendero, oyeron unos sollozos, unos lloros de perro.

Poco después vieron aparecer en la penumbra una silueta maciza.

Los pelos de Nenu se erizaron y el perro enseñó los colmillos. Pero cuando el animal llegó a su altura, Nenu se calmó súbitamente y saltó muy ágil al sendero, frotando enérgicamente el aire con el plumero de su cola.

El animal, espantado, pegó un salto hacia atrás y se echó en la hierba, temblando.

Nenu fue y lo olió, y entonces tuvo la confirmación de lo que ya había sospechado: aquel perro desconocido era... una perra.

Tenía ésta un pelo demasiado corto, un hocico negro tan chato que parecía como si no tuviese. De su cabeza, redonda, salían dos orejillas puntiagudas y triangulares; la izquierda, plegada, le daba continuamente un aire interrogante. Sus formas redondas acababan en una pizca de rabo.

—¡Hola! —dijo Nenu.

—¡Hola! —murmuró la perra, que se puso a temblar al ver cómo los otros perros se acercaban para olerla.

Solamente Loa permanecía al margen, con los pelos erizados, gruñendo.

—¿Qué hace usted aquí, llorando sola por los caminos? —preguntó Nenu.

La perra empezó de nuevo a gemir.

—¡Vaya llorica! —ladró Loa con desprecio.

—¡A ti nadie te ha preguntado nada! —le contestó Nenu. Se volvió hacia la otra perra y prosiguió—: ¡Venga, cuéntenoslo...!

—Me he perdido... —dijo la perra llorando.

Los otros perros ladraron a carcajadas.

—¡También nosotros estamos perdidos! —dijo Mally-Pop—. Todos nosotros somos perros perdidos. Y nadie llora por eso. Excepto Tritus.

Enfadado, el cachorro le dio un ladrido.

—Sí, pero es que yo... lo mío no es igual —dijo la perra—. Yo no soy una perra de campo, yo soy de ciudad, ¿entienden? Por eso... ¡tengo miedo!

—No tiene por qué tener miedo —dijo Nenu—. Para eso estoy aquí yo.

—Para eso estamos aquí *nosotros* —rectificó Mally-Pop.

—¿Cómo te llamas? —preguntó Nenu.
—Vicky —respondió la perra.

—¿Eso es todo? ¿Vicky a secas? ¿No tienes un verdadero nombre de perro?

—No, ni siquiera sabía que existiesen...
Los otros perros se presentaron. Menos Loa.

—En fin... ya ustedes me comprenderán, ¿no? Yo no alterno mucho con otros perros. A mis amos no les gusta. Es que, la verdad, hay algunos más mal educados...

Hasta me ladran cuando voy por la calle
con mi correa.

—¡Seguro que Nenu no haría tal cosa!
—dijo burlona, a media voz, Mally-Pop.

—Habíamos venido a dar un paseo en

coche para tomar un poco el aire y estirar las piernas —prosiguió Vicky—. De pronto vi un gato... Debo aclararles que a mí no me gustan los gatos. Corrí y corrí, y cuando perdí de vista al gato ya estaba oscuro, y yo estaba sola, y no sabía dónde estaba...

Y empezó de nuevo a lloriquear.

—¡Ya está bien, para ya! —gruñó Loa—. ¡Que nos estás hartando con tantas lamentaciones!

Vicky se irguió y le faltó poco para tirarse contra Loa.

—¡Paz! —ordenó Nenu poniéndose entre las dos perras—. Aquí mando yo y no quiero peleas.

Las dos perras se calmaron, aunque sin cesar de echarse unas miradas furiosas.

—¿Por qué tienes así las orejas? —preguntó Mally-Pop.

—Me las recortaron cuando yo era pequeñita.

—¿Y también el rabo? —preguntó el cocker.

—Sí, es para que haga más bonito. Es lindo, ¿verdad? —preguntó Vicky a Nenu y a Mally-Pop, moviendo nerviosa los cuartos traseros.

—¡Puaf! —dijo Loa.

—¡Pero eso es horrible! —gritó Mally-Pop—. ¡Tus amos deben de ser malísimos!

—Los hombres están locos —dijo Pompón.

—¡No señor! Mis amos son muy simpáticos. Me gustaría encontrarlos. ¡Ay! ¡Cuánto me gustaría encontrarlos...!

—¡Esta también está loca! —dijo Pompón—. ¿Pues no que los hombres le han cortado las orejas y el rabo, y encima quiere volverse con ellos?

—¡Pero es que los quiero! —aseguró Vicky con un sollozo—. Y ellos también me quieren. No me tienen más que a mí. Antes había niños en la casa, pero ahora ya no estamos más que los tres. Yo tengo que ocuparme de mis amos, ese es mi oficio, para eso es por lo que yo existo. ¡Ay! ¡Si no hubiese echado a correr detrás de aquel horrible gato!

—¡Está loca! —repitió Pompón.

—No... sé —dijo en voz baja Mally-Pop, que de repente se había acordado de su ama.

—Te quedarás con nosotros —le dijo Nenu— e iremos en busca de Gran-Lobo-Salvaje.

—¡A la porra su Gran-Lobo-Salvaje!
—dijo Vicky—. ¡Yo quiero irme con mis
amos!

—Pero si aquí te querremos mucho...
Acabarás por olvidarlos —dijo Nenu.

—No creo —dijo la perra bóxer—. No
creo.

EL GRUPO empezó a caminar, engrosado
con Vicky, que marchaba tristemente al
lado de Pompón. Tritus, con sus cabriolas,
hacía por alegrarla.

Al cabo de una hora llegaron a una
carretera y empezaron a cruzarla.

De repente, apareciendo tras una curva,
surgió el ruido de un motor y todos se
quedaron paralizados por un haz de luz
brillante.

Los faros se detuvieron a unos pocos
metros de los perros y se oyó un grito muy
fuerte de mujer:

—¡Vicky! ¡Eres tú, hijita! ¡Ven acá, mi
niña! ¿Qué haces tú ahí con esos gamberros

de perros vagabundos? ¡Ven, querida, hija mía!

Sin una mirada a los otros perros, Vicky saltó al coche. No hacía más que ladrar de alegría.

Los faros se alejaron. Liberados de su parálisis, los perros se precipitaron a la cuneta.

9 *La caza de Mally-Pop*

¿LLEGAMOS ya a la montaña? —preguntaba Pompón a Nenu.

—No —respondía el perrazo—. Yo conozco muy bien esta región, aquí veníamos a guardar nuestros rebaños. Primero llegaremos a una llanura. La montaña está más lejos.

Llegados a la llanura, seca, árida, pedregosa y salvaje, no encontraron nada que comer.

Allí no había aldeas, ni basureros, ni carreteras, ni animales muertos en ellas, aplastados bajo las ruedas de los automóviles.

Caminaron durante dos días, dirigidos por el perro marrón que los conducía adonde había agua.

A la tarde del tercer día, cuando llegó el momento de reanudar la marcha, Loa continuó tumbada en el suelo, con la lengua fuera.

—Yo ya no sigo más —dijo, gimiendo en voz baja—. ¡Al diablo Gran-Lobo-Salvaje! Ustedes están locos... Me estoy muriendo de hambre y ya no puedo ni dar un paso.

—Yo *tapoco* —se quejó Tritus.

Nenu vino, los olfateó, y pasó su lengua por el hocico seco de Loa. Como la perra no reaccionase, intentó moverla empujándola por la espalda; luego, empezó a gruñir:

—¡Levántate, vámonos!

La perra no obedeció. Se limitó a mirarlo en silencio con sus grandes ojos tristes.

—Estamos todos demasiado hambrientos —dijo Mally-Pop—. Como no comamos, no llegaremos muy lejos.

Se llevó a Nenúfar un poco aparte.

—Fíjate en el viejo Pompón. No dice nada. No se mueve. Está decidido a seguir, pero estoy seguro de que, como no coma, se morirá en seguida. Sin haber visto a Gran-Lobo-Salvaje.

—¡Gran-Lobo-Salvaje no existe! —gruñó Nenu.

—¡Y qué más da! —dijo el cocker—. El

cree que sí existe, y tenemos que ayudarle.

—¿Pero cómo?

—¡Cazando!

—¿Cazando? —dijo Nenúfar—. ¿Y cómo? Yo nunca he sido más que un perro pastor. Nunca aprendí a cazar. Al contrario, me castigaban cada vez que dejaba las ovejas para echar a correr detrás de un conejo o una liebre. Y tú... perrito mono... ricura... encanto... ¡tú no me irás a decir que sabes cazar!

—Yo podré ser una monada y una ricura —dijo Mally-Pop—, pero nunca abandono a mis amigos. Además, tengo muy buen olfato. Y he hablado mucho de caza con mis amigos, en particular con mi amigo Nadau, un cocker negro que es un verdadero campeón.

—Vale, vale —dijo Nenu asombrado por la seguridad y aplomo de Mally-Pop—. Pero, ¿cómo vamos a hacer?

—Tú quédate aquí, puesto que no sabes cazar —dijo el cocker con una pizca de desprecio—. Quédate aquí, oculto bajo ese arbusto, ten los ojos bien abiertos. Ya me ocupo yo de ello.

Subyugado, el perrazo color marrón fue a echarse a la sombra de un enebro.

En silencio, pegada la nariz al suelo, el cocker comenzó a caminar describiendo círculos cada vez más grandes alrededor del lugar donde reposaba el grupo de perros.

Su nariz captaba, de vez en cuando débiles olores de animales vivos, pero demasiado tenues o demasiado antiguos. No le interesaban.

Buscó durante largo tiempo, y ya se disponía, por fin, a abandonar, humillado por volver adonde Nenu con las manos vacías, cuando, de repente, palpitaron las aletas de su nariz. Entre dos matas de tomillo, un olor fuerte acababa de hacerle cosquillas en el hocico. Era un olor áspero a hierbas pisoteadas, a piel de animal, a orina ácida; un olor que le hizo estremecerse de los pies a la cabeza.

—¡Diablos! —se dijo—. Ahora es cuando necesito recordar las lecciones de mi amigo Nadau, el as de los cazadores.

Siguió el rastro de aquel olor, vio dos pelos grises en una espina de una zarza. La pista era fresca.

De repente, el cocker dorado se quedó inmóvil, completamente inmóvil, con una pata replegada. Debajo de un matorral estaba acurrucada una enorme liebre marrón, con sus ojos redondos clavados en él.

Los pensamientos se entrecruzaban a gran velocidad por la cabeza del perro.

—¡Cuidado! ¡Está ahí! ¡Me ha visto! ¿Qué tengo que hacer ahora? Nadau decía que él se quedaba así, quieto, hasta que llegase su amo con el fusil, pero yo no tengo amo ni tampoco fusil... Es mejor que haga ahora lo que me decía Taió, el perro vagabundo.

Sin previo aviso, se abalanzó hacia adelante dando un ladrido.

La liebre pegó un brinco prodigioso y echó a correr con toda la fuerza de sus cuatro patas, como un resorte. El cocker arrancó tras ella.

La liebre corrió durante largo tiempo. Iba mucho más deprisa que el perro, pero cada vez que creía haberlo despistado y empezaba a descansar, con sus flancos agitándose frenéticamente, volvía a oír a poca distancia la voz clara del cocker que seguía sus huellas.

En varias ocasiones, la liebre intentó hacerle perder la pista. Iba hacia un lado, recorría varios metros, volvía atrás, caminaba en otra dirección, repetía varias veces la misma operación. Luego, pegando unos grandes brincos, saltaba por encima de las piedras, tocándolas solamente con la punta de sus patas.

Pero Mally-Pop no se dejaba engañar por las numerosas pistas falsas. Daba vueltas en círculos cada vez más anchos y, cuando estaba seguro de haber vuelto a encontrar el buen camino, echaba a correr, pegada la nariz al suelo, aspirando con todas sus fuerzas las menores partículas de olor de su presa.

Y, poco a poco, después de una larga persecución por la llanura, Mally-Pop obligó a la liebre, fatigada y angustiada, a volver a su punto de partida.

Por unos instantes, la liebre se creyó a salvo. En su cabecita, loca de miedo y de fatiga, veía ya la imagen de un tronco de árbol hueco que varias veces le había permitido escapar, ocultándose en él, de los zorros o de los cazadores.

Hizo acopio de sus últimas fuerzas y enfiló por entre unos enebros.

Como un rayo, Nenúfar, que desde hacía un rato había oído acercarse la caza y que estaba preparado, alerta los cinco sentidos, cayó sobre ella y le partió el espinazo de una sola dentellada con sus poderosas mandíbulas.

DESPUES de que todos se hubieron hartado, Nenu se volvió hacia Mally-Pop y dijo:

—Nunca más volveré a llamarte *perrito lindo*.

—Gracias —dijo el cocker.

10 *Cómo cayó prisionero Mally-Pop*

PROSIGUIERON su camino y, finalmente, llegaron al borde de la meseta.

Al otro lado de un valle estrecho, excavado como una garganta, aparecían los primeros contrafuertes de la montaña, cuyas cimas se difuminaban en medio de la bruma.

Pompón se detuvo y, sentándose, contempló el paisaje.

—Gran-Lobo-Salvaje está allí. Lo sé. Lo presiento.

Fueron bajando con cuidado las abruptas laderas de la meseta. De vez en cuando, Nenu tenía que agarrar al cachorro por la piel del cuello, para ayudarle a salvar algunos sitios más difíciles.

Cuando llegaron al fondo del valle, todos se precipitaron hacia el río. ¡Por fin tenían agua buena, fresca, pura, después de la de las charcas de la meseta, más o menos corrompida!

Sintieron renacer sus fuerzas y, alegres, Loa, Tritus y Mally-Pop empezaron una serie de carreras y peleas, pero jugando, en plan de broma.

—Deberíamos descansar aquí varios días —dijo Nenu a Pompón—. Tenemos agua, un camino que no pasa muy lejos, y estoy oliendo a pueblo.

—Hagan como quieran —dijo el viejo perro—. Yo voy a continuar. Siento una cosa helada dentro de mí que me dice que me queda poco tiempo. Quédense aquí, ya no estoy lejos de la montaña ni de Gran-Lobo-Salvaje.

—No —respondió el gran perro marrón—. No te abandonaremos. Sin embargo, antes de cruzar el río y de subir por la otra ladera tenemos que encontrar algo que comer. Ya hace dos días que Mally-Pop no ha cazado nada. Porque no ha tenido suerte, claro, porque es un gran cazador.

El cocker agradeció el cumplido.

—Gracias, Nenu —dijo—. Pero aquí es

posible que tenga más suerte. Ven conmigo y te enseñaré. Como tú corres más que yo, seguramente podrás cazar algún conejo o alguna liebre a la carrera, después que yo te levante la caza.

Y se fueron los dos a lo largo de un seto. Mally-Pop husmeaba el suelo como un experto.

—¿Ves? —le decía a su amigo—. Este es un rastro viejo de conejo, no merece la pena seguirlo... Ahí se detuvo una perdiz para comer en ese hormiguero... ¡Hombre, esto ya está mejor! Es un camino por donde pasan los conejos a menudo. No debemos andar lejos de su madriguera...

El rastro llevaba hasta el seto y luego se metía por un agujero. Nenu se disponía a introducirse en él cuando, de pronto, se oyó un ruido de hojas pisoteadas y un gemido. Echó a correr. Tumbado sobre un costado, el cocker respiraba con dificultad.

—¡Mally! ¿Qué sucede, amigo? ¿Qué te ocurre?

—Mi cuello... mi cuello... —gimió el cocker con una voz muy extraña.

Nenu olfateó a su amigo. Alrededor de su cuello había un alambre de acero muy apretado, un nudo corredizo cuyo extremo estaba atado al tronco de un árbol.

—¡Un cepo...! —rugió—. Una trampa como las que mi amo, el pastor, ponía para cazar conejos. No te muevas, no te muevas por lo que más quieras. Si no, te ahogarías.

—¡Me duele mucho! —gimió Mally-Pop.

Nenúfar arremetió a dentelladas contra el tronco del árbol. Hizo volar la corteza, y sus poderosas mandíbulas empezaron a roer la madera. Roía y roía lo más aprisa que podía. Pero pronto, agotado, tuvo que parar. El tronco, apenas estaba desgastado.

Respiró un poco y ya iba a reemprender su trabajo cuando oyó un ruido.

—¡Un hombre! —dijo con un gruñido en la garganta—. Ha sido él quien ha puesto el lazo. Ya verás éste...

—No —dijo Mally-Pop haciendo un esfuerzo—. El me soltará.

Los pasos se acercaban, pesados, tranquilos. Nenu se pegó al suelo en silencio debajo de un matorral, quedando invisible. Pero tenía erizados los pelos del lomo y enseñaba unos colmillos brillantes. ¡Como el hombre se atreviese a hacerle daño a su amigo...!

Apareció el hombre, se dirigió hacia el seto, se agachó. De repente pegó un bote hacia atrás.

—¿Esto qué es? —exclamó.

De nuevo se agachó.

—¡Pero si es un perro! ¡Y nada menos que un cocker! ¿Qué demonios hace aquí? ¡Y está atrapado en mi cepo! No te muevas —le dijo a Mally-Pop—, no te muevas, voy a librarte.

Con sus manos expertas libró al perro del horrible apretón del alambre de acero. Mally-Pop lanzó un gran suspiro. Levantó un poco la cabeza, lamió la mano del hombre y luego se tumbó de costado.

—Pobre amigo —dijo el hombre—. Se diría que estás en un apuro. Te llevaré a mi casa, te cuidaré y luego buscaremos a tus amos... Y tal vez hasta me den una buena recompensa...

Levantó al perro, lo cogió en brazos.

—Ya debes llevar bastante tiempo perdido, amigo. No pesas casi nada.

Y se alejó en dirección al pueblo.

Por un momento, Nenu había pensado atacarle. Pero el tono de la voz del hombre le indicaba que no tenía ninguna mala intención para con su amigo. Además, en lo más hondo de él, toda su infancia, toda su educación le impedía hacerlo.

—¿Y AHORA qué vamos a hacer? —preguntó Nenu al acabar su relato a los otros perros.

—Nada. No podemos hacer nada —dijo Pompón—. El hombre lo cuidará y lo tratará bien. Y volverá a casa de su dueña. Tenemos que cruzar el río y seguir.

—No —dijo Nenu—. Yo no lo abandonaré.

—En ese caso me marcharé solo —dijo el viejo perro—. Yo no puedo esperar más.

—Nos vamo a í —dijo Tritus.

—¡Los niños se callan! —gruñó Nenu—. Escucha, Pompón; voy a llegarme al pueblo a ver lo que puedo hacer por Mally-Pop. Si al amanecer no he vuelto, puedes marcharte. Tritus y Loa que se queden aquí, esperándome, y ya después procuraremos encontrarte.

—De acuerdo —dijo Pompón—. Esperaré, pero en cuanto salga el sol, me marcho.

A grandes zancadas ágiles, Nenúfar se dirigió hacia el pueblo.

Nada más arrimarse a las primeras casas, se armó un concierto de ladridos de todos los perros domésticos encerrados durante la noche. Insultaban a ese perro libre cuyo olor desconocido llegaba hasta ellos, en sus casetas o bajo las mesas.

Nenu se sentó en el cruce de dos calles y movió las orejas en todas las direcciones.

En medio de todos los insultos, de todos los retos que le lanzaban los otros perros, logró, de pronto, oír una voz muy débil que le llamaba:

—¡Ne...nu! ¡Ne...nu!

Con un ladrido de alegría, echó a correr hacia adelante y, guiado siempre por las llamadas de su amigo, llegó por fin cerca de una granja un poco aislada.

Otra voz se mezcló con la de Mally-Pop.

—¡Largo de ahí, vagabundo, sigue tu camino! Vete, que se va a despertar mi amo y te va a pegar un tiro. ¡Que te vayas, ladrón, estás en mi territorio! ¿Acaso no has olido mis marcas?

Al acercarse un poco más, Nenu oyó a Mally-Pop que decía:

—Cállate, Karás, es mi amigo Nenúfar

que viene a ver qué pasa. Sé amable, no grites, es un amigo.

El otro perro se calmó, pero siguió gruñendo.

—Nenu —dijo en voz baja el cocker—, avanza, estamos detrás de una alambrada.

El perrazo rojo se acercó y descubrió a su amigo. Mally-Pop estaba ahora de pie y no parecía que hubiese sufrido demasiado con el lazo.

—¿Cómo estás? —preguntó Nenu.

—Bien, muy bien. Aún me duele un poco el cuello, pero ya desaparecerá. He comido muy bien, ¿sabes? La comida es realmente de primera. ¿Verdad, Karás?

Nenu distinguió un enorme perro lobo que se acercaba. Sus pelos se erizaron, pero el cocker lo calmó con la voz:

—Es un amigo, Nenu. Es un perro muy valiente. No olvides que estás en su territorio; eres un invitado, pórtate, pues, como un invitado.

Para mostrar su buena voluntad, Nenu movió la cola, y Karás y él se olfatearon a través de la alambrada.

—Bueno, vamos, Mally-Pop. Tenemos que marcharnos ya. El viejo Pompón no quiere esperarnos. Y yo no quiero que se marche solo. Ven, vámonos ya.

—Pero... ¿es que no te has dado cuenta? —preguntó el cocker extrañado—. No puedo irme. Estoy encerrado.

11 *Cómo Loa procuró alimento a sus amigos*

NO pareces muy listo, que digamos —refunfuñó Karás—. ¿Crees que tu amigo Mally-Pop se habría quedado aquí si se hubiera podido escapar?

—¡Y yo qué sabía! —dijo Nenu—. Yo creía que estaría enfermo, demasiado débil para marcharse.

—Si yo estuviese ahí fuera abriría fácilmente la puerta —dijo el perro lobo—. Me he fijado cómo lo hace mi amo. No hay más que levantar un picaporte.

—¡Prueba a ver, Nenu! ¡Inténtalo! —dijo el cocker.

—¡Ya me extraña que tu amigo lo consiga...¡ No parece muy despabilado —dijo Karás.

Sin hacer caso de la burla, Nenu dio la vuelta a la cerca. Había, en efecto, una puerta y se puso de pie contra ella. Vio una pieza de hierro que entraba en un agujero y que estaba, toda ella, impregnada del olor del hombre. Empezó a morderla y a tirar con todas sus fuerzas.

—¡Así no! —dijo el perro lobo—. Así lo único que conseguirás será partirte los dientes. Levántalo un poco con el morro.

Nenu lo hizo así. Sintió el frío del metal en la punta, tan sensible, de su hocico y empujó. Pero en vano.

—Está muy duro —dijo resoplando—. Me hace daño.

—Prueba otra vez —gimió Mally-Pop—. No quiero quedarme aquí, quiero irme con vosotros.

El perrazo rojo empujó con todas sus fuerzas el vástago de hierro. Sintió desgarrársele la punta del hocico, y notó el sabor áspero de la sangre que le llenaba la garganta. Pero la barra se levantó y, cuando Nenu cayó sobre sus patas, el cocker no tuvo más que empujar la puerta para encontrarse fuera.

—Gracias, Nenu —dijo.

—Ya ves que no soy tan idiota como

creías —dijo Nenu a Karás, que había ido a tumbarse al fondo de su caseta.

—Es verdad —reconoció el perro lobo.

—¿Te vienes con nosotros? —le preguntó Mally-Pop.

—¿Irme con vosotros...? —gruñó Karás—. ¡Ni hablar! Vosotros debéis de estar un poco locos. ¿Para morirme de hambre como vosotros? ¿Para que me estrangule un lazo? ¿Para verme encerrado en la casa de cualquier hombre? No, gracias, aquí estoy muy bien. La comida es excelente, me la sirven a sus horas, y mi amo no es malo. Eso es todo lo que necesito. Me quedo, me quedo. Y cerrad bien la puerta antes de marcharos.

—¿Que cerremos la puerta? —preguntó Nenu con un poco de desprecio.

—Sí, si no, a lo mejor me entran ganas de escaparme... y no quiero hacerlo.

Apoyándose en la puerta, Nenu dejó caer la barra en su posición.

—Eres un tipo muy raro —le dijo al perro lobo, que parecía haberse dormido ya en su rincón—. Lo que es yo, prefiero morirme de hambre, morirme de frío, pasar miedo, que me duela cualquier cosa, pero ser libre.

Y el cocker y el perrazo rojo se fueron por las calles desiertas de la aldea dormida.

—¡LOA se ha marchado! —les dijo Pompón cuando los otros dos llegaron adonde él estaba.

—¡No! ¡No puede ser verdad! —gimió Nenu lamiéndose el hocico dolorido.

—Se fue sin decir nada —prosiguió el viejo perro—. Yo pensé que había ido a reunirse con ustedes.

En aquel preciso instante, por la dirección de la aldea, se oyó un jaleo enorme de ladridos, y un alboroto de plumas y cacareos de aves de corral. Luego, poco después, un escopetazo.

—¡Loa! —gritó Nenu—. ¡Es Loa!

Siguió un momento de silencio. Y ya se disponía el perrazo a volver al pueblo, cuando la perrita apareció tras el recodo del camino. Temblando a más no poder, llevaba en la boca un enorme gallo muerto.

—¡Loa! —le gritaron todos, lo que despertó a Tritus, que desde largo rato es-

100

taba dormido, apoyado contra Pompón.

—¿Qué pasa con Loa? —dijo la perrita—. Traigo comida. Si no estuviese yo aquí, me pregunto cómo se las arreglarían ustedes. Ea, aquí está el almuerzo —dijo, dejando a sus pies el pollo que aún estaba caliente—. No ha sido difícil. ¡Vaya gozada! Para una vez que atrapo un pájaro...

—¿Y el disparo? —preguntó Nenu— ¿Estás herida?

—¿El disparo? ¿Qué disparo?

—Desde aquí lo hemos oído nosotros —exclamó Mally-Pop.

—¿Ese ruido tan grande que oí era un disparo? —gritó la perra, temblando.

CUANDO ya no quedaba del pollo más que unas plumas desperdigadas por la hierba, el grupo de perros se dispuso a marchar.

—En el pueblo hay un puente —dijo Nenu—, pero no podemos ir por ahí. Todos los hombres estarán en alerta después de la hazaña de Loa, y acaso también hayan descubierto ya la fuga de Mally.

Nos exponemos a que nos peguen unos escopetazos. Hay que cruzar el río por un vado.

Bordearon río abajo, procurando distinguir, en la semiclaridad del alba, el lugar más a propósito para salvar aquel obstáculo.

La cosa parecía difícil. Encajonado entre dos tajos cortados a pico, el río corría a mucha velocidad y sólo se ensanchaba en pocos lugares.

Por fin encontraron un sitio en el que, en una curva, el agua se ensanchaba un poco más y parecía reducir su velocidad.

Nenu se adentró, y en seguida le llegó el agua al pecho. Empezó entonces a nadar y pocos metros después sus patas hicieron pie. Subió a la otra orilla.

—¡No es demasiado difícil! —gritó a los otros perros que, apretados los unos contra los otros, aguardaban.

Con precauciones casi cómicas, como si el agua fuese a manchar su hermoso pelaje plateado, Loa se adelantó; luego, nadando ágilmente, se reunió con Nenu y se estuvo sacudiendo durante un buen rato para secarse.

Mally-Pop la siguió, con sus largos pelos

flotándole alrededor como si fuesen algas.

—¿Y yo? ¿Y yo? ¿Y yo? —gimió Tritus horrorizado por la corriente.

Nenu volvió, lo cogió con la boca por la piel del cuello y, manteniendo la cabeza por encima del agua, lo pasó a la otra orilla.

Ya sólo quedaba el viejo Pompón.

Se metió valientemente en el agua y, en cuanto sus patas dejaron de tocar el suelo, empezó a nadar.

Pero la corriente era, con mucho, demasiado fuerte para sus pobres fuerzas, y fue arrastrado lejos de la orilla de arena en donde le aguardaban sus compañeros.

—¡Pompón! —gritó Nenu corriendo por la orilla.

Se veía la cabeza del viejo perro hundirse y salir a la superficie en los remolinos. Bajaba con la corriente a una velocidad de locura, girando sobre sí mismo.

Corriendo, Nenu le cogió un poco de delantera y, cuando tuvo al viejo perro a su alcance, se lanzó al agua espumante, le agarró con la boca donde pudo, en una oreja, y, nadando con todas sus fuerzas, consiguió arrastrar a su amigo hasta la orilla, en un lugar donde se calmaba el agua gracias a las hierbas del fondo.

Sus uñas se clavaron en la arena y su cuerpo poderoso sostuvo el de Pompón.

Agotados, remontaron la orilla y se desplomaron jadeantes.

Los ojos del viejo perro parecían haber adquirido el tono verdeclaro del agua, y respiraba con unos pequeños resoplidos roncos; su cuerpo entero estaba temblando.

—¡Gran - Lobo - Salvaje...! ¡Gran - Lobo-Salvaje...! —murmuraba.

12 *Gran-Lobo-Salvaje*

DOS días tardó el viejo Pompón en restablecerse. Los otros perros, turnándose, venían a echarse junto a él para procurarle un poco de calor, y a lamerle una y otra vez la punta de su hocico, agrietada por la fiebre.

Para proporcionarles alimento, Loa hizo nuevas incursiones por los gallineros de la aldea. Pero los hombres estaban ya sobre aviso y el último día la perra regresó con las manos vacías.

—Creo que ya tengo bastantes fuerzas para continuar —dijo el viejo perro—. Tenemos que largarnos; si no, los hombres vendrán con sus escopetas y no quisiera yo que os ocurriese nada por mi culpa.

Dejaron, pues, la orilla del río y escalaron con dificultad la pendiente casi a pico, por unos senderos estrechos y traidores.

Nenu y Mally-Pop sostenían al viejo Pompón en los pasos difíciles y Loa se ocupaba de Tritus. Aunque éste ya no tenía mucha necesidad de ayuda: se había convertido en un joven perro fuerte, bastante sensato y ya no se alejaba demasiado.

Llegados a la cima, la pendiente continuaba, pero más suave.

Día tras día continuaban subiendo, siempre subiendo.

El otoño había desnudado los árboles después de haberlos pintado con sus colores más hermosos, y el aire se hacía cada vez más frío.

De cuando en cuando les caía encima una lluvia helada y, temblando, se acurrucaban los unos contra los otros, y de sus gargantas salían bocanadas de vapor.

Un día empezó a nevar.

Una especie de locura pareció apoderarse de Tritus y de Loa. Corrían tras los blancos copos, querían atraparlos a mordiscos con grandes «clacs» de sus mandíbulas, se perseguían el uno al otro dando unos grandes brincos, se echaban a rodar por la fina capa que cubría el suelo.

Ahora, la alimentación ya no era un problema. Abundaba la caza y Mally-Pop había afinado sus sentidos. Con sólo descubrir un rastro, ya sabía lo que iba a encontrar; y ya no echaba a correr, como antes, detrás de un joven gazapillo a quien costaba casi el mismo esfuerzo atrapar que a un viejo macho lleno de experiencia, pero que no proporcionaba al grupo más que unos pocos bocados de carne insulsa.

También Nenu había realizado progresos, aunque lo más a menudo, se contentaba con esperar detrás de un arbusto a que el cocker dirigiese la pieza hacia donde él estaba.

Cazando, comiendo, caminando durante la noche, atravesaron los bosques sombríos y, un día, llegaron a la cima de la montaña.

Era un lugar desolado en donde el viento glacial soplaba a sus anchas.

El grupo se detuvo y se sentó. En toda la extensión de tierra que la vista podía abarcar, sólo se veían bosques y más bosques, pintados de nieve por arriba, oscuros más abajo.

Aguzaron la oreja y olfatearon en todas las direcciones. En ninguna parte se dejaba sentir la presencia del hombre.

—Ya estamos en la cima de la montaña —dijo Nenu volviéndose hacia Pompón—. Ya hemos llegado.

—Sí —dijo el viejo perro.

—Hemos llegado, pero no hemos encontrado a Gran-Lobo-Salvaje —dijo Nenu suavemente.

El viejo Pompón recorrió melancólicamente el paisaje con la mirada.

—No —murmuró con pena al cabo de un momento—. No hemos encontrado a Gran-Lobo-Salvaje...

Y como el viento arreciase más fuerte y empezase a caer una tormenta de nieve, bajaron tristemente hacia el bosque.

La noche era glacial. Acurrucados, apretados todos alrededor de Pompón, a quien sacudían unos fuertes temblores, los perros se durmieron.

De repente, a medianoche, Nenu se despertó sobresaltado. A su lado, el sitio de Pompón estaba vacío, frío ya.

¡Arriba todos! —gritó el perrazo incorporándose sobre sus cuatro patas— ¡Arriba! ¡Pompón se ha marchado!

Los otros se levantaron en silencio, sacudiéndose.

—Está enfermo, no podemos dejarle solo —dijo Nenu—. Mally, ve tú delante, sigue su rastro.

El rastro era ya un poco viejo para el olfato, pero se distinguía perfectamente en la espesa alfombra de nieve. En fila india, los perros lo siguieron.

Las huellas subían entre los árboles. Se veía perfectamente que el viejo perro había comenzado a andar lentamente y que, a veces, agotado, se había dejado caer en la nieve en un hueco que aún conservaba un poco de su olor.

Caminaban lo más aprisa posible, casi corriendo. De repente, Mally-Pop lanzó un ladrido de aviso.

Delante de ellos, negro sobre la blancura de la nieve, divisaron al viejo Pompón que, más que andar, se arrastraba.

De unos cuantos saltos llegaron adonde él.

—Pompón, Pompón —dijo Nenu con un nudo en la garganta—. ¿Por qué te has ido? ¿Por qué nos has dejado, a nosotros, tus amigos?

El viejo perro se volvió hacia él y plegó los labios con aquella sonrisa que le era tan particular y que ya hacía tiempo que no veían. Sus ojos brillaban.

—¡Gran-Lobo-Salvaje! —murmuró—.
¡Gran-Lobo-Salvaje!

—Vuelve con nosotros, Pompón, ven al
refugio —dijo Mally-Pop llorando.

—Está delirando —murmuró Nenu.

—No —dijo Pompón—. Gran-Lobo-Salvaje está ahí. Lo sé. Lo he olido.

Y antes de que los otros, pasmados,
pudiesen reaccionar, reunió todas sus fuerzas y se lanzó corriendo hacia lo alto de la
pendiente.

Cuando los demás llegaron adonde él,
Pompón se encontraba delante de un agujero negro que se adentraba en la roca.

—¡Está aquí! ¡Os digo que está aquí!
—dijo temblando de emoción—. ¡Gran-Lobo-Salvaje está aquí!

Y entró en la cueva, y los otros, tras un
momento de duda, le siguieron.

El estrecho camino excavado en la roca
daba vueltas y más vueltas.

A medida que iban descendiendo, un
olor fuerte y raro subía hasta ellos.

Finalmente desembocaron, siempre detrás del viejo Pompón, en una sala más
grande, donde el olor se hizo tan fuerte
que los pelos de sus lomos se erizaron, al
tiempo que de sus gargantas brotaba un
gruñido.

Del otro lado de la sala llegó hasta ellos otro gruñido, ronco, poderoso, desconocido.

Una vez que sus ojos se acostumbraron a la oscuridad, los perros distinguieron en las tinieblas dos ojos brillantes que enmarcaban un hocico alargado que salía de una masa enorme de piel color aleonado.

—¡Gran-Lobo-Salvaje! —gritó Pompón— ¡Por fin te he encontrado, Gran-Lobo-Salvaje! ¡Soy feliz!

Dio un gran suspiro, se desplomó por tierra... y ya no se movió más...

Epílogo

DURANTE un largo rato no hubo en la gruta más que silencio, entrecortado por los aullidos lejanos del viento y los gemidos de Tritus, que se apretaba contra el cuerpo sin vida de su viejo amigo Pompón.

Finalmente habló el lobo. Su voz era fuerte pero cansada, con un cansancio extremo:

—¡Por fin me habéis encontrado! Tiempo os ha costado, pero me habéis encontrado. ¡Llamad a vuestros amos! ¡Ea, cumplid con vuestra obligación!

—¿Nuestros amos? ¿Nuestra obligación? —dijo Nenu asombrado—. Nosotros no tenemos amos, Gran-Lobo-Salvaje. Sólo hemos venido para verte a ti, el antecesor de todos nosotros. ¡Te saludamos, Gran-Lobo-Salvaje!

El lobo lanzó un largo aullido que semejó una carcajada.

—¿Gran-Lobo-Salvaje? ¿Gran-Lobo-Salvaje? ¿El antepasado de todos vosotros los perros? Así que no sabéis quién soy yo...

—Tú eres Gran-Lobo-Salvaje —dijo Mally-Pop con la voz que le temblaba.

—No —dijo el lobo—, yo no soy Gran-Lobo-Salvaje. Ni siquiera sé si existe el tal Gran-Lobo-Salvaje. No soy más que un viejo lobo que vivía en un zoo, allá abajo, lejos, cerca de la ciudad, solitario en una jaula entre un mono y unos canguros.

—¿Qué es un mono? ¿Qué son canguros? —preguntó Tritus, olvidando por un instante su tristeza.

—Un pobre lobo viejo —prosiguió el otro sin hacer caso de la interrupción—. Un pobre lobo viejo nacido en un cajón, alimentado por los hombres, cuidado por los hombres, observado por los hombres, burlado por los hombres. Un día, mi guardián cerró mal la jaula, y me escapé; y me vine aquí, a la montaña, para morir en ella. Yo no soy vuestro antepasado, yo no soy Gran-Lobo-Salvaje, ni sé si Gran-Lobo-Salvaje existe. Y ahora, si realmente no me deseáis ningún mal, dejadme en paz, por favor, dejadme en paz.

Con la cola gacha, sin una mirada atrás hacia el cuerpo de Pompón ni al viejo lobo moribundo, se alejaron los perros, lleno de tristeza el corazón.

ACAMPARON en un valle, en una cueva poco profunda, alfombrada con hojas muertas.

Loa cazaba con los dos perros, y pronto, Tritus, crecido, empezó a seguirles. Cazaban en grupo o de dos en dos, y las piezas temblaban al acercarse ellos.

Un día en que Mally-Pop, acompañado de Tritus, volvía a la guarida llevando en sus fauces una liebre con la columna vertebral partida, Loa arremetió contra ellos, erizada, gruñendo. De un empujón tiró a Tritus rodando por la hierba recién nacida y, lanzándose contra el cocker, le mordió en el costado.

—¡Se ha vuelto loca! —gimió Mally-Pop retrocediendo precipitadamente, mientras

Tritus huía aullando con el rabo entre piernas.

—No —dijo Nenu que llegaba en aquel momento—. No, no está loca, lo que pasa es que acaba de tener perritos. Unos críos guapísimos por cierto, enteramente mi retrato —dijo Nenu muy orondo—. Loa no consiente que nadie se acerque a ellos. Ni siquiera yo —añadió con aire triste.

—¡Ah, bueno, conque se trata de eso! —dijo Mally-Pop.

—Creo que va a ser necesario que nos separemos. Mucho me temo, amigo Mally, que se hayan terminado tus vacaciones.

—Bueno, por una parte casi me alegro —dijo el cocker—. Aquí, entre nosotros, y que nadie se entere... ya empezaba yo a estar un poco harto de esta vida. Tengo muchas ganas de volver, a ver si mi dueña me sigue queriendo todavía. Y luego... ¡psché...!, en el fondo... un poco de perfume, eso sí, ¿eh?, sólo un poco... eso no puede hacerle mal a un perro.

—Yo... yo me quedo aquí, con Loa y la camada —dijo Nenúfar—. Soy feliz. Soy libre. Aguardaré la llegada de Gran-Perro-Amarillo.

CON un último ladrido de despedida, Mally-Pop y Tritus emprendieron el regreso.

Detrás de ellos, la recia silueta del gran perro rojo se erguía sobre una roca.

Mucho tiempo después de haberlo perdido de vista, oyeron un último y sonoro concierto de ladridos.

Descendieron de la montaña, atravesaron de nuevo el río y la meseta, cruzaron las colinas y llegaron a las afueras del pueblo de Mally-Pop.

—¿De verdad que no, Tritus? —preguntó el cocker al joven perro—. ¿No quieres venir para que te adopte mi dueña?

—No —dijo Tritus—. Me apetece ver un poco de mundo. Además... tengo la impresión de que no me iba a gustar el perfume...

Se olieron para decirse adiós, y luego, con un nudo en la garganta, Mally-Pop se fue corriendo hacia su casa, sin mirar para atrás ni una sola vez.

AHORA, Tritus ha adoptado a un hombre, una mujer y sus dos hijos. Sus dueños son muy simpáticos y le preparan unas comidas suculentas.

Es feliz, da unos largos paseos por el campo, juega con los niños.

Tiene cantidad de perros amigos que le respetan. Es un luchador temible, pero leal.

A veces, echado bajo la mesa de la cocina, mueve las patas como si estuviese corriendo y gime.

—Está soñando —dice su dueño.

Está soñando...

Sueña con interminables correrías por praderas cubiertas de rocío, con chapuzones en rápidas corrientes de agua, con cacerías desenfrenadas bajo los altos árboles del bosque, con juegos alocados en la nieve fría.

Sueña...

Y a su lado corren un viejo perro blanco y canelo, que sonríe, un cocker dorado, un perrazo rojo y una perra plateada.

Y sobre ese sueño flotan los dos ojos brillantes y llenos de misterio de Gran-Lobo-Salvaje.

Índice

Marjorie

Letters From A
Professional Nuisance

Michael A. Lee

Best Wishes

Michael A. Lee
(Tory)

To my wife, Ann-Marie, and my two sons, Tom and George.

First published in Great Britain in 2010 by
Portico
10 Southcombe Street
London
W14 0RA

An imprint of Anova Books Company Ltd.

Some of the contents of this book have previously appeared in: *Written in Jest!*, *Wanted: One Freudian Slip* and *Nothing to Complain About?*

ISBN 9-781-9060-3288-3

10 9 8 7 6 5 4 3 2 1

Printed in Great Britain by TJ International Ltd, Padstow, Cornwall

This book can be ordered direct from the publisher at www.anovabooks.com

Letters From A Professional Nuisance

Improbable Jobs, Impossible Items and Implausible Complaints

Michael A. Lee

PORTICO

Introduction

Welcome one and all to my new book.

It is made up of three distinct and yet closely related collections of letters that I have written over a number of years to a vast range of people in high profile positions, and, indeed, the many engaging and entertaining replies I have received as a result. Some relate to a vigorous search for an improbable job, others were constructed as part of a relentless quest for an impossible item, and the rest were written as part of an obsessive project to engineer the most implausible complaint imaginable.

It all began in October 2000, almost 10 years ago. I had only recently turned 40 and, like thousands of other men at this awkward phase of life, decided that my career was only partially addressing my needs and interests and that it was high time I took some positive action and change my daily priorities and perspectives.

As something of a country music fan and enjoying many of the old favourite ballads such as Marty Robbins ' El Paso 'it seemed quite obvious to me that what I needed to do was to apply to become Mayor of the town featured in a foot-tapping cowboy song.

So I did.

A letter was sent to the Town Hall in El Paso, Texas, and within it a glowing self-appraisal presenting a good case for my becoming the next Mayor of El Paso. Whether or not El Paso actually needed a new Mayor was not something I had particularly considered but I posted the application anyway and then duly forgot all about it and continued with my longstanding work and social routines. At least that was the story for 3 weeks.

And then, late one night, the phone rang. 'Hi there Mr Lee, this is Suzanne Michaels of CBS Channel 4 News in El Paso, Texas ringing with regards to your application to be the next Mayor. In relation to the forthcoming Spring elections The Town Hall has passed on a copy of your letter to us and we were interested to contact you. How did you first hear about our elections and why would an Englishman living in England want to be the Mayor of an American City where 80% of the 750 000 population is of Hispanic origin anyway?'

'Oh, ah, yes,' I eloquently replied. 'Well you see – I didn't actually know there were any elections about to take place but of the three types of people you might have applying to be Mayor; those that make things happen, those that watch things happen and those that ask "what happened?". I would be someone who could make things happen and ensure El Paso becomes a better place for everyone. Why do you ask?'

I was a little fazed at such late night questions for which I had a lack of prepared answers but felt I was surviving the situation reasonably well so far.

'Mr Lee, in 60 minutes we are broadcasting a Spring Election programme to the local population and as our 6th Mayoral candidate it would be great to have some background relating to your interest and abilities. Also would it possible for you to send a photo of yourself attached to an Email and we will broadcast your picture along with your comments?'

'I see,' I said, 'that's fine. I'll send the photo right away and I'm only too happy to answer any questions you have for me. Incidentally I didn't realize that El Paso was so large. In the old song which inspired me to write I had the impression of a one street town with a Sheriffs Office, a Saloon and a jail. It sounds that the place is a tad bigger! Does Felina still live there?'

As a consequence of our telephone conversation my face and Yorkshire accent was heard by hundreds of thousands of people around Texas and, as it turned out, in parts of Mexico too! Despite the fact that I could not technically run for mayor without living in the city as a U.S resident for at least a year fame had nevertheless finally crossed my threshold and I was now something of a celebrity albeit in a rather limited capacity. Unlike Andy Warhol's suggestion that everyone is famous for 15 minutes my time frame could be measured in seconds. However it was interesting to observe that, due to a moment of madness or creative letter writing or whatever one would like to call a fleeting desire to be a Texan Mayor, a seed of an idea was planted deep in the core of my convoluted brain and began to grow. As the seed grew so roots were planted in the stuff of imagination and various shoots of opportunity began to appear. My wife suggested that I might be presenting with the first signs of insanity and that it might be a good idea to suppress such unconventional thinking for the sake of comfort and security. I disagreed with her. My mind was made up. I would begin writing letters of application for jobs that were either impossibly beyond my capability or for which I would be deemed massively under-qualified or under-skilled or for jobs that don't exist at all but just possibly might if reality were viewed from a different angle.

I would also write to organisations and institutions asking for items that are generally impossible to acquire and send letters of implausible complaints to anyone who I considered fair game. I would collect the replies, put together a best-selling book or books and perhaps become a wealthy author and lecturer in no time at all. I would then have more time for my wife and my two fine sons, an opportunity to enjoy more fell running and gardening and the money to drink as many Guinness as I would wish without counting the cost. In short I had become within a few short days a man with a mission.

Initially I experienced the odd moment of doubt about my unusual endeavours. 'You should not write letters of that kind to The British Special Forces,' my wife scolded one day. 'First of all they might take offence at your insolence and have you arrested or shot and secondly, even if they don't, whoever heard of a person applying to be a Regimental Mascot!?'

I did worry about the 'being shot' suggestion especially when there was nothing but silence from the Special Air Service or Royal Marine Commandos but when at last a reply arrived from The Parachute Regimental Association in a style of obvious appreciation and humour I was fired up with enthusiasm and self-confidence. For a short time I actually believed I would become the next mascot!

In the following pages you will read my various letters to a variety of organizations and institutions, societies and federations , businesses and individuals and indeed a host of wonderful responses. Of the many, many letters compiled and posted during the last few years I have been interested to note that 75% of them receive a reply and of these a substantial number are written in a manner which has restored my faith in the presence and power of humour.

Even when humour has not been high on the agenda of the person replying to a letter it has still surfaced in the way in which obvious madness, sarcasm and sheer brass-neckedness has been purposefully ignored for the sake of political correctness, process or laziness.

In itself this can be rather amusing.

In these pages are great lessons in lateral thinking, in communication styles, in pursuing unusual opportunities and perhaps even elements of challenging convention. Most of all there is the enjoyment of a jolly good belly-splitting laugh. Most of the following letters are accompanied by their replies. How would you have replied? What would you have said?

There is an old proverb ; 'A Merry Heart Maketh Good Medicine.' I believe that most of you reading these letters will find their mouths turning up at the corners and experience a little levity and lifting of spirits. A page or two read on the tube or plane may put into context the stresses and strains of the day ahead or the day just endured and my guess is that you will begin to think about the sort of letters you yourselves would write if you were exploring your own creative masterpieces. The writing journey that these letters represent has taken me into places I would never have dreamed of and brought me into contact with a wide variety of people from myriad backgrounds.

When I wrote my first letter little did I realize that I would be interviewed by Phil and Fern on 'This Morning Show' or by Nicky Campbell on 'Five Live' just before Christmas one year.

Neither did I envisage drinking wine with Sir Richard Body in the Reformed Club in Pall Mall, dressing in a big cat outfit to be inaugurated as The Beast Of Bodmin Moor in The Jamaica Inn in Cornwall or addressing The Royal College of GPs as after dinner speaker at their annual dinner in Bristol. From a simple idea sprang a plethora of circumstances which are a story in themselves. What ideas have you swimming around in your head that, once released, would create new worlds of experience and opportunities? What will you do with your brainwaves and creative concepts?

Please read on, be amused and be inspired.

MICHAEL PALIN
SOMEWHERE IN
LONDON

Michael A. Lee
10 Woodlea Avenue
Reinwood Manor
Oakes
Huddersfield HD3 4EF

10th January 2002

Dear Michael Lee,

I know you got my letter recently and, fearing that it might be included in your next book, I think a follow-up is required. The problem is I am sent a lot of things to read, some of which frankly aren't worth the time spent, and as I've been filming abroad for most of the last year the time I have to look at unsolicited work is very tight. Hence my somewhat curt reply.

I've now had time to look through the letters and replies you sent me, and I must say they made me laugh a great deal. I think there is something intrinsically funny about the relentlessness of your quest to be these various strange things, and I also like the somewhat obsessive use of certain qualifications, e.g. fell running, to bait the hook.

But what makes it work for me, apart from your creative approach, are the length and detail of some of the replies. There are clearly a lot of very bored people in offices, doctors' surgeries and Lambeth Palaces around the country who have been stirred to imaginative replies by your own batty approach. The joke builds very well the more you read, and I think in the right hands it could make a very funny book indeed.

All good wishes, and apologies for not having really had time to savour the letters the first time round.

Yours,

Michael Palin

PS Do you really exist?

The Commanding Officer
Headquarters
The Parachute Regiment
Aldershot GU11 2BY
Hampshire

Dear Sir

I am writing to you a most unusual letter, namely to apply for the position of 'Regimental Mascot' should that vacancy become available in the near future.

It has always struck me as a rather unusual quirk of many British army regiments to have as a mascot an animal of some non-human kind to parade alongside some of the best trained and most professional soldiers in the world.

Would it not be better instead to employ for a modest sum of money a human mascot such as myself to march, without lead or handler, in a respected fashion dressed in suitable mascot attire along with the troops at various events and offer a human perspective to the role?

Aged 40, I am a seasoned fell-runner so exceptionally fit for my age, educated to degree standard, and though it is quite some time since I donned a uniform I am told by my long-suffering wife I can be a rather dapper chap in a rugged sort of way. If as mascot I am required to dance or sing, this too I am capable of though I would probably require a ration of alcohol beforehand.

In summary I would make an ideal mascot for the Parachute Regiment and look forward to hearing from you reference the appropriate application/interview process.

Sincerely

Michael A. Lee

UTRINQUE PARATUS

AD UNUM OMNES

THE PARACHUTE REGIMENTAL ASSOCIATION

Patron: HIS ROYAL HIGHNESS THE PRINCE OF WALES, KG, KT, PC, GCB, AK, QSO, ADC

BROWNING BARRACKS
ALDERSHOT, GU11 2BU
HAMPSHIRE

From Major (Retd) R D Jenner

13 November 2000

Michael A Lee
Somewhere in West Yorkshire

Dear Mr Lee,

Thank you for your letter and the offer of your services as Regimental Mascot. Should such a vacancy occur and a human selected to replace our Shetland pony you would find yourself against some stiff opposition. We would of course be obliged to advertise nationally for the post in accordance with current legislation. Naturally we would determine the terms and conditions of service. The post would be unpaid, the accommodation rudimentary and the diet agricultural. The attire would best suit someone who is accustomed to wearing leather next to the skin. As silence and steadiness on parade are prerequisites for the job there would be no requirement to dance and /or sing. With this in mind any consumption of alcohol would be out of the question.

The present incumbent has only been in post two years. He is considerably younger than you and whilst no fell-runner could probably give a good account of himself on the flat. I do not anticipate that he will be replaced in the short term. However don't give up hope and keep your eye on the "Situations Vacant" columns of the national press. Remember that these days change is the natural order of things!

Yours sincerely

Roger Jenner

Copy to : Regimental Mascot

3

Major [Retd] R. D. Jenner
The Parachute Regimental Association
Browning Barracks
Aldershot GU11 2BU
Hampshire

Dear Major Jenner

First and foremost let me thank you for an excellent reply dated 13 November 2000 to my application for the job of Regimental Mascot to the Parachute Regiment.

At first I was exceedingly disappointed to hear that you not only had a perfectly adequate Shetland Pony fulfilling mascot duties for the regiment but also that this equine individual is considerably younger than myself and consequently I applied for some alternative positions I thought might be of personal interest. Of the many opportunities I sought they included 'Harbourmaster' for Wigan Pier, 'Deputy Raven-Master' at the Tower of London, and even 'The Sheriff of Nottingham'. Alas – none of these applications has borne even the smallest of fruit of potential employment and as in the case of my letter to Prince Andrew applying to be 'The Grand Old Duke of York' I have not even received a reply.

Having re-read your kind response, therefore, I have arrived at the conclusion that it is time to return to the original idea, express my belief in a competitive attitude to career aspirations and to reaffirm my initial desire for 'mascot status.' If, for whatever reason, the Shetland Pony finds himself/herself no longer capable of the requirements demanded by an elite regiment please do consider me an appropriate replacement. I am willing to accept the terms and conditions of service as you mentioned provided that I might supplement this 'unpaid post' with other part-time work, that I am assured of a roof over my 'rudimentary accommodation' and that the 'agricultural diet' includes a healthy selection of vegetables [I am not too fond of sugar beet every meal time!]. With regards to the 'wearing of leather next to the skin'

I have my hesitations but have bought a good quality watchstrap as a starter. Furthermore I am willing to curtail the alcohol-induced singing and dancing as I can fully appreciate your comments around the need for silence and steadiness on parade. Perhaps I might enjoy a pint or two of off-duty Calibre and a little quiet whistling instead? Finally, despite my entering for the third time this coming Spring the Man vs Horse vs Bike Mountain Marathon in Wales and am training on the Yorkshire moors in preparation, I am also applying myself to 'giving a good account of myself on the flat' by running along a local canal towpath from time to time.

I am quite willing to challenge your Shetland Pony to a race on either terrain over a twenty miles distance. Rather than wait until the position becomes vacant and 'advertise nationally in accordance with current legislation' perhaps the winner of such a race should take all and 'win' the mascot post. As you quite rightly say 'change is certainly the natural order of things these days' and I would certainly make a noticeable change to the regimental order of things if you exchanged mascot from the wee pony with the short legs to me; the hairy-chested fell-runner from Yorkshire.

Failing that would there be any chance of an honorary membership of the Parachute Regimental Association?

Yours tenaciously

M. A. Lee

Michael A. Lee

UTRINQUE PARATUS

AD UNUM OMNES

THE PARACHUTE REGIMENTAL ASSOCIATION

Patron: HIS ROYAL HIGHNESS THE PRINCE OF WALES, KG, KT, PC, GCB, AK, QSO, ADC

BROWNING BARRACKS
ALDERSHOT, GU11 2BU
HAMPSHIRE

From Major (Retd) R D Jenner

Somewhere in West Yorkshire

22 February 2001

Dear Mr Lee,

Thank you for your letter. I regret to inform you that at a recent high level regimental conference, confidence in our present mascot was confirmed unequivocally. Given his present tender age and the fact that his predecessor was not retired until well into his teens it will be some time before a vacancy occurs. I suspect that by then in spite of having run up many hills you will be well over the hill. The age of retirement for humans in the services is 55. Exceptions are made for a handful of very senior officers, but not for mascots!

I note that you have applied without success for a number of posts. Have you considered applying to one of those Welsh regiments that has a goat as mascot? With your fell running experience you have much to offer. Why not look them up after your race this spring.

A race is out of the question. For you to compete on equal terms you would have iron shoes nailed to the palms of your hands and soles of your feet. There would be no anaesthetic of course. How is your pain threshold? Quite high I imagine being a fell runner. Nevertheless at some time in the future you would doubtless want some recompense for the trauma and indignity. The bad publicity and costs would be unacceptable to us.

Sadly you do not qualify for honorary membership of the PRA.. Furthermore it is not in my power to grant it. Bribery won't work either, unless you can run to £10000 to refurbish the mascot's horsebox.

In the seventies a chap calling himself Henry Root published a couple of volumes of letters written in a similar vein to yours. They are probably out of print now, but your local library might have them. They will amuse you.

Good luck in the race.

Roger Semms

Yours sincerely

The Mayor
The Town Hall
Wigan
Lancashire

Dear Sir

I am writing to you a most unusual letter, namely to apply for the position of Harbour Master for Wigan Pier.

Aged 40, I have spent most of my career within industry but with a long-standing interest in all things nautical and particularly in port management. I am interested now in pursuing an alternative career and would be most grateful if you could advise me of any Harbour Master positions currently available within your own world-famous port within the Wigan area.

I am a conscientious and industrious individual sporting a full naval-style beard and moustache and believe not only could I fulfil any duties allocated to me in my capacity as Harbour Master but would look the part as well. I can even sing a rousing selection of sea shanties which might be a useful motivational capability for those individuals reporting to me.

I thank you for your time and consideration in this matter and look forward to hearing from you in the very near future.

Sincerely

M. A. Lee

Michael A. Lee

LEISURE AND CULTURAL SERVICES DEPARTMENT

Director : Rodney F Hill

Wigan
COUNCIL

Our Reference RFH/GHC/Lee/35.00
Your Reference
Please ask for Rodney Hill
Extension 3500
Direct Line (01942) 828500
Date 2 November 2000

Mr M A Lee
Somewhere in West Yorkshire

Dear Mr Lee

Thank you for your letter dated 26 October 2000, which was addressed to the Mayor of Wigan.

Unfortunately, I am unable to help you. Wigan Pier is in fact based on the Leeds/Liverpool canal and, as such, does not have a harbour. Neither do I have any knowledge or expertise on the career opportunities for a Harbour Master.

I suggest that you visit your nearest and largest reference library; they should have advice on career opportunities and what training would be required to become a Harbour Master.

I hope you achieve the position you wish. In the meantime, I enclose publicity about Wigan Pier, which I hope you will visit some time in the future.

Yours sincerely

Rodney F Hill
DIRECTOR OF LEISURE & CULTURAL SERVICES

c.c.   The Mayor

Please address all communications to the Director of Leisure and Cultural Services.
Leisure and Cultural Services Department, Wigan Council,
The Indoor Sports Complex, Loire Drive, Robin Park, Wigan. WN5 0UL
Telephone: (01942) 244991 Telex: 677341 Fax: (01942) 828540
Web Site: www.wiganmbc.gov.uk E-Mail: g.clarke@wiganmbc.gov.uk

Building the future together

Director of Marketing
Lea & Perrins Worcestershire Sauce
HP Foods Limited

Dear Sir/Madam

I am writing to you a most unusual letter, namely to ask what opportunities there might be to become 'Lea & Perrins Worcestershire Sauce Man'.

Might I suggest that L&P Worcestershire Sauce is probably one of the most important food products within its range on the British supermarket shelves and yet, though appreciated by significant numbers of people, has so much consumer potential yet untapped. Should this potential be exploited to the full I believe that your company would benefit from increased profitability and indeed even more consumers would benefit from the enjoyment and indeed nutrition that L&P Worcestershire Sauce offers.

So, having presented my situational analysis you may well be eager to hear my proposed solution? Do you remember what the Milky Bar Kid did for the sales of white milky bar chocolate? Even now, aged 40, I can remember every word from the Milky Bar Kid's song from the 1960s and as a consequence the thought of white chocolate makes my mouth water. I eat so much of it I should be a company shareholder.

If you were to employ me as 'L&P Worcestershire Sauce Man': a reasonably fit 40-year-old, and dress me in a suitable L&P Worcestershire Sauce costume, I could be filmed doing all sorts of fitness-friendly things such as running, cycling, climbing, dancing, canoeing and so on having consumed L&P Worcestershire Sauce with my eggs for breakfast or in a delicious lunchtime sandwich and broadcast with huge success on TV and placed in magazine adverts.

L&P Worcestershire Sauce could be pigeon-holed and advertised for that adult section of the market where nutrition and fitness are becoming more and more interrelated. As probably the most interested man in L&P Worcestershire Sauce in the whole of the UK I am certainly the man for the job. Will you please consider me?! Between us we could establish an L&P Worcestershire Sauce fan club, perhaps even an Internet website for members and start a new business-focused consumer cult following.

I thank you for your time and consideration and look forward to hearing from you in the very near future. Also in the meantime, would there be any courtesy sample bottles of L&P Worcestershire Sauce I could request in order to stock up my Christmas cupboard?

Sincerely and mouth-wateringly

M. A. Lee

Michael A. Lee

HP Foods Limited

Please reply to :-
HP Foods Limited, Tower Road, Aston Cross, Birmingham, B6 5AB
Tel : 0121 - 359 4911 : Fax : 0121 - 380 2335

Our Ref: 4449

01 December 2000

Mr Lee
Somewhere in West Yorkshire

Dear Mr Lee

Re: L&P Worcestershire Sauce

Thank you for your recent letter and your compliments on our L&P Worcestershire Sauce. We are extremely pleased that you find our product so versatile and economical.

We enclose a product voucher so that you may sample and enjoy some of the other products in our range and have passed your interesting offer to our marketing department for their consideration!

It is always pleasant to receive comments and opinions from valued customers, such as yourself, and we thank you for taking the time to write. These comments help us to assess the market and our consumers which hopefully helps us to meet their demands.

We hope that you continue to enjoy our products in the future.

Yours sincerely

Caroline Saunders
Consumer Services

Registered Office: Mollison Avenue, Enfield, Middlesex EN3 7JZ.
Telephone: (44) 0990 326663 Facsimile: (44) 0990 134881
Registered in England No. 2251694

The Manager
John Lewis
Oxford Street
London W1A 1EX

Dear Sir/Madam

I am writing to you a most unusual letter, namely to apply for the position of 'The Rather Jolly Mobile Christmas Tree' at the John Lewis Department Store of Oxford Street. I guess that it is fair to say that although the idea of a Christmas Grotto complete with Santa Claus is a well established and popular tradition in many department stores that of a 'Rather Jolly Mobile Christmas Tree' is probably a novel one. So, here is the idea in detail.

If you were to employ me as the aforementioned Christmas tree dressed appropriately in coniferous foliage and decorated with a range of suitable baubles and lights I could spend my time planting myself at various key locations within the store to greet the customers in a festive and hearty manner. Every now and then I could uproot myself and wander off in as tree-like manner as possible to the next location and repeat the whole process to the delight of your many customers. The benefits I am sure would include the drawing of curious individuals into your store swelling the ranks of potential shoppers, raising the Christmas spirit in a way conducive to relaxed spending and indeed increasing even further the profitability for your business as a result. In addition I could keep an arboreal eye open for the odd dastardly shoplifter and wrap my branches around that person whilst security was summoned.

I believe it is 'fir' to say that once 'spruced' up I would offer an interesting and mood elevating attraction and dare I say it am 'pineing' to hear from you reference my application.I trust that you have not had a 'forest' of similar letters and consequently will still be able to see the 'wood from the trees'. Many thanks for your time and consideration and I look forward to hearing from you in the very near future.

In the meantime should you feel that my letter deserves an acknowledgement in the form of a small hamper of delicious John Lewis food, if indeed you have hampers of this kind, I am sure that my family saplings and I would do enormous justice to its' mouth-watering consumption.

Sincerely, with seasons greetings and ever the Yorkshire Opportunist,

M. A. Lee

Michael A. Lee

JOHN LEWIS
Oxford Street

18 December 2000
REC/JEB/31

A branch of the
John Lewis Partnership

Oxford Street
London W1A 1EX
Telephone (020) 7629 7711

Direct Line 0171 514 5337

Personal
Mr M A Lee

Somewhere in West Yorkshire

Dear Mr Lee

Thank you for your recent letter enquiring about possible employment with John Lewis.

I regret to inform you that we have no suitable vacancies at present, and are, therefore, unable to consider your application. We are rather concerned that you would have to 'uproot' yourself from Huddersfield but if you would like to contact any of our other 'branches' , we would of course 'leaf' that decision to 'yew'.

I would like to mention however that I very much enjoyed reading your letter and I would like to wish you a very happy Christmas.

I am sorry I cannot be of more help, but would like to thank you for the interest you have shown.

Yours sincerely

Mrs J E Britton
Staff Office

CALEYS
Windsor

BY APPOINTMENT TO
HER MAJESTY THE QUEEN
SUPPLIERS OF HOUSEHOLD
AND FANCY GOODS

BY APPOINTMENT TO
HER MAJESTY QUEEN ELIZABETH
THE QUEEN MOTHER
SUPPLIERS OF HOUSEHOLD
AND FANCY GOODS

**A branch of the
John Lewis Partnership**

High Street
Windsor
Berkshire SL4 1LL
Telephone (01753) 863241

FIH/CW
29 December 2000

Mr Michael A Lee
Somewhere in West Yorkshire

Dear Mr Lee,

Thank you for your letter of 7 December 2000 which has been forwarded to us by one of our other '*branches*'.

After '*conifering*' with other members of management, I believe that the option of a jolly mobile Christmas tree is not viable for Caleys and this '*leaves*' me no choice but to decline your kind offer.

May I wish you and yours a happy and prosperous New Year.

Yours sincerely,

Frances Hickman
General Manager

The Commanding Officer
Marine Nationale
2, Rue Royale
PARIS 8
00350 Armees
France

Dear Sir

I am writing to you a most unusual letter, namely to ask what opportunities are available to me in securing a job with the French Navy as a 'Submarine Periscope Polishing Executive'.

I have for many years been fascinated by the concept of travel beneath the ocean and particularly by the notion of observing objects which are above the surface of the water through the periscope of a suitably submerged submarine. It concerns me to think that should the eyepiece of a periscope be dusty or greasy, appropriate military observation could be severely compromised and, of course, in a critical battle situation could mean the difference between victory and defeat.

If you were to employ me as a 'Submarine Periscope Polishing Executive' I would endeavour to ensure all my periscopes were as clean as clean can be and 100 per cent operational all of the time. I am a jolly good polisher at the best of times and should you require references my wife has agreed to supply them on request. She has also asked whether I might be assigned to a submarine that spends a considerable time away from port and is often deep under the ocean far from land. In addition she felt a French naval training programme would be an interesting contrast to my present work in the UK and although she knows we would not see each other as often as we do at present, thought it a potentially enriching and horizon – widening experience. I am not wholly sure why this would be her wish but I respect her greatly.

Many thanks for your time and consideration and I look forward to hearing from you in the very near future.

Sincerely

Michael A. Lee

P.S. I am most willing to learn to speak French.

MINISTÈRE DE LA DÉFENSE

**MARINE
NATIONALE**

SERVICE D'INFORMATION
ET DE RELATIONS PUBLIQUES
DE LA MARINE
2, RUE ROYALE - PARIS 8ᵉ
00350 ARMÉES
TÉLÉPHONE 01 42 92 16 39 (MARINE 21 639)
FAX 01 40 20 04 90

Paris, le **.15 JAN. 2001**

N°   86   SIRPA/Marine/NP

Sir Michael A. Lee
Somewhere in West Yorkshire

Dear Sir,

I have been very interested in your proposition of becoming the french navy first 'submarine periscope polishing executive'. The inconvenience of our dusty and greasy periscopes has been thouroughly and extensively analysed by the international press (La Dépêche de Montauvert 10.01.2000, The Times 30.02.2000, The Longwood Chronicle 07.05.2000).

Moreover, your private and wise initiative reinforces the close military cooperation between our two countries.
I suggest a slight extension to your proposition in order to cover both our submarine and outerspace activities. Spy satellites also require clean glasses. By the way, the human physical requirements to rotate around the planet, attached to a satellite are close to those required for operational deep sea periscope polishing.

May I propose that we meet to examine the details related to your future employment of 'submarine periscope & spy satellite glasses polishing executive'. A convenient place for me would be on the top of the mid-Atlantic ridge (depth minus 1054 meters) by 40°N in two weeks. Just knock at the door of my greasy periscope.

Sincerely.

Capitaine de vaisseau Olivier Lajous

The Director General
MI5

Dear Sir/Madam

I am writing to you a most unusual letter, namely to suggest to you that I might have been approached in a rather clever but round-about fashion to become a French spy and thought it best to air my concerns to yourself or indeed MI6 if more appropriate.

Shortly before Xmas 2000 I wrote a spoof job application to the Commanding Officers of various world navies asking to be employed as a 'Submarine Periscope Polishing Executive' in a bid to receive some interesting replies for a book I am writing. [I attach a copy of the letter sent to the French Navy]

To my great delight and indeed amusement I received an excellent reply from a Captain in the French Ministry of Defence embracing my job idea with significant enthusiasm and indeed encouraging some extended duties to include cleaning the glasses on the French Spy satellites. He also suggested we met to discuss the idea further as you will read in a copy of his reply as enclosed.

Now call me old fashioned if you will but does this not appear to be a classic spy recruitment scenario? It has all the elements of foreign surveillance strategy; calling me 'Sir' to create rapport and goodwill hence buttering me up for the recruitment process, a mention of space-based spy satellites, and indeed a suggestion of a covert meeting in a far less than visible place where secretive liaison could take place. What's more Captain Lajous has suggested that my employment might 'reinforce close military co-operation between our two countries.' The whole thing makes my spine tingle!

I can assure you that I am a loyal and patriotic citizen of the UK, a born and bred Yorkshireman, and in no way inclined to spy for the French but would be most interested to hear from you with any words of advice you might have for me. Should there be any need for me to write to MI6 separately or indeed send a copy of my concerns to any MI6-employed personnel with an interest in recruitment matters, please do let me know.

Sincerely

M. A. Lee

Michael A. Lee

PO BOX 3255
LONDON
SW1P 1AE

Mr M Lee   7 March 2001
Somewhere in West Yorkshire

Dear Mr Lee

Thank you for your letter of 14 February 2001.

It would appear that the reply you received from the French Ministry of Defence is nothing more than a humorous response to your spoof application.

Yours sincerely,

The Director General

The Duke of Edinburgh
Buckingham Palace
London

Dear Sir

I am writing to you a most unusual letter, namely to apply for the position of 'Gentleman Usher of the Black Rod' at the House of Lords.

Aged 41, I have almost twenty years' experience working within an industry which depends greatly on communication skills and as a consequence have developed a strong, clear voice should I be required to announce my presence to those of the Commons in any verbal manner.

More importantly I have had substantial experience beating on my own front door when returning from the local public house late in the evening in an attempt to persuade my disgruntled wife to release the door-bolts and let me in and this I have done on many occasions. Usually she has agreed to an admission!

Although I have not undertaken this 'summoning' with an ebony stick surmounted with a gold lion – as I would with my staff of office should I be successful in my application for the job – I have brandished various large sticks that have fallen from oak, ash and beech trees in my back garden and knocked heartily in a way that has helped me significantly refine my knocking skills.

If I was employed for the aforementioned job and became a personal attendant of the Sovereign, I can assure you that I am a Royalist and wholeheartedly support our Royal traditions and ceremonies.

I do hope that you will consider me for the job and look forward to hearing from you in the very near future.

Sincerely

M. A. Lee

Michael A. Lee

From: Captain Jamie Lyon, Grenadier Guards

BUCKINGHAM PALACE

9th January, 2001.

Dear Mr Lee,

The Duke of Edinburgh has asked me to thank you for your letter, the contents of which have been noted.

Yours sincerely

Temporary Equerry

Mr. Michael A. Lee

BUCKINGHAM PALACE, LONDON. SW1A 1AA

The Chief Executive
The Guildhall
Nottingham NG1 4BT

Dear Sir/Madam

I am writing to you a most unusual letter, namely to ask whether there still exists the position 'Sheriff of Nottingham' and if so, if I might apply for the position when it next becomes available.

Ever since I was a small boy I have had an interest in the ancient stories of Robin Hood and his merry men, of Sherwood Forest, and in the swashbuckling adventures of all concerned. It strikes me however that stealing from anyone, whether rich or poor, is not exactly the most civilised way of going about the pursuit of justice and has led me to believe that the historical Sheriff of Nottingham was probably not quite the scoundrel he was made out to be. If in 2001 a band of sword-wielding, forest-dwelling rascals came around to my house, threatened my family and I and stole our computer, I would be most aggrieved and keen to seek the help of the local police.

Should therefore a position be available for me to apply to become the current Sheriff of Nottingham I believe I would be a worthy candidate for several reasons; I am an honest, hardworking member of the community. I like Nottingham and, should the need arise, could travel there easily from West Yorkshire by car or train. I once rode a horse in Canada and so could pose for the press when required although I guess it is fair to say that a motor vehicle of some description would be more suitable these days. Should any modern day criminals take refuge in local woods I am an experienced orienteer and fell runner and would almost certainly track them down. Finally, I love banqueting and would relish the chance to dine at Nottingham Castle.

I thank you for your time and consideration and look forward to hearing from you in the very near future. May I also wish you a very happy New Year.

Sincerely

M. A. Lee

Michael A. Lee

Corporate Affairs

Chief Executive's Department
The Guildhall
Nottingham
NG1 4BT
Tel: 0115 915 4725
Fax: 0115 915 4434
~~email: julie.gunn@nottinghamcity.gov.uk~~
Email: chris.bowron@nottinghamcity.gov.uk

Mr Michael Lee
Somewhere in West Yorkshire

15 January 2001

Dear Mr Lee

Thank you for your letter dated 1st January 2001, in which you state your desire to be considered for the role of Sheriff of Nottingham.

It is traditional that the following requirements should be met before assuming this role:

🏹 You must be elected as a councillor to represent a ward of Nottingham

🏹 You are nominated by your fellow councillors to be elected as the Sheriff of Nottingham.

I hope that this information is useful to you.

Nottingham City Council would like to thank you for showing a great interest in our city and would like you to accept the enclosed gift as a token of our appreciation.*

Yours sincerely

Chris Bowron
Service Manager
Corporate Promotions

(*This was a tie embroidered with the Nottingham heraldic crest.)

Nottingham
our style is legendary

Printed on recycled paper ♻

Chief Executive
ABTA
68–71 Newman Street
London W1P 4AH

Dear Sir

I am writing to you a most unusual letter, namely to ask if you might help me find a rather different holiday based on a travel book I read recently involving journeys to several remote parts of the world and therefore become a 'Holidaymaker with a Difference'. Whether it would be possible to visit all of the places mentioned in the travel book over a single extended holiday or whether I would have to plan the complete package of journeys over a series of holidays I am not sure, but would be most grateful for your help either way.

I understand that the journey between many of the island destinations described by the author was by boat but I am unable to pinpoint the exact location of some of these islands in my world atlas. I do, however, have in front of me a list of place-names which might be of help and are as follows: Brobdingnag, Laputa, Balnibarbi, and Luggnagg. I believe that there was a visit to 'the country of the Houyhnhnms' also.

I was extremely interested to read the descriptions of these places in the aforementioned travel book which, incidentally was written by a Mr J Swift, and must admit that my imagination and desire to visit them has been significantly stimulated. The thoughts of wading through fields of giant corn beneath a blue sky, warm sun and close to the sea is most appealing when considered in the midst of an English Winter. I was not particularly excited by the prospect of meeting pirates as was the case in one of the travel books' chapters but thought that since there is significantly more security in international waters than was the case when the book was written this would not be a real modern-day threat.

I do hope that you will be able to assist me in my search for a holiday which involves some or all of the places I have mentioned and would be grateful for advice around holiday costings, recommended times to travel and other relevant information, such as required vaccinations, and look forward to hearing from you in the very near future.

Many thanks for your time and consideration.

Sincerely

M. A. Lee

Michael A. Lee

ABTA

The Association of British Travel Agents Ltd
Registered in England No: 551311 London

London W1P 4AH
Telephone: 020 7637 24
Telefax: 020 7637 07
Email: abta@abta.co.

Mr. M.A. Lee,
Somewhere in West Yorkshire

ITR/JDA/3566

11 January, 2001

Dear Mr. Lee,

Thank you for your letter, 9 January 2001, from which I was interested to learn of your planned journey.

I fear that it may be inadvisable to visit the islands you have identified, as I understand the natives may be hostile particularly the extremely large citizens of Brobdingnag and the rather superior horse-like inhabitants of Houyhnhnms. Accordingly, the Foreign and Commonwealth Office have consistently issued advice not to visit these destinations except in your dreams.

With regards to our advice as to whether it would be best to make a single extended trip or a series of individual holidays, I would caution that unless you can assemble an extremely large group of children with powerful lungs you currently lack the propulsion available to Mr. Gulliver when making his voyage, and therefore may find it difficult to reach your intended destination in either case.

I am sorry to send you such a disappointing reply but hope you will not be deterred from making alternative holiday arrangements this year with one of our members.

Yours sincerely,

I.T. REYNOLDS
CHIEF EXECUTIVE

INVESTOR IN PEOPLE

22

Select World Travel

31 Haven Road . Canford Cliffs . Poole . Dorset . BH13 7LE . United Kingdom
Telephone: Bournemouth 01202 709881 • Fax: 01202 707662
E-mail: info@selectworldtravel.co.uk • Web: www.selecttravel.co.uk

10 January 2000   RR/MAL

Mr Michael Lee
Somewhere in West Yorkshire

Dear Mr. Lee,

Thank you for your letter of 9th January requesting help in arranging a somewhat different type of holiday.

The book that you refer to as having recently read must, I think, be "Gulliver's Travels" and I regret to advise you that it is in fact a work of fiction and none of the places you mention actually exist.

I have to admit that on first reading your letter it occurred to me that maybe it was a "wind up", if you will excuse the expression. But, on reflection it occurred to me that perhaps the writer, having become disillusioned with the service offered by most travel agents, had hit upon an unusual way of sorting the wheat from the chaff.

At Select World Travel we do pride ourselves on finding the right holiday for even the most exacting of clients – and am sure we could assist you in finding that very unusual holiday.

If you would like to pursue the matter further, please do not hesitate to call me so that we may discuss your requirements.

Yours sincerely,

Robert Readman
Manager.

Select World Travel is a division of Select Worldchoice Limited
Registered Office: 1 St. Stephen's Court, St. Stephen's Road, Bournemouth BH2 6LA
Registered in England Number: 3514295   VAT Registration Number: 717 5498 05

worldchoice

Mr R. Readman, Manager
Select World Travel
31 Haven Road
Canford Cliffs
Poole BH13 7LE
Dorset

Dear Mr Readman

First and foremost I would like to thank you for your letter of the 10th January concerning my enquiry around visiting the Islands of Laputa, Brobdingnag, Balnibarbi, Luggnagg and the 'country of the Houyhnhnms'.

I am grateful to you for pointing out to me that these islands do not actually exist other than in the mind of the writer Jonathan Swift and learning that his was a work of fiction 'Gulliver's Travels' and not a travel book as such has certainly helped explain why I could not find them in my world atlas. It is also clear now why some of the descriptions concerning rather small people and giants appeared to be so exaggerated!

As far as priding yourselves at Select World Travel at 'finding the right holiday for even the most exacting of clients' I am indeed sure that you might be able to assist me further and find for me an 'that very unusual holiday' alternative to my previous request especially in the light of my obvious and recent disappointment.
In this regard I would be most interested to know if you could offer suggestions regards my enjoying an activity holiday this coming summer which would, I suggest, offer an enormous amount of fun and indeed add a significant element of education also.

Very recently I was reading a well-thumbed copy of a book by a certain Mr Archy O'Logy; an Irish writer I presume, who described a place famous for its' fossils and ancient history called Gondwanaland. I have not had a great deal of time over the last few weeks to research this place or indeed to look at holiday options as my workload has been particularly heavy and so would be most obliged if you could help me in finding a package that would include travel to and from Gondwanaland, accommodation and including potential for some fossil-hunting excursions. I would also be grateful for any information around currency required in Gondwanaland and any well-written and informative travel-guides that you might recommend. I have already bought myself a new magnifying glass and pith helmet and am really looking forward to firming up a holiday booking and setting out on a refreshing and exciting summer vacation.

Many thanks indeed for your time and consideration and I appreciate the interest you have shown in finding for me that 'very unusual holiday alternative'.

Sincerely   M. A. Lee   .

Select World Travel

31 Haven Road . **Canford Cliffs** . **Poole** . **Dorset** . **BH13 7LE** . **United Kingdom**

Telephone: **Bournemouth 01202 709881** • Fax: **01202 707662**

E-mail: **info@selectworldtravel.co.uk** • Web: **www.selecttravel.co.uk**

10 January 2000   RR/MAL

Mr Michael Lee
Somewhere in West Yorkshire

Dear Mr. Lee,

I am in receipt of your letter dated 13th March regarding the possibility of a holiday in Gondwanaland.

However, I fear that once again I must disillusion you. Gondwanaland does not in fact exist. Gondwanaland or Gondwana are the names given to a hypothetical supercontinent in the Southern Hemisphere which comprised the land masses that now make up Africa, Australia, India and South America some 200 million years ago.

So, while Gondwanaland itself does not in fact exist, it would be possible to visit the continents which at one time supposedly formed it. Probably the best way of doing so would be to take advantage of one of a number of extremely good value Round-the-World fares that are available these days. One of the best being the Star Alliance fare of £1399.00 for Economy travel and £3199.00 for Business Class travel. These fares are valid for 1 year of travel, allow a minimum of 3 stops and a maximum of 15, with a maximum permitted mileage of 29,000 miles. This fare does not include airport taxes.

If you care to let me know which places your are interested in visiting I will be happy to work on a provisional itinerary for you.

We do require a non-refundable payment of £25.00 to be paid before we undertake involved, tailor-made enquires. This payment would however, become part of your payment should you decide to go ahead with the booking.

I look forward to assisting you with your travel arrangements.

Sincere regards,

Robert Readman, Manager.

Select World Travel is a division of Select Worldchoice Limited
Registered Office: 1 St. Stephen's Court, St. Stephen's Road, Bournemouth BH2 6LA
Registered in England Number: 3514295 VAT Registration Number: 717 5498 05

worldchoice

Mr R. Readman
Manager
Select World Travel ...

Dear Mr Readman

First and foremost I would like to thank you for your letter dated 21 March 2001 concerning my enquiry around visiting Gondwanaland.

I am most grateful to you for pointing out that once again my interest has been misplaced in a region that doesn't actually exist; or at least has not existed for many years if ever at all.I intend to revisit the book that described this non-existent land and perhaps even write to the author; a certain Archy O'Logy, and complain about the misinformation supplied therein.

I also thank you for taking the time and effort to write to me about ways in which I might visit many of the continents that were thought at one time to form Gondwanaland. This information has been most helpful.

However, having already been disappointed on two occasions as a direct consequence of reading what I believed were authoritative travel books, I have decided to obtain some ideas for my summer holiday from personal recommendations instead. In this regard, I would be most grateful for any advice you might have for me reference a holiday destination of significant interest.

Only last week I met an old friend of mine in the local doctors surgery waiting room who explained that he had, a little while ago, been feeling significantly below par and in need of a holiday. He had felt constantly tired, somewhat depressed and was gaining weight. Having spoken to his GP I gather he found the solution to his problems in what I presume to be a group of islands called the Islets of Langerhans.

My friend described the degree of contrast he had experienced after hearing about the Islets of Langerhans and told me that not only was he refreshed and back to normal weight but that even his great thirst had been quenched. I have never seen a man so changed by a holiday!

Once again I have been scouring my world atlas but cannot find this group of islands anywhere. I presume that the word 'Islets' suggest a relatively small landmass and so would require a more experienced search than is possible with my own reference source. Mr Readman, if you were able to help me in my quest for this destination I am sure I will have found the answer to my 2001 holiday needs. Incidentally, I seem to remember my friend mentioning something about travelling there by Pan Creas Airlines or Shipping; I wonder if that might be of help in your research.

Once again many thanks indeed for your time and consideration and I look forward to hearing from you in the very near future.

Sincerely   M. A. Lee   .

Select World Travel

31 Haven Road . Canford Cliffs . Poole . Dorset . BH13 7LE . United Kingdom

Telephone: Bournemouth 01202 709881 • Fax: 01202 707662

E-mail: info@selectworldtravel.co.uk • Web: www.selecttravel.co.uk

10 January 2000   RR/MAL

Mr Michael Lee
Somewhere in West Yorkshire

Dear Mr Lee,

I am in receipt of your latest letter regarding your ongoing quest for that 'rather different holiday' in which you express an interest in visiting the Islets of Langerhans.

However, I fear that yet again you have been misled.

I do not know if you ever saw a film entitled "The Incredible Journey", in which a researcher was shrunk to a microscopic size, placed in an equally microscopic submarine and injected into the vein of a another person and then proceeded to explore that person's body?

This, I am afraid, is the only way in which you could ever visit the Islets of Langerhans as they are located on one's pancreas – and are named after the doctor who discovered them.

As a matter of interest, "Where are the Islets of Langerhans?" is a trick question often included in travel quizzes.   And I seem to recall that the same question is also included in the game of "Trivial Pursuit".

I am sorry to have to disappoint you once again, but I suspect that the friend you met at your doctor's surgery thoroughly enjoyed pulling your leg!

For myself, I am intrigued wondering just where this is all leading.

Sincere regards,

Robert Readman
Manager.

  Select World Travel is a division of Select Worldchoice Limited
Registered Office: 1 St. Stephen's Court, St. Stephen's Road, Bournemouth BH2 6LA
Registered in England Number: 3514295 VAT Registration Number: 717 5498 05

Mr R. Readman, Manager
Select World Travel
31 Haven Road
Canford Cliffs
Poole BH13 7LE
Dorset

Dear Mr Readman

First and foremost I would like to thank you for your letter dated 9 April 2001 in reply to my enquiries around visiting the Islets of Langerhans. I am grateful to you for explaining to me that these 'islets' are not small islands as I first thought but rather specialised organs located on the pancreas and, as I have since discovered, apparently responsible for secreting the hormone insulin.

When I realised that yet again my search for an interesting and restful holiday had been misdirected I contacted the old friend I had met in the doctor's surgery and asked him why he had so cruelly led me up the garden path. I am a little embarrassed to tell you that the fault was not his; alas it was confusion in my own understanding of what he was telling me. This unfortunate fellow had indeed felt constantly tired, somewhat depressed and was gaining weight but the focus mentioned to him around the Islets of Langerhans by his GP was in reference to his development of Type 2 Diabetes and his apparent refreshment to the initiation of appropriate medical treatment. I cannot believe I misunderstood his tale to the degree that I would apply for a 'similar holiday' as a result!

On the subject of medical matters I am amazed to read in your recent letter that modern technology has now enabled 'a researcher to be shrunk to a microscopic size, placed in an equally microscopic submarine and injected into the vein of another person' and moreover that a film has been made of this. This documentary surely deserves the title The Incredible Journey and I will certainly look out for it on my Cable TV Discovery channel. It sounds truly amazing.

Do you think there will be any commercial applications as far as this technological advance is concerned in the context of holiday excursions? If there were I would, within certain price constraints, be most interested in being shrunk to the same size as the aforementioned researcher and submarine and be injected into the bodies of various notable individuals. It may be quite revealing to explore the unknown cerebral depths of grey matter belonging to various British politicians or indeed the workings of the ears of certain rap musicians.

For pure relaxation, however, I think I would have to choose, if in agreement, the bodies of various supermodels simply to marvel at their construction and general fitness.I would be most interested to know if there is anything currently available in this regard or whether this would be something to consider at some point in the future. Finally, Mr Readman, as far as your intrigue is concerned as to where 'all this is leading' I would say simply that I am looking for 'that very unusual holiday' to make 2001 a year to remember and relish and to achieve my ambition of becoming a 'Holidaymaker with a difference'.

Many thanks again for your time and consideration and I look forward to hearing from you in the very near future.

Sincerely

M. A. Lee .

Michael A. Lee

Select World Travel

31 Haven Road . Canford Cliffs . Poole . Dorset . BH13 7LE . United Kingdom
Telephone: Bournemouth 01202 709881 • Fax: 01202 707662
E-mail: info@selectworldtravel.co.uk • Web: www.selecttravel.co.uk

10 January 2000   RR/MAL

Mr Michael Lee
Somewhere in West Yorkshire

Dear Mr. Lee,

My apologies for the delay in replying to your letter of 17th April, but I have been away on vacation.

I am pleased to forward four brochures that I feel may offer suggestions for that rather special holiday you are looking for.

I have included the Tauck World Discovery Antarctica brochure – although it is for the period January/February 2002 (the Antarctic Summer).

Australia, of course, offers unbounded possibilities for the adventurous, But I have included the Australasia By Rail brochure as I do feel that train travel is one of the best ways to see a country.

Costa Rica has not yet been spoilt by mass tourism and is one of the most eco-friendly nations in the world.

I do hope that you may find something in these brochures that stimulates your interest.

Once you have had a chance to study them, please do not hesitate to call if you have any questions or would like further information on a particular holiday or destination.

Sincere regards,

Robert Readman
Manager.

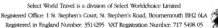

Head of Personnel
North Cornwall District Council
Higher Trenant Road
Wadebridge
Cornwall PL27 6TW

Dear Sir

I am writing to you a most unusual letter, namely to apply for the position of 'Beast of Bodmin Moor' if indeed this position is currently available.

I would be most grateful for your advice on this matter but it does seem to me as though a significant time period has passed since any news of the so-called 'Beast of Bodmin Moor' appeared in the media and I can't help wondering whether the incumbent of past years has disappeared from the scene through retirement, career change or as the quarry of a successful hunter.

Aged 41, I am presently employed within industry as a sales executive but am keen to pursue alternative opportunities that might offer some new interest, challenge and indeed variety to life. I believe I would be an ideal candidate for the position of 'Beast of Bodmin Moor' since I have a great love of the great outdoors and am, as I believe was the previous 'Beast', a very hairy individual. I am well known for my roaring and howling and am as happy sleeping in a wooded copse or cave as I am in my own bed at home. In addition, I am rather fond of lamb-chops and though I generally buy mine at a supermarket or restaurant I would certainly consider a more natural supply if this would help the cause of the 'Beast of Bodmin Moor' legend to continue in a vigorous fashion.

As a member of the Fell Runners Association I am in excellent physical condition and experienced in the navigation of and survival in challenging terrain and well able to keep ahead of the majority of potential trackers.

I would not expect a particularly high salary although I would be most interested to know if, as part and parcel of the job package, there would be the funding for a new pair of Walsh fell-running shoes and some equipment with which to create panther tracks. An assorted bag of big-cat teeth would also be helpful.

I thank you for your time and consideration and look forward to hearing from you in the very near future.

Yours sincerely

Michael A. Lee

NORTH CORNWALL DISTRICT COUNCIL

Mr. M.A. Lee
Somewhere in West Yorkshire

Higher Trenant Road
Wadebridge
Cornwall
PL27 6TW

Telephone
01208 893231

Fax
01208 893232

Email

Dear Mr. Lee

Beast of Bodmin Moor

Please ask for
Mr C C Burnham

Your Ref

My Ref
CCB/JMS

6 March 2001

H Chapman CPFA IRRV
Director of Finance &
Administration

Thank you for your letter applying for the above position.

Despite qualities and characteristics which would seem admirably to suit you for this role, as detailed in your letter, regrettably I have to inform you that, owing to financial constraints, the Council is having to withdraw its support for this post at the end of the current contract.

The present postholder, who is on a seasonal "as and when" contract, has had his hours of work steadily reduced over the past few years, to the point where they are, quite frankly, a mere remnant of their former heyday and some elements of the community are beginning to ask "what's the point?"

This is all very disappointing for us in the Personnel Department, who see the Beast as one or our more enterprising Staff Development initiatives. You may like to know that, like yourself, for years the current Beast, Ebeneezer Peabody, occupied a Senior Management position, but following a stringent selection procedure, including psychometric testing, he embarked on a specially tailored "deconstruction programme", whereby he was systematically stripped of the goal-orientated, focused behaviour which had dampened his spirits and held back the development of his inner aura for so long. In parallel, his perverse leanings towards leadership qualities, performance management and teamwork and his predilection for phrases culled from the latest management textbooks were successfully reduced to a sequence of pre-cultural pounces, jumps, yelps and grunts. However, as you may imagine, this was a very resource-intensive operation, which in the current economic climate we cannot afford to repeat.

I am grateful for your interest in applying for the post and for bringing a ray of sunshine to these rather gloomy winter days. I wish you well in your search for alternative employment and am certain that in time you will find a niche to suit your evident talents. Please accept a copy of the 2001 North Cornwall Guide with my compliments for perusal in your quieter moments and of course, if you are ever down here in the vicinity of Dozmary Pool, do drop in.

Yours sincerely

Chris Burnham

Head of Personnel

THE BEST OF BODMIN MOOR
MARKETING GROUP

Hon. Secretary: Colliford Tavern
St Neot
Liskeard
Cornwall
PL14 6PZ

Tel: 01208 821335

8th May 2001

Mr M A Lee
Somewhere in West Yorkshire

Dear Mr Lee

With reference to your letter of 25th February 2001, which has been referred to our group. Firstly, thank you for your excellent application for the position of 'Beast of Bodmin Moor'. The present incumbent may well wish to stand down for a time, as the rigours of public notoriety and endeavours to avoid the papparrazi are becoming a strain on his family life.

If you will kindly forward your curriculum vitae, references and a recent photograph, we will be pleased to give your application further consideration.

Yours sincerely

Laura Edwards

Laura Edwards (Miss)
Hon. Secretary
The Best of Bodmin Moor Marketing Group

Mr C. Burnham
Head of Personnel
North Cornwall District Council
Higher Trenant Road
Wadebridge PL27 6TW
Cornwall

Dear Mr Burnham

Many thanks indeed for your excellent reply with reference to my application to become the next 'Beast of Bodmin Moor'. I was understandably disappointed to hear that financial constraints within the council are such that this position is no longer sustainable but can sympathise with such resourcing challenges.

It sounds as though the 'deconstruction process' in which your current Beast, Mr Peabody, was involved was an interesting and indeed arduous one and that his consequent development of a 'sequence of pre-cultural pounces, jumps, yelps and grunts' have made him a fitting role-model for his adventures on Bodmin Moor. He sounds to me as someone who might well have replaced the character 'Father Jack' in that memorable TV series Father Ted had there been such a need and should Mr Peabody have been seeking an alternative job. Here in Yorkshire I currently work with several people who make similar yelps and grunts but who sadly have never actually been deconstructed as such. Neither are they able to pounce or jump very quickly at all! They are beasts of a sort but would not survive the moors for long.

Many thanks also for your kind invitation to 'drop in' when in the vicinity of Dozmary Pool. Having looked at the 2001 North Cornwall Guide that you kindly sent me I have decided to do just that. I am currently packing my swimming trunks and making some plans to travel southwards. In the meantime I wondered if I might be so bold as to apply for the position of Sir Bedivere the Second. I assume that the original Sir Bedivere would have passed away many years ago and that his demise has left a rather important role when it comes to the casting of swords.

As a member of the Fell Runners Association I can assure you that I am reasonably strong and believe I would be an exceptionally good sword-caster. I would also be most pleased to entertain the immortal Lady of the Lake if this was part and parcel of the job description.

I trust that the ghost of Jan Tregeagle has not managed to empty the pool with his limpet shell by the time this letter reaches you, thus making the responsibilities of Sir Bedivere obsolete, and I look forward to hearing from you in the very near future.

Yours sincerely and hoping soon to be knighted

Michael A. Lee

NORTH CORNWALL DISTRICT COUNCIL

Mr M A Lee
Somewhere in West Yorkshire

Higher Trenant Road
Wadebridge
Cornwall
PL27 6TW

Telephone
01208 893231

Fax
01208 893232

Email
chris.burnham@ncdc.gov.
uk

Please ask for
Chris Burnham

Your Ref

My Ref
CCB/SS

16 March 2001

H Chapman CPFA IRRV
Director of Finance &
Administration

Dear Mr Lee

Thank you for your letter of 8th March 2001.

I note your continued interest in working for the Council in some capacity and your inventive suggestion of assuming the role of Sir Bedivere the Second.

I am afraid that with your limited experience of swordsmanship you would not be cut out for this sort of work. I am concerned too at your reference to 'entertaining' the Lady of the Lake; the Council simply cannot afford any bad publicity as a result of a harassment case.

I am sorry to be the bearer of bad news but if you are dissatisfied may I suggest you take up your complaint with the Swordcasting Standards Council.

Yours sincerely

Chris Burnham

Head of Personnel

Somewhere in West Yorkshire
31 March 2001

Himself The Pope
Vatican City
Rome
Italy

Dear Sir,

I am writing to you a most unusual letter, namely to apply for the position of Quasi Modo theSecond, the New Hunchback of Notre Dame Cathedral.
Presently residing in the North of England I am a mature 41-year-old man with facial featuresthat are suitably weathered and full of character. One might say that
I have an angular and rugged appearance with a slightly twisted nose and countless craggy lines upon my forehead and at the sides of my piercing eyes. I am unusual in the extent and thickness of my ginger-brown body hair and have a rug-like preponderance of the above across my chest, back and arms. If ever there was a case to be made for a possible link between the orang-utan and man, I would be a notable example. In summary, with the exception of the hump, I would be the ideal candidate to fill the role of Quasi Modo the Second, the New Hunchback of Notre Dame, on the basis that I have many of the notable physical characteristics that have come to be associated with the original resident of your fine cathedral.

In addition to the above I must tell you that as a long-standing member of the Fell Runners Association in England I am a considerably fit individual and would find it relatively easy to run up and down the cathedral steps to and from the bell tower where   I assume I would be provided with suitable lodging. I have a great love of church music and would be most grateful for the opportunity to ring the bells of Notre Dame to the highest standard for the people of Paris and for France. I would also be happy to ensure the bells are cleaned and polished and kept in good condition at all times.

I would add that although I do not have a hump on my back, I would be only too pleased to wear an artificial substitute if this is a necessity of the job. I would also be willing to learn to speak French and Latin.

Many thanks indeed for your time and consideration and I look forward to hearing from you in the very near future.

Sincerely

Michael A. Lee

From the Vatican, 15 May 2001

Dear Mr Lee,

His Holiness Pope John Paul II duly received your letter and has directed me to reply in his name.

His Holiness appreciates the sentiments which prompted you to write and he will remember you in his prayers.

Yours sincerely,

Monsignor Pédro López Quintana
Assessor

Mr Michael A. Lee
10 Woodlea Avenue
Reinwood Manor

Head of Personnel
Kerrier District Council Offices
Dolcoath Avenue
Cambourne TR14 8SX
Cornwall

Dear Sir/Madam

I am writing to you a most unusual letter, namely to apply for the position of 'Official Kerrier District Council Ghost Hunter and Exorcist' in the tradition of Parson Richard Dodge of the 1700s.

Aged 41, I have taken quite an interest in recent months in the many haunted sites and noted apparitions around the Cornwall region and believe I could offer an appropriate service in managing the ghosts and phantoms responsible for the aforementioned activity within your councils' jurisdiction.

As with all institutions the ethereal ghostly inhabitants of Cornwall would doubtless benefit from a more structured framework than exists at present and would permit a more co-ordinated and timed approach to entertaining-by-haunting the local people and indeed many visitors to the area. A predictable sighting [by efficient planning on my part] of Charlotte Dymond walking the slopes of Roughter, for example, would permit the rather satisfied observer more time to enjoy himself/herself at a local restaurant or theatre and by arranging the various Cornish Phantom Coaches to appear at specific times in various places a system could be introduced to allow the committed coach-watcher to enjoy several apparitions in a single night. As a consequence the various spirit entities would be fully occupied with less time to make nuisances of themselves, the human population given regular opportunities for trans-dimensional experiences, and moreover the tourism industry encouraged. Should any particular disincarnate entity refuse to comply with such applied management strategy I am sure that the reputation of my experience in exorcism would be sufficient to deter further disorder or alternatively provide the means for eternal dismissal.

I have already had some psychic communication with 'Flo' of Duporth Holiday Village and, although bitter about the demolition of the old Manor, expressed her belief that my proposal for an ordered Cornish Otherworld community could well be a solution to the present chaos that exists in the county. Despite the opposition these changes will meet from some of the more discontent sprites and poltergeists I am of the opinion that the implementation of this new approach can be completed efficiently and with success should you employ me in the afore-mentioned capacity. I would be most grateful for the chance to discuss this position with you further and thank you for your time and consideration.

Yours sincerely,

N. A. Lee .

KERRIER DISTRICT COUNCIL

Council Offices Dolcoath Avenue
Camborne Cornwall TR14 8SX

Telephone: Camborne (01209) 614000
Fax: Camborne (01209) 614496
Email: Geoff.Cox@kerrier.gov.uk
Web: www.kerrier.gov.uk

Mr M A Lee
Somewhere in West Yorkshire

GEOFFREY G COX, LLB, Solicitor
Chief Executive Officer

Please ask for:	Mrs Chapman
Direct Dial:	01209 614362
Your Ref:	
My Ref:	MEC/pers
Date:	12 April 2001

Dear Mr Lee

Official Kerrier District Council Ghost Hunter and Exorcist

Thank you for your letter dated 6 April seeking employment by this Council in the above capacity.

As far as I am aware, the Council has never felt the need to make such an appointment so regret to say that I cannot help you at this time.

Thank you for your interest in the Kerrier District.

Yours sincerely

Margaret Chapman.

Margaret Chapman
PA to the Chief Executive

Somewhere in West Yorkshire
29 April 2001

Dr M. J. Adam
Waterloo Surgery
615–619 Wakefield Road
Waterloo
Huddersfield

Dear Dr Adam

I am writing to you a most unusual letter, namely to apply for a position at Waterloo Health Centre as a Partner in General Practice.

Aged 41, I have been for many years a longstanding member of the Fell Runners Association. As such I am experienced in matters of map reading and believe this would be of great benefit when it comes to finding my way around the areas serviced by the Waterloo Practice.

Despite the complexity of the local road system around various parts of Huddersfield my accomplished navigational skills should overcome any challenges involved in home visits and indeed finding my way home after a long and stressful day at work.

In addition to a rather comprehensive file of fell race records demonstrating my tenacity at seeing a race through from its' beginning to its' end, a necessary characteristic for General Practice in these demanding times, I can also boast various swimming certificates assuring you of my ability to keep my head well above the water.Considering how much administration there is as an added necessity to the patient-orientated workload for the New Millennial family doctor this will doubtless serve as a useful survival trait should you employ me as your new partner.

Amongst my many other pastimes I have for some time now had a keen interest in gardening and have learned to tell the difference between the wood and the trees as well as recognise the shrubs and plants that possess hidden thorns. Along with a substantial knowledge that specific garden pests and diseases require specific treatments I believe that I can offer you assurance that I fully understand the need for a structure in General Practice that provides for efficient diagnosis and indeed medicinal or surgical solutions as appropriate.

Amongst my many books I have two sturdy volumes of the *Oxford Textbook of Medicine* which I believe will serve me well in aiding my diagnostic duties at Waterloo and although the majority of my writing has been in the field of job applications, I am sure I could write letters of referral when required.

As someone who has experienced various strains of the Common Cold, worried about mild anxiety connected to pressures at work and suffered from painful verrucae,   I would be most able to empathise with 80 per cent of the patients visiting surgery on a daily basis. As far as the others are concerned I may require a little mentoring!

In summary I would be most interested to be considered as a General Practitioner in your highly regarded practice and despite my lack of any suitable medical qualification relevant to the aforementioned role I am sure my interests and experience would nevertheless serve me well in a somewhat liberal context.

I would like to take this opportunity of thanking you for your time and consideration and look forward to hearing from you in the very near future.

Sincerely and ambitiously

M . A . Lee

Michael A. Lee

615-619, Wakefield Rd.,
Waterloo,
Huddersfield.
HD8 0LS

17th Sept 2001

Dear Mr. Lee,

I must apologise to you for not replying earlier to your frank and very interesting application for the position of partner at Waterloo Surgery as a partner in General Practice.

I regret to inform you that the post has now been filled but I feel that you would be interested to hear of my views on your wish to enter General Practice.

I do not see that your lack of a medical qualification should in any way bar you from pursuing this career. It has become very obvious that nowadays the patients know considerably more than the doctors they profess to consult and indeed, usually they get what they ask for. A GP's job now seems to be an aid to the technical and ludicrous notion that he or she alone can sign prescriptions, organise investigations and refer patients to hospital. The concept that the patient is 'God' and the patient 'knows best' is well established as evidenced by the 'lay down and kick me' attitude of the General Medical Council. I do not see you should have any difficulty convincing the authorities to enter General Practice – might I suggest that you buy a medical qualification in Dubai where I understand there is the biggest duty free outlet in the world- and respond to the Government's appeal for more doctors from abroad in the first place. This would certainly provide you with the appropriate certification to practice in this country and pursue your ambition.

I was most impressed by your achievements in fell running. In my opinion all fell runners are crackpots and let's face it you have to be mad to enter General Practice. I am not sure as to the usefulness of your swimming experience but certainly there is a vogue for underwater births and you may find this a specialty you might wish to develop or even expand e.g. underwater genito-urinary medicine or gynaecology. Clearly a life-saving certificate would circumvent the need for Cardiopulmonary Resuscitation accreditation – a bronze should suffice.

Administration is no problem. The state of the health service is such at the moment that it works entirely on the chaos theory principle. As such no one person or practice can be deemed to be accountable for anything, audits can be invented and the only requisite is the ability to be creative. Given the style of your application I do not think you will have much trouble here.

... continued

The interest in horticulture and garden pests and diseases will certainly be an asset to any practice fortunate to have you as a partner. General Practice does involve long periods of boredom so what better way of spending the time other than tending a garden. I am sure that a bid could be placed to the Primary Care Group for a therapeutic garden for the benefit of your patients on the assumption that they work in it for therapeutic reasons and so you should be saved the chores such as digging, weeding and grass cutting. In practice, plants and patients tend to suffer the same sort of problems e.g. wilt –'tired all the time' and mildew - Athletes foot, and will respond to similar treatments. A little inventiveness may be required but basically anything you use on plants will, as with patients, either kill or cure. I have often wondered what the human equivalent of 'Round-Up' would be. Perhaps there is an M.D. in this?

Don't worry about textbooks. They are far too thick, unreadable and unimaginably boring. Listen to the patients. They know it all and all you have to do is agree with them, get them to sign a disclaimer and hand them what they want. Patients always feel the best doctors are the ones that do what the patient wants.

NEVER admit to having an illness. In spite of your previous history of colds and verrucas, to admit to a patient that you are anything but superhuman and immune to all illness and therefore able to work 365 days a year non-stop 24 hours a day will beg the question whether you really are fit to practice and may land you in front of the General Medical Council. Similarly ditch this idea of empathy. It is like an infectious illness and you might find yourself developing symptoms and hypochondriacal ideas which may lead you to suspect that you are not really fit to practice –an absurd notion!

I hope that in spite of your disappointment in not being successful with your application to the Waterloo Practice that you will be reassured and I hope a little encouraged, or even inspired to become a General Practitioner and try again.

Best wishes for the future.

Yours sincerely,

Dr. M.J. Adam

Head of Personnel
Penwith District Council
St Clare
Penzance TR18 3QW
Cornwall

Dear Sir/Madam

I am writing to you a most unusual letter, namely to apply for the position with Penwith District Council of 'Jack the Giant Killer [the Second]' should this position become available in the near future.

Aged 41, I am presently employed as a sales executive within industry but have had for quite some time now a particular dislike for giants and their evil ways. I have also had a desire to relocate to the South West and have quite a liking for Cornwall. In these times of increasing criminal activity it angers me to think of cattle-stealing giants following in the ancient warped tradition of Cormoran of St Michaels' Mount and creating even more work for an already stretched police force not to mention providing a less than ideal role model for the youth of today. I am sure that you would agree that there is a clear need for both community vigilance and indeed someone at hand to fulfil the role of 'Jack' should there be a local Giant problem that requires immediate attention.

As a long-standing member of the Fell-Runners Association I am a fit individual well trained in the art of race and pursuit and am able to run for long periods of time and at a significant pace when the occasion arises. This is a useful ability when pursuing or indeed evading or ambushing giants that possess a large stride or urgency. In addition to my flight of foot, I am a keen gardener and as such am adept at digging efficiently so that should there be a requirement to excavate large pits for the purpose of trapping your troublesome giants I would certainly be the person for the job. In terms of despatching the aforementioned giants, once again I am suitably qualified as a strong and determined individual and would not be averse to tapping these enormous criminal brutes on the head as did the original Jack. [I may need to acquire from one of your local council services a suitable pickaxe for this purpose.]

I am fully aware that unlike the time of the original Jack there are few if any wolves or pirates remaining in Cornwall, and so I realise that my responsibilities would be relatively restricted to the larger pests in the area. However, doubtless it would be fair to say that from a cost-effectiveness perspective my role would be fully justified as far as savings to police-time, livestock and indeed copycat behaviour is concerned if just one troublesome giant was culled in a particular season.

In conclusion, I am looking forward to the opportunity of discussing this matter with you further and thank you for your time and consideration.

Yours sincerely

M. A. Lee

Penwith District Council

St. Clare Penzance Cornwall TR18 3QW
Telephone (01736) 362341 Fax (01736) 336575
Jim McKenna BA CPFA **Chief Executive**

David Hooper LL.B(Hons) Solicitor
Head of Legal and Personnel Services

Your Ref:
My Ref: DAG/CGE
Ask For: **MRS D A GROVES**
Direct Dial: (01736) 336536
Date: 25 April 2001

Dear Mr Lee

RE: POSITION OF "JACK THE GIANT KILLER (THE SECOND)"

Thank you for your recent offer of availability for employment if the above position should become created.

Fortunately, for us, our Giants although temperamental can be quite reasonable and we see no need for a slayer of Giants at this particular time.

If however, in the future, our resident Giants become unruly any such vacancy would be advertised through our local employment service and in the local press therefore reference to these from time to time is recommended.

In the meantime, good luck with your Giant killing!

Yours sincerely

pp . *Amanda*

Personnel Officer

Mr M A Lee
Somewhere in West Yorkshire

Somewhere in West Yorkshire
14 May 2001

Tony Blair
10 Downing Street
London SW1A 2AA

Dear Mr Blair

I am writing to you a most unusual letter, namely to apply for the position within the present government of 'Official Scapegoat'.

There have been numerous occasions over the last few years when I have switched on my television to hear the evening news or indeed read with interest various articles about current governmental policy within the national press to find the word 'scapegoat' bandied about. It seems to me as if there is always someone, often a Conservative or a Liberal Democrat, keen to find a particular individual on whose shoulders the responsibility and blame for decisions made by the Labour Government but that find opposition elsewhere can be firmly placed. Much time and energy is devoted to this hunt for the so-called 'Scapegoat' but never have I heard of anyone actually claiming responsibility and accountability for such a role. How handy it would be to have a particular person at whom the hordes of bitter dissenters could point and wag their bony fingers whenever the need arises! On this basis I presume there is a vacancy for which I would like to be considered and provided that there would not be included in the terms and conditions of the job an expectation to bear any financial or legal penalties associated with duties undertaken, I would like to become the 'Official Scapegoat' forthwith.

Aged 41, I am currently employed as a Sales Representative and as such am resilient and thick-skinned. In so saying I would be able to bear the brunt of many policy criticisms on behalf of the government far better than the average person. I am also a skilled communicator and would be a competent choice when it comes to explaining why exactly I am taking the blame for a particular unpopular decision or resolution. Although I do need a new pair of quality shoes for the role, I can assure you that I am of a smart, intelligent appearance and believe I would prove to be a highly efficient and popular scapegoat should I be successful in my application.

As a longstanding member of the Fell Runners Association I can assure you that I am able to 'go the distance' and my possession of various swimming certificates should offer proof that I can easily keep my 'head above water'. Amongst the usual assortment of GCE 'O' Levels, 'A' Levels and degree, I also have a Garden Design Certificate which would serve me well in deciding how exactly to construct a watertight story or a retaining excuse that will effectively prevent a political landslide. In short and in figurative terms I could be the pond-liner in the great government lake of Westminster!

I thank you for your time and kind consideration regards my application and look forward to hearing from you in the very near future.

Sincerely

M . A . Lee .

1O DOWNING STREET
LONDON SW1A 2AA

From the Direct Communications Unit   23 May 2001

Mr Michael A Lee
Somewhere in West Yorkshire

Dear Mr Lee

The Prime Minister has asked me to thank you for your recent letter.

Yours sincerely

AEMER LODHI

Her Royal Majesty The Queen
Buckingham Palace
London

Your Royal Highness

I am writing to you a most unusual letter, namely to apply for the position within the House of Lords of 'Principal Prodder and Nudge-Master'.

Having observed with great interest on many occasions the gatherings of our many eminent Lords, Ladies, Earls and other titled persons within the House of Lords I have been regularly amazed at the number of individuals who have clearly nodded off to sleep in the midst of the proceedings. Whilst, on one side of the House a learned Baron provides his fellow Lords with the latest information around the dangers of atmospheric pollutants on the worlds' ozone layer, three or four other members of the House are away in the 'Land of the Sandman' totally embroiled in a pleasant dream or snoring contentedly after an earlier glass of sherry.

Despite the vast number of people listed as Principal Officers and Officials within the House of Lords holding a miscellany of titles ranging from 'Lord Chancellor' through 'Counsel to the Chairman of the Committees' to 'Principal Doorkeeper' I can find no-one whose job it is to wake the Lords from their slumbers and ensure their leadership is not lost to the Land of Nod.

Aged 41, I have spent half a career in industry and consider myself an industrious, conscientious, astute and moreover alert individual and believe that it is of benefit to any team proceedings to have fully conscious members who can play a full part in the work at hand. Blessed with a loud voice and reasonably bony fingers I am sure I would be a most efficient candidate for a role which involved rousing a sleeper from his alternative state of mind by a short, sharp shout in the ear and a prod in the ribs.

As a rather tenacious individual, I am not one for giving up on a task easily and even those who have perhaps added a little too much whisky to their water would not be too much of a challenge to me. As 'Principal Prodder and Nudge-Master' at the House of Lords I am sure I could ensure an attendance of Lords who would become brighter eyed, bushier tailed and more capable of at least appearing to help lead the House in the way they are expected to.

Doubtless you would agree with me that this role would carry significant responsibility and would certainly require a character of the highest calibre and commitment. I believe I am that person! I thank you for your time and kind consideration and I look forward to hearing from you in the very near future.

Sincerely

M. A. Lee

Michael A. Lee

BUCKINGHAM PALACE

Dear Mr. Lee,

Thank you for your recent letter to The Queen suggesting that your particular skills would be appropriate for the mythical post of *Principal Prodder and Nudgemaster* in the House of Lords. Your thoughtfulness in putting your name forward for this office is appreciated, but it is not within the gift of the Palace and so it would seem you will have to dream on .....

Yours sincerely,

MRS. DEBORAH BEAN
Chief Correspondence Officer

M.A. Lee, Esq.

Lieutenant General Sir Michael Willcocks KCB

GENTLEMAN USHER OF THE BLACK ROD
HOUSE OF LORDS LONDON SW1A OPW
TEL: 020-7219 3100
FAX: 020-7219 2500

Dear Mr Lee,

Thank you for your letter in which you apply for the position of Principal Prodder and Nudge-master. I am afraid that at present there is no such vacancy.

To be fair to the Members, however, I should point out that the acoustics in the Chamber are dreadful and to counteract this loudspeakers have been set into the backs of the benches. What may appear to the general public therefore as sleepy postures are actually the result of the Member in question having to position his/her ear to the nearest loudspeaker in order to catch the debate.

I wish you luck in your quest for service to the Nation.

Yours sincerely,

Michael Willcocks

Michael A Lee Esq
Somewhere in West Yorkshire

49

The Marketing Director
The Dulux Dept/ICI Paints
Abbott Mead Vickers – BBDO Ltd
151 Marylebone Road
London NW1 5QE

Dear Sir/Madam

I am writing to you a most unusual letter, namely to apply for the position of 'Hairy Human Dulux Dog' to feature in your paint adverts.

Along with many other people in the UK I have been a longstanding admirer of your highly successful advertising scheme involving the loveable Dulux dog and I suppose it is fair to say that the image of the dog has become synonymous with your brand of paints. My only concern regards your canine Dulux dog adverts is that, whilst appealing to a large section of dog-loving UK residents, it may not actually convert to usage of Dulux paints the many individuals who actually dislike the creature with a vengeance. Could it be that whilst gaining the allegiance of one section of the population you may actually be discouraging another pool of potential customers from using your products and perhaps even losing them to the competition? Having so defined a need in the paint advertising market place let me therefore propose a solution to you!

Aged 41, I am a rather weathered but friendly looking Northerner with a reasonable level of fitness and blessed with a rug-like preponderance of ginger-brown body hair across my back, chest, shoulders and arms. One might say that I am slightly reminiscent of a hairy domestic dog exuding a certain primal enthusiasm and energy whilst at the same time adding a very human element to the equation and image.

My proposal is simply this – employ me as your next advertising image: the 'Hairy Human Dulux Dog' could add sales potential for your existing customers whilst encouraging those previously unconvinced by the original dog or dogs to think more kindly of a paint associated with a real person, albeit a rather hairy wolven one. By adding to your original theme whilst injecting a measure of humour you might well find that demand for your Dulux paints quickly increases and the year-end sales bonuses become very attractive indeed!

I can hold a paintbrush between my teeth and would be quite willing to appear in a range of colours to suit particular marketing strategies, as well as jumping through the occasional hoop if necessary. I can already visualise the upturn of the Dulux cash sales growth in my mind's eye!

Doubtless you will want to discuss this idea further with me and perhaps we could meet at an appropriate time and place for a bowl of something thirst-quenching and a juicy steak. I thank you for your time and consideration and look forward to hearing from you in the very near future.

Sincerely   M . A . Lee .

ABBOTT MEAD VICKERS · BBDO LTD

151 Marylebone Road
London NW1 5QE
Telephone 020 7616 3500
Fax 020 7616 3600
amvbbdo@amvbbdo.com

June 21, 2001

Michael Lee
Somewhere in West Yorkshire

Dear Mr Lee

Application for Dog Role

Thank you for your letter dated 24th May.

We were most interested to read of your market insights concerning non-dog loving paint users, and intrigued by your proposal to audition for a role as 'the Hairy Human Dulux Dog'.

Whilst we do not anticipate the immediate demise of our current canine talent, we are grateful for your concern over our future options.

Holding a paintbrush between your teeth would certainly be a minimum performance requirement. However, some 46% of paint is now applied via roller. Are there any innovative tricks you can perform with one of these?

Best wishes

Yours sincerely

Tom Nester-Smith
Board Account Director – ICI Paints

Registered in England
Registration Number
1935786
Registered Office
151 Marylebone Road
London NW1 5QE

Head of Personnel
Pendle Borough Council
Town Hall
Market Street
Nelson
Pendle BB9 7LG
Lancashire

Dear Sir/Madam

I am writing to you a most unusual letter, namely to apply for the position of 'Witchfinder General' for Pendle Borough Council.

I would be most interested indeed to follow in the footsteps of Mathew Hopkins of the 17th century whom I believe was born in the town of Manningtree within the boundaries of Tendring District Council, Essex, but who had an enormous effect on life around the Pendle area and whose role is currently vacant.

Aged 41, I have for quite some time been significantly concerned about the upsurge of interest in matters related to the occult by large numbers of people within the UK and particularly those involved in the ancient practice of Witchcraft. Only last week I was myself the witness of a troublesome incident here in the North of England when my sister-in-law visited the home of my wife and I one warm and humid afternoon. On her departure and to my great distress I found that the milk had curdled on top of the fridge, my prize daffodils had irreversibly drooped and all the family was struck down with an almost unearthly thirst.Having tentatively mentioned these occurrences and my understandably well-founded suspicions of my sister-in-law's leanings towards the dark arts to my dearly beloved, I then found that my wife could not bring herself to speak to me for almost a month. Isn't this appalling? Quite frankly I am shocked to think that such obvious sorcery and demonic spellbinding is so evident and even permissible in today's so-called civilised 21st-century England!

I understand from my research of times past that the approach towards finding women of the kind mentioned above was rather different to that of present times and similarly that the penalties for the practice of such devilry were far more severe if proven. Indeed it is interesting to read of the fate of the infamous witches of Pendle in Lancashire or those of Chelmsford four hundred years ago. Should my sister-in-law, who incidentally also lives in Lancashire, have had the opportunity to consider that her fate could be a similar one to that of the Pendle or Chelmsford Witches if she did not return to the righteous path, I am convinced that the milk on the fridge would still be fresh and the daffodils in full flower.

In addressing my concerns I trust that you can now see my reasoning for applying to be the new 'Witchfinder General' and will be suitably convinced that the re-establishment of this role would be pivotal in dowsing the wiccan embers once and for all.

Having spent half a career in the world of industry I am experienced in the techniques of interviewing people. This would indispensable in my role as 'Witchfinder General' both in terms of recruiting my team of 'Witchfinder Technicians' and also within the process of extracting confessions from those practicing their evil ways either on a solitary basis or as part of a larger coven. I am reasonably strong and believe that once my suspects are found and captured I could easily bind them prior to undertaking the well-known water test; if they sink they are innocent and if they float they can be justifiably hung, burned at the stake or perhaps more appropriately in 2001 be given the obligation of community service.

I know that the great Witchfinder General of the 1600s, Mathew Hopkins, received just twenty shillings for each witch he discovered and of course at that time this would have been an ample reward for his efforts. Should I be successfully appointed as his 21st-century successor I believe we would need to discuss further the salary and bonus package taking into consideration factors of inflation and job equivalents. There is also the matter of obtaining an appropriate uniform.

Doubtless you will be interested to take this application forward to the interview stage and with such in mind I would be grateful if you could send to me details about the selection process.

I thank you for your time and consideration and look forward to hearing from you in the very near future.

Sincerely

Michael A. Lee

CORPORATE POLICY UNIT
Town Hall, Market Street, Nelson, Pendle, Lancashire BB9 7LG

Telephone:	**(01282) 661984**	Fax:	**(01282) 661630**
Ext:		My Ref:	
Ask for:	Sarah Lee	Your Ref:	
Date:	18 June 2001		

Somewhere in West Yorkshire

Dear Mr Lee,

Thank you for your letter promoting yourself as a Witchfinder General, although I think you may be several centuries too late.

I'm enclosing a Pendle Discovery Guide so that you can find our more about the Pendle Witches of 1612.

At the back of the guide is a mail order section where you can order any publications about the witches, including a Pendle Witches Trail guide. We also have an audio guide to the Pendle Witches Trail which you can contact our Tourist Information Centre about (address and telephone number on inside back cover).

The world famous trial documents of the Pendle Witches were used as a guide by the Witchfinder General. However, I understand that he himself was executed as a witch some years later, which might make you re-think your position.

With best wishes,

Sarah Lee
Principal Promotions Officer

Corporate Policy Manager: Brian Astin

Switchboard: (01282) 661661   Minicom: (01282) 618392   Fax:(01282) 661630

Head of Communications
Michelin Tyre PLC
Campbell Road
Stoke-on-Trent ST4 4EY

Dear Sir/Madam

I am writing to you a most unusual letter, namely to apply for the position of 'Michael the Merry Mobile Michelin Man' with Michelin Tyres PLC.

Aged 41, I have spent many years working as a sales executive within British industry and have reached that crossroads in life where I am exploring other potential career pathways. In this regard I was most interested to read on your website that 'ongoing individual career plans and personal progress are fundamental to the Michelin philosophy' and decided on this basis that you would be an excellent choice for my employment aspirations.

The Michelin Man logo and model has been a longstanding and memorable part of the Michelin Tyre business and I doubt that there would be many individuals unfamiliar with such a unique and outstanding image. I firmly believe, however, that you could further strengthen the business generated by such an image by employing an individual like myself to fulfil the role of 'Michael the Merry Mobile Michelin Man' in a human capacity at various exhibitions, PR events and occasions of hospitality. In other words, you could bring to life your logo in the same way that Disneyland has brought to life the cartoons Mickey Mouse and friends for thousands to see and with whom they can interact. The implications as far as sales promotion are concerned would doubtless be significant.

I would encourage you to consider me for this position on the basis of the following characteristics, skills and competencies.

First and foremost, my first name is Michael and so there would be no great challenge in my coming to terms with being addressed as 'Michael the Merry Mobile Michelin Man.'It might of course be a more complex process if I were a Cedric, Hubert or Zachariah!

Secondly, I have a natural propensity for weight-gain around the stomach and as in so saying would provide a basic costume-friendly shape for a Michelin Man outfit.

Indeed individuals would notice, and quite rightly so, that 'Michael the Merry Mobile Michelin Man' not only promotes spare tyres, but even carries them around himself!I am sure that you would agree this would be an ideal association to encourage.

Thirdly, I can assure you that as a longstanding member of the Fell Runners Association I am a relatively fit, be it slightly overweight, man with a substantial mobility and stamina. This would serve me well in the capacity of attending events of reasonable duration where there would be an expectation for committed socialising and promotional effort to take place. One might say 'I can go round for a long time!'

Finally, I have had a longstanding interest in tyres in their many forms and as a consequence could bring to the role a natural enthusiasm and interest that would help in the promotion of the company, Michelin Tyres PLC, and its well-established product range. I perform well under reasonable pressure and have no history of personal punctures.

I thank you for your time and consideration in relation to my job application and I look forward to hearing from you in the very near future.

Sincerely

M. A. Lee .

Michael A. Lee

Mr M A Lee
Somewhere in West Yorkshire

24 July 2001

Dear Mr Lee

Job application - Michelin Man

Thank you for your two letters dated 29 June recently received in this office. Your notion of 'Michael the Merry Mobile Michelin Man' is novel, to say the least! Over the years we have used Michelin men (and women) to wear our Bibendum (Michelin Man) suits for the types of function which you highlight in your letter. Today, these suits are made in the USA and considerably easier to wear than the stiff nylon ones of the 1960s-90s. It has therefore become easier to press-gang our volunteer employees, often apprentices, in to action!

We note your offer and should our Michelin men and women 'go on strike', we'll make contact!

Yours sincerely

Paul Niblett
Head of Communications

paul.niblett@uk.michelin.com

Michelin Tyre
Public Limited Company

Campbell Road
Stoke-on-Trent
ST4 4EY

Tel: +44 (0)1782 402000
Fax: +44 (0)1782 402011
Website: www.michelin.co.uk
Registered in England no. 84559
Registered Office: Stoke-on-Trent ST4 4EY

INVESTOR IN PEOPLE

The Chairman
The Ancient Order of Foresters Friendly Society
904–910 High Road
North Finchley
London N12 9RW

Dear Sir/Madam

I am writing to you a most unusual letter, namely to enquire about the possibility of being employed by the Ancient Order of Foresters Friendly Society as a 'Woodsman'.

Aged 41, I have spent many years as a sales executive but have reached that time of life when I am exploring alternative employment opportunities.

Indeed I have recently begun considering a return to the work I was involved in on the North Yorkshire Estate of Aldwark, now National Trust I believe, where I spent many months trimming branches from coniferous trees and clearing drainage ditches with a billhook and a scythe shortly after graduating in 1981. Although the weather was harsh, the salary poor and conditions challenging there was a certain contentment associated with a hard day's work in the woods and certain benefits as far as physical fitness and harmony with nature were concerned. Indeed I look back with a certain pleasurable nostalgia at my time as a Woodsman.

As you will doubtless understand I was therefore significantly excited at discovering your organisation on the Internet and although I have not fully absorbed all the information on your well-presented website, I decided you may well be an ideal choice for my application for a return to the trees.

I am an affable, industrious, conscientious and well-educated individual with 18 years of scientific sales beneath my career belt but more importantly am fit and strong and already experienced in many techniques of forestry maintenance and management. Although my recent career has been one of involvement with health-care professionals I am just as able to communicate easily and clearly with farmers, fire-fighters and local village families. In short, I would be an ideal candidate to consider for the position of 'Woodsman' with your organisation.

I noticed also that there was an entry on your website describing 'The Band' of The Ancient Order of Foresters Friendly Society and may I take this opportunity to say that should you be short of musicians I am also something of a dab hand at playing the kazoo. Indeed I often play my kazoo here in our leafy garden in Huddersfield.

Thank you for your time and consideration as far as this application is concerned and I look forward to hearing from you in the very near future.

Sincerely

M. A. Lee

Michael A. Lee

Ancient Order of Foresters Friendly Society

London United District
Foresters House, 904-910 High Road, Finchley, London N12 9RW
Telephone: 020-8445 8878 Fax: 020-8343 8510
E-mail:lud@aof.co.uk

Friends you can trust

Our Ref: GDL/BP

Your Ref:

Mr M A Lee
Somewhere in West Yorkshire

19th July 2001

Dear Mr Lee,

Thank you for your letter dated 12th July 2001 and the information contained therein.

Unfortunately, I am unable to assist you with employment as the Society does not need "Woodsmen" nor does it require it a kazoo player in its Brass Band.

However, may I take this opportunity to enclose a leaflet, which gives a brief history of the Society and I wish you every success with your quest for an alternative career.

Yours sincerely,

G D Lloyd
District Secretary

H. E. Mr Tarald O. Brautaset
Ambassador to the Court of St James
Royal Norwegian Embassy
25 Belgrave Square
London SW1X 8QD

Dear Sir

I am writing to you a most unusual letter, namely to ask whether I might purchase or lease the Island of Jan Mayen from the Norwegians who currently own and govern this most interesting land in a bid to fulfil my desire to become a 'Recluse'.

Aged 41, I have for some time been looking for an unusual piece of real estate that I might acquire on either a freehold or leasehold basis which would offer me a significant degree of peace and solitude. As the father of two small children and having a demanding wife, I have often dreamed of the type of island typified by Jan Mayen as a place for refuge and respite. In other words I am looking for a holiday home with a difference!

As a place located between the Greenland and Norwegian Seas at 71 00 North and 8 00 West and enjoying an arctic maritime climate with frequent storms and persistent   fog,
I believe there is little risk of mass tourism spoiling the remote nature of Jan Mayen. Indeed I gather that, with the exception of a few brave souls manning the meteorological station located on the island, there is absolutely no indigenous population whatsoever to interfere with the natural environment and its' intrinsic character.

Since Jan Mayen offers no natural resources, has no arable land, no crops, no pastures and no woodland but instead presents simply as a barren volcanic island of moss and grass, I can see no possible reason why the Norwegian Crown and government would want to maintain ownership of the island when presented with an offer of purchase or lease such as mine.

Should you be happy to proceed with the sale or lease of Jan Mayen as I fully expect you to do may I assure you that I will be quite happy for you to continue with your meteorological endeavours and indeed maintain the one airport that offers access to the interior. I would also be more than happy to permit any scientists interested in studying the active volcano Haakan V11 Tapen/Beerenberg to visit whenever they wished.

As for myself I would be most content to have free range to pitch my tent wherever I wanted on this most fascinating of islands and perhaps build a modest cabin for the more inclement times of the year where I could rest and meditate with at least a degree or two of comfort.

I can think of no better place than Jan Mayen in which I could avoid my many household chores here in the North of England and permit my eardrums, damaged by many decibels of small children shouting over long periods of time, to recuperate and recover.

May I suggest that should you be happy to proceed with my purchase option a sum of £10 be paid for freehold possession forthwith and should you be more comfortable with the idea of a leasing contract that we run with 50p per year.

Many thanks indeed for your time and consideration regarding this matter and I look forward to hearing from you in the very near future.

In the meantime I had better go and entertain my family or I will be in serious trouble again.

Sincerely

M. A. Lee

Michael A. Lee

ROYAL NORWEGIAN EMBASSY
LONDON

Mr Michael A Lee
Somewhere in West Yorkshire

Dear Mr Lee,

I am writing in reply to the generous offer contained in your letter of 24 July to the Norwegian Ambassador.

While appreciating your predicament, the Embassy regrets to inform you that the island of Jan Mayen is currently not up for sale nor lease. However, should there be any changes in this situation, you will probably be among the first to be notified.

In the meantime, you might like to consider spending a holiday on the Norwegian mainland, and I enclose "The official travel guide Norway 2001" for your perusal.

Yours sincerely,

Erik Svedahl
1st Secretary

Postal Address:
25 Belgrave Square
London
SW1X 8QD
Great Britain

Office Address:
25 Belgrave Square
London
SW1X 8QD
Great Britain

Telephone:
(+44) (0)20 7591 5500

Telefax:
(+44) (0)20 7245 8993

Website:
http://www.norway.org.uk

E-mail:
emb.london@mfa.no

Somewhere in West Yorkshire
1 August 2001

The Archbishop of Canterbury
Lambeth Palace
London SE1 7JU

Dear Sir

I am writing to you a most unusual letter, namely to apply for the position of 'Principal Stable Boy for the Four Horses of the Apocalypse'.

Having recently re-read parts of the Book of Revelation I was fascinated to consider the four horses that are described in Chapter Six and their pivotal but certainly unenviable roles in carrying around the four horsemen who are to be given power over a quarter of the earth in the last days.

I am particularly perturbed at the thought of these white, black, red and pale horses having to play host to four individual horsemen who, we are told in verse eight, will kill people by war, starvation, disease and wild animals. What a mean team of heartless souls they must be!

Quite frankly I would not wish to meet any of them on a dark night!
With respect to the horses, however, I assume that whilst they await their future briefings at the opening of the first of seven seals they will require kind and committed attention. In this regard employ me as 'Principal Stable Boy for the Four Horses of the Apocalypse' and I will ensure that these animals are suitably groomed, their saddles and bridles cleaned and polished, their shoes maintained and that they are properly fed and watered on a regular basis.You can also rest assured that the horses will be suitable exercised and prepared for their release at the end of time in accordance with the graphic descriptions in the aforementioned chapter of Revelation.

Although, as Principle Stable Boy, mine would be primarily a role of equine care perhaps I might also assume a secondary and rather crafty role in supporting a more positive and caring approach to humanity. One could almost describe the role as that of an undercover agent in the apocalyptic stable. In short I could attempt to convince the horsemen themselves whilst visiting their respective steeds to desist from their obsessive interest in war, disease, starvation and nasty animals and concentrate on more wholesome interests such as jogging, fishing, poetry-writing and watercolour painting instead!

If I am successful the prophesied terrors of Revelation Chapter Six may be transformed into a future realism of worldwide self development, new interest and communities of people busy studying at evening classes and involving themselves in more endearing activities. The horses could be re-deployed to riding schools or put out to pasture and the horsemen become role models of true repentance.

Aged 41, I am an individual of tremendous vision and indeed focus. You will find me an industrious and conscientious person possessing a polished eloquence and positive attitude

Moreover I have a particular interest in apocalyptic issues and a desire to ameliorate the consequence of worldwide cataclysm if at all possible. Finally, I am fit and strong so that I might undertake my responsibilities with energy and efficiency, and should one of the horsemen take a particular dislike to me I can put up a jolly good fight.

Many thanks indeed for your time and kind consideration and I look forward to hearing from you in the very near future.

Sincerely

M. A. Lee

Michael A. Lee

Mr Andrew Nunn
Lay Assistant to
The Archbishop of Canterbury

Mr Michael A Lee
Somewhere in West Yorkshire

3 August 2001

Dear Mr Lee

The Archbishop of Canterbury has now left London for his summer break and so I am writing on his behalf to thank you for your 1 August letter. Thank you for putting your name forward for the position of Principal Stable Boy for the Four Horses of the Apocalypse. I regret however that applications for this post are not being handled from this office; the Archbishop is not regarded as the managing employer in this case. Rather you should apply to St John the Divine, c/o The Lamb and Flag, Patmos, Greece. If you are successful in your application, I am sure there will be many who will be grateful for any ameliorating influence you can bring to bear on the Horsemen, in the manner you propose.

Another position you may like to consider – but again the post is not in the Archbishop's gift – is that of stable boy to Balaam's Ass. Though less well remunerated than the position of Principal Stable Boy for the Four Horses of the Apocalypse and perhaps lacking the apocalyptic element that may be of crucial interest to you, this post represents a major opportunity in the field of animal welfare. In this case a history of cruelty and abuse means that the successful candidate must be able to demonstrate a proven track record in palliative equine care. Applications may be sent to Balaam son of Beor, Pethor near the River, Amaw.

With best wishes

[signature]

Lambeth Palace, London SE1 7JU
Direct Line: +44(0)20 7898 1276 *Switchboard:* +44(0)20 7898 1200 *Fax:* +44(0)20 7261 9836
Email: andrew.nunn@lampal.c-of-e.org.uk

65

Jim Cunningham
MP for Coventry South
The House of Commons
London SW1A 0AA

Dear Sir

I am writing to you a most unusual letter, namely to apply for the position of 'The Horse for Lady Godiva' should there be a requirement for such a role in the near future. As MP for Coventry South I thought that you might be the best person to approach for advice with regard to this position.

I am sure that the various carnivals and commemorative events that take place from time to time in the Coventry area providing the public with a theatrical glimpse of that most infamous Midlands maiden will have no end of well-qualified candidates for the part of Lady Godiva herself. I wondered, however, whether this would be the case when it comes to considering likely human candidates for the part of the horse if indeed a real horse is no longer an option.

Considering the current foot and mouth disaster that has restricted the movement of so many animals in so many places I would suggest that it would be far more appropriate to select an appropriate person to fill this role for forthcoming occasions as we move forward into late summer and autumn.

In this regard, I can assure you that I would be an ideal candidate for any events requiring a horse for Lady Godiva and would certainly like to be considered for such.

Aged 41, I am a moderately large but fit individual with a thick covering of ginger-brown body hair. As a member of the Fell Runners Association I am accomplished at completing various paced runs and courses and would be adept at 'trotting', 'cantering' and indeed 'galloping' when appropriate. Furthermore, I would be quite willing for the female playing the part of Lady Godiva to sit on my muscular back whilst I parade with joyful whinnying through the streets of Coventry.

I am a fit and healthy individual and apart from my 'Athletes Foot' which is well contained I have no other communicable diseases that would be of concern to the local population.

I would be most pleased to provide you with a copy of my CV if you wish to take this application process forward.

May I say, however, that should my services be required I would need a firm offer of employment as soon as possible as various other organisations have expressed significant interest in my obvious career aspirations and flexibility and in this regard there is substantial interest in my becoming the new Beast of Bodmin Moor or possibly the new mascot for the Parachute Regiment.

Between ourselves I must say that I would prefer working more closely with a charming Lady Godiva in Coventry than either the angry, war-hungry men of Aldershot or wandering the bleak and lonely heights of Bodmin Moor with no fixed abode. In these difficult times, however, one needs to keep options open.

I thank you for your time and consideration and look forward to hearing from you in the very near future.

Sincerely and hopefully

M. A. Lee

Michael A. Lee

JIM CUNNINGHAM MP
COVENTRY SOUTH

HOUSE OF COMMONS
LONDON SW1A 0AA

Immigration Assistant:
Liz Hasthorpe
Tel: (024) 7625 7870
Fax: (024) 7625 7813

Constituency Office:
Tel/Fax: (024) 7655 3159
London Office:
Tel/Fax: (020) 7219 6362

JC/PB

15th August, 2001.

Mr. M.A. Lee,
Somewhere in West Yorkshire

Dear Mr. Lee,

Thank you for your recent letter offering your services as "The Horse for Lady Godiva" at any carnivals or commemorative events that may take place in Coventry.

I have forwarded a copy of your letter onto the City Centre Company (Coventry) Limited, New Union Street, Coventry, who promote such events in the City.

My secretary has spoken to the Company, who have advised her that the Carnival has not been held in Coventry for some time, but that that your letter would be kept on record, should any events occur in the future.

Yours sincerely,

Jim Cunningham, MP
COVENTRY SOUTH

Our Reference   :   CM/RJB
Direct Dialling No. :   02476 834022
Fax No.   :   02476 832017
Date   :   16th August 2001
Reply to   :   E.Millett

CITY CENTRE COMPANY
COVENTRY

M.A.Lee Esq.
Somewhere in West Yorkshire

Dear Mr. Lee,

A copy of your letter to Jim Cunningham, MP re the above has been forwarded to me for my attention.

Your offer has some interesting possibilities and given your CV stands scrutiny with the Royal Veterinary Society I would be delighted to pursue the matter further.

I should however bring one important point to your notice. It is not well known by people outside the Coventry area but Lady Godiva's horse was never a "whole" animal. A prerequisite of any work we do with the delightful lady will be the necessity for you to be gelded, presupposing that has not already taken place of course.

I do hope the last item has not dampened your enthusiasm and look forward to receiving your CV in due course.

Liz Millett

Liz Millett
Chief Executive

Cc H. Root

City Centre Company (Coventry) Limited · New Union Street
Coventry · CV1 2NT
Tel: 024 7683 3671/2   Fax: 024 7683 2017
www.coventry.towntalk.co.uk
Registered No: 3365320 Registered Office: The Council House · Earl Street · Coventry · CV1 5RR

Liz Millett, Chief Executive
City Centre Company [Coventry] Ltd
New Union Street
Coventry CV1 2NT

Dear Ms Millett

First and foremost may I thank you for your recent letter dated 16 August in response to my application for the role of 'The Horse for Lady Godiva'.

I am absolutely delighted to hear that my offer has 'interesting possibilities' and that should my CV stand scrutiny with the Royal Veterinary Society, which I am confident it will as I am a most credible creature, you will be delighted to pursue the matter further. I am not as delighted, however, to hear that a prerequisite of my work within the role of 'The Horse for Lady Godiva' would be for me to be gelded. In fact, such a notion brings tears to my eyes! Aged 41, I consider myself to be at a prime time of my life and indeed am pleased to say that I am in good condition and operational in every capacity and wish to remain so for many more years .

After considerable consideration I have come to the conclusion that the original horse for Lady Godiva which, as you explained, was not a 'whole' animal must have been gelded on account of a character which included an element of uncontrollable bestial behaviour. The poor fellow was probably a little too frisky for his own good and   I can fully understand why Lady Godiva and her entourage would have been eager to err on the side of caution and remove any possibility of the unthinkable.

In contrast, you may be relieved to learn that my own carnal nature has been trained and disciplined over the years to conform only with convention and even though un-gelded I would pose no immediate threat to the lovely Lady Godiva herself. At least not during public events! If this information itself is not sufficient to convince you that I could still be employed in the above capacity in my natural state, may I also suggest that for added peace of mind you might provide me with a specially designed bridle which will prevent the raising of unexpected interest in the lady in a mechanical manner.

In summary, although I do understand your initial suggestion regards emasculation, you will hopefully be now reassured that you can employ me despite the necessary surgery and rely instead on the well-honed discipline of a seasoned fell-runner and indeed on the restraints of the bridling.

Doubtless you will now be keen to take this interview process to the next stage and I look forward to hearing from you in the very near future.

Sincerely

M. A. Lee   .

Michael A. Lee
cc H.Root & his horse

Our Reference	: CM/RJB
Direct Dialling No.	: 02476 834022
Fax No.	: 02476 832017
Date	: 16th August 2001
Reply to	: E.Millett

CITY CENTRE COMPANY
COVENTRY

M.A.Lee Esq.
Somewhere in West Yorkshire

Dear Mr Lee

LADY GODIVA'S HORSE

Thank you for your most recent letter regarding the above.

Unfortunately I had suspected that, as with other steeds before you, you would find difficulty in complying with the essential criteria of the job specification.

Whilst you offer a comprehensive account of your conformity to convention, it would be remiss of me to place Lady Godiva or the citizens of Coventry in a situation which may prove in any way unseemly, distressing, dangerous or illegal. You will recall that simply seeing the fair lady in a state of undress caused a permanent visual impairment to one of our previous residents. The risk is simply too great to contemplate.

However, whilst I have some difficulty in understanding your aversion to the knife, I am told that there are several products on the market which chemically can produce the same effect as physical gelding. May I invite you to consider this alternative route?

Yours sincerely

Liz Millett

LIZ MILLETT
Chief Executive

City Centre Company (Coventry) Limited · New Union Street
Coventry · CV1 2NT
Tel: 024 7683 3671/2   Fax: 024 7683 2017
www.coventry.towntalk.co.uk
Registered No: 3365320   Registered Office: The Council House · Earl Street · Coventry · CV1 5RR

Coventry City Council

Members' Support Unit

Council House
Earl Street
Coventry
CV1 5RR

Please contact Janet Ford
Direct line 024 7683 1173
Fax 024 7683 1009
janet.ford@coventry.gov.uk

Mr M Lee
Somewhere in West Yorkshire

Our reference AL/jf/lee 2
16 October 2001

Dear Mr Lee

I have been asked by Mr Geoffrey Robinson MP to respond to your letter which was sent to him on 10 August 2001. I am the Cabinet Member (Area Co-ordination and Leisure) within Coventry City Council and therefore Mr Robinson feels that a response to your letter falls within my portfolio.

I must firstly apologise for the delay in responding to you but I have been away on holiday.

The post which you mention ie. 'The Horse for Lady Godiva', has been vacant for quite a number of years! After some research we believe that the salary which was last recorded for this post to be in the region of 3 bushels of hay, free stable and free horse shoes (up to a maximum of 4 sets per year).

I would be interested to receive your CV and specifically what attributes you can bring to this role and any references you are able to provide. Once I have received your CV, and should I consider you to be a suitable candidate, I shall contact you and invite you to Coventry for an audition. Perhaps we could ask Lady Godiva along to audition you.

I note that you mention that you suffer from athlete's foot and although you assure me that it is contained, I think it would be irresponsible if I did not request a 'Movement of Livestock' certificate from the Ministry of Rural Affairs if you were to visit Coventry.

I must say that sometimes my duties as Cabinet Member seem onerous but I look forward to receiving your CV and personally checking your fetlocks. I am a woman of indeterminate years and my fetlocks have been known to attract admiring glances but not for a number of years now!

Perhaps you could enclose a picture of yourself which may help us to decide if you are a suitable candidate?

I hope that you have not already been recruited by some other organisation and will be able to send me further information in the next few weeks.

Kind regards.

Yours sincerely

Councillor Mrs Ann Lucas
Cabinet Member (Area Co-ordination & Leisure)

Somewhere in West Yorkshire
7 August 2001

Sir Richard Body
MP for Boston & Skegness
The House of Lords
London

Dear Sir Richard

I am writing to you a most unusual letter, namely to ask how I might be considered for the position of 'Lincolnshire Poacher' should there be a suitable vacancy available at present or in the near future. As MP for Boston & Skegness I thought you would be the ideal person to whom I should turn for advice.

Inspired both by the fact that my father was from Lincolnshire and indeed by the images conveyed by the traditional folk song that shares the name of the job I am applying for, I believe that I would be an ideal candidate for the position.

Adept at walking and creeping around at night with little sound, I believe I could remain hidden and undetected for long periods of time in the copses and woods, hedgerows and ditches of the Lincolnshire countryside from both animals and indeed the gamekeepers. I have a love of the great outdoors and it could indeed be my delight on a moonlit night at any season of the year to stalk a prospective meal across the vast tracts of Lincolnshire farmland, riverbank and forest.

In terms of equipment there would be no need for you to worry about any cost to the local council; I have a full set of cold weather clothing, including a warm woolly hat, as well as appropriate gear for the warmer nights. I am a bit short when it comes to the department of tools used in the despatch of my quarry but will be only too pleased to acquire my own snares, ropes, knives and catapult. [A gun, I fear, would be too noisy!]

If you could advise me with reference to a place where I could buy a large thermos flask for the winter months ahead, I would be much obliged.

I thank you for your time and consideration and look forward to hearing from you in the very near future.

Sincerely

Michael A. Lee

Jewell's Farm,
Stanford Dingley,
Reading,
Berkshire,
RG7 6LX

August 15th
2001

Dear Mr Lee,

Thank you for your letter about being the Lincolnshire Poacher.

Ferreting is a good form of poaching. What experience of it have you?

If a gamekeeper catches you by surprise, you need to catch your ferret quickly and run with it.

How fast can you run with a ferret in your pocket?

Yours sincerely

Rinus Bury

Sir Richard Body
Jewells Farm
Stanford Dingley
Reading
Berkshire RG7 6LX

Dear Sir Richard

First and foremost, may I say thank you for your swift reply to my enquiries with regards to becoming 'The Lincolnshire Poacher'.

I wholeheartedly agree with your comments that ferreting is a 'good form of poaching' and has indeed proven itself an integral and popular element with many individuals within the poaching profession. My own experience of ferreting is, however, rather limited as I have a rare ferret phobia and consequently the associated fear of being savaged by these small but strong creatures has left me no option but to explore ferret-less techniques.

With respect to your valid and poignant question 'How fast can you run with a ferret in your pocket?' I hasten to add that I am a long-standing member of the Fell Runners Association and, although my track-record of running with a small furry creature in my pocket is a non-starter, I have been known to run for several hours on tough terrain and in inclement conditions at a reasonably noteworthy pace and often with a weighty rucksac on my back.

When pursued by a worthy competitor during the odd fell race I can also report that my veins run thick with adrenalin and make my pursuit a most challenging endeavour for even the hardiest individual. The same would certainly be true in the event of my being caught by surprise by a vigilant gamekeeper.

In the light of this new information would you agree that my credentials for becoming the officially recognised 'Lincolnshire Poacher' are worthy enough for further consideration?

I trust that you will be interested to take my application for employment in the above capacity to the next stage and look forward to hearing from you in the very near future.

I will not be available for interview next week as I am having a short holiday to restore my catapult and clean my boots but will back in the throw of things the week beginning 3 September.

Sincerely

M. A. Lee

Michael A. Lee

Jewell's Farm,
Stanford Dingley,
Reading,
Berkshire,
RG7 6LX

August 24th
2001

Dear Mr Lee,

You seem hopelessly
unqualified.
                Yorkshires are
world class timewasters.

                Why not become
The champion Yorkshire timewaster?
                Write to every
Yorkshireman your challenge to the
title.

                Once acclaimed the
champion, a song will be written
about you to be sung by millions.

                    Yours sincerely
                    Ringo

76

Managing Director Courts [UK] Ltd
The Grange
1 Central Road
Morden
Surrey
SM4 5PQ

Dear Sir/Madam

I am writing to you a most unusual letter, namely to apply for the position of 'Courts' Jester' at a store of your choosing within the UK.

Having recently wandered around your Huddersfield store looking at various pieces of furniture and electrical goods it occurred to me that, despite present business appearing to be healthy, there may well be an unusual but memorable way for you to create further interest in your stores and merchandise and indeed increase overall business returns to an even greater extent.

Long ago in the courts of kings around various parts of the world, there were to be found colourfully dressed clowns or jesters whose job was to entertain the gatherings of people at state functions and generally add a little merriment to the proceedings at hand. Dressed in multicoloured costumes and often with accompanying bell-festooned hats of character and distinction these jesters would hop, dance and tumble their way around the courts making people laugh and adding to the spirit of the occasion.

Aged 41, I am an accomplished hopper, dancer and indeed tumble-turner and I can also sing like a lark, recite poetry and generate infectious laughter at will. As a long-standing member of the Fell Runners Association I have a significant strength and stamina and am able to maintain an energetic and vigorous mobility for long periods of time. In short, and in the absence of any Royal vacancies at present, I would make an ideal 'Courts Jester' whom the crowds of customers within your chosen store could watch and marvel and whose reputation and novelty would help attract an additional number of prospective purchasers to the store also.

Doubtless this concept will be of interest to you and perhaps you might consider piloting the position here in Huddersfield?

Should my jolly acrobatic antics be a success you might then wish to promote me to the position of 'Jester Recruitment and Training Executive' and permit me to interview and employ sufficient individuals of suitable character to jump, twist and twirl their individual ways throughout every Courts Store in the UK. Not only would your crowds of customers achieve their intended purchases and enjoy a certain shoppers' satisfaction but a trip to Courts could also become a multi-dimensional event and offer an additional element of circus for the benefit of the whole family. One can almost hear a small child saying to his father; 'Dad, please can we forget the theme park next week and come here again instead?' The father, in his wisdom, would reply of course, 'I'm glad you said that, son!'

Your sales would doubtless become a logarithmic growth phenomenon and those earning bonus and qualifying for shares will be chuffed to grollies. This is probably one of the few win-win suggestions you will hear in today's competitive market places.

I thank you for your time and consideration with regard to this unusual suggestion and I look forward to hearing from you in the very near future.

In the meantime I intend to add a few more bells and bobbles to my patchwork hat and will continue practicing my backward flips and ancient ballads with hope and commitment.

Sincerely

M. A. Lee .

Michael A. Lee
PS I also juggle!

The Grange, 1 Central Road, MORDEN, Surrey, SM4 5PQ, United Kingdom
Telephone: 0208 640 3322 Fax 0208 410 9244
Direct Line: 0208 410 9381 Email: alison@COURTS.PLC.UK

21st August 2001

Mr M Lee
10 Woodlea Avenue
Reinwood Avenue
Oakes
Huddersfield
West Yorkshire HD3 4EF

Dear Mr Lee

Thank you for your letter dated 9th August 2001, which has been passed to me for a response.

Reading through your letter I must firstly say how very impressed I was by the diversity and number of your skills. You are clearly a very talented man.

Although you do not mention salary in your letter we unfortunately have a policy of no new recruitment in the UK at the moment due to difficult trading conditions. It would also not be right to favour one store over another in the current climate so we would not be able to open a new position just in one store.

However, when we open new stores we are always looking for novel acts to keep children amused so maybe this is somewhere we would be able to work together? Perhaps you could send me a video of your 'act' and then I would be able to decide whether or not it would be suitable for our purposes.

Thank you again for taking the time to write to us.

Yours sincerely

Alison Cohen
PR Manager

Courts plc. Reg. No. 272534
Courts (UK) Ltd. Reg. No. 737130. Courts (Overseas) Ltd. Reg. No. 461239
All companies registered in England with registered offices at The Grange, 1 Central Road, Morden, Surrey SM4 5PQ

The Very Reverend C. Lewis
The Dean
The Deanery
Sumptor Yard
St Albans
Hertfordshire AL1 1BY

Dear Sir

I am writing to you a most unusual letter, namely to apply for the position of 'Gargoyle Model' for the Cathedral & Abbey Church of St Alban.

It was with great interest that I heard recently of the replacement of some of the traditional monstrous stone gargoyles around the outside of the Cathedral & Abbey

Church of St Alban with new and appealing gargoyles depicting the faces of certain prominent 20th Century church figures and well-known individuals. I was immediately struck by the similarities of such an unusual development with the ways in which the Rotary Club or Round Table organisations choose their members from a variety of different backgrounds and professions.

In so saying, perhaps you would consider adding to your gargoyle collection of monsters and clergymen one or two stone depictions of a Yorkshireman with a business background famed for surviving a lightning strike six years ago and known locally for his fell-running and love of the hills.

Aged 41, I am an individual with a craggy face, misshapen nose, balding head and a less than handsome appearance. When on occasions I open my eyes in a wide, startling manner, my wife becomes rather nervous and usually scuttles off into another room to avoid my troublesome appearance. It is most disconcerting to be the one person in a city street of hundreds that small dogs always attack and at whose appearance babies begin to scream!

In short, I would be an excellent choice of model on which a modern-day gargoyle could be based offering an element of contrasting professional background to the existing entourage whilst maintaining the tradition of grotesque looks and propensity for scaring away those elemental beings who have no business creating mischief near the Cathedral.

Doubtless you will be interested to consider this proposal further and I look forward to hearing from you in the very near future.

Many thanks for your time.

Sincerely

M. A. Lee

Michael A. Lee

CATHEDRAL
AND ABBEY CHURCH
OF SAINT ALBAN

Sumpter Yard, St Albans, Hertfordshire, AL1 1BY, UK

Direct Dial: 01727 890202   Evenings/weekends 01727 890203   Cathedral: 01727 860780   Fax: 01727 890227
email: dean@stalbanscathedral.org.uk

Mr Michael Lee

Somewhere in West Yorkshire

11 September 2001

Dear Mr. Lee,

Thank you for your letter of 7th September and I think that is a wonderful idea. We will hold you as a gargoyle reserve, as we unfortunately are not currently in production.

There was once a party for people who had their picture on the front of Time magazine and one of the speakers, apparently, remarked on the fact that looking round it must be the only magazine which did not choose their cover people for their good looks.

Yours sincerely

Christopher Lewis

The Very Reverend Christopher Lewis *Dean*
The Deanery, Sumpter Yard, St Albans, AL1 1BY

Head of Marketing – Strongbow
Bulmers Worldwide
Plough Lane
Hereford HR4 0LE

Dear Sir/Madam

I am writing to you a most unusual letter, namely to apply for the position of 'Archer' within the marketing team working with Bulmers Strongbow Cider. Aged 41, I have reached that stage of life where I am considering a change of career direction and pursuing an alternative pathway which will offer new challenges and perhaps include interests I would normally explore outside of my work .

In this regard I am pleased to inform you that not only am I a keen cider drinker but also somewhat accomplished in the ancient skill of archery. At the age of ten I purchased my very first bow and arrow set and, though inhibited in utilising the full potential of such ancient tools by black, plastic suckers on the end of the arrows, I very quickly became adept in the art of launching my arrows in a manner supportive of fast and straight flight. There were many other children of a similar age whose mothers demanded retribution from my own poor parents for the hair-loss that their offspring suffered when removing stuck-fast suckered arrows from their tender heads. Since I was eventually forced to leave home in a hurried and permanent fashion and take refuge in Storthes Hall Woods near Huddersfield, avoiding the many searches by the newly named One-Eyed Inspector Tallbody and his boys in blue, there came a stage when I was faced with innumerable occasions to hone and master the art and indeed science of archery. There were few young rabbits safe from my eager eye and keen appetite when striding out amongst the bluebells and bracken with my taught bow I can tell you!

Having watched many TV adverts for Strongbow Cider where various archers fire their arrows at a selection of bars, tables and other furniture types associated with places of cider appreciation I am convinced I could do a far better job. Not only could I be of use in drawing attention to the pint of Strongbow Cider itself in the tradition of your well-established adverts but also my presence as the 'Mad, Bald Archer of Storthes Hall Woods' might convince certain publicans to stock more of your product. This would doubtless be a novel marketing strategy!

In terms of salary I am reasonably flexible provided I am paid enough to purchase a new tarpaulin for the roof of my woodland shelter and a ball of good quality string. Perhaps we could come to an agreement in terms of a reasonable allocation of cider samples on a weekly or monthly basis also? I trust that my credentials have persuaded you to consider taking my job application to the next stage and I look forward to hearing from you in the very near future.

Sincerely

M. A. Lee .

HP Bulmer Limited
The Cider Mills, Plough Lane,
Hereford HR4 0LE, England

Telephone +44 (0)1432 352000
Facsimile +44 (0)1432 352084
Web Site www.bulmers.com

Bulmers

Mr M A Lee
Somewhere in West Yorkshire

NEC/YJ   21 September 2001

Dear Mr Lee

Thank you for your entertaining letter applying for the roles of "Archer" with this
Company.

We have, at present, a full complement of skilled Bowmen across the Company but are
always interested in hearing from those who possess this increasingly rare talent. I have
passed your letter to our Marketing Manager in charge of the Strongbow brand and I am
sure that she will be in contact if any suitable opportunities arise.

In the meantime may I urge you to continue to explore the refreshing taste of Strongbow
cider but ask that you refrain from practising your archery after enjoying a pint of two of
the above.

Yours sincerely

Neil Chambers
UK HR Director

TBWA\LONDON

Mr. Michael Lee
**Somewhere in
West Yorkshire**

November 1st 2001

Dear Mr. Lee,

Many thanks for your interest in Strongbow and your application for the position of 'Archer'.

Unfortunately, we commission a special effects company who use an automated rig for the firing of the Strongbow arrows. This ensures we comply with health and safety regulations, and insurance requirements, on our film shoots. Hence, the position of archer is not currently available.

I do hope you find an alternative opportunity for your archery skills.

Kind regards,

Rebecca Tickle,
Account Director.

cc. Annie Neil
     Neil Chambers

TBWA\LONDON LTD
76-80 Whitfield Street
London W1T 4EZ

+44 (0)20 7573 6666 t
+44 (0)20 7573 6667 f
www.tbwa-london.com

The Managing Director
Sentinel Lightning Protection
& Earthing Ltd
Unit C
Thornfield Industrial Estate
Hooton Street, off Carlton Road
Nottingham NG3 2NJ

Dear Sir

I am writing to you a most unusual letter, namely to apply for a job with your company as a 'Lightning Conductor'.

Aged 41, I am at that interesting time of life where half a career in sales has led to my looking at alternative challenges that might better suit my character and abilities whilst offering direction of a rather different nature to the one in which I am presently involved.In short I am looking for a job with an added degree of excitement and one which would be 'charged' with possibilities.

On Wednesday 15 February 1995 I was struck by lightning during an early evening run on the hilly outskirts of Huddersfield during a thunderstorm. I am filled with awe when I think back to the instant when I watched my own hand and foot illuminate with brilliant white light.Fortunately for me, the long-sleeved running vest and long-legged Ronhill Tracksters that I was wearing at the time were as wet as is conceivably possible due the driving rain that accompanied the storm and I presume that the lightning tracked around my wet garments and earthed through my rubber soled training shoes. The subsequent ECG at the local hospital showed no damage to the heart and there were no burns either. I do, however, sometimes wonder whether a small charge of electricity created short circuits in my cerebral cortex but that is hypothesis rather than proven fact!

In this respect I would be most interested to know whether you might have any requirement for a human lightning conductor provided of course you could supply the equipment to safeguard any personal injury whilst the lightning is actually being conducted. I would be most interested once again to observe the electrical surge of a lightning strike pass safely around my protected self but perhaps in a different location to the one previously.

Perhaps there might be some potential for my deployment, not on the summit of a hill, but at the top of a church steeple, mill chimney or strapped to the wing of a light aircraft in thunderous conditions. The subsequent experience would certainly make interesting reading in terms of an article in the newspapers or as a news feature on TV thus creating some free advertising for your, or should I say 'our' business, and would also safeguard the structure to which I was assigned from high voltage damage. In addition I would have the opportunity to add extra dimensions to my CV and to my overall experience in the wilder side of life.

I trust that you will be interested to take this application to the next stage of the interview process and I look forward to hearing from you in the very near future.

Sincerely

M. A. Lee .

Michael A. Lee
PS In terms of luncheon arrangements I am willing to provide my own bread and toasting fork!

SENTINEL

Nationwide service in design and
installation of Lightning Protection systems,
including Earthing and Testing to B.S. 6651: 1999

**Sentinel Lightning Protection
and Earthing Ltd.**

UNIT C
THORNFIELD INDUSTRIAL ESTATE
HOOTON STREET
NOTTINGHAM NG3 2NJ
Telephone 0115 985 9222
Fax 0115 985 9393
Web Site www.sentinel-lightning.co.uk
E-mail enquiries@lightning-conductors.co.uk

Our ref. SJC/LMF

19th September 2001

Michael A Lee
Somewhere in West Yorkshire

Dear Mr Lee

Further to your letter dated 16th September 2001.

We were most intrigued to hear of your encounter with one of natures most spectacular phenomena, namely an electro-magnetic discharge to earth, or in laymans terms, "LIGHTNING".

Such discharges are of course not unusual in themselves, but it has to be said that seldom are such events witnessed at such close quarters and subsequently reported in detail.

Needless to say, upon hearing of your unusual conductive properties, we immediately set about examining our field of operations in search of a possible opening for your talents, but we were unfortunately unable to isolate such an opening within or normal scope.

However, so unusual are your particular dissipative attributes that we considered expanding our normal scope of operations into the following areas, with the specific aim of creating a previously non-existent position.

A) Radcliffe on Soar Power Station lies directly in the final approach path of aircraft landing at the East Midlands airport, and as such it's 600 foot chimney stack is fitted with the mandatory array of aircraft warning lights, which have been on occasion known to fail during electro-magnetic storms.

This prompted us to examine the possibilities of "renting" you out on an hourly basis, your brief being to stand atop the 600 foot stack, waving a red spotlight at the cockpits of approaching aircraft and holding a large illuminated placard clearly emblazoned with the words "*TEMPORARAY TRAFFIC LIGHTS*", with also the slightly less prominent sub-script "*courtesy of Sentinel Ltd*", together with our telephone and fax numbers.

Unfortunately however, we had trouble getting this idea through the Health and Safety executives risk assessment procedure, since it was the general consensus of opinion within the executive that an unacceptable degree of risk was attached to airline pilots in trying to write down our telephone and fax number whilst attempting to land a large passenger jet during such inclement weather conditions.

№ 9902

Registered No. 2627073

Certificate number 2407/00

87

Continued......

B) We made representation to the National Association of Fish Farmers with a view to reducing their labour costs for the maintenance of stock ponds.

When a stock pond is due for maintenance, it is often necessary to remove the fish to a holding pond using the "electro-netting" procedure. This involves several staff members wading around for several hours using low voltage shock devices until the large number of fish are removed.

Again, we considered renting you out on an hourly basis, to stand barefoot, somewhere close to the centre of the relatively shallow pond, whilst holding on tightly to a length of steel wire armoured 36kV power cable carrying some 36,000 volts of direct current, thus effectively electrifying the entire pond with a single short voltage pulse.

We were however politely informed that whilst the merits of the speedy removal of stock were obvious, it is nevertheless desirable for at least the bulk of the fish to actually survive the removal process and subsequently be returned ALIVE to the stock pond after maintenance.

It is with regret therefore that at this particular time we are unable to find a suitable outlet for your talents within our current scope of operations.

Rest assured however, that we are actively engaged in the consideration of other options, which at a later date may indeed prove to be profitable for both ourselves and yourself alike.

One option, although in the early stages of the development process, is the one man operation *HUMAN UNDERWATER WELDING SYSTEM* (how long can you hold your breath?), which requires no equipment other than the weighted harness which allows you to sink to the desired depth whilst attached to a high voltage welding cable.

Welding operations will be carried out with "fingertip" accuracy since the necessary charge will be delivered to the weld site by simply touching it with your index finer, and subsequently running said finger around the joint.

In the meantime however, as a possible financially lucrative aside, one wonders if the manufacturers of RON HILL TRACKSTERS have ever considered the thermal and electro-magnetic dissipation properties of their sportswear as a possible selling point, and whether or not they may wish to consider entering into a contract with your goodself, featuring a series of time lapse colour photographs, taken at an incredibly high shutter speed, of yourself in a suitably darkened environment, whilst being subjected to an artificially induced electrical discharge of say in the region of 100kA for a duration of 100 micro-seconds, whilst standing in a bucket of water and wearing RON HILL SPORTSWEAR.

As an advertising aid, or indeed as the main thrust of a campaign aimed at perhaps runners who live in an area with a high concentration of high voltage overhead power lines, the above photographs would surely attract a substantial dividend for the subject of the pictures.

It has to be said that the photographic effect is spectacular, although I must admit that I have only ever seen one such sequence of pictures, taken during a recent execution in America.

For now at least, we shall keep your details on file with a view to possible future contact.

Yours sincerely

S J CARGILL
MANAGER

Himself The Pope
The Vatican
Rome
Italy

Dear Sir

I am writing to you a most unusual letter, namely to apply for the position of 'Fisher King', a role for which I believe the previous incumbent had responsibility to guard that most treasured of ancient objects, the Holy Grail. Since the Grail has been an object of great interest and quest by those within the church for many centuries I thought it appropriate to approach your good self as a leader of the worldwide church is my first point of contact.

As an individual who is reasonably fit in body and mind I believe I would be an ideal candidate for the aforementioned position as it is well within my capacity to offer a degree of physical strength combined with an astute attention as far as general security of the Grail is concerned. Like the original Fisher King I am quite willing to relocate to a castle situated in a remote place surrounded by a sufficient amount of wasteland and, as a highly self-motivated individual, would be most content to undertake my duties in such a challenging and unusual environment. As far as the Grail itself is concerned I have it on good authority by a friend of mine that it has been seen on show in the window of an antique shop in the Glastonbury area of England and is available for a modest price. [I am not entirely sure that the proprietor of the shop realises the value of the object in his possession either materially or more importantly as far as church significance is concerned so it will be best for everyone if ownership changes hands.] I understand that my friend will complete a purchase of the Grail very shortly.

You will doubtless be most interested in my timely enquiry around this vital position and I look forward to hearing from you in the very near future.

Once again may I thank you for your time and consideration.

Sincerely

Michael A. Lee

SECRETARIAT OF STATE

FIRST SECTION · GENERAL AFFAIRS

From the Vatican, 2 October 2001

Dear Mr Lee,

I am directed to acknowledge the letter which you sent to His Holiness Pope John Paul II and I would assure you that the contents have been noted.

His Holiness will remember you in his prayers.

With good wishes, I remain

Yours sincerely,

Monsignor Pédro López Quintana
Assessor

Mr Michael A. Lee
10 Woodlea Avenue
Reinwood Manor
Oakes
HUDDERSFIELD
W. Yorks.
HD3 4EF

Stephen Byers
Minister for Transport, Local
Government & the Regions
The House of Commons
London

Dear Sir

I am writing to you a most unusual letter, namely to apply for the position with the present government of 'King of the Road' and as Minister for Transport I thought you might be the ideal person to approach in this regard. Like you, I am a keen fell-walker and in so saying I have spent much time on many occasions travelling to various countryside regions around the UK in order to prowl the hills and mountains of our more scenic regions. When time and a demanding family permit and I like nothing better than to indulge myself in hours of solitary hiking for relaxation and enjoyment.

In this regard, I am sure you will appreciate the time spent anticipating the sense of freedom that precedes these therapeutic expeditions into the hills and dales and the fact that it is often necessary to do so whilst travelling by car or train via our busy motorway, road and rail network. Similarly, I am sure that you will also be familiar with that legend of travelling stalwarts who not only travelled extensively across the USA for many years but also captured the aforementioned freedom and pure enjoyment of such travel in song, the one and only Boxcar Willie. His rendition of that all-time song 'King of the Road' has inspired me on many occasions in the past in a musical sense and has now fuelled my ambitions for a new job at a time of life when I would relish the chance of facing new challenges and job responsibilities.

As the officially appointed 'King of the Road' I could be employed a three-fold capacity. First, I could act in an advisory capacity to provide best route information for those members of parliament who are taking to the roads and rail for either recreational or indeed business reasons. Second, I could attend the House of Commons Christmas Party and sing my own version of Boxcar Willies' 'King of the Road' to lift the spirits of all the members and prepare everyone for their seasonal break. Finally and most importantly, I could have my craggy self dressed in a similar fashion to Boxcar Willie broadcast on TV and in the national papers as the image of the Department of Transport and provide a figure of familiarity and fondness to help forge rapport between the department and the public. Mine could be the facial focus of your bill-board advertising and letterhead imagery.

Doubtless you will want to spend some time considering me for this exciting role and I look forward to hearing from you in the very near future regards details of how we will take my application to the next stage of the employment process.
Sincerely

N. A. Lee .

DTLR
TRANSPORT
LOCAL GOVERNMENT
REGIONS

Teresa Stembridge
PS to Michelle Banks
HR - Customer Service

Department for Transport,
Local Government and the Regions
Zone 5/01
Great Minster House
76 Marsham Street
London
SW1P 4DR

Direct Line: 020 7944 6041
Divisional Enquiries: 020 7944 6041
Fax: 020 7944 2215
GTN No: 3533
teresa.stembridge@dtlr.gsi.gov.uk

Web Site: www.dtlr.gov.uk

29 November 2001

Michael A Lee
Somewhere in West Yorkshire

Dear Mr Lee

I am writing in response to your letter of 16 October 2001, addressed to Stephen Byers.

My apologies for the delay in responding to you – your letter does not appear to have reached the Minister's office until 2 November, and was subsequently passed on to us here in the Human Resources Division for response.

Unfortunately we do not have any vacancies within the Department for the position mentioned in your letter. We will, however, keep your details on file and contact you again should any similar positions become available.

Yours sincerely

Teresa Stembridge

INVESTOR IN PEOPLE

Document2

The Manager/Director
Jodrell Bank Planetarium
Jodrell Bank Science Centre
Macclesfield
Cheshire

Dear Sir/Madam

I am writing to you a most unusual letter, namely to apply for the position at Jodrell Bank Planetarium of 'The Man in the Moon'.

There have doubtless been millions upon millions of children throughout British history who have been taught by their parents and through countless books that there exists a character called 'The Man in the Moon'. Indeed, as a small child in the 1960s I not only believed in this legendary figure myself, but was quite convinced at the time that I could in fact see this person as I looked at a full moon on a rare, clear night. [Even today I am similarly convinced that such is the case after a few glasses of a good red wine!] It was with significant distress, therefore, that I watched the first human beings land on the moon in 1969 – or so it was portrayed by the Americans – as I wondered if they might frighten off the age-old guardian of our bright night light and somehow change the lunar face for good.

As the present generation of children visit your world-famous planetarium in London there must be a huge expectation for many to catch sight not only of the whirling galaxies, solar flares and planetary wonders but also to see, be it even for a few moments, their familiar friend 'The Man in the Moon.' I would imagine that for a not insignificant few an absence of such a sighting might be grossly disappointing and detrimental to the satisfaction of their visit.

Aged 41, I am an individual with a craggy, cratered face that is suitably rounded and I also have a pair of blue, twinkling eyes with a happy sort of smile to boot. In short I would be an ideal candidate for the role of 'The Man in the Moon' should you decide that such a character be employed forthwith. I am a gregarious individual with a certain enthusiastic eloquence and would be only too happy to provide an informative presentation on the origins, geology and exploration of the moon from my seat high up in the roof of the planetarium to the awe and fascination of the audience below.

Doubtless you will want to take this job application to the next stage of your selection process and in this regard I look forward to hearing from you in the very near future.

Many thanks for your time and consideration.

Sincerely

M. A. Lee .

Michael A. Lee

PS As far as meals are concerned I would anticipate bringing my own packed lunch which usually contains a generous helping of green cheese, and so there would be no need on your part to worry about a food allowance of any kind.

Jodrell Bank
Science Centre & Arboretum

Michael A Lee,
Somewhere in West Yorkshire

Dear Mr. Lee,

Thank you for your 'most unusual' letter which I read with interest. Currently we do not have any vacancies at the Science Centre and our programme of events when external organisations provide activities, drama workshops etc., are fully booked for 2001/02.

Thank you however for writing to tell us of the unique experience that you could provide.

Yours sincerely,

Sylvia Chaplin
General Manager

Macclesfield   Cheshire SK11 9DL
Fax: 01477 571695   Tel: 01477 571339

Administered by The University of Manchester
VAT Registration No. 148581834

Head of Corporate Personnel
Chief Executives Department
Greenwich Borough Council
2nd Floor
29–37 Wellington Street
Woolwich
London SE18 6RA

Dear Sir

I am writing to you a most unusual letter, namely to apply for the position with Greenwich Borough Council of 'Old Father Time' should this become available in the near future.

The name of Greenwich is doubtless one of world renown as far as its' connection with Greenwich Mean Time is concerned and its' association with it marking the very meridian where East officially meets West. I am sure that without such a location of time reference the world might be a far more confused place than it is already and there would be countless individuals involved in endless arguments around the subject of past, present and future time and the setting of various timepieces. The working day of the world population would perhaps begin and end in a variety of unacceptable ways according to the whims and fancies of the employees concerned and lunch hours might be extended indefinitely and without timed discipline. Bars might stay open far too long into the night and small children might never reach their respective schools before the cessation of the days' lessons. Society and its' economy would descend miserably into chaos very quickly indeed.

I am sure that the key reason that our society has not sunk in such a fashion to the dark depths of irretrievable disorder is credit to the legendary figure of timekeeping and temporal management himself, 'Old Father Time'. My great concern, of course, is that being 'Old' may well mean the near-future arrival of the present incumbents' demise and the urgent need for a credible and able replacement. I have certainly in all my years never heard of any replacement of the existing holder of this office and presume he must be approaching retirement or, worse still, due to receive a visit from his cousin The Grim Reaper!

As a 41-year-old fell runner and long-standing member of the Fell Runners Association I am officially recognised by the rules of the organisation as a 'veteran'. Indeed, I have to tell you that my creaking knees and back are in collusion with this definition also, although, needless to say, that my mind is keen and alert and my life expectancy over the next forty years or so significantly positive and optimistic. Add to this the fact that I am actually a father of two small children and also have a 1961 Omega Seamaster watch that keeps exact time if wound up every day and you will understand that I would be an ideal candidate for the role of 'Old Father Time' should a candidate be sought. I am a man who balances prospects with maturity.

Many thanks for your time and consideration as far as this job application is concerned and, although you will no doubt receive many letters of a similar ilk to this each month, I do look forward to hearing from you in the very near future and taking this application to the next stage of the employment process.

I feel confident that we could work efficiently together and maintain the worlds' many endeavours in the timed fashion to which it is accustomed.

Sincerely

M. A. Lee .

Michael A. Lee

Reply to Jim Parrott

Telephone 020-8921-5003

Facsimile 020-8921-5718

email jim.parrott@greenwich.gov.uk.

To Mr M A Lee
Somewhere in
West Yorkshire

Corporate Personnel

Chief Executive's Department

2nd Floor
29-37 Wellington Street
Woolwich
London SE18 6RA

Our Ref JP/cc/H09/1

Your Ref

Date 30 October 2001

Dear Mr Lee

Thank you for your recent application for the position of 'Old Father Time'. Whilst Greenwich Council is proud of its position on the meridian the responsibility for time itself lies with the Royal Observatory and you may wish to pursue your enquiries with them.

However, my understanding is that the current incumbent has achieved unusual longevity and that no vacancy is expected imminently. This may be connected with some blurring of the calendar in relation to the meridian although that might be more readily understandable in the other hemisphere where the meridian becomes the international dateline and at least one hostelry, which claims to lie directly upon it, circumvents local licensing laws by operating three bars in different parts of the building known as yesterday, today and tomorrow.

I also fear that it would be impossible to provide fells in this vicinity. However, I can vouch for the local hills providing a more than adequate challenge a decade, or so, on from formal recognition as a 'veteran'.

With best wishes

Yours sincerely

Jim Parrott

JIM PARROTT
HEAD OF CORPORATE PERSONNEL

Somewhere in West Yorkshire
22 October 2001

The Manager/Director
Maritime & Coastguard Agency
105 Commercial Road
Southampton SO15 1EG

Dear Sir/Madam

I am writing to you a most unusual letter, namely to apply for the position with the Maritime & Coastguard Agency of 'Iceberg Warden' should such be available either presently or in the near future.

Living in West Yorkshire, I am a 41-year-old sales executive looking to pursue an alternative career pathway that would offer a certain degree of new challenge as well as providing the route to focusing my attention on coastal issues, rather than those pertaining to an inland environment as is my present situation.

Living in the heart of the industrial backwoods you will doubtless sympathise with the shock I felt when I read just last week of the sinking of the *Titanic*. [The postal service is always a little slower here than in most other British towns!] It occurred to me that in order to avoid a similar tragedy happening in British waters it would surely be of the highest priority to appoint someone to monitor the movement of icebergs and perhaps even paint them in a noticeable luminescent colour so that even at night our brave sailors could see them from a distance as they float precariously around our sea and ocean territory. [The icebergs, that is, not the sailors!]

Although I would certainly require some specialist training to satisfactorily fulfil my duties I can assure you that I would be an ideal candidate for the job. As a geographer I spent much of my youth armed with a trusty watch and sturdy pair of training shoes timing the progress of oranges down stretches of various local Yorkshire streams in order to gauge speed of various rivulets and wild waterways, and hence you can rest assured that the movement of natural phenomenon is not a new concept to me. I am also a dab hand at calculating the possible pathways that moving objects might take given a miscellany of variables and the application of my Physics 'A' Level and natural psychic ability.

Finally, I have had an abundance of painting and decorating experience over the years and would find the painting of roving icebergs a bright and noticeable colour a relatively straight-forward task. I am sure that you will process many letters requesting employment with your well-respected organisation but feel confident that my credentials will convince you to take my application to the next stage of consideration. Many thanks indeed for your time and I look forward to hearing from you in the near future.

Sincerely

PS Should I be successful in my bid for employment would you provide the cold weather overcoat and mittens or would I be expected to purchase them myself?

Maritime and Coastguard Agency

Bay 3/25
Spring Place
105 Commercial Rd
Southampton
SO15 1EG

TEL: 023 8032 9100
DDI: 023 8032 9277
GTN: 1513 277
FAX: 023 8032 9122
richard_wilson@mcga.gov.uk

Michael A Lee Esq
Somewhere in West Yorkshire

Your ref:

Our ref:

24 October 2001

Dear Mr Lee,

Thank you for your interesting letter about the possibility of employment as an Iceberg Warden.

I am pleased to tell you that the United Kingdom is a signatory to the North Atlantic Ice Patrol Service operated by the United States and Canada. The service uses aerial surveillance to spot icebergs and modern communications and navigation equipment at sea ensures that ships are warned of the dangers.

Against the background of that tried and tested arrangement, we will not need to take up your proposal.

Thank you again for your interest in maritime safety.

Yours sincerely,

Richard Wilson
Head of Strategic Planning

INVESTOR IN PEOPLE

An executive agency of the Department for Transport, Local Government and the Regions

The Manager/Director
Tate Modern
Bankside
London SE1 9TG

Dear Sir/Madam

I am writing to you a most unusual letter, namely to explore the possibilities of the Tate Modern purchasing or exhibiting a series of what I am sure are unique pictures created by none other than a house spider that has taken a shine to living in our home here in West Yorkshire and thus become a recognised 'Northern Exhibitionist'.

Doubtless you recall the recent media coverage of 'Thai Elephant Art' discussing the artistic accomplishments of elephants that had been supplied with canvas, paint and brushes. I believe that these works of art have become very popular and indeed rather chic.

In the same way I am convinced that the many 'spider footprint paintings' we have collected on quality cartridge paper through the colourful wanderings of our very own 'Boris' the house spider would be of huge interest to many people through a wonderful combination of novelty and aesthetic appreciation of fine spider artwork.

Much of the work is at present unframed but should you be interested in either purchasing it or perhaps exhibiting it and selling it on my behalf we could always organise the framing also. I have had a rather clever idea to frame the pictures using a cobweb-like frame made of silk or similar!

I thank you for your time and consideration and look forward to hearing from you in the very near future regards the suitability for taking this idea forward.

Sincerely

M. A. Lee

Michael A. Lee

Bankside
London SE1 9TG

call
+44 (0) 20 7887 8000
fax
+44 (0) 20 7401 5052

visit
www.tate.org.uk

MODERN
TATE

Michael A Lee
Somewhere in West Yorkshire

23-11-2001

Dear Michael

Thank you for your recent letter regarding an acquisition.
The Tate Gallery is a British national museum. This means that it is a state organisation
and is funded by the government through the Department of National Heritage.
Acquisitions are decided upon ultimately by the Board of Trustees.
In the field of contemporary art, acquisitions reflect those artists who have already
made a significant contribution and have achieved national or international recognition.
Potential acquisitions of contemporary art generally come from artist's dealers, other
commercial galleries or collectors.
I have enclosed a leaflet which may help you find a more suitable gallery to approach.
Thank you for your interest in the Tate Gallery.
I hope this is helpful.

Yours sincerely

Anita Dalchow
Information Assistant

Nigel Peel
North Cotswold Hunt
The Kennels
Broadway
Worcestershire

Dear Sir

I am writing to you a most unusual letter, namely to apply for the position with the North Cotswold Hunt as 'The Rather Nimble Two-Legged Fox' should this vacancy arise in the near future.

There have, of course, over the last months and years been substantial discussions in many circles, including those of government, around the possibility of a ban on fox-hunting. There are understandably many people outraged at this possibility and should this scenario be realised there would doubtless be many packs of foxhounds and huntsmen disappointed and somewhat redundant as far as their sport is concerned.

However, having thought long and hard about this issue, I believe I could offer a positive solution to your own pack which would, in the event of disappearance of the traditional quarry from the equation, continue to offer you a significant degree of fun whilst maintaining a strong element of serious hunting.

Aged 41, I am a reasonably fit individual with a great love of the countryside and for country sports. Although bald as a coot on the top of my head, I am most remarkable in the thickness and extent of ginger-brown body hair elsewhere on my chest, back, arms and shoulders and from a distance, with shirt removed, have a slight resemblance to our furry friend, the red fox. I am rather crafty by nature and just like Old Foxy I love to eat fresh chicken and rabbit when available, although be it said I usually acquire mine from the butchers shop. Most importantly I am a long-standing member of the Fell Runners Association and, not only am I skilled as far as map and compass work is concerned, but also I can run like the wind when being chased.

In short then my proposal is this: provided the foxhounds are trained to stand back once they have caught me – if indeed they are successful enough to do so – and leave me unravaged, I am perfectly happy to play the part of the fox at any of your future hunts.

Dressed either in a lightweight fox outfit or in my own running attire you could provide me with a five- or ten-minute lead time and I would provide chases such as you have never seen before. You would marvel at the ability I have at negotiating high walls and fences, at hopping over streams, wading rivers and vanishing like some mysterious sprite in the heart of a wooded copse. In the space of a minute I would sprint like a cheetah, lay low like a very low thing and canter gracefully like a thoroughbred horse. I would be a challenge for any pack of hounds and huntsmen no matter how experienced or keen their approach. Finally, I would add an interesting touch to the end of the proceedings by joining the hunt concerned for a pie and a pint at the nearest appropriate hostelry and even provide the team with a fox's perspective of the occasion.

The hunts would be saved, the hounds exercised and thrilled, and the huntsmen offered a day of exceptional sport. Moreover, I would have in these uncertain times a secure role as 'The Rather Nimble Two-Legged Fox'.

I trust that this job application is of interest to you and, thanking you for your time and consideration, I look forward to hearing from you in the near future.

Yours sincerely

M. A. Lee .

Michael A. Lee

Kineton Hill
Stow-on-the-Wold
Cheltenham
Gloucestershire
GL54 1EZ

M A Lee Esq

Somewhere in West Yorkshire

1 December 2001

Dear Mr Lee

Thank you so much for your most unusual letter. As you can imagine, the hounds and I are rather hoping that we will not need to take up your offer! My wife and I were particularly struck by your willingness to wear a lightweight fox costume. We felt that, although it would add a splendid touch of authenticity, it might well unnerve the large number of sheep that roam the Cotswold hills.

Once again, thank you very much for your letter, which has brightened up a rather dull start to the hunting season.

Yours sincerely

Nigel Peel .

N D B Peel

Somewhere in West Yorkshire
13 November 2001

David Butterfield
Human Resources Services Manager
Kennett District Council
Brawfort
Bath Road
Devizes
Wiltshire SN10 2AT

Dear Sir

I am writing to you a most unusual letter, namely to apply for the job of 'White Horse Jockey' for one of the many famous white horses present within the Wiltshire Downs area that falls under your own geographical jurisdiction.

Over the years I have heard mentioned on several occasions the names of various white horses such as Westbury, Pewsey, Marlborough and Broad Hinton and can imagine no better place in which they could reside than the beautiful chalk downs of Wiltshire. Never, however, have I heard mention made of either rider or jockey for these wonderful animals and I assume that perhaps the absence of such reference suggests a job opportunity.

I am neither the tallest nor the heaviest person to have walked the streets of West Yorkshire but am agile, keen and nimble as of course all jockeys should be. I am as bald as the proverbial coot and consequently can offer a degree of aerodynamic efficiency when sat in riding position. Even when stationary the wind tends to blow over me rather than against me thus preserving my balance and dignity.

I am also smart and well presented and would offer the many tourists who visit the area in a bid to see the famous white horses a certain enjoyment in the appreciation of quality and the art of dapper dressing.

Although doubtless you will receive many letters of a similar kind to this rest assured that you would find me a candidate of superior standing and an ideal man for the job.

Sincerely

M. A. Lee

Michael A. Lee

KENNET District Council

Chief Executive: M.J. BODEN, T.D., M.B.A., LL.B.(Hons)
CHIEF EXECUTIVE'S GROUP.
Browfort, Bath Road, Devizes, Wilts. SN10 2AT.
Tel: Devizes (01380) 724911 Ext. **627**
Fax (01380) 720835.   DX 42909   www.kennet.gov.uk

Mr M A Lee
Somewhere in West Yorkshire

Please ask for   **Anne Ewing**

Your reference

Our reference   **HR/AE/LM**

Date   **11 December 2001**

Dear Mr Lee

Thank you for your letter of 13 November 2001 addressed to Mr Butterfield which, has been passed to me for attention. I apologise for the delay in responding to you, but I wished to discuss your proposal with our Tourism Manager.

You are quite right that we have a number of White Horses within our local area. Whilst your agility and nimbleness would be very useful in order to climb the horses, riding them is not a practical proposition as they are two dimensional.

If however, you would wish to pursue a career in tourism within the local area, our Tourism Manager says that she would be happy to consider you if you would care to let us have further details about yourself.

In the meantime I enclose some information on the White Horses within the area which you may find of interest.

Yours sincerely

Anne Ewing
Principal Human Resources Officer

Head of Personnel
Dudley Metropolitan Borough Council
Council House
Dudley DY1 1HF

Dear Sir/Madam

I am writing to you a most unusual letter, namely to apply for the position or nominal title of 'King of the Castle' at Dudley Castle – and since you are the individual at the Head of the Borough Councils' Department of Personnel, I thought you would be an ideal person to write to in the first instance in this regard.

Aged 41 and experiencing something of a male mid-life crisis, I recently wrote to the Garter King of Arms at the College of Arms in London asking whether I might obtain a title and become a member of the peerage. I have always felt I might have missed being born into the aristocracy by a mere cats whisker but I have nevertheless always carried around with me the intrinsic self-belief in my upper-crust potential. Unfortunately, my wish to become a Duke, Earl, Viscount or Baron is dependant on honours emanating from the crown and sadly there is no emanation forthcoming. Similarly, a Knightage which would bring with it the prefix of 'Sir' is presently and similarly elusive and sad to say I am still as always the ever faithful and aspiring but simply named Mr Lee. Much as I would like to be a Lord, I am not.

Having said this I could not help being influenced and impressed by an experience I had on holiday with my family earlier this year on a Brittany beach when, stood at the very top of a monumental sandcastle that my two fine sons and I had built with great pride, I heard myself uttering the words of the immortal chant: 'I'm the King of the Castle'. At that very moment I felt that the occasion was one of prophetic significance and decided in the blink of a French gnat's eye that indeed my destiny would be to apply for and win the coveted title or even role of 'King of the Castle', dependent, of course, on finding an appropriate castle for which I could be king – even if it meant being a king in spirit and absence rather than necessarily one who resides in the castle itself.

As a reasonably ambitious, intelligent and regal individual I therefore believe I would be an ideal candidate for the role of 'King of Dudley Castle' and I would be very grateful indeed for your time and consideration in this regard.

I am quite happy to relinquish any claims to ownership of any brick, mortar or lands associated with the castle and I would not be particularly discouraged should I be granted the title or role without any royal subjects to whom I could wave. In a similar vein, I have no collateral to bring with me either for the finance of banquets or political purposes, and so there would be as little expected of me as I would expect in return.

Perhaps I could appear at certain formal occasions complete with crown and cloak to introduce an event or function and add to the magic and splendour of the occasion as members of the public say such things as, 'Ee, who would have thought that the King himself would be here; wait until we tell Aunty Edith!' Doubtless you will require a little time to consider my application but I do look forward to hearing from you at a convenient time in the very near future.

Sincerely

Michael A. Lee

Chief Executive's Department
Andrew Sparke, L.L.B., Chief Executive
Council House, Priory Road, Dudley, West Midlands, DY1 1HF
Tel: (01384) 818181 Fax: (01384) 815226 www.dudley.gov.uk
Minicom Number for the Hearing Impaired (01384) 815273

Your ref: Our ref: Please ask for: Direct Line:

Dear Mr Lee,

Thank you for your recent application to become King of the Castle at Dudley Council.   Thank you for also sharing your life experiences with us.   It's gratifying that someone with such a strong sense of purpose, self-belief and regal destiny wishes to be so closely associated with Dudley.

Dudley Council undertakes a range of civic duties and mandatory responsibilities. Whilst our brief is wide ranging, sadly it does not extend to creating Kings, either for Dudley Castle or elsewhere. If it did I'm sure that your commitment and ambition would make you an excellent candidate to fulfil the role. As it is, I am sorry that we must disappoint you.

Please don't be downhearted.   Someone of your spirit, determination and evident style is sure to realise an appropriate destiny. If you think of yourself as regal, doubtless regal you will become.

In a gesture of goodwill and in an effort to allay your obvious disappointment we would be delighted to welcome you to Dudley at some point in the future. Whilst we would be unable to offer you official duties, we would be happy to show you a vibrant, confident and exciting Borough and introduce you to some wonderful people who like you, we suspect, do not suffer from taking themselves too seriously.

If you would like to accept our invitation of a day out in Dudley, please contact me on 01384 815228 and I would be delighted to make the arrangements.

Yours sincerely

Jayne Surman

Jayne Surman
Head of Marketing and Communications

The Honourable Mr Howard
Castle Howard
York
North Yorkshire

Dear Sir

I am writing to you a most unusual letter, namely to apply for the position of 'Locum Globe Carrier' during holiday periods at Castle Howard.

Let me explain. Yesterday my wife and I and our two angelic children visited Castle Howard for the first time and enjoyed with great admiration the beauty and opulence of your wonderful house as well as the aesthetic pleasures of your expansive grounds and myriad statues, monuments and fountains.

It was also with tremendous admiration and indeed awe that I observed the actor playing the part of Atlas in the midst of the great fountain holding the zodiac encircled globe on his muscular shoulders without even a hint of movement or fatigue. What a professional!

It occurred to me, however, that there must be periods of time when the house and gardens are open to the public but when this gentleman has time away from the job for holidays or perhaps to receive physiotherapy or shoulder massage. Doubtless therefore this will mean you have a requirement for someone to stand in as a locum Globe Carrier. Herein may lay a job opportunity for me and a solution in staff recruitment for you!

Aged 42, I am a reasonably fit, strong individual with an interest in stately homes and houses, an enjoyment of the great outdoors and a desire to be more involved in classical culture. In short, I would be an ideal candidate for the task of holding up the great globe in the midst of the fountain in a committed, be it motionless manner for the pleasure of your visitors and indeed for your family and your good self.

I am also an affable individual and should there be occasions when small children have become bewildered by the activities of the day or disappointed at parental refusal of an ice-cream treat, they could be brought to the fountain and receive a hearty smile from Atlas himself. Mum could say to her precious son or daughter, 'There is no need for you to cry over a busy day is there? That man has the whole world on his shoulders but still finds cause to smile!'

I am sure that you will receive many letters of this kind on a regular basis and so thank you for your time and kind consideration and I look forward to hearing from you in the very near future.

Sincerely

Michael A. Lee

CASTLE *H*OWARD

Our Ref: SBGH/SLB/Est.HO.
Date: 21 march 2002

Michael Lee Esq
Somewhere in West Yorkshire

Dear Mr Lee

Thank you for your letter dated 18 March applying for the position of 'Locum Globe Carrier' during holiday periods at Castle Howard.

As you can appreciate, this is indeed a testing position and one that requires great strength, patience and resilience to the cold.

I am sure that our visitors would much enjoy meeting Atlas while he takes his well earned rests in the same way that they are now to find Sir John Vanbrugh, the 5th Earl of Carlisle, and other members of my family stalking the corridors of the house itself.

In order to progress your application further we will need your measurements of the following muscles; Latissimus Dorsi, Deltoids, Teres Majors, Trapezius, Gluteaus Maximus, Biceps Femoris, Gastocnemius. Pectoralis Majors, Biceps Brachii, Brachioradialis, and Rectus Femoris. Furthermore, we will of course require 3 references, and would expect Zeus to provide one of these. How are your relations with Poseidon these days? Can he help!

We would assume that you would provide your own outfit, and please let us know the size and make-up of your entourage.

Yours sincerely

The Hon. Simon Howard

Chairman: The Hon Simon Howard. Tel: +44 (0)1653 648444 Fax: +44 (0)1653 648462
E-mail: sbgh@castlehoward.co.uk

Epilogue ...

After many months of applying for the most bizarre jobs I could think of and receiving a host of replies that were essentially rejections of variable amusement, I was overjoyed to eventually receive a firm offer of employment. Despite the fact that the original holder of the position is reputed to have been a big cat of some description, I received a wonderful job contract to become the very latest, contemporary 'Beast Of Bodmin Moor' and, I might add, subsequently invited to be inaugurated as such in Cornwall. How could I refuse such a unique opportunity?!

I was duly inaugurated as the aforementioned 'Beast' in 2002 and am that very animal to this very day. Here is a copy of the contract for you to read and, with it, a rather fetching picture of me in my furry tiger outfit hired specially for the occasion (the fancy dress shop neither had a leopard nor a panther outfit!) If there is one thing to be learned from this lateral venture it is that 'Where there is a will there is a way.' Initiative and improvisation can bring surprising results to the table!

The Best of Bodmin Moor

The Best of Bodmin Moor
Mount Pleasant Farm
Mount
Nr. Bodmin
Cornwall
PL30 4EX

Dear Mr. Lee

The committee of The Best of Bodmin Moor would like to offer you the position of The Beast of Bodmin Moor. It appears that the previous holder of the position has taken an unauthorised sabbatical or has been poached, (we hope the same fate does not befall you).

There are of course a few conditions of employment, which must be met. You must promise not to steal milk from other cat's saucers, leave deposits in people's gardens or 'presents' by their back doors. You may not eat such things as fresh lamb or beef that has not been sourced through the appropriate channels, though as we are currently inundated with rabbits (they cleared out all my carrots and lettuces again!) I'm sure the odd one would not go amiss. You must have up to date vaccination certificates for feline flu and be wormed regularly, only bonafide sickness as diagnosed by our vet would qualify for sick pay, a 'gippy' tummy after a night out on the tiles or fur balls would not suffice.

We reserve the right to terminate your employment forthwith should you make a nuisance of yourself of frighten anyone, severe misconduct will result in incarceration in Newquay zoo for an indeterminate period. Holiday pay would not be appropriate, as this is such a lovely place to live, you could not possibly want one.

Finally the perks of the job include the aforementioned rabbits, as many mice as you can eat, the right to roar wherever and whenever you see fit and a warm welcome in front of the fire at Jamaica Inn.

I hope you feel up to the task and will enjoy becoming the official Beast of Bodmin Moor.

Yours sincerely,

Chairman Best of Bodmin Moor

Promoting the Hidden Heart of Cornwall
www.bodminmoor.co.uk

Impossible Items ...

Customer Service Manager
Next Retail Ltd
Desford Road
Enderby
Leicester LE19 4AT

Dear Sir/Madam

I am writing to you as part of my quest for an unusual item; namely a pretty 'Freudian Slip' for my wife.

Only last week my wife and I threw a dinner party here at our home in Huddersfield and enjoyed a wonderful meal along with several glasses of wine with some friends. The conversation was varied and delightful and we touched on areas as diverse as psychology and lingerie.

It was during this relaxed and stimulating conversation that I seem to recall one of my friends saying he had purchased a Freudian Slip for his wife and it occurred to me afterwards that a similar gift might well also provide an excellent present for my own wife on the occasion of her next birthday.

In this regard I wondered, as a national retailer of ladies and gentlemen's fashion, if you might be able to advise me with reference to the styles and colours of slips you sell and whether any of them carry the Freudian brand name. In asking for such advice may I say that my wife is almost 41 years old and therefore not such a Jungian as she used to be and so a reasonably conservative style of slip would be more appropriate than something too obviously suggestive.

Many thanks indeed for your time and kind consideration in this matter and I look forward to hearing from you in the very near future.

Sincerely

M. A. Lee

Michael A. Lee

NEXT

Customer Service Department
Desford Road, Enderby, Leicester, LE19 4AT

Our Ref:2048664/PE
09 April 2002

Mr M A Lee
Somewhere in West Yorkshire

Thank you for your recent letter, which has been forwarded for my attention by the Customer Service Manager, requesting advice on where to obtain a 'Freudian Slip' for your wife's Birthday present.

Our Lingerie Department stocks a stunning Black Slip M41669 for £19.99, which perfectly fits the requirements stated in your letter and is both sexy and sophisticated.

Alternatively I have the details of three very pretty and becoming Jersey Slips from our Spring/Summer 2002 Nightwear range. These are:

M37435	Blue 'Cheeky Devil' Slip	£14.99
M37437	Pink Jersey Slip	£16.99
M52816	Lilac Embroidered Woven Slip	£16.99

I have forwarded a copy of your letter to our Ladieswear Product Director for her future reference and consideration. Your interesting comments will be greatly appreciated when considering future ranges for our Ladieswear Lingerie Selection. I am sure she will endeavour to investigate the Freudian Brand Name further, as this is a Nietzsche of the market we are currently looking to expand.

Thank you for taking the time and trouble to write to us concerning this matter. Next considers customer feedback to be essential in helping to improve our goods and services. I hope this information has been of some assistance.

Yours sincerely,

Portia D Edmiston
Customer Services Department

Contact Customer Services on 0870 243 5435. Our opening hours are 9.00am - 5.30pm Monday to Saturday; 11.00am - 5.00pm Sundays. Fax: 0116 284 2318 E Mail: enquiries@next.co.uk.

NEXT RETAIL LTD. DESFORD ROAD, ENDERBY, LEICESTER, LE19 4AT. TELEPHONE: 0116-286 6411
TELEX 34415 NEXT G. FACSIMILE: 0116 284 8998.

REGISTERED IN ENGLAND 123434. REGISTERED OFFICE, DESFORD ROAD, ENDERBY, LEICESTER LE19 4AT.

Portia D. Edmiston
Customer Services Department
Next Retail Ltd
Desford Road
Enderby
Leicester LE19 4AT

Dear Portia

First and foremost may I thank you for your response dated 9 April 2002 to my letter enquiring about the acquisition of a Freudian Slip for my wife. Your recommendation of various items was enormously helpful. I was pleased also to hear that the Ladieswear Product Director will look further at the Freudian brand name and indeed plans to exploit fully the opportunities within this Nietzsche of the market. I trust that the range will be sold at prices that do not convince your customers to Hegel!

Since you were so helpful previously I wondered if I might once again ask your advice regarding another acquisition; that of a shirt which changes colour according to its surroundings.

As an avid viewer of TV programmes connected with wildlife, I recently watched with great interest and enthusiasm a documentary concerning animals such as the chameleon and the squid that have the ability to change colour and patterning according to the environment. I cannot specifically remember how many variations of colour, shade and patterning were involved in the case of these creatures but it was certainly comprehensive, to say the least, and offered them camouflage when required as well as a means of efficient communication. These reptiles and beasts of the oceans literally make biological fashion statements.

Although I assume that the acquisition of a shirt that mimics the versatility of the skins of the aforementioned species will involve significant expenditure, I would be more than willing to spend my hard-earned cash on such an item as a long-term clothing investment. Furthermore, as you are a large, established purveyor of items such as men's shirts whose range is deemed to be of the highest calibre with an admirable variety, I have no doubts that you will be more than able to help me in my enquiries.

I would indeed be proud to experience my shirt changing rapidly from a shade of grass green whilst I mow the lawn to a blue, mauve and sunshine-yellow patchwork as I step into my tasteful utility room for a cooling drink. I could blend into the background if faced with a threatening situation by adopting a pebbledash shirt effect against a nearby house wall or present myself as a dynamic individual by changing my shirt colour to one that contrasts in a bright and even gaudy fashion with the bland and grey shades and hues adjacent to it. It is with great amazement that I look at the many developments of our 21st-century hi-tech world and with great anticipation that I look forward to wearing a shirt of this type with an incredible and obvious difference.

Many thanks indeed for your time and kind consideration in this matter and I look forward to receiving any advice you believe will be helpful in my search for the above garment.

Sincerely

M. A. Lee

Michael A. Lee

Our Ref:2048664/PE
17 June 2002

Mr M A Lee
Somewhere in West Yorkshire

Dear Mr Lee,

Thank you for your very interesting letter. I was very impressed that so much contemplation has gone into formulating the fantastic idea that you have presented.

Shirts such as you describe would certainly put Next at the cutting edge of modern fashion. It could lead to a whole new dimension of colour coding as we know it. For example, our Home department could produce sofas and curtains that change colour to co-ordinate with different people as they enter the room depending on what mood they are in. The possibilities of this idea are limitless and I would therefore like to thank you for writing in with your suggestions.

I have passed a copy of your letter to our Menswear Product Director and hopefully, being a man of reason and integrity, he will see what he can do about transforming your dreams to reality. Please be assured that when the first phase of ChaMichael A Leeleon Shirts are released onto the market, you will be rewarded for your inspiration. Next, as an ethical retailer, will not forget your hand in our future success.

In the meantime, the following Men's shirts are extremely comfortable and change colour slightly when you squint your eyes. They are part of our Autumn/Winter 2002 range and will be available from the middle of August:

M70517 Soft Touch Microcheck Shirt £19.99 short and long sleeves available in 4 colours
M23710 Long Sleeve Soft Touch Textured Shirt £26.00 available in 5 colours

Thank you for another thought-provoking letter. Please rest assured that you will be the first to know if I happen to discover that these shirts have already been made. Until that time, I wish you a great deal of sunshine to assist your gardening exploits. It was lovely to hear from you again.

Yours sincerely,

Portia D Edmiston
Customer Service Department

Contact Customer Services on 0870 243 5435. Our opening hours are 9.00am - 5.30pm Monday to Saturday; 11.00am - 5.00pm Sundays. Fax: 0116 284 2318 E Mail: enquiries@next.co.uk.

NEXT RETAIL LTD. DESFORD ROAD, ENDERBY, LEICESTER, LE19 4AT. TELEPHONE: 0116-286 6411
TELEX 34415 NEXT G. FACSIMILE: 0116 284 8998.

REGISTERED IN ENGLAND 172434 REGISTERED OFFICE DESFORD ROAD, ENDERBY, LEICESTER, LE19 4AT

120

Head of Geography
Durham University
Durham
County Durham

Dear Sir/Madam

I am writing to you as part of my quest for an unusual item; namely details about a place I have heard mentioned many times over the last 40 years or so but about which I can find little in the way of concrete geographical information. I cannot even locate it in my world atlas. The place to which I allude is none other than Cloud Cuckoo Land!

It is with a sense of wasted time and effort that I must tell you of my many hours and perhaps days spent searching in a keen yet futile manner for further information about this intriguing place in libraries, on the Internet and in countless bookshops. I have searched high and low for further knowledge about a land I would love to visit and explore but which seems to elude even the greatest minds in the worlds of geography, travel and anthropology.

Even some of the better-known High Street travel agents were unable to help in my desperate search, although they did manage to mention their cut-price travel insurance during their feeble attempts.

It is for this reason that I decided to approach an institution regarded as one of England's finest as far as academia and learning is concerned: Durham University and its world-famous Department of Geography.

Doubtless there have been many other men and women of curious and searching minds who have also approached you for some clues regarding the whereabouts of Cloud Cuckoo Land and I am proud to join their ranks. In this regard I would be most grateful for any advice you can provide and I look forward to hearing from you in the very near future.

Sincerely

M. A. Lee

Michael A. Lee

**University
of Durham**

Department of Geography

*Science Laboratories
South Road
Durham DH1 3LE, UK
Fax:* **0191 374 7307**
Direct Line: **0191 374 2458**
E-mail: **R.J.Allison@durham.ac.uk**

187.02

12th April 2002

Professor Robert J. Allison B.A., Ph.D.
Chairman of the Board of Studies

Mr M A Lee
Somewhere in West Yorkshire

Dear Mr Lee

Cloud Cuckoo Land

Thank you for your letter dated 8th April 2002.

I suspect that you may be looking in the wrong sources. Rather than searching for an answer to your query in an atlas, please refer to the Oxford Companion to English Literature. The attached may be of interest.

Yours sincerely

pp.

Professor Robert J. Allison
Chairman of the Board of Studies

⊠ xrefer   select a topic ▮ [   ]   (GO)   Help

xreferences

Aristophanes (c. 448 - 380 bc)
The Oxford Companion to English Literature

adjacent entries

Clorin
Clorinda
Cloten
Cloud-cuckoo-land
Cloud of Unknowing, The
Clough, Arthur Hugh (1819 - 1861)
Club, The

Cloud-cuckoo-land

(Nephelococcygia), an imaginary city built in the air in *The Birds* of Aristophan

The Oxford Companion to English Literature, © *Margaret Drabble and Oxford 1995* ❶

Home ; About ; Feedback ; Help
Title List ; Testimonials ; Add xrefer to your browser ; Add xrefer to your site
© 2002 xrefer ; Privacy

122

Somewhere in West Yorkshire
8 April 2002

The Director
RSPB HQ
The Lodge
Sandy
Bedfordshire SG19 2DL

Dear Sir/Madam

I am writing to you as part of my quest for an unusual item; namely some information about a particular type of bird I heard about whilst flicking from channel to channel on NTL cable television last week.

For many years now I have been a keen amateur ornithologist and have a reasonable though not exhaustive knowledge of birds both in the UK and from around the world but I had never before heard of a 'Culture Vulture' until my semi-concurrent Friday-evening viewing of the 'Animal Planet' and 'Discovery' channels, and the programme 'Frazier'. Indeed, for a moment or two I actually thought I might have been a little confused!

I seem to remember that this particular type of vulture is a cut above the rest when it comes to vultures generally and enjoys a range of more select food than its less fussy cousins. It prides itself on a nicely groomed appearance and enjoys observing with a critical eye the theatrical comings and goings of other birds and animals on the stage of its tropical home. In addition to these facets of behaviour, its cry is more refined than that of other birds and it hops in a way suggestive of particularly good breeding and class.

I would be most grateful if you could provide me with any other details you have regarding this strange and interesting bird and I look forward to hearing from you in the very near future. I thank you for your time and consideration but really must fly.

Sincerely

M. A. Lee

Michael A. Lee

for birds
for people
for ever

UK Headquarters
The Lodge, Sandy
Bedfordshire SG19 2DL
Tel: 01767 680551
Fax: 01767 692365
DX 47804 SANDY
www.rspb.org.uk

12/4/02

Dear Mr Lee,

Thank you for your letter dated 8/4/02.

I am not so sure what to make of your letter but in general terms, this is indeed true of all species of birds. There is always one individual that is in someway different (I hesitate to use the word superior). These individuals tend to be the most successful in attracting mates and competing for food. I should add that appearance is not always the defining characteristic so much as strength. I had to smile a little at the reference for your information and without wishing to be critical; it is typical of the Americans to coin an anthropomorphic term to label this with.

Anyway, I certainly do not want to be picking over the bones of this subject because it is a bit of a soar point. You can groan now!

Yours sincerely

Ian Peters

Ian Peters

Patron Her Majesty the Queen President Jonathan Dimbleby Chairman of Council John Croxall Chief Executive Graham Wynne

Registered charity no 207076

Somewhere in West Yorkshire
25 April 2002

Ian Peters
RSPB
UK Headquarters
The Lodge
Sandy
Bedfordshire SG19 2DL

Dear Mr Peters

First and foremost I would like to thank you for taking the time and effort to reply to my letter asking for advice about the 'Culture Vulture'. Armed with the information you sent to me I have now begun asking various travel agents whether they might organise a reasonably priced holiday for me so that I might visit the natural habitat of these creatures in a bird-watching and photographic capacity. I am looking forward to the trip with great excitement and a sense of the 'unknown'!

Inspired by this recent addition to my knowledge about our feathered friends, I turned on my TV again last night and to my astonishment heard the phrase 'pigeon's milk' in reference, I believe, to nutritional foods. (I was at the time channel hopping between 'Animal Planet' and a cookery programme.)

I wonder in this regard whether you might be able to advise me of any retail outlets in the North of England that specialise in the sale and supply of 'pigeon's milk' and whether you know anything of its packaging in terms of volume or of the availability of full cream, semi-skimmed and fat-free varieties.

Once again I thank you for your time and kind consideration and look forward to hearing from you in the very near future.

Sincerely

Michael A. Lee

for birds
for people
for ever

UK Headquarters
The Lodge, Sandy
Bedfordshire SG19 2DL
Tel: 01767 680551
Fax: 01767 692365
DX 47804 SANDY
www.rspb.org.uk

29/4/02

Dear Michael,

Thank you for your letter dated 25/4/02.

I am not sure what context "pigeon's milk" was mentioned on the TV programme but I found the following information on a web search.

Food for young: Both male and female parent pigeons produce a special substance called "pigeon milk," which they feed to their hatchlings during their first week of life. Pigeon milk is made in a special part of the bird's digestive system called the "crop." When hatchlings are about one week old, the parents start regurgitating seeds with crop milk; eventually seeds replace the pigeon milk.

Sleeveless Errands

The most common prank was to send someone on a 'sleeveless errand,' which meant sending them to search for a non-existent product. Young apprentices working in the shops of tradesmen were frequent victims of this trick. For instance, they might be sent to the market to search for hen's teeth, pigeon's milk, a history of Eve's grandmother, striped paint, a soft-pointed chisel, a box of straight hooks, sweet vinegar, a stick with one end, or a penny's worth of strap-oil or elbow grease. Alternatively, they might be sent to a saddler's shop to ask for some strong strapping, at which point, if they were not careful, they would receive what they asked for across their shoulders. Or they might be sent to ask for a 'long stand,' whereupon they would be told that they could stand for as long as they wished.

Yours sincerely

Ian Peters

Ian Peters

Jenny Plackett
Assistant Director
Devon Guild of Craftsmen
Riverside Mill
Bovey Tracey
Devon TQ13 9AF

Dear Ms Plackett

I am writing to you as part of my quest for an unusual item; namely details about courses in the ancient craft of epoch-making.

Having chanced upon your guild on the Internet it occurred to me that since the Devon Guild of Craftsmen involves so many craftsmen of various backgrounds there might well be the chance of my obtaining some substantial advice about the aforementioned craft which I am so eagerly trying to study and, indeed, at which I might try my hand.

Over the years I have applied myself to the study and practice of various arts and crafts ranging from compiling framed pictures from tamed slug trails to building scale models of plague villages from pieces of dead elm wood. Sadly, my attempts have left much to be desired and I have not found the satisfaction I have sought in these areas.

It is for this reason I would like to join the ranks of some of the great names of history, such as Columbus, Drake and Genghis Khan, by learning to mould the materials of the present to influence the happenings of the future. In short I would love to become a qualified epoch-maker.

Doubtless you have many requests of this kind on a regular basis and so I thank you for your time and kind consideration and look forward to hearing from you in the very near future.

Sincerely

M. A. Lee

Michael A. Lee

The Devon Guild of Craftsmen

Riverside Mill
Bovey Tracey, Devon
TQ13 9AF

Tel: 01626 832223
Fax: 01626 834220
E-mail: devonguild@crafts.org.uk
Website: www.crafts.org.uk

Mr M A Lee
Somewhere in West Yorkshire

16th April 2002

Dear Michael Lee

Re: Courses in Epoch-making

Thank you very much for your recent letter, which my colleagues and I read with much interest.

Unfortunately we cannot recommend any particular courses to you because, as far as we know, none exist. Obviously a niche in the market, should you find such an Epoch-Maker, perhaps you could offer yourself as an apprentice and, having acquired the necessary skill and experience, run training courses for the benefit of other interested novices? Please keep us advised of your progress – part of our role as an educational charity is to provide exactly this sort of information on continuing professional development to the public.

Whilst writing, I must mention that we were particularly fascinated to read of your framed slug trail pictures – do you happen to have any images on slide of this work? It would indeed be a marvellous addition to our already comprehensive slide library.

I wish you the best of luck in the development of your work, and look forward to hearing of your progress.

Yours sincerely

Jenny Plackett
Assistant Director

Somewhere in West Yorkshire
26 April 2002

Head of Customer Services
Boots the Chemists
PO Box 5300
Nottingham NG90 1AA

Dear Sir/Madam

I am writing to you as part of my quest for an unusual item; namely an effective anti-wrinkle cream for the mirror in my en suite bathroom here at home in the northern town of Huddersfield.

It is fair to say that at 42 years of age there are few things that readily surprise or shock me. Over the years I have observed a wide range of phenomena in a variety of locations and situations and rarely am I taken aback at events around me. Just yesterday, however, there occurred a rather shocking exception to the rule when I looked into the bathroom mirror and noticed with a degree of horror that it had developed wrinkles. Sad to say, these wrinkles are positioned on the surface of the mirror in such a way as to correspond with various parts of my own face when I am standing in my usual position in readiness for teeth-cleaning and tie-fastening.

In this regard I would be most grateful if you could advise me with reference to the range of available anti-wrinkle creams that could remove these worrying bathroom furniture wrinkles as well as ensuring that the underlying reflecting surface is left intact and without damage. I am also in the process of writing to the Professor of Physics at Oxford University to better understand how this strange phenomenon has developed and will keep you informed if appropriate.

Many thanks indeed for your time and kind consideration and I look forward to hearing from you in the very near future.

Sincerely

M. A. Lee

Michael A. Lee

By Appointment to
Her Majesty The Queen, Chemists,
Boots The Chemists Ltd, Nottingham.

CS\1221146

Mr M A Lee
Somewhere in West Yorkshire

 **BOOTS**
THE CHEMISTS

Customer Service
PO Box 5300
Nottingham
NG90 1AA

Tel: 08450 70 80 90
Fax: 0115 959 5525
Minicom: 08450 70 80 91
Email: btc.cshelpdesk
@boots.co.uk

30 April 2002

Dear Mr. Lee

Thank you for your letter dated 26 April. I am sorry to learn of the problem you have experienced with your en-suite bathroom mirror.

I can appreciate the distress this has caused you. Have you found this with just the one mirror or are others in your house affected?

We do have a wide selection of anti-ageing products in our stores. As this is quite an unusual problem I would suggest you call into one of our larger stores and speak to the No7 Consultant. She will be able to advise you on what products are more suitable for your requirements. Alternatively we do have selected stores which offer beauty treatments.

I personally have experienced a similar problem and now use Boots Time Delay products which I can highly recommend. The range has creams which protect, conceal and repair.

I do hope you are able to find a product to help and that you can return to normal tie-fastening and teeth-cleaning without the worrying wrinkles.

Yours sincerely

Pam Summers
Customer Manager

Pam Summers
Customer Manager
Boots the Chemists
PO Box 5300
Nottingham NG90 1AA

Dear Ms Summers

First and foremost may I thank you for your swift and helpful reply to my enquiries about my wrinkle-festooned bathroom mirror. In answer to your question about other mirror involvement I am sad to say that the problem is now house-wide and all the mirrors are similarly affected. I very much appreciate your advice and will endeavour to heed your suggestions as soon as possible.

In the meantime I wonder if might ask for help in a second area of concern that is creating something of a personal challenge to me at present?

It was with great consternation that I heard my wife suggest to me recently that I ought to involve myself to a greater degree in the everyday household chores such as cooking, washing-up and ironing here in our Huddersfield home. She provided a long and eloquent summary of my existing shortfalls as far as the practicalities of domestic activity are concerned and also intimated that the solution to the present predicament would be the application of copious amounts of 'elbow grease'.

Since I am a firm believer in the principles of both constructive criticism and taking a literal view of feedback presented to me I decided that I would indeed pursue the option of applying some of the aforementioned grease to my own elbows if only I could find an appropriate brand. Doubtless you will appreciate the cold shoulder my wife will show me if I don't show her a greased elbow or two as soon as possible!

Although I have already contacted various companies that specialise in heavy-duty industrial greases that might prepare me for the certain onslaught and challenges of increased home-based duties, I would also be most interested to know if Boots the Chemists offer a brand of tailor-made elbow grease that would fit my requirements.

Many thanks indeed for your time and kind consideration and I look forward to hearing from you in the very near future.

Sincerely

Michael A. Lee

By Appointment to
Her Majesty The Queen, Chemists,
Boots The Chemists Ltd, Nottingham.

CS\1221146

 **BOOTS
THE CHEMISTS**

Customer Service
PO Box 5300
Nottingham
NG90 1AA

Mr M A Lee
Somewhere in West Yorkshire

Tel: 08450 70 80 90
Fax: 0115 959 5525
Minicom: 08450 70 80 91
Email: btc.cshelpdesk
@boots.co.uk

8 May 2002

Dear Mr. Lee

Thank you for your reply dated 1 May.

I have to say I thought it would spread to all the mirrors in your house. Hopefully by using the products recommended the problem will be reduced in a few weeks.

With regard to 'elbow grease,' this is something not widely asked for any more. However if you speak to a Pharmacist in store they should be able to make some up to your requirements. Alternatively our Botanics range have Intensive Moisturisers and creams which may be of help to you.

Should you find this extra work tiring we also sell a very good range of vitamin tablets which will help to build you up and give you extra energy.

I am a great believer in shared household chores and am pleased to learn that you will be getting involved.

Yours sincerely

**Pam Summers
Customer Manager**

Boots The Chemists Ltd
Registered office
Nottingham NG2 3AA
Registered London 928555
A subsidiary of
The Boots Company PLC

Somewhere in West Yorkshire
30 April 2002

The Director General
MI5
PO Box 3255
London SW1P 1AE

Dear Sir/Madam

I am writing to you as part of my quest for an unusual item; namely a recipe for the tastiest chicken madras in the UK.

Surfing the net a little earlier this evening, I was delighted to read through a section of MI5's official website entitled 'Myths and Misunderstandings' and subsequently felt both reassured as far as security measures are concerned as well as inspired as far as cooking is concerned. Let me explain.

I was left in no doubt by the clarity of communication within the aforementioned section that members or former members of MI5 are not at liberty to disclose without lawful authority any information, reference, security or intelligence matters to the public since this would be in breach of the Official Secrets Act. This makes eminent sense to me and I am pleased to learn that there are still, in this chaotic and confused century, vital safeguards to preserve the high and necessary standards of British intelligence and its confidential status.

I was equally pleased to read, however, that such security measures do not preclude the disclosure of information relating to the colour of the carpets at MI5 HQ, which I understand are blue – a good choice – and the fact that a rather tasty chicken madras is served at the in-house restaurant. In this regard I wonder if you might advise me regarding the amounts of coriander and chilli peppers that are included in this mouth-watering dish and I will try out the MI5 recipe in the very near future.

If this recipe finds its way into the public domain it could well be featured on the menus of Indian takeaways as dish number 007!

Many thanks indeed for your time and kind consideration and I look forward to hearing from you in the near future.

Sincerely

Michael A. Lee

PO BOX 3255
LONDON
SW1P 1AE

30 May 2002

Mr M A Lee
Somewhere in West Yorkshire

Dear Mr Lee

Thank you for your letter of 30 April. I apologise for the delay in replying.

Our catering department use a commercially available madras paste as a basis for the Chicken Madras served in our restaurant.

Yours sincerely,

The Director General

Head of Customer Services
Nestlé UK Ltd
York YO91 1XY

Dear Sir/Madam

I am writing to you as part of my quest for an unusual item; namely a chocolate fireguard.

Involved as I am in industry and specifically in the complex world of sales and marketing, I work with a large number of individuals whose range of skills, attitudes and indeed performance achievements are amazingly varied.

Doubtless you would agree that it is a straightforward task to choose rewards of a tangible and motivational kind for those whose abilities and achievements are noteworthy and require explicit recognition of a material nature.

However, it proves an endless and far more difficult task to provide gifts that involve a message of stark and obvious meaning to those whose successes could be best summarised on the back of a postage stamp and who require a hint of sarcastic encouragement before finding that the regional manager is standing next to them in battle fatigues with a P45. It is for this reason that I write to you.

If you could supply me with a number of modestly priced chocolate fireguards, certain of my colleagues could receive a symbolic item providing integral feedback in the sweetest way I can currently conceive.

There would certainly not be a bitter taste left in their mouths and perhaps the significant uptake of energy-providing glucose would provide the impetus for action and future industry.

Many thanks for your time and consideration and I look forward to hearing from you in the near future.

Sincerely

Michael A. Lee

P.S. All this word-processing has given me an appetite. Feel free to send samples of your more conventional chocolate creations if appropriate. I have two small children and very little money!

Nestlé UK Ltd

YORK YO91 1XY

TELEPHONE (01904) 604604
FACSIMILE (01904) 604534

www.nestle.co.uk

Mr M A Lee
Somewhere in West Yorkshire

DIRECT LINE: 0800 000030

0888216A   **3 May 2002**   DIRECT FAX: (01904) 603461

YOUR REF   OUR REF   DATE

Dear Michael

Thank you for your recent amusing letter.

We are sorry to hear that you are having trouble motivating your Sales Force.

We are sorry to inform you that Chocolate Fireguards have been withdrawn from our range due to the vast amount of them being returned due to heat damage.

We hope that this is not too disappointing a reply, however we have included some goodies for your children. Thank you once again for taking the trouble to contact us and good luck in your task .

Yours sincerely

Joanne Nudd
Call Centre Supervisor
Consumer Services

The Archbishop of York
Bishopthorpe Palace
Bishopthorpe
York
North Yorkshire YO23 2GE

Dear Sir

I am writing to you as part of my quest for an unusual item; namely the title 'Son of a Gun' within the Church of England.

As a 42-year-old Yorkshire man, I have, over the course of many years, watched with great interest a vast selection of Westerns both on TV and in the cinema, and have even read a number of paperbacks of a cowboy nature. When reviewing these films and books it is rather staggering to note how often a character appears who is known as the 'Son of a Gun' and who, in many cases, provides the viewer or reader with a figure of moral fortitude and example in comparison to the pistol-toting father who rode the Wild West before him.

As an upright and honest individual who believes in the law and order of contemporary society, the importance of family life and of open and honest government based on Judaeo-Christian traditions, I would myself like to be considered a 21st-century 'Son of a Gun' in the England of today and specifically within the structure of the Church. I could then be seen as a modern-day 'Anglican Shane' travelling from place to place representing all things bright and beautiful and embodying the principles of strength and peace.

My greatest difficulty in claiming a right to the title is the fact that my blood lineage does not actually involve a father who possessed or made use of any form of gun. (All he owned in the potential weapons department was a small penknife!)

Consequently I wondered if, in order to provide a bona-fide basis for my application for the aforementioned title, I might be adopted, at least in a symbolic manner, by a canon! I would then truly be the 'Son of a Gun' and could wear my robes and stetson with pride and dignity.

Many thanks for your time and consideration. I look forward to hearing from you in the very near future regarding how to take this application forward to the next stage.

Sincerely

Michael A. Lee

THE BISHOP OF WAKEFIELD - The Right Reverend Nigel McCulloch

Bishop's Lodge   Woodthorpe Lane   Wakefield   West Yorkshire   WF2 6JL
Tel: 01924-255349   Fax: 01924-250202   E-mail:bishop@wakefield.anglican.org

09 May 2002

Mr M A Lee
Somewhere in West Yorkshire

Dear Mr. Lee,

Thank you for your interesting letter concerning your desire to serve as a modern day 'Church of England Shane' and to obtain a bona fide basis for your claim to the title 'Son of a Gun'.

However, your request poses real problems as Wakefield is an 'equal opportunities' diocese. If I were to grant such a request, it might well open the floodgates to many other applicants for the said title. Some of these may be women and that would necessitate the creation of a precedent, as we would be forced to create the title 'Daughter of a Gun'. In fact the whole project may be perceived as politically incorrect. Perhaps the best compromise would be the title 'Offspring of a Gun'.

There again we run into the murky waters of political incorrectness. Referring to a person by their job title, ethnic origin or medical condition is now unacceptable. To be the son of a 'Gun' would not be permissible. The 'Son of a person who has/had, owns/owned, uses/used a Gun' would be more acceptable.

Your suggestion of adoption by a Canon, symbolic or otherwise, also poses problems. As defined in the 'Concise Oxford Dictionary', a Canon is a 'member of a cathedral chapter', but the weapon of war to which I believe you meant to allude is defined by that publication as 'Cannon: a large, heavy gun'. Over the former I have a certain amount of influence, but over the latter, regrettably none. Therefore I find myself unable to accede to your request.

/I

I believe that the term 'Gunner' is still in current use by Her Majesty's armed forces. It may be that a request made to the appropriate department of that authority might meet with more success.

May I wish you every success in your quest to become an 'Offspring of a Gun (Gunner)' that it might enable you to wear your Stetson with pride. I too, as a boy, enjoyed games of Cowboys and Native Americans.

Yours sincerely

+ Noel Wakefield

THE OFFICE OF
THE ARCHBISHOP OF YORK

Bishopthorpe Palace
Bishopthorpe
York
YO23 2GE

Tel: (01904) 707021
Fax: (01904) 709204
E-mail: office@bishopthorpe.u-net.com
www.bishopthorpepalace.co.uk

The Venerable Alan Dean
Special Adviser to the Archbishop

01 May 2002

Dear Mr Lee,

I write in acknowledgement of your letter to the Archbishop, dated 29th April 2002 - but whose contents cannot but lead one to suppose that it might have been more appropriately dated 1st April 2002.

Be that as it may, I have to tell you that - with or without the adoptive lineage of which you speak - the formal appointment which you have in mind simply does not lie within the Archbishop's gift.

Accordingly, any representational role in the matter of 'all things bright and beautiful'(etc.) would have to be undertaken solo: that is, without commissioning or benefit of letters patent.

With all good wishes - and with thanks for brightening our day!

Yours very sincerely

Mr M A Lee
Somewhere in West Yorkshire

The Venerable Alan Dean
Special Advisor to the Archbishop
Bishopthorpe Palace
Bishopthorpe
York YO23 2GE

Dear Sir

First and foremost may I thank you for your letter dated 1 May 2002 in reply to my enquiries about becoming a 'Son of a Gun' within the Church of England. I was disappointed to hear that the appointment of such a person does not lie within the Archbishop's gift but am nevertheless appreciative of your response as it has allowed me to consider alternative opportunities for my attention and midlife aspirations.

In this regard I am writing to you once again as part of my quest for an unusual item; namely the title 'Spire Straightener' in relation to the age-old problem regarding the crooked spire of Chesterfield's ancient church. I presume this falls within the geographical area managed by the Archbishop of York. Let me explain. Fascinated by myths and legends, I recently focused on a website while surfing the net. This related the well-known theory that the famous crooked spire of St Mary's was caused by the uncontrolled rage of the Devil as he fled, cloven foot pierced by a hoofing nail, from the Blacksmith of Bollsover, damaging the spire en route. Call me a cynic if you will, but this I find hard to believe as historical fact!

In stark contrast, however, I do think that the alternative explanation – that the twisting was the result of the spire leaning in an attempt to watch in astonishment as a virgin was joined to her husband in the wonderful union of matrimony – is highly plausible. I also happen to believe that it is eminently likely that the spire will straighten itself if another virgin marries in the church at a later date.

This is where I may be able to help. My wife, who is, incidentally, a midwife, mentioned to me in a rather discrete fashion that one of her colleagues, a shy and somewhat introverted lady in her late 40s, has neither enjoyed the pleasures of a stable marriage nor indeed those of an unstable marriage, common-law relationship or even a passionate moment through the eyes of indiscretion or the base of an empty wine glass. Strange as it sounds in these modern times, this spinster is nothing less than a virgin!

It occurred to me that should you know of any bachelors of the Chesterfield parish who have, to date, struggled with the challenges of relationship and are willing to meet with this lady we might, between us, have a plan for free spire restoration. If you were to choose a bachelor who is happy to forego pre-nuptial activity of any physical kind and enjoy a wedding ceremony with the chaste lady to whom I have already referred, the spire will, as tradition states, return to its original non-crooked state. A cunning plan, I am sure you will agree!

I am not at all interested in seeking monetary reward for such information but would get my satisfaction from seeing two lonely hearts gain comfort and companionship and also by receiving the official title, 'Spire Straightener', an accolade that will doubtless serve my future reputation and career path well.

Doubtless you receive many letters of this kind on a regular basis and so I thank you for your time and kind consideration and I look forward to hearing from you in the very near future.

Sincerely

M. A. Lee

Michael A. Lee

THE OFFICE OF
THE ARCHBISHOP OF YORK

Bishopthorpe Palace
Bishopthorpe
York
YO23 2GE

Tel: (01904) 707021
Fax: (01904) 709204
E-mail: office@bishopthorpe.u-net.com
www.bishopthorpepalace.co.uk

The Venerable Alan Dean
Special Adviser to the Archbishop

23 May 2002

Dear Mr Lee,

How good it was to hear from you again - and that so soon!

However, I fear that, once again, your plan falls at the first hurdle. The fact is that the affections of the good people of Chesterfield are so very firmly wedded to their church's twisted spire that the mere thought of its being straightened would be entirely anathema to them. In short, there is simply no call for a 'spire straightener'.

Disappointing though this may be to you, I have every confidence that you will be able to put the bravest of faces upon your chagrin and resume your search for that elusive 'something' which beckons to you from beyond the shores of that more pedestrian reality which detains the rest of us.

Doubtless you will give us news of progress - and, needless to say, we ourselves are a-tiptoe in fascinated anticipation!

*With all good wishes
yours sincerely*

Mr M A Lee
Somewhere in West Yorkshire

The Venerable Alan Dean
Special Advisor to the Archbishop
Bishopthorpe Palace
Bishopthorpe
York YO23 2GE

Dear Sir

Once again, may I take this opportunity to thank you for taking the time and effort to respond to my recently suggested plan to untwist the spire of Chesterfield Parish Church.

I was a little disappointed that the plan will remain a concept without application and, indeed, disappointed for my wife's friend whose future appears to be one of bleak though committed spinsterhood but I do appreciate your comments and explanation regarding safeguarding the continuity of 'things familiar' for Chesterfield's community. I will, as you quite rightly suggest, move forward in my quest for the unusual and focus on activities other than spire straightening.

In this respect I wonder if you may be able to help me in my desire to acquire the position of 'Officially Recognised Parish Worm Charmer' in the wonderful parish of Fatfield in County Durham, famed, of course, for the fabled Lambton Worm of times past.

I did write to the Bishop of Durham in reference to this matter several months ago. Sadly, I failed to receive a reply and concluded that the appointment of such a key position might well lie more within the remit of the Archbishop.

Having recently read on an Internet website the story of the Lambton Worm, it occurred to me that had the original worm been female and cast into the fabled well by Sir John Lambton while pregnant, there is a jolly good chance that other monstrous worms of gargantuan proportions may well have been born before the slaying of the mother and have been living undetected beneath the ground for several centuries and perhaps in large numbers.

It is not beyond the bounds of possibility that one of these days another large, milk-stealing, baby-eating worm might emerge from its subterranean burrow or well corner and create mayhem among the community within the Fatfield parish.

This could have catastrophic consequences for church attendance on Sunday mornings and indeed at evensong though it may well keep the grave diggers rather busy. Herein lies a potential job opportunity for me and hence the reason for my writing this application to your good self! In a similar manner to the Indian snake charmer, I have developed an intriguing mastery of hypnotising worms by playing an Irish penny whistle. Within seconds of my playing a ballad these slithering beats of the ground become transfixed and hence are ready for capture or despatch.

As a longstanding member of the Fell Runners Association I am reasonably quick on my feet and can move around the worm with a fleetness of foot a little reminiscent of Mohammed Ali in his earlier days.

I am rather nimble with a sword and I have no particular sympathy for worms other than those normal-sized creatures that live in my compost heap and herbaceous borders and carry out the marvellous task of breaking down and aerating my soil. I would therefore have no difficulty in trapping or slaying the monstrous offspring of the original legend should the occasion arise and indeed would feel such a deed fully justified if community safety was threatened.

Doubtless you receive many enquiries of this kind as I appreciate the market for employment is rather competitive these days and so thank you for your time and kind consideration. Please rest assured, however, that candidates with skills and abilities such as mine are few and far between.

I look forward to hearing from you in the very near future and in anticipation of receiving an invitation for interview can assure you that I will continue my regular rehearsal of the penny whistle and fine tuning my swordsmanship.

Sincerely

M. A. Lee

Michael A. Lee

**THE OFFICE OF
THE ARCHBISHOP OF YORK**

Bishopthorpe Palace
Bishopthorpe
York
YO23 2GE

Tel: (01904) 707021
Fax: (01904) 709204
E-mail: office@bishopthorpe.u-net.com
www.bishopthorpepalace.co.uk

The Venerable Alan Dean
Special Adviser to the Archbishop

26 June 2002

Dear Mr Lee,

My grateful thanks for your latest offering of 26th May 2002.

It was heartening to learn of your continued readiness to offer your services in ways which are, to say the least, imaginative.

However, whilst I am filled with admiration for your facility upon the (Irish) penny whistle and whilst your physical agility and swordsmanship (would it be foil, epee or sabre?) leave me trembling and breathless, I remain concerned that once again you seem intent on seeking to deploy your skills to combat problems in areas where no discernible problem exists.

Could it simply be that you are exhibiting an extraordinary degree of prescience ? - or could it be something rather more disquieting?   We shall, as they say, continue to watch this space.

Yours very sincerely

Mr M A Lee
Somewhere in West Yorkshire

146

The Vicar
Chesterfield Parish Church
Derbyshire

Dear Sir

I am writing to you as part of my quest for an unusual item; namely the title 'Spire Restoration Manager' with relation to the age-old problem regarding the crooked spire of your ancient church. Let me explain.

Fascinated by myths and legends, I recently found a website relating the well-known theory that the famous crooked spire of St Mary's was the result of the spire leaning over in an attempt to watch in astonishment as a virgin was joined to her husband in the wonderful union of matrimony. I also believe that it is eminently likely the spire will straighten itself if another virgin marries in the church at a later date. This seems to me entirely within the realm of credibility!

This is where I may be able to help. My wife, who is, incidentally, a midwife, discreetly mentioned to me that one of her colleagues, a shy and somewhat introverted lady in her late 40s, has neither enjoyed the pleasures of a stable marriage nor indeed those of an unstable marriage, common-law relationship or even a passionate moment through the eyes of indiscretion or an empty wine glass. Strange as it sounds, this aforementioned spinster is nothing less than a virgin! I am not, at this point in time, willing to divulge her name.

It occurred to me that should you know of any bachelors of the parish who are willing to meet with this lady we might, between us, have a plan for free spire restoration. If you were to choose a bachelor who is happy to forego pre-nuptual activity of any physical kind and enjoy a wedding ceremony with the chaste lady to whom I have already referred, the spire will, as tradition states, return to its original non-crooked state and not one single penny will need to be paid to surveyors, tradesmen or builders' labourers for the work involved. A cunning plan, I am sure you will agree!

I am not at all interested in seeking monetary reward for such information but would get my satisfaction from seeing two lonely hearts gain comfort and companionship in their togetherness, and also by receiving the official title, 'Spire Restoration Manager' which would be a wonderful addition to my rather brief and uninteresting C.V. Doubtless you receive many letters of this kind on a regular basis and so I thank you for your time and kind consideration and I look forward to hearing from you in the very near future.

Sincerely

M. A. Lee .

P.S. Failing this, I also undertake basic gardening duties and can dig graves by the bucketful provided there is not too much pebble-strewn boulder clay in the area.

Chesterfield
Parish Church

28 CROMWELL ROAD
CHESTERFIELD
S40 4TH

Mr M A Lee
Somewhere in West Yorkshire

19 June, 2002

Dear Mr Lee,

Thank you for your letter, and your novel answer to our architectural oddity. I am sorry it has taken a while to reply but I have been busy identifying suitable candidates for your lady friend's hand. I have now managed to find three suitable bachelors of mature years who might fulfil the role you had in mind, which at least allows her a degree of choice.

However, I perceive a difficulty. As you will know, the marriage ceremony must be public but the marriage itself is not effected simply by the ceremony in church, but must also be consummated. My three candidates are willing, even enthusiastic so to do, granted the frustrating purity of their lives hitherto. The problem arises because the people of Chesterfield have an emotional – and indeed an economic –attachment to the spire of such intensity that anyone who managed to straighten it might well be strung up from the nearest lamppost. My friends are feeling their necks, rather anxiously.

How may I put this with appropriate delicacy? They are asking me what guarantees are on offer to ensure that the pleasure of the marriage bed will be sufficient to offset any dire consequences? A man may be willing to die for love – but for an uncertain one night stand?

Yours sincerely,

PS My gardener is a total disaster, and any help would be gratefully received.

148

The Duke & Duchess of Devonshire
Chatsworth House
Matlock
Derbyshire

Dear Sir & Madam

I am writing to you as part of my quest for an unusual item; namely a permit to pan for gold in the four large reservoir lakes, the Emperor Fountain, the Cascades and the river belonging to your wonderful Chatsworth House estate.

Rather than accompany members of a recognised gold-panning or prospecting club to the aforementioned areas of potential water-borne fortune, I would much prefer to undertake my own gold-panning enterprise as a solo venture and play the part of a modern-day Klondike prospector both for relaxation and perhaps to make the lucky discovery of an obscenely large gold nugget. I would even be happy to bring along my own Thermos flask!

I can assure you that my gold-panning activities would not interfere with any of the other concerns undertaken in, on or around Chatsworth and I will be careful not to leave any trace of my endeavours. I have no mule to disgrace itself and am myself a clean and fastidious person.

Should I be fortunate enough to find that most precious of minerals in the area I can assure you that I will keep such a discovery to ourselves and thus avoid any consequent gold rush that would doubtless be detrimental to the integrity of the countryside and surrounding flora and fauna. Would a 50/50 share of the findings be agreeable to yourselves?

As a Yorkshire man with a pioneering spirit and desire to become a self-made millionaire, I would be most interested in any help and advice you can provide.

I thank you for your time and consideration and look forward to hearing from you in the very near future.

Sincerely

M. A. Lee

Michael A. Lee

13 May 2002

RBW/vmb/024

Mr M A Lee
Somewhere in West Yorkshire

Dear Mr Lee

Gold-panning on Chatsworth Estate

I refer to your letter of the 30th April addressed to the Duke and Duchess of Devonshire who have asked me to reply on their behalf.

I am afraid I am going to disappoint you by saying it will not be possible to give you permission to pan for gold at Chatsworth. As you might imagine, we get a considerable number of requests from people wishing to search for treasure of one sort or another and it has therefore been necessary for us to adopt a policy of dealing only with one recognised group. If we were to accede to individual requests, it would be unfair to all those who have been turned down in the past and so it simply remains for me to wish you good luck with your pioneering spirit and desire to become a self-made millionaire.

Yours sincerely

R B Wardle
Agent

Marketing Manager
Ready Brek Brand
Weetabix Ltd
Burton Latimer
Northants NN15 5JR

Dear Sir/Madam

I am writing to you as part of my quest for an unusual item; namely the variety of Ready Brek cereal advertised on TV a few years ago that helps children to glow in the dark.

Now aged 42, I remember well the memorable advertising for your most excellent breakfast cereal, demonstrating the way small children who ate Ready Brek on a regular basis were provided with a bright and distinct aura around their bodies and were protected from the chill winds of winter. I presume that the film of these luminous children was taken before the introduction of special effects and the impact of such viewing has certainly had a significant and long-lasting effect on me. A few weeks ago I bought a 750g box of Original Ready Brek for the first time in many years and served a generous portion of this tasty breakfast food to my three-year-old son George. Possessing a voracious appetite, he ate the contents of his bowl with enthusiastic haste and soon afterwards showed all the signs of restored energy levels and an associated degree of boisterousness in his play.

However, sad to say, he did not glow even in the remotest sense of the word. Over the next week or two I increased the amount of Ready Brek for George's breakfast by an additional bowl a day. At the end of this period and several boxes of Ready Brek later he was consuming the equivalent of ten bowls of cereal each morning. Although the side effects – which included severe bloating and abdominal distension, intractable wind and a tendency to lie still for long periods of time – were a little disturbing, I persevered with the regime hoping for luminescence. Alas, not a single shaft of light was to be seen anywhere.

I came to the conclusion that perhaps today's Ready Brek is a modified version of the brand I saw advertised so often many years ago. I wondered if I might be able to purchase the original 'Original' cereal, if indeed you are still able to manufacture and supply this. You will be pleased to know that since I cut back George's rations to just one bowl of cereal a day, along with a piece of buttered toast, he has recovered from his overfeeding and has begun to smile again. He still doesn't glow in the dark but, since the lighter spring mornings have arrived, he doesn't need to. When autumn arrives, of course, the same challenges will doubtless arise.

Many thanks for your time and kind consideration in this matter and I look forward to hearing from you with appropriate advice in the very near future.

Sincerely

M. A. Lee .

248-46-5/ajl/V1.50

Mr M A Lee
Somewhere in West Yorkshire

May 9, 2002

Dear Mr Lee

Many thanks for your letter of May 1, though we were sorry to hear how disappointed you were that your son did not 'glow', even after such a large helping of Ready Brek.

Please tell George not to worry. Times have changed and with the success of that memorable campaign, we no longer feel it necessary to make, what now appears, such an obvious statement. Those who need to know have the knowledge and appreciation of how healthful and satisfying a bowl of Ready Brek can be. And those who, for whatever reason, do not know, well what more can I say?!

For old times sake, you can see the 1980s advert in the Time Machine section of our new Internet site. We hope you will be able to visit www.weetabix.co.uk very soon.

In the meantime, we trust you and young George will continue to enjoy the great taste of Ready Brek

Yours sincerely

Paul Blomley

Paul Blomley
Consumer Services Officer
e-mail: consumerservice@weetabix.co.uk

Weetabix Ltd
THE LEADING BRITISH BREAKFAST CEREAL MANUFACTURER
Weetabix Limited, Burton Latimer, Kettering, NN15 5JR

Head of Customer Care
Warburtons Ltd
Hereford House
Hereford Street
Bolton BL1 8JB\

Dear Sir/Madam

I am writing to you as part of my quest for an unusual item; namely a sliced loaf whose slices, when buttered, are guaranteed to fall butter side up. In this regard I could think of no better organisation to which I could direct my initial enquiries than your good selves at Warburtons.

Doubtless there are innumerable people across the UK who stand in amazement at the scientific and technological achievements of Western man in the 21st century. Each day the newspapers contain information about the very latest developments in space exploration and exciting medical breakthroughs, super-computers and even robotics.

The children of the early Warburton family several years ago would be amazed to see the world in which we now live, with its complexity of microwave ovens, widescreen TVs, interactive laptop gadgets that can recognise and respond to human voices, and even cloned sheep.

Perhaps in the light of contemporary automation, they would regret so much time spent in days gone by kneading dough by hand! Yet, despite all the time, effort and energy that has been invested over the years to create this hi-tech society and the opulence and convenience that this permits, I have yet to find a solution to an age-old problem: how to avoid the buttered side of my sliced bread or toast from landing face down on a dusty linoleum surface or hairy carpet smeared with my children's cast-off bananas. I am significantly stressed at the very thought of this regular occurrence repeating itself once again.

Many thanks indeed for your time and kind consideration in this matter and I would be most grateful for any help and advice you can offer.

Sincerely

M. A. Lee .

Michael A. Lee

ODE TO A LOAF

What a pity, what a shame
Your plight we feel is clearly plain

Much to our regret we have to say
Its our bet it's just the way

It's sods law or so they say
That buttered bread falls that way

We would suggest you keep tight hold
Once buttered our bread becomes quite bold

There is no more that we can say
"Respect the Bread", it's the best way.

Anon. Circa 2002

Warburtons Limited
Hereford House
Hereford Street
Bolton BL1 8JB

Telephone 01204 556600
Facsimile 01204 532283
www.warburtons.co.uk

INVESTOR IN PEOPLE

Registered Office
Back o'th' Bank House
Hereford Street
Bolton BL1 8HJ

Registered in England
No. 178711

Head of Lost Property
Transport for London
Transport Trading Limited
Lost Property Office
200 Baker Street
London NW1 5RZ

Dear Sir/Madam

I am writing to you as part of my quest for an unusual item; namely my lost 'umph' which I may well have mislaid somewhere within the London Underground network a few weeks ago.

Aged 42, I have spent the best part of 30 years enjoying the spare-time activity of cross-country and fell running. For many years I enjoyed a position in various races in the top 50th percentile and could run with fleetness of foot without any significant effort of lung or muscle. Although a little tired the day after a race or long training run, I would nevertheless recover quickly and be as fresh as the proverbial daisy for the next event in no time at all. The same was true of my daily working life. I would begin in the morning with energy levels of the highest, work with all cylinders firing and still have the time, inclination and wherewithal to party late into the night at the end of a busy and productive day. In short I had lots of 'umph'.

Sadly, I have to inform you that much of my 'umph' has disappeared. My 'get up and go' has regrettably 'got up and gone'! I now run more slowly with far more effort required and my recovery time has increased considerably, to the point where legs and lungs still show the signs of stiffness and stretch several days after a bout of training or a short fell-race. I wake up for work feeling tired, fulfil my daily obligations with a sense of fatigue, and retire to my bed in an exhausted and worn-out fashion.

In this regard I have searched high and low for my lost 'umph' but cannot find it anywhere and I have begun to wonder if I lost it when travelling on the Underground earlier this year. If it has turned up in your lost-property office I would be grateful to have it back again!

Many thanks for your time and kind consideration in this matter and I look forward to hearing from you in the very near future.

Sincerely and anxiously

Michael A. Lee

Mr M A Lee
Somewhere in West Yorkshire

Dear Mr Lee

Thank you for your letter of the 5 May 2002.

It must have come as quite a shock
To find that time had slowed your clock

To notice that your 'umph' had gone astray
You must have realised there had to come that day

A day that your 'umph' just ran out
A day that you no longer sprint about

A day when things get lost and start falling out
Because many people come in here and shout

I've lost my hair my teeth as well
Like some of us here, so let me tell

If I had found your 'umph' I'd have spread it around
But unfortunately it was never found

Yours sincerely

Maureen Beaumont

Transport Trading Limited, Lost Property Office, 200 Baker Street, London NW1 5RZ

Registered office: Windsor House, 42-50 Victoria Street, London SW1H 0TL. Registered in England and Wales. Company Number 391 4810. VAT Number 756 2770 08

Head of Customer Service
Met Office
London Road
Bracknell
Berkshire RG12 2SZ

Dear Sir/Madam

I am writing to you as part of my quest for an unusual item; namely a silver lining from a used cloud.

Despite the passage of over 20 years since I graduated in Geography, I clearly remember one of my college lecturers explaining that once a cloud has shed its moisture in the form of rain, sleet, hailstone or snow there will, ultimately, be no cloud left as it is the very moisture that forms most of its integral structure. He did, however, fail to mention a very important if not vital piece of information; specifically, what actually happens to the silver lining once the bulk of the cloud had vanished.

Having thought long and hard about this puzzle, I initially came to the conclusion that the majority of silver cloud linings are so thin and lacking in depth that they break apart into countless minute fragments as they fall from great heights to earth and are lost among the soil, vegetation and water on the earth's surface.

However, analysing this concept a little more closely, I began to wonder if this were true also of low cloud since, as the silver lining has less far to fall, there is less chance of fragmentation and disintegration and the consequential possibility of complete sections of silver lining surviving for the picking.

It is in this regard that I write. I am not a wealthy man by any stretch of the imagination and would love nothing better than to find either a complete silver lining or indeed part of a silver lining of any recognised cloud type. I would be most grateful, therefore, if you could advise me of any locations within the UK where the chances of realising my lofty dream could be accomplished more readily. This would make me a very happy man indeed.

I realise that you must deal with many enquiries of this type on a regular basis and so I thank you for your time and kind consideration and look forward to hearing from you in the very near future.

Sincerely

M. A. Lee

Michael A. Lee

Customer Centre
PD9 Powell Duffryn House
London Road
Bracknell
RG12 2SX
Tel: 0845 3000300
Fax: 0845 3001300
e-mail: customercentre@metoffice.com

May 22, 2002

Dear Mr Lee,

Thank you for taking the time to write to the Met Office. Unfortunately we cannot advise you as to purchasing or finding a silver lining.

The proverb "Every cloud has a silver lining" has been widely used to mean "*Every difficult or depressing circumstance has its hidden consolations. There is always a reason for hope in the most desperate situations*".

It has been used in 1915 by the First World War troops in war time song "Keep The Home Fires Burning" in Charles Dickens' "The Bleak House" written in 1852 to a quote by Radio 4 in 1994.

If you would like any further information about Meteorological events please don't hesitate to contact us.

Yours Sincerely,

Andy Marriott
Customer Centre Duty Manager

INVESTOR IN PEOPLE

The New Mayor
The Town Hall
Hartlepool

Dear Sir/Madam

I am writing to you as part of my quest for an unusual item; namely the position of Hartlepool's 'Monkey Hanging Executive' should this role become available in the near future. As the new and creative Mayor, I thought it best to seek your advice about securing this position since neither your predecessor nor your MP were inclined to consider me when I wrote to them at an earlier date.

Although currently living in Huddersfield, West Yorkshire, I remember as a child hearing on many occasions the tale of the hanging of the infamous 'French spy' from my dear Grandmother of the once flourishing Eden Street in West Hartlepool. As a consequence I have wondered for many years if indeed the simian creature that suffered his or her demise from the end of a north-eastern rope had actually been craftily trained by the Napoleonic enemy and if perhaps the hanging was therefore a justified act of anti-terrorism. It is my opinion that an invasion from the Continent may well have been averted by this timely execution and that releasing this enigmatic French agent could have led to events of catastrophic significance, changing the very history of British Isles. It is possible that, had the hanging not occurred, we might even now be suffering under a despotic Norman presidency rather than living in a democratic British society with a caring Royal Family, as we do.

Aged 41, I am most concerned at the many contemporary occasions when the French look northward with a Norman nose for trouble, complaining about our various industries and institutions and criticising our British way of life. I wonder if at some point in the near future they might once again try a dastardly trick of subterfuge and repeat their insertion of a spy, as they did so long ago.

Should this possibility become a reality, the local Hartlepool community would doubtless require the services of a competent monkey hangman and I would suggest that I am an ideal candidate for the job. Should the spy need arresting in coastal waters I am a good swimmer with a strong and determined grip. I am also a seasoned fell-runner and, being fast on my feet, believe I could outrun a monkey over distance should there be a need to catch a desperate escapee. I can jump quite a height and even climb trees! I have also had experience of scouting and am so adept at tying knots and nooses that I was once awarded a knot-tying badge.

Having spent much of my youth in the Hartlepool area, I would be quite happy to relocate. Of course, I have a good grasp of local geography, which is always of benefit if any form of hunting or tracking is involved.

I thank you for your time and consideration and look forward to hearing form you with regards to this matter in the very near future.

Yours sincerely

M. A. Lee

STUART DRUMMOND
Mayor of Hartlepool

Civic Centre
Hartlepool TS24 8AY

Our Ref: SFD/DB

Tel: 01429 266522
Fax: 01429 523701
DX: 60669 Hartlepool-1

Your Ref:

HARTLEPOOL
BOROUGH COUNCIL

16th May 2002

Mr M A Lee
Somewhere in West Yorkshire

Dear Mr. Lee

Thank you for your letter dated 8th May 2002.

If the position of 'Monkey Hanging Executive' ever becomes available in Hartlepool, I will keep you in mind.

Yours sincerely

STUART DRUMMOND
Mayor

Head of Enquiries
National Maritime Museum
Romney Road
Greenwich
London SE10 9NF

Dear Sir/Madam

I am writing to you as part of my quest for an unusual item; namely some space at the National Maritime Museum that would lend itself perfectly to my present condition, which is most accurately described as a 'complete wreck'.

Aged 42, I am a rather craggy, weather-beaten individual whose hold has been filled to capacity one too many times, causing significant leaning and the beginnings of a sinking process. It has surprised and indeed concerned me in recent months to experience an increasing stiffness in my muscles and joints early in the morning and greater weariness earlier in the evening than used to be the case; in seafaring terms my timbers are beginning to rot even though the mast is, at least for the time-being, still upright.

The waves that were visible on the top of my head a few years ago have permanently retreated and instead there is but a bare, sandy beach that provides a home only for sunburned tissue and settling dust. In short, I could be likened to a ship on the rocks and am probably good for very little but as an example of a complete human wreck.

It is on the basis of the aforementioned state of deterioration that I write to you for help. Please could you find a section of the museum where I might be seen by members of the public both as an interesting and unusual seaside exhibit as well as a stark warning of what can happen when a landlubber forgets to wash his decks, varnish the hull and replaces his lime allocation with far too much rum?

Many thanks indeed for your time and consideration and I look forward to hearing from you in the very near future.

Sincerely

Michael A. Lee

...illustrating the importance of the sea, ships, time and the stars...

Mr M A Lee
Somewhere in West Yorkshire

16th May 2002

Dear Mr Lee

Thank you for your message in a bottle dated 10th May 2002.

I am so sorry to hear about your present rather distressed state, but at least we may take comfort in the fact that you have sailed the high seas and must have many a yarn to while away the hours.

I am very sympathetic having been holed below the waterline myself only recently, although in my case it did allow for a full refit and I am now back with the fleet.

Should you be interested in any employment opportunity with us which may allow similar treatment in your case, please forward your latest curriculum vitae for our consideration. In the meantime, try to maintain a leeward station so as not to spill the rum.

Yours sincerely

A.N.Bodle

Andy Bodle
HR Director

Patron: HRH The Duke of Edinburgh, KG, KT
National Maritime Museum, Greenwich, London SE10 9NF
Tel: 020 8858 4422 Fax: 020 8312 6632 www.nmm.ac.uk

INVESTOR IN PEOPLE

Maritime GREENWICH
A WORLD HERITAGE SITE

Lord Harewood
Harewood House
Harewood
Leeds
West Yorkshire

Dear Sir

I am writing to you as part of my quest for an unusual thing; namely permission to remodel a specific part of the statue of Orpheus crafted by Astrid Zydower that stands outside your magnificent house in the midst of the formal terrace garden. Just last week my wife and I visited Harewood House so that our two small children could meet Noddy and his friends who were visiting for the weekend, and also to see your impressive gardens and wonderful collection of birds. The day was most enjoyable with the exception of one 'not so small' detail. Let me explain.

As my family and I walked through the terraced gardens, the eyes of my wife and I fell upon the heroic figure of naked Orpheus supporting the big cat upon his muscular shoulders and standing without shame in a pose both classical and boastful. We were both shocked at the size of his sculpted inheritance but, whereas my own shock turned quickly into jealousy, my wife's became an annoying combination of glassy-eyed admiration and complete distraction. Over a week has passed and she still looks into space and frequently sighs in a most distressing manner, oblivious of my presence or obvious annoyance.

Doubtless there are scores of male visitors who share my experience of envy and utter disbelief in the dimensions of Orpheus' tail-end Charlie, and I am sure that there must be an equal number of besotted women whose beguilement following their visual encounter hinders their progress in everyday life. Perhaps you would consider my suggestion that I once again visit Harewood House, this time with hammer, chisel and sandpaper and remodel the offending member of Orpheus so all families can return home in as content a manner as possible and learn to live life with modest expectations intact.

Doubtless you would agree that my act of mercy can lead to nothing but good and perhaps, as well as helping to maintain an element of contentment for the many married and courting couples that chance upon a single sight of Orpheus, it may also help Lady Harewood and your good self in whatever emotional difficulties regular sightings of 'The Big Fellow' may have caused.

Many thanks for your time and kind consideration and I look forward to hearing from you in the very near future.

Sincerely

M. A. Lee

Michael A. Lee

P.S. I am now going out to my garage where I keep my chisel sharpener!

14th May 2002

Mr M A Lee
Somewhere in West Yorkshire

Dear Mr Lee

Thank you for your letter raising a most important point, to wit the not inconsiderable endowment of Orpheus as sculpted by Astrid Zydower.

It may interest you to know, but will probably not surprise you, that I frequently see young couples out of my window, the male with a camera and the female standing on the edge of the central fountain with her hand held up suggestively in front of Orpheus. I can only guess at what she is attempting to address.

If you warn me when you are likely to come again to Harewood, a visit which we should naturally anticipate with much pleasure, we will have the fountain filled a little fuller than usual and maybe some sinister fish deployed within it in order to withstand your assault on Orpheus and his endowment.

Yours sincerely

Lord Harewood

Chief Magistrate
Bow Street Magistrates Court
Bow Street
London

Dear Sir/Madam

I am writing to you as part of my quest for an unusual item; namely membership of the athletics club associated with the Bow Street Magistrates Court known as the Bow Street Runners.

Aged 42, I first began running almost 27 years ago as a rather chubby 15-year-old. At first my efforts were restricted to short road runs but soon developed into longer cross-country ventures and finally into long-distance fell races. I am sure that I am hooked to the fun that running brings but, apart from a £9 annual subscription to The Fell Runners Association, a national organisation that provides a fell-race agenda and a magazine, I have never actually become a member of any particular running club before.

Since the Bow Street Runners are so well known and are associated with a group of people recognised for their discipline and enforcement of order, I would be delighted to be considered for membership forthwith. I realise that there is a significant distance between Huddersfield, where I live, and Bow Street in London but the accolade of belonging to such a club would make the travelling to and fro a worthwhile task.

I would be most grateful if you could send to me the relevant membership application forms and would also like to take this opportunity to ask whether I need to purchase blue PT kit and a flashing light for winter evening training.

Many thanks for your time and consideration.

Sincerely

M. A. Lee .

Michael A. Lee

BOW STREET MAGISTRATES' COURT

LONDON WC2E 7AS

Tel: 020-7853-9232
Fax: 020-7853-9298

Mr M A Lee
Somewhere in West Yorkshire

22 May 2002

Dear Mr Lee

I was delighted to receive your letter of the 18th May and read about your achievements in running.

I am sorry to have to break the news to you that the Bow Street Runners no longer exists, the age and state of health of the District Judges was such that there was grave risk of injury to their health.

However, every cloud has a silver lining and this disappointment means you will not need to purchase all the equipment and the flashing light.

May I wish you every success in your fell running and cross-country ventures.

Yours sincerely

Penelope Hewitt.

Head of Customer Services
Consignia PLC
148 Old Street
London EC1V 9HG

Dear Sir/Madam

I am writing to you as part of my quest for an unusual item; namely a 'Poetic Licence'.

Having spent a little time this afternoon wondering whom I might approach in my search for the aforementioned item, I came to the conclusion that, as the contemporary face of The Post Office which has had decades of selling and supplying various licences, you might be the ideal starting point in my enquiries.

While surfing the web I was most interested to read of the vast array of licence possibilities available within certain UK towns, ranging from dog-breeding and late-night café licences to pig-movement and scrap-metal-yard licences. There is, I notice, even a pool-betting licence available in some places, presumably for those who share a love of both the races and the swimming baths!

It seems that there are licences to cater for a substantially wide range of interests and tastes, business needs and hobbies, although many of these appear to be supplied by local-council departments. It was not immediately evident, however, whether there exists the opportunity for applying for and obtaining a poetic licence and I wondered if this was simply a quirk of the sites I visited or whether I was searching in the wrong places. I wonder if perhaps the good old established Post Office could shed more light on the subject!?

Having been both a writer and a salesman for quite some time, I often find myself in situations where exaggeration and focus seem to be par for the course and in this regard I wondered if it might be best to ensure that the claims I make in writing and in storytelling were protected by an officially purchased licence even if they are not actual objective facts. In this regard I would be most obliged for any advice and help you can provide in my quest for such an item.

I thank you in anticipation of your time and kind consideration in this matter and look forward to hearing from you in the very near future.

Sincerely

Michael A. Lee

31 May 2002

1-80000976

Mr M A Lee
Somewhere in West Yorkshire

Dear Mr Lee

Thank you for your letter of 29 May 2002 to Consignia plc Headquarters.

With regard to a "Poetic Licence" acquisition outlined in your letter, I refer to the Oxford English Dictionary " A poetic licence is a poet's or writer's departure from strict fact or correct grammar, for the sake of effect."

It is a phrase used to describe the use of exaggeration or storytelling in everyday life. Unfortunately, there is no "Official" licence of this sort provided by the Post Office.

I thank you for contacting Consignia plc.

Yours sincerely

Caroline Chaplin

Caroline Chaplin
Consignia Headquarters Customer Service Manager

Group Centre, 5ᵗʰ Floor, 148 Old Street, LONDON, EC1V 9HQ
Tel: 020 7250 2888 Fax: 020 7250 2030

Consignia plc is registered in England and Wales. Registered number 4138203. Registered office: 148 Old Street, LONDON, EC1V 9HQ

cc Royal Society for the
Prevention of Cruelty to Animals

Head of Enquiries
Battersea Dogs Home
4 Battersea Park Road
London SW8 4AA

Dear Sir/Madam

I am writing to you as part of my quest for an unusual item; namely 'the hair of a dog'.

Although I have occasionally enjoyed a glass of beer or wine during the course of the last few years, rarely have I consumed sufficient to warrant any of the well-documented side effects that are described the next day by many people as 'hangovers'. Au contraire, my own meagre and infrequent ration of alcoholic beverage has usually created a certain sense of warmth and inner contentment during the evening of my self-indulgence, led me perhaps to the joyful and melodious singing of 'Danny Boy', and then created a pleasant fatigue conducive to a deep and restful night's sleep. By morning the alcohol has normally cleared from my system and I am fresh as the proverbial daisy, fully prepared to face a new and wonderful day.

Last Saturday, however, was an exception to the rule and it is for a related reason that I now write to you for help. Over the course of the evening I somehow consumed two flavoursome and fortifying glasses of a dark stout, a tumbler of homebrew mango wine and a little saké. I suspect that the host of the party that I was attending also added a little whisky to my cup of late-night cocoa.

As a consequence, next morning my head felt a little like a piece of two-by-two pine when it is placed in a vice for sanding, my mouth like the surface of the sandpaper had it been left out in the desert for a week or so and my sense of vitality similar to that of an inmate of Death Row. In short, my moderation of a lifetime was shaken and stirred, turned upside down and then punched. It took me almost three days to recover.

During my recovery period a friend suggested that should I obtain 'a hair of the dog' I might endure the symptoms of my self-induced suffering to a greater degree and make a swifter recovery than was the actual case. I did not manage to find one, however, as I do not own a dog and know few if any friends who do. Should I happen to experience a repeat of the foolish behaviour already described, however,

I believe it would be prudent for me to obtain 'a hair of the dog' and keep it in my wallet or bathroom cabinet 'just in case'.

As a well-established organisation involved in the care of many different types of dog, I wondered if it might be possible for you to supply me with a hair of a dog proven to be of benefit in the circumstances I have described. My friend did not provide details about whether any specific breed of dog offered more success than another as far as hair was concerned, but if you believe that a German shepherd dog might provide a better hair than a poodle, or a terrier than a bulldog, in the provision of healing benefits, I will take your advice and, if convenient, an appropriate sample of hair as authoritative medical aid.

Many thanks indeed for your time and kind consideration and I look forward to hearing from you in the very near future.

Sincerely

Michael A. Lee

Mr M A Lee
Somewhere in West Yorkshire

Battersea Dogs Home

Patron: Her Majesty The Queen
President: His Royal Highness Prince Michael of Kent

4, Battersea Park Road, London SW8 4AA
Tel: 020-7622 3626   Fax: 020-7622 6451
www.dogshome.org

31st May 2002

Dear Mr Lee

Thank you for your letter, which we were delighted to receive.

I can certainly sympathise with the dreadful condition and symptoms that you have described and it would truly be a miracle of modern science if these could be alleviated at a faster rate than nature.

We usually find that the "Hair of the dog" treatment involved another alcoholic drink during the "morning after" suffering, and have no cases on file involving the consumption of a real dog's hair for this condition!

I am consequently sending you a selection of hairs taken from our groomer's dog brush and we would be delighted to hear back from you about any success that you encounter. We would however strongly suggest that this experiment be conducted steadily over a lengthy period of time, as we would never wish to cause you any further discomfort. We would also advise a consultation with your GP.

I would be happy to share the news of any success that you encounter with the staff at the Dogs Home. It would make a topical alternative to Aspirin or Resolve.

Yours sincerely

Head of Enquiries
Battersea Dogs Home

Battersea Dogs Home
4, Battersea Park Road,
London SW8 4AA
Tel: 020-7622 3626
Fax: 020-7622 6451

Battersea at Old Windsor
Priest Hill, Old Windsor,
Berkshire SL4 2JN
Tel: 01784 432929
Fax: 01784 471538

A Member of The Association of British Dogs and Cats Homes
Company Limited by Guarantee. Registered in England No. 278802   Registered as a Charity under t
VAT Registration No. 726 5204 47 Registered Office: The Dogs Home Battersea, 4 Battersea Pa

Royal Society for the Prevention of Cruelty to Animals

Patron HM The Queen *Vice Patron* His Grace The Archbishop of Canterbury

Registered charity no. 219099

Our Ref: 2557669/chv

Mr M A Lee
Somewhere in West Yorkshire

Dear Mr Lee

Thank you for your most unusual and poetic letter of 28 May. I apologise for the delay in replying and hope that in the meantime you have made a fine and full recovery from your evening of alcoholic indulgence.

I have pleasure in enclosing, as requested, a very special "hair of the dog" (indeed, a few!) most generously donated by our canine companion, Bailey, which, although unproven, may I hope prove useful to you in the event of any future occurrence of over-indulgence of the tippling variety. Please keep them in a safe place.

I am sure you will appreciate that the fulfilment of such rare and peculiar requests, whilst introducing a leavening element to an otherwise routine day of enquiry handling, places an unusual drain on the RSPCA's charitable resources, serving as in this case not the furtherance of the welfare of animals but the enhancement of the quality of human life. In token thereof, I hope you may consider this august organisation worthy of your future support and perhaps make application for an RSPCA affinity credit card or feel driven to make a small donation towards our future animal welfare work. I am therefore seizing the opportunity of enclosing a few leaflets which I hope may capture your interest.

A toast to your good health and to the welfare of all animals (and especially to Bailey, our doggie hair donor).

Yours sincerely

Caroline H Vodden (Mrs)
Head of Supporter Care

Royal Society for the Prevention of Cruelty to Animals

Patrons HM The Queen, HM Queen Elizabeth The Queen Mother *Vice Patron* His Grace The Archbishop of Canterbury

Registered charity no. 219099

" Hair of the dog"

from Bailey.

with compliments

Enquiries Service (Direct lines: Tel 0870 3335 999 Fax 0870 7530 284)

RSPCA Headquarters, Wilberforce Way, Southwater, Horsham, West Sussex RH13 7WN
Tel 0870 010 1181 Fax 0870 7530 284 DX 57628 HORSHAM 6 Website: http://www.rspca.org.uk

Head of Customer Services
Thomas Crapper & Co
The Stable Yard
Alscot Park
Stratford-upon-Avon
Warwickshire CV37 8BL

Dear Sir/Madam

I am writing to you as part of my quest for an unusual item; namely the job title and suitable employment as 'A-Cistern Director' within a well-established waste-disposal solutions company. Since I chanced upon an advertisement for your own company within a magazine I was reading in a doctor's waiting room last week I decided that you might be the ideal place to begin my enquiries.

Aged 42, I have spent a significant amount of time in the vicinity of cisterns of the type you manufacture. As a matter of interest I have, since the age of 2, spent approximately 10 minutes each day or, if recalculated, 146,100 minutes, 2,435 hours, or 100 days and nights close to a variety of toilet cisterns and am therefore more than familiar with this range of products as far as appearance, mechanics and even colour schemes are concerned.

As an industrious and conscientious individual, I can assure you that I have a committed attitude to my various daily duties and I am known for my consistency and my regularity, which to some extent I am sure relies on my possession of adequate moral fibre.

I am a well-read and well-educated person, as the bookshelves in various rooms within my house would suggest, and pride myself as a traditionalist who has great respect for the great British institutions, a strong work ethic and successful organisation, as well as for our royal family and indeed our sovereign on the throne.

Should you be interested to consider me further for 'A-Cistern Director' I would be pleased to meet with you for interview and will be only too glad to bring with me a strong and very, very long CV for your perusal. (This, you will be glad to hear, is printed on soft and recycled paper to support the use of sustainable timber resources and to avoid the need to involve a drain-clearing company should the document be thoughtlessly discarded.)

Many thanks indeed for your time and kind consideration in regard to my hoped-for employment and I look forward to hearing from you in the very near future.

Sincerely

Michael A. Lee

THOMAS CRAPPER & COMPANY, LTD.

SANITARY ENGINEERS

By Warrant of Appointment to their Late Majesties Edward VII and George V.

ESTABLISHED 1861.　　　　INCORPORATED 1904.　　　　COMPANY No. 82482.

Somewhere in West Yorkshire

8th June 1902.

Dear Mr. Lee,

I am grateful to be in receipt of your's of the third instant, being an application for a situation at Crappers. My fellow directors and I have been much impressed to read your missive in all its detail. However this led us inexorably to the conclusion that you are greatly over-qualified for the post.

Therefore I regret to relate that we are unable to offer a position to you but we wish you well in your endeavours. You might try Messrs Boggs & Co. of Looe, Cornwall.

I am, yours sincerely,

S.P.J.Kirby.

Simon Kirby.

THE STABLE YARD,　　ALSCOT PARK,　　STRATFORD-ON-AVON,　　WARWICKSHIRE.　(CV37 8BL)

ELECTRIC MESSAGES: wc@thomas-crapper.com　　　TELEPHONE: ALDERMINSTER (01789) 450 522.

MANAGING DIRECTOR – S.P.J. KIRBY.　　　　　　FACSIMILE:　"　"　"　"　523.

The President
Camberwell Society
38 Camberwell Grove
Camberwell

Dear Sir/Madam

I am writing to you as part of my quest for an unusual item; namely an opportunity to meet a world-famous 'Camberwell Beauty'.

It is with a certain degree of regret that I look back over the last 20 years to the countless organisations to which I have belonged and from which I have resigned, which have been unable to point me in the direction of anything more than Painted Ladies in Pontefract and fragile Lacewings in Halifax. So many of my past leads have offered neither the charms, character nor looks of my expectations and consequently they have simply fluttered by on damaged wings or on flight paths quite different to my own journey through life.

As a northern man living in the town of Huddersfield I am not familiar with the Camberwell area nor of places locally where a Camberwell Beauty might be seen and so I am writing to you for your kind help and advice.

I would be grateful if you could recommend places I could visit where I might observe the 'Beauty' of my dreams and so permit my adding the consequent encounter to my trusty logbook. This is at present collecting dust on an office shelf and looking more and more like a large cocoon each day.

Doubtless you have many similar requests concerning the search for a Camberwell Beauty and I thank you for your time and kind consideration in this matter.

I look forward to hearing from you in the very near future.

Sincerely

Michael A. Lee

Mr M A Lee
Somewhere in West Yorkshire

Dear Sir,

Thank you for your letter of June 2nd.

As I imagine you will not be surprised to learn, I am not sure whether in your letter you are by Camberwell Beauties referring to butterflies or women. If the former, I will try and make enquiries to find out. If the latter, I suggest you either place an advertisement in the Society's journal - the Camberwell Quarterly - or move to Camberwell and join the Society where several of our members in my opinion deserve this accolade.

So far as the Quarterly is concerned I don't think we have ever before carried general invitations to particular social encounters with members of the opposite sex but if tastefully drafted and likely to cause no offence I daresay the Editor might be willing to publish one.

Yours faithfully,

Conrad Dehn

Head of Customer Services
Wilkinson
JK House
Roebuck Way
Manton Wood
Worksop
Nottinghamshire S80 3YY

Dear Sir/Madam

I am writing to you as part of my quest for an unusual item; namely a 'corporate ladder'. I thought that, as a large retail organisation involved in the sale of a wide range of do-it-yourself and gardening equipment, you might be able to advise me.

Over recent months there has been much reference at the company for which I work to individuals who have gained promotion in their various careers, and indeed salary increases also, as a consequence of their 'climbing the corporate ladder'.

Although I have worked consistently hard at my job and been rewarded in a reasonable and satisfactory manner for my efforts to date, I would be keen to move even further forward in my employment and am eager to obtain one of the aforementioned corporate ladders for this purpose.

I have never actually seen a corporate ladder and thought that rather than showing my ignorance and asking one of my management team where I would find one I ought first to make enquiries elsewhere. The added benefit of this approach is that it avoids the possible scenario of my making a calculated guess at purchasing a corporate ladder from someone such as yourselves but making a mistake and bringing home a step-ladder or roofing ladder instead.

Doubtless you receive many similar letters to this over the course of the year and so I thank you for your time and kind consideration and look forward to hearing from you in the very near future, telling me where I might purchase such an item.

Sincerely

M. A. Lee

Michael A. Lee

Wilkinson

JK House
PO Box 20
Roebuck Way
Manton Wood
Worksop
Nottinghamshire
S80 3YY
Tel: (01909) 505505
Fax: (01909) 505777

Mr M A Lee
Somewhere in West Yorkshire

17 June 2002

Dear Mr Lee

Thank you for your recent enquiry regarding your quest for a 'corporate' ladder.

I too have heard many references to such an item and, like you, have been attracted to the benefits that such an item appears to bring. Those who own one clearly enjoy the positive outcomes that can be gained – indeed I've found that people who must own a corporate ladder of their own are reluctant to lend me theirs even for a week or two. I can sympathise with your predicament in not wanting to show your ignorance by asking your management as I know from experience the unusually vacant expression and strange reply that one can get from making such enquiries.

However, only a few months ago I believed that I had made some progress and actually acquired a corporate ladder of my very own, but this turned out to be one of the older models of the 'corporate kick-step' and so my personal search continues.

I am aware that our buying team is currently working hard in the Far East, searching for a supplier who is willing to trade openly in the market of corporate ladders. I understand that there are difficulties however, as in line with our marketing strategy such a product must be available for us to sell at the most competitive price and be of the highest quality. Our understanding of this product is that it must be handled and used with the greatest of care, for not only can it be climbed, but one can also fall off (or indeed be pushed). Therefore, the buyer's search is complicated by the need to risk-assess every product sample to evaluate its safety.

I am sorry that on this occasion I am unable to help any further and wish you well in your own search for a corporate ladder. In the meantime, may I suggest purchasing Wilko Broad Beans at 89p as an alternative, as perhaps an almighty beanstalk will develop, enabling you to achieve your dreams another way.

Many thanks for your letter and best wishes in your quest.

Assuring you of our best attention at all times.

Yours sincerely
pp WILKINSON

David Bosworth
Customer Relations Manager

Head of Enquiries
College of Optometrists
42 Craven Street
London WC2N 5NG

Dear Sir/Madam

I am writing to you as part of my quest for an unusual item; namely a pair of 'context lenses'.

For many years I have suffered from a degree of myopia or short-sightedness and would like to take this opportunity to mention that I have been very pleased with Boots Opticians both for offering me an excellent eye-testing service during this time and for providing me with various high quality lenses and indeed spectacle frames when required. It is with reference to another area of vision, however, that I write today. Let me explain.

Although I am perfectly capable of observing physical detail at a distance through my everyday glasses or, if out of the normal range of vision, through my handy binoculars, as well as being capable of reading easily and performing the full range of tasks that require watching objects close to the eyes I am, on occasion, challenged to position things in context.

My understanding of the relative importance of various issues and priorities at home and at work as well as during various aspects of social life is sometimes exaggerated and poorly focused. The complexity of everyday life with its countless demands is often unclear to me and at times significantly blurred around the edges.

It is for this reason I would find it enormously helpful to acquire the aforementioned context lenses so that my sense of perspective is restored and I can see life for what it really is. As the College of Optometrists, I thought that you might be the ideal starting point for my enquiries!

Doubtless you receive many letters of this kind on a regular basis and so I thank you for your time and consideration and look forward to hearing from you in the near future.

Sincerely

Michael A. Lee

THE COLLEGE OF OPTOMETRISTS

Mr M A Lee
Somewhere in West Yorkshire

24th July 2002

Dear Mr. Lee,

Thank you for your letter which has been passed to me.

I am very interested to hear of your request, as I too would find such lenses useful on occasion. They would go well with my Round Tuit. Unfortunately the College is unable to help you in your search, but you may find that the British Context Lens Association (www.bcla.org.uk) will be able to give you more information.

Please let me know if you succeed in your quest.

Kind regards

Yours sincerely

Dr. Susan Blakeney
Optometric Adviser

Somewhere in West Yorkshire
19 June 2002

Jill Silander-Hatch
Garden Gifts of Distinction
32 Beaconsfield Way
Frome
Somerset BA11 2UD

Dear Sir/Madam

I am writing to you as part of my quest for an unusual item; namely a 'Fountain of Eternal Youth'.

Since turning 40 a couple of years ago, I have become increasingly conscious of the way in which my face is wrinkling, my joints are beginning to ache after exercise and my ears and nose are sprouting wiry hairs. It is certainly becoming more difficult for me to maintain a balance between the enjoyment of good food and an acceptable physique and I also find it an impossible task to retain more than a token amount of hair on the top of my head.

Names and places that were once readily available to my system of mental recollection often evade me now and only yesterday I accidentally put on my dressing gown on top of my shirt and tie instead of the desired jacket. In short, my ageing process has kicked in with a vengeance. It is in this regard, therefore, that I write to you.

Surfing the net last night I chanced upon your website advertising, among other things, a range of fountains and wondered with great hope if your range might include that most English of ancient artefacts, a 'fountain of eternal youth'.

I can already imagine such a fountain positioned appropriately in the back garden of my home here in Huddersfield, offering an experience of aesthetic worth as well as readily available draughts of age-repelling and life-preserving water. Doubtless such a fountain will be highly coveted and priced accordingly but may I emphasise to you my substantial interest in acquiring such an item to hasten the day my appearance and physical prowess return to that of my late teens and early twenties.

Many thanks indeed for your time and kind consideration and I look forward to hearing from you in the very near future.

Sincerely

Michael A. Lee

Garden Gifts of Distinction

32 Beaconsfield Way FROME Somerset BA11 2UD
Tel: *(01373) 471749* **Fax:** *(01373) 303113* **Email:** *Gardengiftsfrome@aol.com*
www.Gardengiftsofdistinction.com

Birdbaths - Statues - Sconces - Pedestals - Planters
Plaques & Urns for Gardens, Patios,
Courtyards & Conservatories

20th September 2002

Mr M A Lee
Somewhere in West Yorkshire

Dear Mr Lee

It is with sorrow that I reply to your letter of
the 19th June. I have spent from then till now
testing all my fountains to see if one would meet
your requirements of "Fountain of Eternal Youth".
Though they are all aesthetically beautiful, none
have returned me to my girlhood!

However, gazing at these delightful fountains has
made me realise that youth is not everything! An
appreciation of beauty grows with age - so the
fountains appear more beautiful & ageless though we
do not!

So do return to my website - and order a fountain
today!

Yours sincerely

(Mrs) Jill Silander-Hatch

Distinctive Gifts for the Discerning

VAT No: 753 6910 16

182

Head of Customer Services
Environment & Transportation Service
Kirklees Metropolitan Council
Flint Street
Fartown
Huddersfield HD1 6LG

Dear Sir/Madam

I am writing to you as part of my quest for an unusual item; namely a solution to my present state of 'writer's block'.

Over the last couple of years I have spent an hour or more each evening compiling with great satisfaction a range of creative and grammatically colourful pieces of written material designed to entertain, stimulate and inspire even the most unimaginative hearts and minds of potential readers.

Each day I would see another two or three pages of wonderful word sculpture appear before me as if by magic and I would retire to bed happy with my literary effusions and fall into the deep and refreshing sleep that comes only from true contentment and perceived achievement.

Sadly, however, I must inform you that during the previous few days I have unfortunately developed a 'writer's block' with the result that my adjectives have become sluggish, my nouns full of inertia, my analogies without momentum. My whole system of creative writing has ground to an unexplained and frustrating halt.

It is for this reason that I write in desperation to your good selves.

As a well-established service experienced in the art and science of unblocking pipes and drains, I wondered if you might be able to offer any practical solutions to rid me of my writer's block, ensuring that the sentences and paragraphs that have flown so freely in times past are once again allowed to move in an unhindered fashion and find their intended outlet?

Doubtless, the key to survival in the competitive world of business in these hectic times has much to do with innovative application of existing techniques. I decided I would seek a solution from a team of experts who are used to dealing with the difficulties that often lie just around the bend and whose tools have the characteristics of both flexibility and versatility.

I daresay that you receive many enquiries of this kind on a regular basis and so I thank you for your time and kind consideration and look forward to hearing from you in the very near future.

Sincerely

Michael A. Lee

Kirklees
METROPOLITAN · COUNCIL

ENVIRONMENT & TRANSPORTATION SERVICE

Highway Network Manager
Richard Bunney

Flint Street
Fartown
Huddersfield HD1 6LG
West Yorkshire

Please contact:- Mr F O'Dwyer
Tel: 01484 225529

E-mail: frank.o'dwyer@kirkleesmc.gov.uk
Fax: 01484 225599
Text phone for deaf people: 01484 225531

Our Ref: 3.3.1/HIM043947/FO'D/CAH   Date: 24 June 2002
Your Ref: None

Mr M A Lee
Somewhere in West Yorkshire

Dear Mr Lee

RE: WRITER'S BLOCK

I refer to your letter dated 19 June asking for help with 'Writers' Block'

I must start by explaining that I am nowhere near as eloquent as you; it isn't in the requirements or training for engineers.

I don't feel qualified to offer a solution, but I would like to try and offer an insight and suggest some sources for you to explore.

It is at once understandable and intriguing that you link your problem with ours in maintaining the highway drainage system.

Early work by such people as d'Arcy and Bernoulli derived algorithms to describe the functioning of drainage systems.

For many years there has been a popular understanding of the 'stream of consciousness', perhaps this has encouraged people to think of the working of the brain in similar terms to the working of drains.

However there is no comparison in complexity. Consciousness has been described as 'The last great mystery of science'.

Continued over/....

1405JUN.DOC

Terry Brown - Highways and Transportation Manager

INVESTOR IN PEOPLE

184

Researchers are beginning to question the accepted concept of a stream of experiences passing through the mind. Perhaps this concept has been thought of as similar to gravity driving water through a drain.

Susan Blackmore has recently suggested that consciousness may be an illusion, so if it isn't what it seems, no wonder it is proving such a mystery.

'The Hard Problem' as David Chalmers calls it is 'how can the firing of brain cells produce subjective experience? It seems like turning water in to wine'

Several researchers are working on projects. For example Francis Crick is trying to pin down how brain activity corresponds to the world we see and Susan Greenfield is looking for the particular physical state of the brain which accompanies a subjective feeling.

Accessible sources you may try are New Scientist and Scientific American. The Meme Machine, by Blackmore and a recent Scientific American special edition 'The Hidden Mind' may also provide some insight and possibly inspiration for you.

Understanding the process is one thing but perhaps you would consider maintenance of the brain as well. Two recent items of interest are that the US Environmental Protection Agency have confirmed that burning candles with wicks stiffened by being treated with lead release high levels of lead throughout the house. All candles manufactured in America or Western Europe use alternatives. You will be aware of the effect of lead particles in the air. A small study at Kings College hints at a beneficial effect from eating a diet high in soya.

If, after following up these links, the insight they provide into the working of the brain does not inspire the clearing of the current blockage, perhaps you could accept a challenge and pen 1,500 words on why 'Flying a kite at night is so weird'.

In closing, I must explain that the main function of the brain is to manage resources and, interesting as this may be on a quiet Sunday, it isn't possible to use the Authority's Highways resources on continuing the correspondence. Perhaps you could consider enrolling on a creative writing course. I will leave that as another research item for you.

Best of luck.

Yours sincerely

F O'Dwyer

FRANK O'DWYER
Group Engineer, Maintenance.

1405JUN.DOC

Dr P. Faulkner
Field Head Surgery
Leymoor Road
Golcar
Huddersfield HD7 4QQ

Dear Dr Faulkner

I am writing to you as a part of my quest for an unusual item; namely information about a condition mentioned to me by a friend who has recently completed a period of work at Sizewell Power Station. I thought you might be able to suggest some possible treatment options for a condition that sounds particularly distressing and one which I am convinced I am also suffering from myself.

When my friend mentioned 'The China Syndrome' I had imbibed at least five pints of a rather smooth and palatable real ale, but I nevertheless distinctly remember him mentioning extremely high temperatures and their affect on physical stability as a consequence of this state. I am sure that he told me that the syndrome had critical consequences and was something that should cause a huge degree of concern to all involved.

When last Tuesday I myself began to feel rather hot and feverish, with a significant sinking feeling, I was not convinced that a mere self-limiting virus was to blame; rather this was another manifestation of 'The China Syndrome.'
Unfortunately, I am unable to find out anything more from my small collection of medical textbooks and presume that even my two volumes of *The Oxford Textbook of Medicine* may be out of date. I can tell you, however, that I feel urgently in need of advice before the symptoms become unmanageable and I find myself resting below ground for time immemorial.

Once again many thanks for your time and kind consideration and I look forward to hearing from you in the very near future.

Sincerely

Michael A. Lee

FIELDHEAD SURGERY
Dr. PETER FAULKNER
Dr. OWEN DEMPSEY
Dr. MICHAEL WALLWORK
Dr. SHEILA BENETT
Telephone: (01484) 654504
Fax: (01484) 460296
e-mail: fieldhead@doctors.org.uk

FIELD HEAD
LEYMOOR ROAD
GOLCAR
HUDDERSFIELD
HD7 4QQ

Our Ref; PF/kg

21st June, 2002

Mr. M. A. Lee,

Mr M. A. Lee
Somewhere in West Yorkshire

I read your letter of 19th June 2002 with interest. I have studied your symptoms and have come to the conclusion that the nearest equivalent of a viral illness which you correctly assume, is that of the 'Kawasaki' syndrome. This causes fevers and general malaise with the possibility of sudden, if not, later death from coronary artery involvement. I am fairly sure that this is not the case for you as, I believe, you have no interest in motorcycles and there is certainly no illness known as the 'Japan' syndrome.

I have discovered that the 'China' syndrome is indeed a possibility in your case, as the dysmorphic physiognomy which you possess may have been produced by non-subtle genetic modification through some form of irradiation. I have based this possibility of severe radiation exposure from the fact that you are almost completely bald and it is well known that the hair follicles are particularly radio sensitive.

The disaster scenario of rapidly approaching death is unlikely to be avoided, unless a heroine can be found to rescue you from your plight before total melt-down occurs.

I am glad that you are able to have five pints of your real ale, as I am sure that the time is approaching where you will be completely unable to drink when your gastrointestinal system is stripped of its lining from radiation effects.

I hope that your last days are comfortable but I can be of help, in that I am aware of a number of excellent joiners who should be able to make a coffin suitable for your requirements.

All the best.

Yours sincerely,

Dr. P. Faulkner.

Dr P. Faulkner
Field Head Surgery
Leymoor Road
Golcar
Huddersfield HD7 4QQ

Dear Dr Faulkner

First and foremost may I take this opportunity to thank you for your kind help with reference to my enquiries regarding 'The China Syndrome.'

Having considered the rather gloomy prospects associated with a confirmed diagnosis of 'The China Syndrome' I have looked closely and at length at various other aspects of my current symptomatology, hoping to find a less pessimistic prognosis. Once again, I would appreciate your advice in this matter.

I am beginning to wonder whether my original fears of complete meltdown were unwarranted but am still at somewhat of a loss to explain the following physical manifestations. Let me explain.

Several friends and colleagues have recently pointed out to me that I have a 'brass neck' and am sometimes 'hot headed'. I have certainly been known to 'see red' especially concerning the roll-out of unreasonable company expectations by various members of the senior management team and, when addressing issues connected to the above, have been accused of having a 'nose for trouble'. Doubtless my sharing of these unfortunate medical phenomena would also suggest that I tend to 'wear my heart on my sleeve'.

As a consequence of recognising such a miscellany of disturbing presentations I am now thoroughly confused and am not sure whether I ought to be referred to a neurologist, orthopaedic surgeon, specialist in opthalmology, a clinician in ENT or a cardio-thoracic expert.

I would be grateful for any light you can shed on such an unusual case-history as mine and look forward to hearing from you in the very near future.

Sincerely

M. A. Lee

Michael A. Lee

FIELDHEAD SURGERY
Dr. PETER FAULKNER
Dr. OWEN DEMPSEY
Dr. MICHAEL WALLWORK
Dr. SHEILA BENETT
Telephone: (01484) 654504
Fax: (01484) 460296
e-mail: fieldhead@doctors.org.uk

FIELD HEAD
LEYMOOR ROAD
GOLCAR
HUDDERSFIELD
HD7 4QQ

Our Ref; PF/kg

4th July, 2002

Mr M. A. Lee
Somewhere in West Yorkshire

Dear Michael,

Many thanks for your letter of 27th June 2002. I am afraid that I am not able to be more forthcoming in the possibility of a better outcome with your condition. The position of chaos in to which your body appears to be descending may indeed lead your friends and colleagues to note the fact that you do indeed have a brass neck – this may be easily be put down to the fact that there may be some transition from base materials in to brass - and undoubtedly, your body is made up of extremely base material. I can only assume that colleagues have noticed that you are hot headed due to the lack of insulation on top of your scalp, such that any thermal emission will be completely unhindered.

As mentioned before, bleeding from several sites may cause you to see red if you are stricken with a conjunctival haemorrhage and as for having a nose for trouble, should the condition progress, then you may lose your nose altogether, hence not be troubled with people accusing you of having one of these items.

I am sure the fact that you wish to wear your heart on your sleeve may be indicative of some severe psychological disturbance and hallucinogenic problems induced by many pints of real ale, which will no doubt cause hallucinations of the appearance of various internal organs on exterior parts of your body. This line of reasoning may also account for the fact that you may have, at times, appeared legless.

I can only commiserate with your sad condition and hope that you do take my advice as outlined in the original letter to make yourself comfortable in the short time that you have left upon this Earth, before total disorganisation of your system takes place.

I am sure you have gathered from our correspondence that I regard your condition as completely unique, as indeed I am sure there is only one of a kind with reference to yourself.

Yours sincerely,

Dr. P. Faulkner.

Dr P. Faulkner
Field Head
Leymoor Road
Golcar
Huddersfield HD7 4QQ

Dear Dr Faulkner

Once again may I take this opportunity to thank you for your time and kind consideration in your advice about my broad-ranging miscellaneous presentations as previously described.

I was understandably concerned, though not surprised, to hear that mine is a rather unique condition but have come to the conclusion that, despite the inevitability of the complete disorganisation and eventual meltdown of my physical being, I ought to apply my remaining time to helping other people as best I can. In this regard I am writing a letter of concern related to my dear wife and would again be most grateful for your learned advice and suggestions. I wondered specifically if there might be a suitable treatment regime for a problem with which my wife is currently afflicted, specifically a 'bone of contention'.

Almost every day during the last few months my wife has approached me with a look of sheer agony on her face and a sense of despair in her voice and has exclaimed: 'I have a bone of contention to discuss with you.' I am never quite sure how she manages to move off at a conversational tangent from this musculo-skeletal problem to various shortfalls in my own behaviour and to my various unfinished household and garden tasks and tie the two irreversibly together but it is clear that her suffering is affecting her judgement to a significant degree.

I myself have suffered considerably in the past from low back pain and recall gaining substantial benefit from physiotherapy and massage. I wondered if perhaps my wife might also receive help from a suitably qualified physiotherapist, osteopath or chiropractor so that this 'bone of contention' of hers is manipulated in such a way as to put it to rest once and for all.

Although I have attempted to find the aforementioned bone in my books of human anatomy and indeed on the Internet I have to date been unsuccessful. I am wondering whether my wife is using a local term for what others generally know as 'the funny bone' or perhaps 'the humorous' or whether her description is completely disjointed or even requires a certain amount of reconstruction.

Many thanks indeed for your time and kind consideration in this sensitive matter and I look forward to hearing from you in the very near future.

Sincerely

Michael A. Lee

FIELDHEAD SURGERY
Dr. PETER FAULKNER
Dr. OWEN DEMPSEY
Dr. MICHAEL WALLWORK
Dr. SHEILA BENETT
Telephone: (01484) 654504
Fax: (01484) 460296
e-mail: fieldhead@doctors.org.uk

FIELD HEAD
LEYMOOR ROAD
GOLCAR
HUDDERSFIELD
HD7 4QQ

Our Ref; PF/kg

24th July, 2002

Mr M. A. Lee
Somewhere in West Yorkshire

Dear Michael,

How pleasant it was to hear from you again.

I will have to start charging for giving my professional opinion as I realise that I have been giving it far too freely to date.

You have correctly identified a peculiar anatomical variant present in the female of the species, which is the "bone of contention". This is an interesting ossification found in a very secretive area in the female body.

The origin of this article may be traced to Biblical times, when Adam had a piece of rib removed from his body from which to fashion his partner, Eve. It is apparent that God did not quite manage to fashion an identical skeleton from this, leaving an extra particle which subsequently became the bone of contention.

Although the bone of contention is rarely exhibited, indications of its presence may be given during times of intense annoyance and frustration, hence it is easy to see why your wife is on the point of disclosing its presence more fully.

Management of the bone of contention would be rather drastic, in as much as it would involve a spousectomy to remove the source of annoyance. In your case, this may not be necessary, as your condition does appear to be imminently fatal, so this unpleasant surgical procedure may be dispensed with. Massage does help, giving great pleasure to the woman concerned, but as to whether it is actually a valid treatment for the bone is another matter.

I can reassure you that the bone of contention as an anatomical entity is certainly not the funny bone or humerus and represents a serious development in anatomical study.

I hope my description of the bone of contention is of help to you.

Yours sincerely,

Dr. P. Faulkner.

Head of Customer Services
White Knight
72 George Street
Caversham
Reading
Berkshire RG4 8DW

Dear Sir/Madam

I am writing to you as part of my quest for an unusual item; namely the services of a dry-cleaning organisation that is able and willing to launder my money.

Over the years I have taken my various two-piece suits to a whole range of dry cleaners conveniently located near the homes I have owned or rented. In the majority of cases my suits have been returned to me in immaculate condition and I have been able to present myself at work in a smart and dapper manner.

The same is true of various pairs of casual trousers and indeed also when the occasional need for my curtains to be dry cleaned has arisen. Stains have vanished, creases and folds have been banished and the dust and grime of everyday life have been replaced with a pleasing cleanliness and restoration of the appearance of something new.

In this regard I wondered if you might be able similarly to launder some of the £5, £10 and £20 notes that come regularly and legitimately into my possession but are creased and wrinkled, often dirty and lacking the lustre that one ideally expects of paper currency. There is nothing worse than filthy lucre!

I have certainly heard of various companies and institutions that launder money but sadly cannot find such a reference in *Yellow Pages*. Logic suggests to me that laundering is surely a function of the dry-cleaning industry and this explains the rationale for my writing to you in this regard, especially since you bare the gallant name of 'White Knight' and will probably come galloping to my rescue with much-needed help as soon as possible.

Doubtless you receive many letters along similar lines to this and so I thank you for your time and kind consideration and look forward to hearing from you in the very near future.

Sincerely

Michael A. Lee

White Night Laundry Services Ltd
72 George Street
Caversham
Reading
Berkshire RG4 8DW

20 June 2002

Michael. A. Lee
Somewhere in West Yorkshire

Dear Michael

Thank you for the opportunity to be of service to you.

White Night Laundry Services Ltd is able and willing to launder your money immediately.
Please send by return of post a very large package containing as many £5, £10 and £20 notes as you can get into a suitcase or large laundry box.
We promise to launder your money but cannot guarantee to return it to you.

Do you require the above items to be dry cleaned or washed and pressed if they are as dirty and creased and wrinkled as you suggest?

Awaiting an early reply

Head of Enquiries
British Weight Lifters' Association
131 Hurst Street
Oxford OX4 1HE

Dear Sir/Madam

I am writing to you as part of my quest for an unusual item; namely the services of one of your members capable of lifting a weight from my mind.

Doubtless you would agree with me that we live in an era where life is generally lived by a large proportion of the British population at a far faster pace than ever before. Despite the innumerable leaps forward in home comforts, hi-technology and indeed in medicine, many individuals apply themselves so intensely to the everyday challenges of careers, sports, social and family life that they are often in danger of over-stressing themselves and sometimes even experiencing the so-called 'burn-out syndrome'. I may well be one of these individuals.

Aged 42, I am one of society's many 'task jugglers', attempting to maintain a fine balance between responsibilities and duties at home and at work. As a result I have for some time now experienced the common problem of having much to think about. It all weighs very heavily indeed upon my mind.

Despite trying various relaxation techniques and distractions such as drum beating, making jams and talking to herbaceous perennials in my back garden, I still find it hard to switch off and put aside my many mental burdens. It is in this regard that I write.

Rather than experiment further with various avenues of stress management, I thought I would ask whether you know of a person who is so strong that they could simply lift the weight from my mind and carry it somewhere far from my focus and attention.

I am sure that you receive many enquiries of a similar nature to this and so I thank you for your time and kind consideration and look forward to hearing from you in the very near future with appropriate advice and suggestions.

Sincerely

Michael A. Lee

British Weight Lifters' Association

Grovenor House
131 Hurst Street
Oxford OX4 1HE

Mr M A Lee
Somewhere in West Yorkshire

1st July 2002

Dear Mr Lee

Thank you for your letter of 24th June.

I regret that as we are a voluntary body, and rely on a limited number of volunteers to help us, we are not in a position to be able to assist with your particular enquiry.

Yours sincerely

J Gaul

Director
Natural History Museum
Ipswich

Dear Sir/Madam

I am writing to you as part of my quest for an unusual item; namely official recognition as 'The Long-Lost Missing Link' by the Natural History Museum in Ipswich.

Aged 42, I have for many years been rather concerned at the extent and thickness of my ginger-brown body hair which sits like a doormat across my chest, back, arms and shoulders as well as my legs and, indeed, the soles of my feet. Just recently this preponderance of reasonably soft human fur has been joined by some coarser cousins in my ears and nostrils and, when viewed in profile together with my receding forehead and heavily set eyebrows, does tend to present a rather unlikely modern man.

As a longstanding member of the Fell Runners Association there is nothing I like better than to run through the ancient oak woods and peat bogs of Yorkshire in England and, when the spirit takes me, to sing the odd song. Fellow runners suggest that these are mere grunts and howls of a primeval nature.

I am thrilled when I spot on the hilltops a rabbit or mountain hare and have been known to leave the race at hand to pursue with great glee these small edible creatures as if driven by an uncontrollable but integral part of my inner self. I have no great interest in the comforts and high-technology of modern life and am quite content sleeping beneath the stars or wandering over rocky crag and green dale.

Over the last few months there have been many occasions when I have been pursued by vicious-looking dogs who moments before seeing me were happily enjoying a juicy bone or playing with their master's toddler. My wife has suggested that one possible explanation is that I probably look and smell rather primitive to the dogs and consequently their own natures revert to those times long ago when wolves and tribal man were sworn enemies. In short, she has suggested I may be a throwback to a more ancient time. I am inclined to agree with her!

If then you wish to meet with me for the purposes of an interview and an assessment for validation purposes, confirming my status as an individual displaying the physical and certain cultural traits of early Neanderthal man or perhaps even an example of Dinanthropoides nivalis, then please contact me as soon as is conveniently possible. I am more than happy to appear at your museum as an exhibit.

I thank you for your time and kind consideration of this letter of enquiry.
Sincerely

Michael A. Lee

Ipswich Borough Council Museums & Galleries High Street Ipswich IP1 3QH
Telephone: 01473 433550   Facsimile: 01473 433558
Email: museums.service@ipswich.gov.uk   Website: www.ipswich.gov.uk
Minicom: 01473 432526

Please ask for:

Our Ref: David Lampard

Directline: DJL/JRF [5.3.1]
              22 July 2002

IPSWICH
BOROUGH
COUNCIL

Tim Heyburn
BA PGCE AMA
Head of Museums

Mr M A Lee
Somewhere in West Yorkshire

Dear Mr Lee

Thank you for your letter regarding your status as "The long lost missing link". Unfortunately I do not feel that I have the necessary expertise to comment on your status as I am a marine biologist by training. Also Ipswich Museum does not possess the resources to carry out the more detailed study that your case warrants. At the least this seems to suggest some sort of DNA analysis by a larger institution.

However you have raised a few interesting points. You do not say between what species that you believe you are the long lost missing link between. There are a number of possibilities; the Neanderthals for example are a distinct species and there is only some recent slightly controversial suggestions that they possibly interbred with modern humans in Spain. There are a number of other hominid ancestors, however recreating their physical attributes is a theoretical business.

However it is well known that humans share more than 90% of our genetic material with the other primates and the Orang Utan for example has coarse orangey hair, although it is relatively slow moving and tends to be vegetarian.

Have you discovered whether any other people in Huddersfield have developed the same characteristics? your condition may be part of a local cluster and other examples may allow some sort of statistical analysis to be carried out.

Unfortunately Huddersfield is outside of our collecting area and we are unable to take up your suggestion of appearing as an exhibit. Have you tried museums nearer to your home area. The other problem is that we do not have a licence to exhibit live specimens. Our other specimens are of course stuffed and mounted, which is a permanent, not to say drastic step to take.

I am sorry that I cannot help you any further with your quest. However, good luck in your search.

Yours sincerely

David J Lampard

David Lampard
(*Keeper Natural Sciences*)
Ipswich Borough Council Museums Service

Animal Welfare
Benefits
Housing Advisory Services
Ipswich Borough Homes
Local Tax
Sport and Play
Strategic Planning & Regeneration

This information can be made
available on audio tape, braille or
alternative formats upon request
from the above telephone number

Chief Executive: James D Hehir
Directors: Laurence Collins, Tracey Lee, Michael J Palmer
Printed on environmentally friendly paper

Somewhere in West Yorkshire
5 July 2002

Professor Ian Tracey
Chorus Master
Royal Liverpool Philharmonic
Hope Street
Liverpool L1 9BP

Dear Professor

I am writing to you as part of my quest for an unusual item; namely a 'human dawn chorus' here in the garden of my home in Huddersfield.

Despite the fact that the English summer has numerous days that begin very early in the morning with the first hint of light at 4.00 a.m., when magnificent dawn choruses are provided by every neighbourhood bird with an ear and beak for music, I inevitably sleep through the entertainment and wake around 7.00 a.m. Should I wake any earlier I fear that my sleep deficit would interfere with my demanding work and make the already stretching challenges a more difficult burden to bear.

Unfortunately, this has meant the development of a profound and ongoing sense of loss as I have been missing out on what I believe can be a most uplifting and almost spiritual winged concert. I am now looking for viable and more conveniently timed reproductions. It is in this regard that I write to your good self as primary contact for the Royal Liverpool Philharmonic.

I wondered if there might be a chance that the accomplished members of your choir could put some time aside early one morning in the next few weeks, travel over to my garden in Huddersfield and sing a selection of appropriate harmonious songs to which I might awake with pleasure and contentment. Perhaps the choir could begin with 'Morning has Broken', move on to the old favourite, 'Sunshine on my Shoulder', and finish the medley with 'The Leaving of Liverpool'.

Although I am not a wealthy man and cannot offer any financial reward for such a favour, I can guarantee endless coffee and croissants and I assume that many of the neighbours will join with me in astonished applause as they look out of their bedroom windows to see 116 choir members singing to their hearts' content on my back lawn.

I have no doubt that you are inundated with many requests of this kind and so I thank you for your time and kind consideration in relation to this matter.

Sincerely

Michael A. Lee
P.S. There is usually ample parking capacity for your coaches and minibuses at the side of the road at the top of the cul-de-sac in which the house is situated.
P.P.S. Please let me know approximately how many croissants you will require.

Mr M A Lee
Somewhere in West Yorkshire

12 July 2002

Dear Mr Lee,

Thank you for your letter. The RLPC is indeed inundated with requests but I am bound to say that this is the first time we have been asked to provide a 'dawn chorus'.

After careful consideration of the logistical implications of such a venture, and the possibility that your neighbours may not greet the musical offering with quite the same degree of enthusiasm as yourself, despite the very tempting offer of coffee and croissants I am afraid that we will have to refuse.

As an alternative, may I suggest that you acquire recordings of the choir and set one track up to begin playing at 7am - that way you could ring the changes from day to day, even introducing a seasonal touch at Christmas time. Or as a last resort, you might be able to find a local choir - I believe there is a Choral Society in Huddersfield itself.

With many thanks and best wishes,

As ever,

Professor Ian Tracey
Chorus Master

Philharmonic Hall
Hope Street, Liverpool L1 9BP

Telephone +44(0)151 210 2895
Facsimile +44(0)151 210 2902
Box Office +44(0)151 709 3789

ISDN +44(0)151 709 8746
info@liverpoolphil.com
www.liverpoolphil.com

Patron Her Majesty the Queen
Music Director Gerard Schwarz
Chairman Professor Peter Toyne
Chief Executive Michael Elliott

Royal Liverpool Philharmonic Society
Founded 1840
A company limited by guarantee
Registered in England number 886195
Charity number 230518

The Head Chef
The Savoy
The Strand
London WC2R 0EU

Dear Sir

I am writing to you as part of my quest for an unusual item; namely information about purchasing some rare and specific types of food for my forthcoming Roman Toga Party.

As an accomplished and creative chef, I thought that you would be a good starting point for my enquiries and will perhaps be able to throw some light on the supply of some of the commodities described below.

Ever since leaving grammar school almost 25 years ago in the days when Latin and Roman Civilisation were, quite rightly, part of the syllabus, I have been fascinated by the cuisine and delicacies of the ancient world. This partly explains my motives for organising a toga party here in Huddersfield and also for seeking to set out a banquet that would do justice even to the palates of emperors and kings. It is in this respect that I would be grateful for your help and advice.

I thought that it would be a good idea to begin my Roman era entertainment with a selection of dormice dipped in honey, larks' tongues marinated in olive oil and pearls dissolved in vinegar, all of which I have read about in various history books. This will be followed by a choice of refreshing sea-urchin soufflé or rabbit-testicle soup accompanied by a good-quality Chianti wine.

In the tradition of the Emperor Caligula, this lavish feast of extravagance and culinary excellence will then proceed to a main course beyond belief; a whole roasted donkey stuffed with apples and grapes with parsnips in its ears, set upon a silver-plated platter. There will doubtless also be copious amounts of red Italian wines available at this stage as well as a light side salad.

I am not sure whether my guests will have very much room left for a dessert after this meal with a difference but I will nevertheless supply ice-cream, just in case. Plain strawberry will probably suffice.

It is with respect to the purchase of these ancient, mouth-watering and nutritional foodstuffs that I write. I am not sure whether I might be able to find most of the above in a typical supermarket delicatessen or pre-packed foreign meals section or whether I might need to search further afield. I dare say you deal with enquiries such as mine on a regular basis, and so may I say many thanks indeed for your time and kind consideration. I look forward to hearing from you in the very near future with appropriate advice and helpful suggestions if convenient.

Sincerely

M. A. Lee

Michael A. Lee

Mr M A Lee
Somewhere in West Yorkshire

The Savoy
Strand, London WC2R OEU
Telephone (020) 7856 4343
Facsimile (020) 7240 6040
E-mail info@the-savoy.co.uk
Web site www.savoy-group.co.uk

Reservations
Telephone (020) 7420 2500
Facsimile (020) 7872 8901

15th July 2002

Dear Michael,

Thank you for recent letter dated 7th July.

Unfortunately I am due to go on holiday in the next few days and would not have the time to give you the exact details that you are after.

But I do know the difficulty of designing menus for all kinds of occasions. I can therefore recommend a very useful book called 'The Book of Ingredients' by Phillip Dowell and Adrian Bailey.

I hope that this is some use to you and good luck for your event!

Warmest regards and wishes,

Anton Edelmann
Maître Chef des Cuisine

The Savoy Hotel
Registered in En
No. 5669255
Registered Offic:
1 Savoy Hill
London WC2R 0F

Head of Customer Services
London Art Co UK Ltd
44 Deepdene Road
London SE5 8EG

Dear Sir/Madam

I am writing to you as part of my quest for an unusual item; namely a 'picture of health'.

Aged 42, I have just began to reach that stage of life where, after many years of cross-country and fell running, my knees creak in a most terrible fashion and my back is as stiff as a board each and every morning.

Whether stress is partly to blame or whether it has more to do with the ravages of age I am not sure, but I am now also as bald as the proverbial coot and possess a face like a dried out wash-leather.

I have far less energy than I did twenty years ago, sleep less predictably and rarely feel refreshed as I go about my daily duties at home and at work. I am pasty, slightly overweight and suffer from perpetual rhinitis and blocked sinuses. To top it all, my friends and family have begun to suggest that I should not smile at people who do not know me lest they become anxious or even frightened. It is for these reasons that I am writing to you.

If you could supply me with a picture that features the face and figure of someone who represents the antithesis of myself, I could hang it on my bedroom wall as if it were a mirror. Perhaps if I were to look at the depiction of someone blessed with good looks and a youthful physique on a regular basis I might begin to gain a new self-image that just could have a beneficial effect on my present state. If it is true that 'you are what you eat' and 'you are as young as you feel', there may be some truth in the proposition that 'you become what you look at', and an appropriate 'picture of health' might revolutionise my appearance and indeed, my lifestyle.

Since I have tried and been disappointed with most of the alternative methods with supposedly proven rejuvenating abilities, such as eating prunes and cabbage for breakfast, chanting ancient Sumerian incantations and hanging upside down from my landing banisters I decided it was time to move on to more likely options.

I would value your advice enormously.

I have no doubts that you receive many requests of this kind on a regular basis and so I thank you for your time and kind consideration and look forward to hearing from you in the near future.

Sincerely

Michael A. Lee

London Art Co UK Ltd
24 Deepdene Road
London
SE5 8EG
Tel: 020 7738 3867
Mobile 07711 952808
e-mail: paul.wynter@londonart.co.uk
www.londonart.co.uk

www.londonart.co.uk

Mr M A Lee
Somewhere in West Yorkshire

19th July, 2002

Dear Michael,

Thanks for your letter, I scan sympathize with much of it, especially the blocked sinuses. Having hit 40 myself this year and with three kids to chase around - life certainly does not get any easier.

I'd love to help find someone to paint your portrait, Most of our Artists like to work from photographs so a sitting may not be necessary. Two that spring to mind are **Escha Van Den Bogerd** and **Alan Graham Dick**. Escha lives in Holland (so only works from photographs) she creates wonderful abstract backgrounds and does seem to flatter her subjects, she's also not expensive at between £340 and £600 depending on what sort of size you would like. Alan has painted some wonderful portraits of some of our clients, he also works from photographs but insists on taking them himself, he's Scottish and older so may well sympathize with your needs. He is however much more expensive as he's relatively well known, his fees are between £1,600 and £6,800.

Do let me know your email address and I would be delighted to send you some sample images of their work. They can of course be found on our website.

Haven't sent a letter in years.

Best wishes

Paul Wynter
Managing Director.

Registration no 3373771, Registered office; 187 High Street, Tonbridge, Kent, TN9 1BX.
VAT no 730705655

Head of Customer Services
Shoenet
17 Manderwell Road
Leicester LE2 5LR

Dear Sir/Madam

I am writing to you as part of my quest for an unusual item; namely some advice and perhaps even evidence regarding the survival of shoes after their physical demise.

On the basis that shoes have souls I recently began to wonder whether, after their heels have worn down, their leather or other material uppers have become hopelessly thin and the time has arrived for their departure to the bin, they actually make a spiritual transformation into a different dimension.

Surely it is conceivable that the innumerable items of footwear that have provided their wearers with practical and comfortable service over the years might, as their laces are undone one last time, cross the boundaries of life as we know it and travel to a so-called shoe heaven?!

On this basis, I wondered if you might have any information about occasions when owners of a particularly well-loved pair of brogues or suede shoes, slippers or snakeskin boots, have experienced anything like a paranormal event when the time has come for the disposal of their footwear. Such events may well have been reported by refuse collectors or those who scour skips and tips for used bargains.

Have there, for example, been documented cases of people returning home from work to see the ghostly shape of their previously owned slip-ons sitting happily beneath the telephone table where they were always to be found before they fell apart and were thrown on the November bonfire?

Are there any occasions when objects have been kicked mysteriously around a house as if a pair of jealous working boots, ousted from the home many months earlier, were communicating their outrage at the appearance of a pair of new and adequate successors?

Could it be that the tongues we once thought permanently irreparable are actually wagging throughout eternity and the eyelets we considered closed for threading as open in their new dimension as the day they were made?

Doubtless you will receive many enquiries such as this and so I thank you for your time and consideration and look forward to hearing from you in the very near future.

Sincerely

Michael A. Lee

Livingston & Doughty Ltd. *Inc. ShoeNet*

17 Mandervell Road
Oadby
Leicester
LE2 5LR

Mr M A Lee
Somewhere in West Yorkshire

16th July 2002.

Dear Mr. Lee,

We thank you for your letter of 14th July 2002 but regret
that we cannot help you as we have no evidence of the survival of shoes
in the after-life!

However, we have some fine shoes on our Website and hope that
you will purchase a pair to give you lasting satisfaction in this life!

Yours sincerely,
for LIVINGSTON & DOUGHTY LTD.

Managing Director.

WORLDWIDE SUPPLIERS TO THE SHOE INDUSTRY **Registered in England 80205**
Telephone: 44(0)116 271 4221 Fax: 44(0)116 271 6977 E-mail: orders@shoenet.co.uk
Established over one hundred years

205

Head of Customer Services
Aqualisa Products Ltd
The Flyer's Way
Westerham
Kent TN16 1DE

Dear Sir/Madam

I am writing to you as part of my quest for an unusual item; namely a shower head with a full complement of hair.

Having recently returned from northern France where I spent a rather relaxing two weeks with my family on our annual holiday, it occurred to me that the shower head I used in the bathroom of our rented holiday cottage, like most of the shower heads I have used at home, at the houses of friends and in hotels, was, in effect 'bald'.

If it were not that I am also as bald as the proverbial coot I do not suppose that such follically challenged shower heads would cause me particular concern. But since I am, I frequently note with great anxiety that looking at round, shiny, hairless shower heads during my daily ablutions reminds me of my own ageing state and creates a significant sense of anguish and sadness within the very depths of my being.

It is for this reason that I write to you as a well-established and well-known purveyor of shower-related hardware. If anyone can help me I am convinced it will be you. I would be most grateful, therefore, if you could advice me regarding the availability of alternative shower heads that possess a jolly good head of hair.

Although as a child my own hair was ginger in colour, with a tendency to wave a little when long, I am actually quite flexible when it comes to the colour and style of shower head hair if the current range is restricted. Indeed, a curly Afro-style shower head would be as acceptable to me as one modelling a longer, straighter hippy look, provided the item in question is fully functional and its bare top is completely hidden.

Doubtless you receive many requests along similar lines to this and so I thank you for your time and kind consideration and look forward to hearing from you with appropriate advice in the very near future.

Sincerely

M. A. Lee .

Michael A. Lee
P.S. Do you also provide hats for shower heads in order to keep the hairy ones dry when in use?

AQUALISA PRODUCTS LIMITED
THE FLYER'S WAY · WESTERHAM · KENT TN16 1DE · TELEPHONE: (01959) 560000 · FAX: (01959) 560009
www.aqualisa.co.uk

12th August 2002

Mr M A Lee
Somewhere in West Yorkshire

Dear Mr Lee

Thank you for your letter of 6th August 2002.

Your quest is indeed unusual. As you indicate in your letter, we are a well established manufacturer and supplier of showering products and certainly not a hair today gone tomorrow business. However, our range does not currently contain hairy showers. To be brutally frank, it is not an option for which we have much demand.

I enclose a copy of our current product brochure. These are all of the bald variety although you may find something there you like. If not, may I suggest a wig shop?

Yours sincerely

Martyn Brown

Martyn Brown
Customer Service Manager

Enc

Registered Office: Pentagon House, Sir Frank Whittle Road, Derby DE21 4XA   Registered in England No. 1281596
Ultimate Holding Company   Baxi Group Ltd

Somewhere in West Yorkshire
14 August 2002

Customer Service Manager
Furniture 123 Ltd
Sandway Business Centre
Shannon Street
Leeds LS9 8SS

Dear Sir/Madam

I am writing to you as part of my quest for an unusual item; namely the traditional 'ducking stool' that I read about in a recent magazine article on rebellious and awkward wives. As a well-established supplier of various types of stools, I thought that you would be the ideal organisation to which I could write as a useful starting point.

My reference books tell me that the 'ducking stool' was used widely in centuries past as a chair on which disorderly women were seated and subsequently ducked beneath the waters of a pond or lake as suitable punishment for breaking rules and regulations and presenting themselves as trouble-makers and nuisances.

When I read about this superb piece of furniture I immediately decided that life would never again be complete for me without a similar item for use when my own wife is giving me grief and will not toe the line. This happens regularly!

I would be most grateful therefore if you could send details to me of your full range of 'ducking stools' and any literature you might have on strapping and restraining techniques associated with ensuring those seated in these wonderful pieces of ancient woodcraft cannot escape from their deserved and educational submersions.

Many thanks indeed for your time and consideration and I look forward to hearing from you in the very near future.

Sincerely

M. A. Lee

Michael A. Lee

Date: 16/08/2002

Our ref. enquiry

Mr M A Lee
Somewhere in West Yorkshire

Dear Mr Lee

Thank you for you letter dated 14th August. I have had a look through our website and our manufacturers catalogues and I'm afraid we don't have anything resembling a Ducking stool.

I guess we all have a use for such an item at some time or other so if you do find one please let us know!

Best of luck.

Kind Regards

Jonathan Seal
Customer Services Manager
Furniture 123 Ltd.

Furniture 123 Ltd, Sandway Business Centre, Shannon Street, Leeds LS9 8SS
Tel: 0113 248 2233 Fax: 0113 248 2266 Email: info@furniture123.co.uk Website: www.furniture123.co.uk
Registered in England and Wales. Company No 2696994

Head of English
The University of Bradford
Bradford
West Yorkshire

Dear Sir/Madam

I am writing to you as part of my quest for an unusual item; namely some advice regarding a course of study that might lead to a 'Degree of Comparison' and the possibility of undertaking this at the prestigious University of Bradford.

Ever since I was a small boy I have been interested in comparing the various merits, dimensions and characteristics of innumerable items, objects and creatures within the animal, vegetable and mineral worlds. Had I lived in ancient times I am convinced I would have been the man who invented the vast grammatical array of comparative terms such as 'smaller', 'wider' and 'a great deal more purple' and might well have held the noble title of 'State Comparitor'.

Relative to many of my peers – there I go again – I would estimate my ability at assessing the relation between the majority of things as better than most and at least as good as the remainder. In addition to this long-established skill of objective assessment, that I trust will assure you of my ideal candidacy for the aforementioned degree course, I also have a swimming certificate showing my adequacy at completing a full length in a modern pool. This is surely a more worthy accomplishment than a mere width though admittedly not quite as good as a quarter mile!

Doubtless there will be great interest from many quarters in accessing a course leading to a 'Degree of Comparison' and so I thank you for your time and kind consideration.

I look forward to hearing from you in the very near future.

Sincerely

Michael A. Lee

UNIVERSITY OF BRADFORD

16th August 2002

Mr M A Lee
Somewhere in West Yorkshire

Dear Mr Lee

Your letter of 14th August addressed to the 'Head of English' was delivered to the Language Unit.

I am not sure if we can help you in your quest. Your letter was stranger than many I have seen during my time in the university but not as odd as some.

It will probably come as no surprise that the University of Bradford does not run a 'Degree of Comparison' with the entry requirement of a swimming certificate. However, I am enclosing the current prospectus for the School of Lifelong Education and Development as you may be interested in taking some of the modules offered. You may find some better than others.

Yours sincerely

[signature]

Elspeth Allcock
Administrator

Lang/comparison
UNIVERSITY OF BRADFORD   WEST YORKSHIRE   BD7 1DP   UK
TEL +44 (0)1274 235208/234578   FAX +44 (0)1274 235207
EMAIL langunit@bradford.ac.uk.   www.bradford.ac.uk/acad/langunit

MAKING
KNOWLEDGE
WORK

Head of Customer Services
Dickinson & Morris Ltd
Ye Olde Pork Pie Shoppe
8–10 Nottingham Street
Melton Mowbray
Leicestershire LE13 1NW

Dear Sir/Madam

I am writing to you as part of my quest for an unusual item; namely a substantial supply of 'humble pie'.

Only yesterday my dear wife confronted me after an episode of disagreement around evening meal arrangements, looked straight into my eyes and suggested that I should eat a large portion of 'humble pie'.

To be perfectly frank with you I am not sure whether she was worried that I am not eating sufficiently well at present or whether she thought that a bite of something tasty and nutritious might compensate for our angry words and differences in opinion and thus ameliorate my negative mood.

It is in this regard, therefore, that I am writing to you as a well-established manufacturer and purveyor of pies in an attempt to order the aforementioned pie for consumption as soon as is conveniently possible, assuming, of course, that this type of pie features within your product range.

Although I have seen many, many varieties of pork pie, game pie and indeed apple pie, I have never actually seen or tasted a humble pie and would, as a consequence, be most grateful for your advice and suggestions regards obtaining such.

Doubtless you receive innumerable letters of a similar nature to this and so I am most grateful for your time and kind consideration and I look forward to hearing from you in the very near future.

Sincerely

Michael A. Lee

DICKINSON & MORRIS

ADMINISTRATION

PO BOX 580

LEICESTER LE4 1ZN

TELEPHONE (0116) 235 5900

FAX (0116) 235 5711

E-MAIL dickinson&morris@porkpie.co.uk

www.porkpie.co.uk

DICKINSON & MORRIS

8 - 10 NOTTINGHAM STREET

MELTON MOWBRAY

LEICESTERSHIRE

ENGLAND LE13 1NW

TELEPHONE (01664) 562341

FAX (01664) 568052

Mr M A Lee
Somewhere in West Yorkshire

11th September 2002

Dear Mr Lee,

I am in receipt of your recent letter regarding whether or not we have "humble" pies within our product portfolio.

At Dickinson & Morris we produce not only the Rolls Royce equivalent of pork pies, but probably the finest pork pie in the world. Dickinson & Morris have been baking and selling this delicious English delicacy from Ye Olde Pork Pie Shoppe, in Melton Mowbray, since 1851. Our pies are made with hand-trimmed shoulder and belly of fresh, British pork, seasoned with traditional spices, encased and hand-crimped in a hot water pastry, baked until golden and then jellied with a natural pork bone stock. The resultant pie is a glorious combination of tasty and succulent pork with a rich and crunchy crust.

We therefore think that this would make it a good contender for a "humble" pie, being nutritious, satisfying and excellent value for money. I have enclosed a copy our brochure, should you wish to sample one.

Yours sincerely,

ANDREA TOMLIN
BRAND MANAGER

BORN AND RAISED IN MELTON MOWBRAY

REGISTERED OFFICE: CHETWODE HOUSE, LEICESTER ROAD, MELTON MOWBRAY, LEICESTERSHIRE.   LE13 1GA. REGISTERED NO. 03116767 ENGLAND

Dickinson & Morris is a division of Samworth Brothers Limited.

Samworth Brothers

213

Epilogue ...

It is with a certain degree of light-hearted disappointment that I must tell you of my abject failure in acquiring a single specific product, title or membership as a consequence of my many letters enquiring after impossible items.

Granted, I did receive a box of sweets from Nestle and a selection of hairs from the dog groomers brushes at the RSPCA and Battersea Dogs Home but these did not really resemble either the chocolate fireguard or the hangover cure I had initially envisaged.

However, there is always a silver lining to even the darkest of clouds, a ray of hope in the dingiest of dungeons and a hint of water beneath the sands of even the driest deserts.

Indeed, in collecting together the myriad letters and replies that comprised my unusual quest for that 'elusive thing' I have acquired the material for the second section of this very book.

Perhaps there is nothing unusual about a book per se but this, I am sure you will agree, is very unusual one indeed and so, serendipitously, my quest was actually realised.

This section of the book represents a product that has been created from the parts designed to find a product.

Something was ventured and something has been gained.

Implausible Complaints ...

HRH Prince Charles
Buckingham Palace
London

Dear Sir

I am writing you a letter of complaint.

In early April of this year I wrote to your father, HRH The Duke of Edinburgh, asking whether I might acquire membership of the Order of The Bath. Sadly, and to my extreme annoyance, my letter remains unanswered. Perhaps you would be so good as to point out his oversight in responding to me when you next sit down to enjoy a glass of port together?! In the light of such an absence of communication as regards the aforementioned matter, I have duly decided that you might be the ideal person to whom I should address my enquiries instead.

As a committed and devoted father of two small and energetic sons aged two and five, I find myself early each evening issuing orders with regard to the urgency of commencing the bathing process. As the father of two sons yourself, you will doubtless appreciate that the implementation of such orders is often both challenging and indeed time-consuming, particularly when, in my case, both of my heirs have recently discovered the principles of early anarchism and temporarily refuse to comply with instructions.

Having mentioned the inherent difficulties of bath-time management, however, I am pleased to say that the process is normally completed to the reasonable satisfaction of everyone concerned and the boys are put to bed in a clean and orderly state. On the basis of such success, therefore, I wondered if I might be considered for membership of the aforementioned Order of the Bath and perhaps with time even aspire to become a 'Deputy Night Commander'.

Once again I thank you for your time and kind consideration and look forward to hearing from you in the very near future.

Sincerely

M. A. Lee

Michael A. Lee

From: The Private Secretary to HRH The Prince of Wales

Tuesday, 11th June 2002

Dee K. Lee

Thank you for your letter of 31 May to The Prince of Wales.

Membership of the Order of the Bath is an honour granted, particularly to members of the Armed Services, for outstanding service to the Crown. I hope you will understand, therefore, why your letter is not something to which His Royal Highness would be able to respond.

I am sure, however, that His Royal Highness would want me to pass on to you and your family his best personal wishes.

Yours ever

Stephen Lamport

Michael Lee Esq.

217

Head of Consumer Relations
A Large Tissue Company
Somewhere in the South of England
(Who wishes to remain anonymous!)

Dear Sir/Madam

I am writing you a letter of complaint.

Despite the availability of a wide range of tissues, many of which are manufactured and supplied by your good selves, I am currently frustrated in my search to find and procure a type of tissue that will 'wipe the smile off a face'.

Doubtless you will agree that within any organisation involving a variety of individuals whose aspirations and personalities range from the sublime to the ridiculous, there usually exist a host of social and inter-personal challenges that need to be addressed by everyone concerned. Fortunately many of the processes required by such challenges are relatively simple to initiate and most people manage to work with a reasonable degree of collaboration.

It is with a great sense of regret, however, that I admit ultimate defeat in my dealings with one particular character within my present place of occupation. This certain individual happens to possess an insincere smile that is wider than that of the Cheshire Cat in the story Alice in Wonderland and brings as much joy to those around as Ivan the Terrible did to his victims. This fixed excuse for an expression of goodwill and contentment has, in the course of the last year, curdled milk in the office fridge and caused the wallpaper to peel off the walls in desperation.

I myself have taken to wearing darkened sunglasses on even the gloomiest of days simply as an aid to avoiding all the details of a smile that could solidify melted butter in the middle of the Sahara Desert and would easily persuade the most resilient of heroes to cry in a horrible and distressing fashion. Even the postman turns and runs when he catches sight of the aforementioned individual and often before delivering the post!

It is for these understandable reasons that I come to you for help and information. Should you have advice with reference to tissues that can wipe the smile off the face of the archetypal Beelzebub, I, and a team of many, would be most grateful indeed.

Many thanks for your time and kind consideration and I look forward to hearing from you in the very near future.

Sincerely

Michael A. Lee

Head of Consumer Relations
'A Large Tissue Company'
Somewhere in the South of England

20 June 2002

Mr M A Lee
Somewhere in West Yorkshire

Dear Mr Lee

Thank you for your recent letter of complaint regards your difficulty in obtaining an unusual type of tissue.

I have pondered long and hard about the challenge you have posed and guess that much depends upon the type of face and the characteristics of the smile concerned. The prospect of applying our tissues to a fiendish leer probably presents more challenges than those of a supercilious smile as the contours would create fewer problems if the face is smoother and less strained. Nevertheless I can, I think, offer a potential solution.

As a well-established company involved in the manufacture and sales of multipurpose tissues we at 'A Large Tissue Company' strive to produce tissues that are as soft as possible. Softness is one of the key attributes demanded by our customers, whether using kitchen towel, toilet tissue or – more appropriately in your case – facial tissue. The fact that softness is achieved with great effort – R&D work, special technology, exotic machinery, special materials et al – means that with very little effort it would be possible to create a product that is far from soft.

In short, the use of a strong, harshly creped tissue, which could be easily made on many of the machines in our possession, could solve your problem. If applied vigorously and continuously to any face, it would be easily capable of removing the face itself, let alone the smile attached to it, and by applying a little care the smile alone could be disposed of, leaving the rest of the visage relatively unaffected.

The use of softer tissues would be less effective in this respect and would require substantial time involving extended rubbing but, as evidenced by the end of one's nose during a heavy cold, even soft tissue will eventually cause erosion to begin.

I enclose a sample of the roughest tissue we currently have at hand but declare that we can bear no responsibility for any change in facial appearances that occurs to your colleague as a result of the use of such.

Sincerely

John Doe Esq.

Head of Complaints
H. J. Heinz Company Ltd
South Building
Hayes Park
Hayes
Middlesex UB4 8AL

Dear Sir/Madam

I am writing you a letter of complaint.

For quite some time now I have been searching for a generous amount of 'canned laughter' and am tremendously annoyed and frustrated at my failure to procure such a commodity to date.

I have written to various people in a number of organisations, including your own, on several occasions but, alas, have received little in the way of advice or satisfactory help and am thus turning to you in heartfelt desperation.

Having spent almost half a career involved in industry and in the world of the sales fast lane, I have often experienced occasions when my environment has been starved of fun and humour and where my fellow employees are so exhausted with their efforts that the mustering of a little levity is a near-impossible objective to achieve. Doubtless the phenomenon of feeling flat is one that innumerable individuals are familiar with across many types of occupation, and the desire for a lifting of the spirit and the injection of humour is a common need. It is in this regard that I write to you today.

As a large, well-established company within the food industry, known far and wide for your manufacture and distribution of excellent food items such as your world-famous beans and soups, I have recently decided that you might well be the beacon of hope in my dark and unproductive quest for the aforementioned cheering commodity, namely cans filled with joyous inspiration. I have no doubt that if anyone knew who may have mastered the art of placing laughter in a tin, it would be your good selves at H. J. Heinz Company Limited.

Should you be able to advise me with regard to the procurement of, or actually provide me with a couple of crates of canned laughter, I will endeavour to carry with me each day a number adequate to ensure that there is always a facility at my workplace for opening up a microcosm of happiness and releasing it into otherwise downbeat and sometimes depressed circumstances.

It will indeed be gratifying to see faces light up with immediate and spontaneous smiles, to hear the noise of instant chuckles issuing from hitherto bored and joyless colleagues, and to experience the startling but reassuring effusion of a guffaw that has just found its freedom.

In short, I am looking forward to obtaining food for the heart in a conveniently packaged form that will be appreciated by everyone who comes into contact with its refreshing and spiritually nutritious contents.

Many thanks indeed for your time and kind consideration in this matter and I look forward to hearing from you in the very near future.

Sincerely

Michael A. Lee

P.S. Would you also be able to supply can-openers?

H. J. Heinz Company Limited

South Building
Hayes Park
Hayes
Middlesex UB4 8AL
England

Tel: +44(0) 20-8573-7757
Fax: +44(0) 20-8848-2325
www.heinz.co.uk

Mr. M. A. Lee
Somewhere in West Yorkshire

18th September, 2002

Dear Mr. Lee,

Thank you for your enquiry.

Every year, we receive hundreds of requests for financial help or the supply of goods. Because our donations budget is severely stretched, it is not always possible to co-operate and we would ask to be excused on this occasion.

Yours sincerely,

Adele Mannering
Trust Administrator

Registered Office: South Building Hayes Park Hayes Middlesex UB4 8AL England

Registered London. No 147624

Somewhere in West Yorkshire
10 September 2002

The Archbishop of Canterbury
Lambeth Palace
London SE1 7JU

Dear Sir

I am writing you a letter of complaint. As I drove, last Tuesday, from Huddersfield towards the village of Holmfirth along a winding country road, I found myself held up somewhat by a slow-moving tractor and was unable to overtake this vehicle directly in front of me due to the sharp bends in the road that obscured a view of possible oncoming traffic.

Deciding to adopt a stoical view of my journey, I switched on the radio and found myself listening to a radio personality interviewing a well-known clergyman. As you will shortly understand, this was a rather serendipitous development which one might say set the scene for what occurred next.

Just as the radio interview came to its conclusion with a rousing and inspirational hymn, the tractor that I had been following for approximately fifteen minutes suddenly and without any prior warning turned into a field. There was no prior indication that this was to be the case!

As you will doubtless appreciate, I was completely unprepared for such a turn of events and, needless to say, was somewhat shaken.

Not only did I have to slam on the brakes with a consequential skid but when I stopped the car and turned around to double-check the reality of what I had experienced, there was absolutely no sign of the tractor ever having existed, only a large field of grass partly obscured by a modest wall-side woodland copse. (Doesn't the recounting of such a strange, albeit true, story make one's spine tingle?!)

As you will surely appreciate, my letter to your good selves within the Church is an attempt to find a rational and perhaps even a theological explanation for such an unusual occurrence, at the same time as venting my frustration that a revelation as regards the existence of such a profound mystery has not been made more apparent by the Church already.

Since the Magic Circle was unable to help in my enquiries, I thought that I ought to write to you as the Head of the Church of England to ask if there may be an element of the supernatural at work here and to seek any words of advice and comfort you might offer to me in this matter.

Many thanks indeed, and should you be able to shed any light on this mysterious happening, I will look forward to hearing from you in the near future.
Sincerely

M. A. Lee

Michael A. Lee
P.S. I also have concerns for the driver of the tractor. If the tractor turned into a field, could the driver have turned into a turnip? It is all so very worrying.

LAMBETH PALACE

Mr Andrew Nunn
Lay Assistant to
The Archbishop of Canterbury

Mr M A Lee
Somewhere in West Yorkshire

12 September 2002

Dear Mr Lee

The Archbishop of Canterbury is overseas at the moment and so I have been asked to write thanking you for the letter you wrote on 10 September and to reply.

I am happy to confirm that there is nothing unusual about a tractor turning off a road and into a field.
Neither – sadly – is there anything unusual about it doing so without prior warning.

With best wishes

Lambeth Palace, London SE1 7JU

Dr P. Faulkner
Fieldhead Surgery
Leymoor Road
Golcar
Huddersfield HD7 4QQ

Dear Dr Faulkner

I am writing to you with a worrying complaint.

The complaint in question rests upon an unusual range of symptoms that have recently emerged reference my general gripping and clasping abilities and I would therefore greatly appreciate any comments and suggestions you might have in this regard.

As you know from our previous conversations in the surgery, I have for some time been aware that I have not been able to grasp facts as I ought nor seize opportunities as I should, although I have thankfully been able to snatch the odd conversation here and there where time permits.

It seems now that these challenges are becoming more complex and I have found myself involuntarily clutching at straws and having to get a grip of myself as a consequence of the anxieties these rather atypical presentations cause me. I fear that I am now either all thumbs or, more seriously, simply do not have my finger on the pulse at all.

I am, as ever, placing myself in your most capable diagnostic hands and look forward to hearing from you in the near future with appropriate advice and possible treatment options.

Sincerely

M. A. Lee .

Michael A. Lee

FIELDHEAD SURGERY
Dr. PETER FAULKNER
Dr. MICHAEL WALLWORK
Dr. SHEILA BENETT
Dr. JAN SAMBROOK
Dr. STEVEN JOYNER

FIELD HEAD
LEYMOOR ROAD
GOLCAR
HUDDERSFIELD
HD7 4QQ
Tele: (01484) 654504
Fax: (01484) 460296

e-mail addresses:-
Our Ref; PF/kg   pete.faulkner@gp-b85051.nhs.uk   mike.wallwork@gp-b85051.nhs.uk   sheila.benett@gp-b85051.nhs.uk
jan.sambrook@gp-b85051.nhs.uk   steve.joyner@gp-b85051.nhs.uk

14th January, 2003

Mr. M. A. Lee
Somewhere in West Yorkshire

Dear Mr. Lee,

I must apologise for my tardy reply to your letter of 3rd January 2003, but it only appeared in my in-tray on the 9th January 2003.

I am interested to read that you have been having difficulties in your "general gripping and grasping abilities". I really feel you ought to pull yourself together and take notice of my comments.

It is clear that your inability to "grasp facts" is due to the gross intellectual deficit from which you suffer. The inability to "seize opportunities" must be partly due to the delusional beliefs that you have, that people are actually prepared to offer you opportunities to gain advantage. There is nothing to suggest that there are any opportunities for you in this life.

I was greatly concerned to hear that you had been able to "snatch the odd conversation here and there", as I am not aware that anybody has deigned to actually engage you in conversation; this is notable when I see people pointing at you in the road and tending to cross the street to avoid you.

The challenges which you describe are indeed becoming more complex and I am surprised to hear that you are "clutching at straws", having told you on many occasions that drinking beer without the use of a straw is probably healthier for you in the long run. This method of drinking may have consequences in not being able to "get a grip of myself" – I was rather hoping that you would be able to use the gripping of one's self as a private issue.

As for having your "finger on the pulse", this is assuming that you are actually a living, sapient being and have a pulse at all. This in fact being the case, I would suggest some anatomy lessons to locate the pulse in the first place. As for you being "all thumbs", well I feel this is a load of pollex.

I am afraid that your sad life continues. I am happy to help in which ever way you would suggest, but feel it only right to point out my limited abilities when faced with such a hapless creature.

Yours sincerely,

Dr. P. Faulkner.

226

Dr P. Faulkner
Fieldhead Surgery
Leymoor Road
Golcar
Huddersfield HD7 4QQ

Dear Dr Faulkner

I am writing to you with another complaint.

Just last Thursday I was preparing myself for my night-time slumber when my wife kindly informed me that a bilateral muscle particularly concentrated above my hip regions was clearly evident and in a way which affected the measurement of my actual waist by a tape measure. I was absolutely astonished.

Although I have been working out in the gym frequently and eating a rather substantial amount of muscle-building food, I had no idea that this would lead to the production of such muscle in the aforementioned parts of my well-toned body.

Having referred to a number of medical and anatomical textbooks in which all known muscle groups are described and defined, I was at a loss to locate the muscle I have so obviously developed over the last few weeks and so decided to write to you as an eminent GP to ask where I should lodge my startling and exciting discovery.

As you would doubtless expect, I have actually named this newfound muscle in the old-fashioned tradition of utilising Latin names and have decided on Flabbius maximus, although I do have some reservation that this may have already been used as a lead character in a poem by Catullus or an epic by Virgil. (I will check this out with the Professor of Classical Studies at Huddersfield University!)

I would be most grateful if you could advise me whether the discovery and naming of this muscle is something that will require patenting and if so, whom I should contact in this regard.

I would also be interested to know if you have had any prior knowledge of this muscle, and whether there is any treatment to decrease its unsightly mass and reduce the folds and wrinkles contained therein.

Sincerely and in anticipation

M. A. Lee .

Michael A. Lee

FIELDHEAD SURGERY
Dr. PETER FAULKNER
Dr. MICHAEL WALLWORK
Dr. SHEILA BENETT
Dr. JAN SAMBROOK
Dr. STEVEN JOYNER

FIELD HEAD
LEYMOOR ROAD
GOLCAR
HUDDERSFIELD
HD7 4QQ
Tele: (01484) 654504
Fax: (01484) 460296

e-mail addresses:-

Our Ref; PF/kg   pete.faulkner@gp-b85051.nhs.uk   mike.wallwork@gp-b85051.nhs.uk   sheila.benett@gp-b85051.nhs.uk
jan.sambrook@gp-b85051.nhs.uk   steve.joyner@gp-b85051.nhs.uk

20th January, 2003

Mr. M. A. Lee
Somewhere in West Yorkshire

Dear Mr. Lee,

Many thanks for your letter of 13th January 2003. I find the contents of your letter most interesting and have to wonder about your powers of personal observation. It is extraordinary that it was only your wife that noticed that you had these protuberances above your hip regions. I can only assume that the prominences to which you refer are extremely subtle and visible only in certain amounts of light. I can reassure you that these are well recognised areas and your ingestion of muscle building foods and working out at the gym will probably have little effect on the appearance of these areas.

I am afraid that you have made the assumption that this tissue is actually of muscular origin and as I have only your opinion that your body is "well toned", I feel duty bound to inform you that this tissue was probably of adipose nature, rather than muscle. The name flabbius maximus is an interesting one for this tissue and I am sure is equally applicable to both muscular and adipose tissue. Flabbius may indeed have been a lead character in a poem by Catullus or an epic by Virgil, but I have not read many Thunderbird's texts of late.

I have also to inform you that the tissue to which you refer is well known to the female of the species and in a way of trying to not hurt their partner's feelings, the colloquial term of "love handles" has been applied to this tissue. This can be put in to classic terms, for example 'cupide grippi' or 'grabaflabbius amore'.

It is possible that this tissue has appeared on yourself over relatively recent years, due to the fact that you have now passed the magic age of 40 and have stated to ingest large amount of foaming brown liquid. The effect may be in the future to produce not only an excess of the said tissue, but also the appearance of the dreaded floppius minimus. I would certainly advise you to be careful on the amounts therefore taken.

In short, I feel that you would be not pursuing fruitful pastures to try and have this area named "flabbius maximus" and just accept that it is and always will be a part of the male anatomy of middle age which helps to make most bodies of that age unattractive to the female species.

Yours sincerely,

Dr. P. Faulkner.

Dr P. Faulkner
Fieldhead Surgery
Leymoor Road
Golcar
Huddersfield HD7 4QQ

Dear Dr Faulkner

I am writing you yet another letter of complaint.

For many years now I have experienced a phase of creativity that has provided me with a certain freedom of thinking and reflection. Indeed, this period of mental pioneering has allowed the green shoots of lateral-mindedness to emerge and, with time, has also brought forth the rich metaphorical blossoms of original concepts and countless writings.

Despite my feeling completely at ease with this right-brained dominance of recent years and enjoying the satisfaction of knowing that countless people around the UK have enjoyed reading my material of a quirky and perhaps satirical nature – along with the many musings it has attracted from an equally large host of scribes, philosophers and comedians in high-profile positions – I am nevertheless at odds with one issue of concern.

Several individuals have suggested, while nodding suggestively in my general direction, that there is 'a very thin dividing line' between genius and madness.

The question I have for you, Dr Faulkner, is not whether I am a bona fide genius, nor whether I am suffering from a rare form of enigmatic psychiatric manifestation of a somewhat positive and industrious nature, but rather, where on earth I can find a 'very thin dividing line'. I have written to rope-makers, large DIY stores and even manufacturers and purveyors of thin-nibbed pens but, alas, to no avail.

Since you are an experienced specialist in the discipline of the mind and its many moods and maladies and have spent years differentiating between those who belong in an institution and those who have become an institution, I have little doubt that you could provide directions in my quest for such an elusive item.

Once I have procured such a 'very thin dividing line' from an appropriate source I will be in a far better position to assess the degree to which genius and madness are actually separated in my own individual case or whether the two dimensions have in fact merged to become a hybrid peculiarity unknown to contemporary medicine.

I trust that all is well with you and look forward to receiving your response as soon as is conveniently possible.

Sincerely and as ever enigmatic

Michael A. Lee

FIELDHEAD SURGERY
Dr. PETER FAULKNER
Dr. SHEILA BENETT
Dr. STEVEN JOYNER
Dr. DAVID OLIVER
Dr. JAN SAMBROOK

FIELD HEAD
LEYMOOR ROAD
GOLCAR
HUDDERSFIELD
HD7 4QQ
Tele: (01484) 654504
Fax: (01484) 460296

Our Ref; PF/kg

14th October, 2004

Mr. M. A. Lee
Somewhere in West Yorkshire

Dear Michael,

How nice to hear from you again. I wonder if your feeling 'completely at ease' has anything to do with the use of mind-bending drugs? I have come to the conclusion that your flight of ideas and verbose communications must be due to the ingestion of illegal substances.

I am aware of your penchant for a nip of Guinness now and again…. have you ever considered that it may have been 'spiked'? I rather doubt that you can be described as a 'genius', even though this word is contained in the word 'Guinness'. The 'right-brained dominance' to which you refer, is probably due to the fact that the sentient and intellectual part of the left brain has completely atrophied in your case. This does bring in to question the possibility that you suffer from delusions of grandeur, linked to tertiary syphilis (though the pattern of bruising on your body from the barge poles, inflicted by various females over your lifetime make this very unlikely). Should, however, you feel the need to don a Napoleon's hat, you may consider this as a possibility. If indeed there is a 'rare' psychiatric condition that you suffer from, then this is it!

As to the subject of your complaint, then I find it difficult to explain what a thin dividing line actually is. I would consider that the line, should it exist, would be no more than a hair's breadth and it would not divide brilliance from madness, but bearable from unbearable. I do not want to seem to be uncharitable, but why try to pick the gossamer thread from one's own eye, when you cannot see the steel reinforced cable in your own? Perhaps you have misheard the phrase and are looking for a thin divining lion? This may be a water seeking cat, or a hungry one about to dine on a missionary. I digress.

I would suggest that you contact a Chain Store for inspiration, or follow the links to your goal. Steer clear of conventional medicine, as we Physicians can only posture and make conciliatory "hmmm" and "ah" noises to people who possess the gift of appearing vaguely normal. You may indeed be a hybrid peculiarity, possibly an alien species, or a product of an interplanetary leg-over, in which case you may be in danger of being carted off for medical research.

I hope my considered reply is of assistance to you.

Kind regards.

Yours sincerely,

Dr. P. Faulkner.

Somewhere in West Yorkshire
1 May 2003

The Managing Director
Luxembourg Tourist Office
122 Regent Street
London W1B 5SA

Dear Sir/Madam

I am writing you a letter of complaint.

In my own humble opinion the country of Luxembourg lacks lustre and requires a complete overhaul.

Should you need someone to help rebuild the place, I am quite a dab hand at mixing sand and cement, have a certain eye for good taste and excellence and would like to volunteer my services forthwith.

I also have friends who can drive and control a variety of demolition and construction vehicles, in addition to fork-lift trucks. Provided they are paid a satisfactory salary, I am certain that they also will agree to help. Between us I believe there is a chance of creating a European location of interest and character. We must, however, move swiftly!

I have packed my suitcase in anticipation.

Sincerely

M. A. Lee .

Michael A. Lee

Grand Duchy
of Luxembourg

Luxembourg Tourist Office

Our Ref: public\complain\M_A_Lee
London, 07/05/03

Mr M A Lee
Somewhere in West Yorkshire

Dear Mr Lee,

Thank you for your letter of May 1. You might as well unpack your suitcase again, because somebody else has got the job. Sorry...

Kind Regards,

Serge Moes
Director

122 Regent Street ■ London W1B 5SA
Tel: 020 7434 2800 ■ Fax: 020 7734 1205
tourism@luxembourg.co.uk ■ www.luxembourg.co.uk

The Archbishop of York
Bishopthorpe Palace
Bishopthorpe
York YO23 2GE

Dear Sir

I am writing you a letter of complaint.

Over the last few years I have attended a modest number of weddings that have taken place in a fine selection of Anglican churches around the UK. Indeed, it has been a great pleasure and privilege to have been part of these wonderful events. They have often involved the marriage of friends or family and, on one specific and particularly notable occasion, the wedding was my own.

I have enjoyed the spirit of community, considered the importance of commitment, and partaken of the food and refreshments with great relish and fond memories. Had it not been for one small matter I would have no cause whatsoever to write to you today.

The reason for my discontentment and the cause of my complaint are large and pretentious hats. Very simply, Archbishop, I would like to see them banned from weddings forthwith. They are at best often confusing to the eye and at worst a hazard to the health of nearby congregational members.

I wonder, therefore, whether you might consider introducing a church bill ensuring that such items will no longer be permitted at the aforementioned events.

Only recently I arrived at the wedding of a close friend, Hubert, and his fiancée, Penelope, with tremendous joy and anticipation when, to my great consternation, an ostrich feather-festooned, saucer-shaped hat of a rather bright orange hue entered the church, carrying with it a small lady in her early sixties who was evidently intent on causing harm to others. Quite frankly I was in fear for my life.

Two young bridesmaids were injured as the rim of the hat impacted with their tender foreheads, necessitating field dressings; the best man was knocked off his feet and landed in the font; and an ancient oak pew was completely overturned, complete with seven residents of the nearby Cloud Cuckoo Residential Home who had come along for the experience. (I refer to the wedding rather than to the consequent trip to Casualty.)

Doubtless you are sympathetic to my concerns and I would urge you to consider my plea for restrictions to the wearing of large hats as soon as is conveniently possible. In the meantime I intend to arrive at any future Anglican weddings to which I am fortunate to be invited in full body armour and a motorbike crash helmet. It is the only way to ensure complete safety and continued survival although, at the end of the day, I believe it is not only inconvenient but a shameful thing to have to do.

Sincerely but gravely concerned

M. A. Lee

**THE OFFICE OF
THE ARCHBISHOP OF YORK**

Bishopthorpe Palace
Bishopthorpe
York
YO23 2GE

Tel: (01904) 707021
Fax: (01904) 709204
E-mail: office@bishopthorpe.u-net.com
www.bishopthorpepalace.co.uk

6 May 2003

Dear Mr Lee

Thank you for your letter of 2 May 2003 concerning your request that large and pretentious hats are banned from weddings.

As a motor cycling priest, I often turn up for weddings in a crash helmet though do find removing it before the service begins is helpful in ensuring I have an unclouded view of the congregation!

At some Churches hats are a mixed blessing - not least when seeking to administer communion beneath a wide brim - but I feel that your suggestion would be something of a hammer to crack a nut!

I am sorry that the Archbishop has been unable to reply to you personally but he is presently away from the Office.

With every good wish.

Yours sincerely

Michael L Kavanagh
Domestic Chaplain to the Archbishop
and Diocesan Director of Ordinands

Mr M A Lee
Somewhere in West Yorkshire

Head of Personnel
The Dairy Council
5–7 John Princes Street
London W1G 0JN

Dear Sir/Madam

I am writing you a letter of complaint.

My dear wife has suffered for a number of years now from an extremely loud snoring condition that regularly impacts upon the quality and depth of my own sleep and wakes me from my slumbers rather earlier in the morning than I would wish. (I have tried sleeping in the garden hut and in the loft to avoid the consequent noise but, alas, the discomfort of such attempts to find a solution has rendered them notably futile.)

In the high summer months when the sun rises earlier than is the case during alternative English seasons, I am pacified by the wonderful singing of the various songbirds in the nearby trees that entertain and thrill me with their dawn chorus, and am not overly concerned at such an untimely arousal. I often lie contentedly beneath my duvet with an appreciation of our fine feathered friends outside the window and contemplate the wonders of nature in all her musical glory.

In the wintertime and early spring, however, my 3.30 a.m. awakenings are met simply by darkness and the distressing rattling of glass bottles as they are carried hither and thither by the local milk vans, ensuring that myriad customers are supplied in readiness for their breakfast cereals and pre-work milky coffees.

This irritates me beyond description and there is not even the comforting consolation of a coughing sparrow at this time of the day. It is not the milkmen I blame for the incessant rattling of bottles but the Dairy Council, whose apparent absence of total condemnation of milk bottles and their rattling capacity is, in my opinion, inexcusable.

In these supposed days of social tolerance and civilisation, I wonder if the Dairy Council might pass a resolution to do away with bottles with the capacity to annoy the sleepless and introduce credible and practical alternatives, such as obligatory foam or badger-hide containers that make little or no sound when colliding with each other.

Doubtless you receive many complaints of a similar nature but I felt sufficiently angry and concerned at this intolerable situation that I decided to write to you also. I must dash now as I can hear a milk van approaching and I want to ask the driver if he has any hazelnut yoghurt for sale.

I look forward to hearing from you in the near future.

Sincerely sleep-deprived but rather peckish

M. A. Lee

Tel 020 7499 7822
Fax 020 7408 1353
info@dairycouncil.org.uk
www.milk.co.uk

The
Dairy|Council

Mr M A Lee
Somewhere in West Yorkshire

21 May, 2003

—

Dear Mr Lee

I am afraid that The Dairy Council does not have a personnel department but in my capacity as Communications Manager I am happy to respond to your recent letter (6 May, 2003)

I was sorry to read about your sleepless nights but feel this letter may not bring you the comfort or resolution that you desire.

The Dairy Council does not have the power to 'do away' with milk bottles, rather this would be controlled by consumer demand in partnership with the dairy companies that supply doorstep deliveries.

As you will see, I have copied this letter to Edmond Proffitt at the Dairy Industry Association Limited (DIAL) as this organisation represents the doorstep delivery service and I thought he might be interested in your suggestion that milk crates are designed with foam or badger-hide to lessen the noise of bottles colliding.

This is the first time that The Dairy Council has received a complaint of this nature and I'm sorry that you felt sufficiently angry and concerned to write to us.

My final comment, and I'm sure you have already tried this, would be to approach your milkman and explain the situation to him so that he may appreciate your concerns while delivering in your area.

Yours sincerely

Michele Stephens
Communications Manager
The Dairy Council

Cc Edmond Proffitt

5-7 John Princes Street, London W1G 0JI
Registered in England (203597). Limited Liability.

The Marketing Director
Andrex Brand
Kimberly-Clark Ltd
1 Tower View
West Malling
Kent ME19 4HA

Dear Sir/Madam

I am writing you a letter of complaint.

For many years now I have been purchasing a relatively large quantity of Andrex toilet tissue in an array of colours for the use of my family and myself here in the West Yorkshire town of Huddersfield. Although I agree with the essential messages you have communicated via television advertising that such tissue is soft, strong and very, very long, and am suitably impressed and indeed content with our own use of Andrex toilet tissue, I am nevertheless a little irritated.

It was my impression that customers of such toilet tissue would qualify for a free Golden Labrador puppy. Despite having bought several tons of the aforementioned product over the last few years from a variety of sources, not once have I discovered a free puppy voucher or even a written explanation of what I need to do to claim my pet. While I understand that an offer such as this might, for budgetary reasons, only apply to a small number of Andrex users, I have not heard of anyone else who has actually obtained a small, playful canine friend either.

Clearly the frustrated though longstanding hope and anticipation that a free dog was coming our way has been a most exhausting experience for all of us and, quite frankly, we are beginning to suffer from bouts of disappointment and despair.

I have asked my two sons if they would accept an alternative animal to love and care for, such as a corn snake or stick insect, but unfortunately they are still hoping for the aforementioned pooch. In fact, so committed to the task of acquiring his 'Andrex' creature is my youngest son, George (aged three), that he has taken to visiting the toilet seven or eight times a day simply to cram as much tissue down the bowl as he can in order to create more product demand and raise the chances of a voucher find. (He is a bright boy with a wonderful understanding of market forces and basic merchandising!)

I wonder as a consequence of our particular situation whether you could advise us of current puppy stocks and whether we might qualify for one as high-volume tissue users.

Should this offer now be obsolete, a year's supply of Andrex toilet tissue, irrespective of colour or shade, would be most welcome.

Sincerely and in anticipation

M. A. Lee

16th May 2003

Dear Sir,

Thank you for your recent letter and we are pleased that you are an Andrex® loyalist. As you may be aware we have a substantial puppy collection from where soft toy puppy items may be purchased (I enclose a leaflet).

However, as I am sure you will understand, we are unable to provide real puppies and indeed have never made such a promise to do so. Dogs could not be given as free gifts as individuals should purchase one on the basis that they are able to love and care for them as well as supporting them financially.

I enclose a limited edition 30 year puppy soft toy as a thank you for buying Andrex® for so long.

Yours sincerely,

Joanna Ball
The Andrex® Team

The Marketing Director
Timotei Shampoo
Lever Fabergé Ltd
Admail 1000
London SW1A 2XX

Dear Sir/Madam

I am writing you a letter of complaint.

A few weeks ago I decided to purchase half a dozen 250 ml containers of your Timotei Shampoo advertised for 'normal hair' and containing 'revitalising herbs' from a local Huddersfield supermarket. (I don't mean that the revitalising herbs were from a Huddersfield supermarket but rather that the shampoo to which the herbs had already been added was obtained from such.)

I was most satisfied with the price and duly returned home with newfound hope, a spring in my step and a primary objective to apply a portion of the aforementioned product to my head as soon as possible. Indeed, not only did I apply the intended portion of shampoo that very day but also continued to apply a similar portion to my head every day for over a month.

Alas, I have been so very, very disappointed with the results and am presently rather distraught and depressed! Your shampoo did not provide me with a single normal hair nor even a dry hair, a greasy hair nor hint of a mere bristle. In fact, at the end of my industrious endeavours to fulfil my expectation that Timotei would be ideal for normal hair, I was just as bald as I was at the start.

I am aghast at the lack of expected potency displayed by Timotei at reversing my balding plight and at the efficacy sadly lacking at providing me with normal hair of any kind whatsoever. Had Timotei promoted the appearance even of abnormal hair I would have been relatively pleased and certainly more impressed than I am at present. No subsequent hair at all, however, has been a tremendous shock to my system and I accordingly feel a significant and understandable frustration.

In the light of my negative experience I would be most grateful if you could suggest a plausible option whereby the sandy beach of my bare head may once again be covered in abundant waves, as was the case in my tender youth?

Sincerely

M. A. Lee

Michael A. Lee

P.S. My wife, on the other hand, uses Timotei for normal hair with outstanding success and I have noticed that her curls, with a long-lasting clean feel, grow rapidly on a continuous basis. Free samples would be most welcome indeed.

Ref: 85431
Date: 28 May 2003

Mr M A Lee
Somewhere in West Yorkshire

Dear Mr Lee

Thank you for your recent letter from which I was sorry to learn of your disappointment with Timotei Revitalising Herbs Shampoo.

From the information provided it would appear that you are following the correct procedure and as such I am at a loss to explain the cause of your disappointment. Please accept our apologies for any frustration this has caused and I hope that you will accept the enclosed as a token of our goodwill.

Following discussion with our technical department we believe that to change the tide of a sandy beach of baldness to abundant waves of normal hair may be too drastic. They have suggested that to find a more humble target such as greasy, or fine hair rather than normal hair may be a more realistic goal. The theory being to start small and work upwards. You may be interested to know that Lever Faberge produce shampoos and conditioners for greasy hair, dry hair, coloured hair, combination hair and many other types. Perhaps you will find more satisfying results if you begin with a shampoo for greasy hair or even one intended for dandruff. Once you have achieved success using these products you could then move up to dry hair, and so on until you reach the dizzying heights of normal hair.

I do hope that this information is of some help and that the desolate security store of your crown may once again be full of the abundant locks of your youth.

Yours sincerely

Mark Walker
Consumer Link Advisor

--
Enclosures:
1 x Lever Fabergé Voucher £5

0250 19262

9 "909368"045009">

04619

TERMS AND CONDITIONS

To the Consumer: This voucher entitles you to a saving of £5 on the retail price of any Lever Faberge product. Redemption of this voucher other than conforming with the above would constitute fraud. Not valid after 30/09/04.

To the Retailer: Lever Faberge Ltd. Department 674 (NDC Corby, Northants. NN17 1NN) will refund the face value of this voucher provided it has been presented in payment against any Lever Faberge products. Lever Faberge Ltd. reserve the right to refuse redemption of vouchers if they have reason to believe that they have been accepted other than in accordance with these terms. Not valid after 31/12/04.

Persil
Cif
Dove
physio sport
SR
Vaseline
Organics
Signal
POND'S
Shield

LEVER FABERGÉ

£5

COMPLIMENTARY
VOUCHER

THIS VOUCHER MAY ONLY
BE REDEEMED AGAINST
LEVER FABERGÉ PRODUCTS
This voucher cannot be exchanged for
cash and no change will be given

Surf
Comfort
Impulse
mentadent P
SURE
LYNX
BRUT
Timotei
Pears
Salon Selectives

HRH The Duke of Edinburgh
Buckingham Palace
London

Dear Sir

I am writing you a letter of complaint.

Having spent some substantial time considering your beautiful and, of course, world-famous home, Buckingham Palace, I am astounded that there is no sign of a traditional hermitage within the grounds of your wonderful residence that is either presently occupied or currently prepared for habitation by a suitably qualified hermit.

I understand that in the eighteenth century many aristocratic families (and perhaps royal families also) had various hermitages built within their spacious estates to house gentlemen of a thoughtful nature who chose to live rather solitary lives and spend undisturbed time considering the meaning of existence and writing poetry about swans, lost love and the starry night-time skies. It is without doubt a great pity that there are, to my knowledge, no hermitages of this kind remaining and a desperate shame that, as a consequence, few opportunities exist for hopeful hermits such as I to secure positions of appropriate and suitable interest.

Please might I suggest, Your Royal Highness, that you consider the construction of a small hermitage within your grounds as a worthwhile venture in the near future.

As a pensive individual in his early forties with a demanding wife and two small and noisy children I would be most interested to travel to Buckingham Palace myself, change into clothing more suited to an outdoors hermit, and spend some quality time in pursuing the creative and cerebral arts that I rarely have the chance to follow here in Huddersfield.

Imagine the tens of thousands of visitors who could be attracted to marvel at a modern-day hermit living for periods of time within the grounds of the palace and what revenue this might generate via entrance tickets, compilations of philosophical poems written by the hermit himself and even illustrated autographs for those willing to make a substantial investment in return for something a little unusual.

Doubtless you receive many letters of this kind and so I thank you for your time and kind consideration, and look forward to hearing from you in the very near future.

I have packed my sandals and a woolly hat in anticipation.

Sincerely

Michael A. Lee

From: Captain George Cordle, Grenadier Guards

BUCKINGHAM PALACE

18th August, 2003

Dear Mr Lee,

I write to acknowledge your letter to The Duke
of Edinburgh and to say that the comments you express
have been noted.

Yours sincerely,
George Cordle

Temporary Equerry

Mr. Michael A. Lee

BUCKINGHAM PALACE, LONDON. SW1A 1AA
TELEPHONE: 020 7930 4832 FACSIMILE: 020 7839 5402

Head of Complaints
Customer Care
The Met Office
FitzRoy Road
Exeter EX1 3PB

Dear Sir/Madam

I am writing you a letter of complaint.

As I am sure is the case with numerous gentlemen of my age who can look back over many years of abundant and indeed enjoyable eating and drinking, I have to confess to the possession of several pounds of unwanted subcutaneous fat. As a consequence I am currently being rather careful about my day-to-day diet and have, to date, been reasonably successful at avoiding such treats as giant, triangular chocolate bars, tasty maple-syrup sandwiches and tins of condensed milk. I have instead turned my appetite to nutritious meats and juicy fruits, low-calorie cereals and essential vegetables and must say that I am rather pleased to note the reduction of my waistline to a small degree.

There is, however, an ongoing element of annoyance as I attempt to pursue my praiseworthy goal of losing weight and it is the Met Office that I presume bears responsibility for the cause of such irritation. It is for this very reason that I write.

As I sit in my garden at the weekends or in my car at lunchtime gazing skyward with a stomach that is never completely satisfied, and surrounded by the grumbling sounds so often associated with hunger, I have begun to notice that the majority of the clouds I see passing above me are either meat-pie shaped or appear so similar to innumerable vanilla slices I have eaten over the years that I am being driven to distraction.

I know that it is now possible with modern technology to seed clouds in such a way that rain is encouraged when necessary and I wondered, therefore, if there may exist other techniques whereby the shapes of the clouds may be changed from warm, buttered meatloaf and wedges of blue Stilton to food-free items such as traditional castles and fluffy farm animals.

Doubtless you receive many letters of this kind and so I thank you for your time and kind consideration. I must sign off now since I have just cast my eyes on some cumulonimbus clouds rather reminiscent of mouth-watering Belgian truffles coming in from the west and must avoid further temptation by obtaining a substitute morsel or two in the form of a green apple from our fruit bowl downstairs.

I look forward to hearing from you in the very near future.

Sincerely

M. A. Lee

Mr M A Lee
Somewhere in West Yorkshire

Direct tel: 0870 900 0100
Direct fax: 0870 900 5050
E-mail:

25 August 2003

Our ref: GL29

Dear Mr Lee

Thank you for your letter dated 18th August 2003. Your comments have been noted.

The Met Office is a world-leading supplier of advice on the weather and the natural environment. As the UK's national weather service for the past 150 years, we provide service to government departments, commerce, industry and the media.

We are sorry that you are finding the formation of clouds, as you put it, "irritating" but you must realise clouds are a natural phenomena and we have no control over their formation nor any need to alter their formation even if it were possible.

Yours sincerely

Mrs Sarah Spedding
Customer Advisor

.

Mrs Sarah Spedding
Customer Advisor
The Met Office
FitzRoy Road
Exeter EX1 3PB

Dear Mrs Spedding

First and foremost may I thank you for your thoughtful letter of 25 August 2003 in response to my complaint about the existence of clouds that resemble the shapes of high-calorie foods and that pay little regard to my desire for a temptation-free diet at my particular time of fat-accumulating life. I was more than a little surprised to read that the Met Office has no control over the formation of these clouds, nor the need to alter their formation even if it were possible. One lives and learns!

I do, however, have another complaint to bring to bear, one that I believe lies firmly within the boundaries of responsibility and accountability as far as the Met Office is concerned. Let me explain.

Only a few days ago there were reports in the newspapers, via the radio and on TV about the supposed 'Big Freeze' that was due to bring severe weather from the Arctic and create a situation resembling Siberian chaos across the UK. To say that I was horrified at the prospect of wild, freezing gales, subzero temperatures and snow several metres deep would be a gross understatement. I therefore decided to take every available precaution possible in the days before the forecast event to protect my family from the ravages of the winter to come and to ensure a plentiful supply of provisions to permit continued warmth, food and mobility, for a period of several weeks if need be.

At the end of my preparation I had not only purchased 100 kilograms of basmati rice, a sack of flour, 200 eggs and a selection of tinned foods that have all but filled our spare bedroom, but also a sledge, eight Alaskan huskies and a wonderful range of outdoors gear including a raccoon-tailed, rabbit-skin hat and an ice-axe. There was so little room left in our house as a consequence of my efficient planning that my wife decided to leave home to lodge with her sister in Lancashire, and the joists of the loft have now begun to bend beneath the weight of the tinned herrings stored up there.

It will come as no surprise to you that I have experienced an extreme degree of disappointment and frustration at the way in which this so-called bout of significantly inclement weather passed this part of the world by almost completely. Although I did see the odd snowflake and observed a young silver birch tree bend slightly in a short-lived breeze, there was no reason to don my thermal underwear at all, and the money and time that I spent on procuring snow goggles, ice-fishing tackle and books on winter survival have been a total waste.

Surely the Met Office owes me an apology for exaggerating the supposed January climate that should have descended on West Yorkshire in the life-threatening manner described so frequently in the media – but that never did – and would also perhaps consider buying from me a number of well-trained dogs and a sledge that are now excess to personal requirements.

I look forward to your swift response.

Sincerely

M. A. Lee .

Michael A. Lee

P.S. Does anyone in your department like tinned herrings?

Mr M A Lee
Somewhere in West Yorkshire

Direct tel: +44(0)0870 900 0100
Direct fax: +44(0)1392 885681
E-mail:

5 February 2004

Our ref: CMC/SS

Dear Mr Lee

Thank you for your letter dated 30th January 2004 concerning the recent cold and snowy weather.

In relation particularly to Huddersfield, I have taken advice from an expert within the Met Office and would draw your attention to the satellite image enclosed. It is interesting to note that it shows the extent of snow that fell during those days. The white areas are mainly snow, although there is some cloud over Wales.

As you will note, there is an area of brown to the south of the Pennines which encompasses Huddersfield. This is where little or no snow fell. This pattern is a result of the shelter the Pennine hills give to that area. The weather systems at the time produced a strong northerly wind across the UK and "shadows" can sometimes be created to the lee of high ground like this. This aspect cannot always be relied upon and thus is difficult to forecast, but as you can see, your area was surrounded by snow. You were lucky or unlucky – depending on your view!

Perhaps this emphasises how the UK's weather is so "local" and after the event it is easy to say why the patterns that we see have been formed. To forecast this level of detail ahead of time is sometimes very difficult.

Many areas *did* experience awful conditions and the general advice issued by the Met Office was essentially correct and helped many to avoid being inconvenienced. Local Authorities and other market sectors were also able to plan how to best meet demand on their resources as a result of their ongoing relationship with the Met Office.

We are sorry you feel you were not served well on this occasion. Met Office forecasts are among the best in the world and we, as an organisation, continually strive to serve the UK public with a high quality service.

Kind regards

Yours sincerely

Sarah Spedding
Customer Advisor

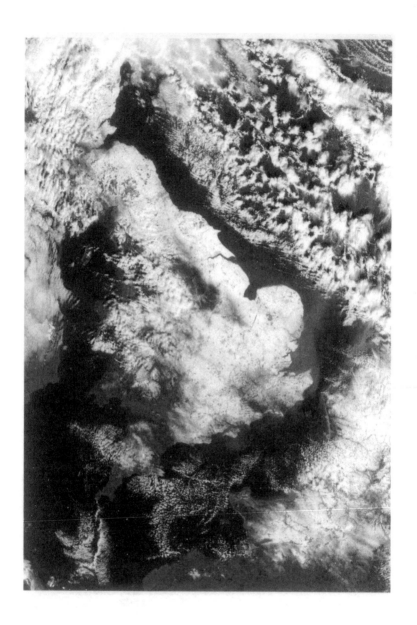

248

The Director
Royal College of Music, London
Prince Consort Road
London SW7 2BS

Dear Sir/Madam

I am writing you a letter of complaint.

May I say from the outset that my complaint, however, does not directly apply either to yourself or to anyone else involved or associated with the Royal College of Music, London. Rather, my complaint is relevant to a somewhat irritating neighbour of mine whose weekends are more often than not spent pottering in his nearby garden and pursuing his favourite hobby of whistling in a most terrible manner that is both distasteful and out of tune to an extreme degree.

Never before have I lived so close to someone in his early fifties who knows so many tunes of little merit, who can render them memorable cacophonies by setting them to a most remarkable though disturbing lip warble and continue in this unenviable fashion from dawn until dusk. I am convinced that such unconscious behaviour will ultimately cause a mind of fragile constitution living in the vicinity to descend into utter and hopeless madness. Indeed, I now fear for my wife on a daily basis!

Having thought long and hard about the possible outcomes of my mentioning to my tone-deaf canary-like neighbour in a direct fashion his dreadful whistling and the warfare that might result from consequential emotional injury, I decided instead to write to you.

I wonder whether you might have in your possession some information on a 'Basic Whistling Course' or 'When Is a Tune Tuneful?' seminar available to those of relevant disposition who would be both interested and likely to benefit from the study of such.

If so I would be most interested indeed to receive this information at the above address. I will duly, though diplomatically, pop it through my neighbour's letter-box when he has retired to bed for the night and when there remains little chance of my being spotted as the guilty party suggesting musical development. (I am also only too happy to anonymously purchase his train ticket should he decide that a suggested workshop or programme of study is appropriate – though whether I could stretch to a return fare I am not sure.)

Doubtless you have been approached on many occasions in regard to matters similar to this and I appreciate your time, consideration and understanding accordingly.

I do look forward to hearing from you in the very near future.

Sincerely

M. A. Lee .

Mr M A Lee
Somewhere in West Yorkshire

Prince Consort Road
London SW7 2BS
United Kingdom

Tel: +44(0)20 7589 3643
Fax: +44(0)20 7589 7740
www.rcm.ac.uk

8 October 2003

Dear Mr Lee

I am afraid that the RCM cannot help you with your enquiry.

I enclose, however, some information available on the Internet. You will be able to judge whether this is of any use in your situation.

Yours sincerely

Charlotte Martin
Secretariat

G:\Secretariat\Correspondence\Correspondence\lee.doc

Whistling

Whistling is good for the lungs.

There have been actual whistling schools set up in the past such
as
Agnes Woodward's school of the 1920s.
There may be courses in whistling available today.

The English term for a professional whistler is *siffleur*.

Some people have mastered the skill of whistling two or even
three notes at once and can whistle in harmony.

If you wanted to say the word 'whistling' to those of a different
language the following might be a useful reference:

Filipino – *sumipol*
German – *pfeifen*
Hebrew – *sharkan*
Icelandic – *flautari*
Norwegian – *lungepipen*
Swedish – *vissian*

In the Disney film adaptation of the story about Pinocchio there
is a cartoon cricket called Jiminy who talks about whistling for
help.
It may be worth checking the Yellow Pages to see if his number
is listed.

The Director
Royal Horticultural Society
80 Vincent Square
London SW1P 2PE

Dear Sir/Madam

I am writing you a letter of complaint.

Just over eight years ago I purchased, from what I believed was an upmarket and reputable garden centre here in West Yorkshire, a Swiss cheese plant that appeared to be in excellent condition and had leaves of a healthy green hue which I thought would fit well with the colour scheme of my home's hallway. I replanted the aforementioned cheese plant in a large, colourful pot full of fresh compost, positioned it to the left of my front door and, while experiencing a certain pleasure at my handsome purchase, waited patiently for harvest-time.

Let me say at this juncture how much I have enjoyed a variety of cheeses over the years and especially the world-famous Swiss cheese itself; consequently I was most excited at having procured a wonderful houseplant both for purposes of admiration by friends and family and also as a source of enjoyable and nutritious food. I went so far as to stock my pantry with a gourmet selection of rather expensive savoury biscuits and a bottle or two of port in preparation for the tasting of my home-grown cheese.

Alas, I have now waited for and been disappointed at the non-arrival of not just one expected harvest-time but several, and quite frankly I am fast becoming disillusioned with the whole episode.

I now have suspicions that the garden centre has sold me a dud cheese plant and I am more than a little dismayed, given the amount of time and loving attention I have given the plant over the years and how little I have gained in return. You will be saddened to hear that I have had to resort to a far less interesting brand of supermarket cheese and feel exceptionally betrayed.

Rather than approach the garden centre manager directly with my grievance – he is a tall chap with a menacing manner about him – I decided that the best course of action was to write directly to the Royal Horticultural Society and lodge my complaint at the highest levels. I thought that you might be able to suggest a course of action appropriate to my terrible situation and offer some direction in this desperate predicament.

Doubtless you receive complaints of this kind on a regular basis and with this in mind I do thank you for your time and kind consideration in this matter.

I look forward to hearing from you in the very near future.

Sincerely though concerned

M. A. Lee

Director General
80 Vincent Square, London SW1P 2PE

T 020 7821 3039   www.rhs.org.uk
F 020 7821 3020

Royal
Horticultural
Society

Mr M A Lee
Somewhere in West Yorkshire

Dear Mr Lee

Thank you for your distressing letter of 5 October. We were all devastated here to learn of your traumatic experience with regard to the non-performance of your Monstera plant.

We believe that you probably have a case for action against the retailer for failing to warn you that, under EU legislation to protect cheese-makers within the EU member states, all Swiss Cheese Plants must be rendered sterile by vasectomy before they can be imported. If you were to lift the plant out of its pot, you might just see the remains of the bits of strangling red tape with which this delicate operation was performed.

If legal action fails, you might consider asking the MOD to intervene with military action on your behalf. I have to warn you, however, that sending a gunboat is not popular as it was and, with Treasury constraints, particularly not to Switzerland.

Finally, you might consider therapy for all your family and friends who may be suffering from this sad episode. After extensive research, we have discovered that the Monstera Raving Loony Party does run a counselling group for those suffering from your affliction. But caveat emptor: the cure may be worse than the problem.

With kind regards and best wishes for a speedy recovery.

Yours sincerely

Andrew Colquhoun
Director-General

Chief Abbot
English Benedictine Congregation
Buckfast Abbey
Buckfastleigh
Devon TQ11 0EE

Dear Sir

I am writing you a letter of complaint.

Despite the increasing popularity over the last few years of a whole range of television programmes focusing on the preparation and serving of various types of mouth-watering foods and the appearance of a large number of so-called TV chefs as a consequence, I am most concerned at the complete lack of representation from our English Benedictine congregations.

Indeed, although there are chefs known to specialise in seafood, chefs who are known for their country of origin and even chefs known for the dimensions of their waistlines, there is currently, as far as I know, no chef known for his connection to a monastery. With regard to this unacceptable situation I would like to suggest a practical solution.

Aged 43, I am an affable and industrious individual able to turn my hand to a wide range of tasks but particularly to the art of cooking and, even more specifically, to the preparation of foods guaranteed to inspire the palates and satisfy the appetites of even the hungriest monks. Among my specialities are the most wonderful lasagnes, roasts and winter hotpots as well as a comprehensive range of summer salads, light soups and delicious sweets and puddings.

I must say, however, that among my cornucopia of imaginative recipes and creative meals there stands one area of distinctive and outstanding kitchen-based accomplishment; namely my excellence as far as the deep frying of chipped potatoes is concerned. In short I believe I should duly be considered a wonderful candidate for Buckfast Abbey as your 'Principal Chip Monk' and perhaps in the future may be thus considered someone worthy of the title 'Chief Fryer'.

Once the BBC hears of such a career development there will doubtless be a place for yet another TV cooking programme and the chance for the Abbey to raise funding through the efforts of their very own culinary master. I even have a few ideas as far as a potential name for the programme is concerned, ranging from 'Preparing the Sole' to 'Meat, Mead and Meditation'. Personally I think we could be on to a winner here!

I look forward to hearing your views on this matter.

Sincerely

Michael A. Lee

Mr M A Lee
Somewhere in West Yorkshire

Buckfast Abbey
Buckfastleigh
Devon TQ11 0EE

20.10.03

Dear Mr Lee,

Thank you for your most interesting letter of the 14th October, which has been passed on to me.

While we appreciate your concern over our lack of celebrity - especially in the culinary field – believe me we are not unhappy to linger in such obscurity. Monks on the whole appreciate quietness and the very thought of televisual attention is enough to send shivers down our collective spine. So all in all we would rather not take up your offer to boost our profile in this way.

We have at present a full complement of staff who, though possibly lacking your own flair, are sufficient for our simple needs.

We will however keep your letter on file and consider you for any future opening in this area of our activities.

Yours sincerely,

Father James Courtney O.S.B.
Bursar

Tel: (01364) 645500
Fax: (01364) 645891

Direct lines: (01364)
Bursar's Office: 645590
Education Department: 645517
Gift shop: 645510
Works Department: 645503
Book shop: 645506
Gardens Department: 645507
Monastic Produce shop: 645570
Conferences & meetings: 645530
Grange Restaurant: 645504

E-mail:
enquiries@buckfast.org.uk
education@buckfast.org.uk
guests@buckfast.org.uk
warden@buckfast.org.uk

Website:
http://www.buckfast.org.uk

Buckfast Abbey Trustees Registered
Charity Commission Number: 232497

Dart Abbey Enterprises Ltd.
Registered in England
Registered Number: 1435171

VAT Number: 381524161

From the Abbot of Downside

Dom Richard Yeo OSB.

Tel.: 01761-235121
Fax: 01761-235156
E-mail: AbbotRYeo@aol.com

DOWNSIDE ABBEY
STRATTON-ON-THE-FOSSE
RADSTOCK BA3 4RH

17 October 2003

Dear Michael,

Thank you very much for your letter which arrived this morning, and for your suggestion that you might come to Downside as a chef, and possibly seek to do a cookery programme on the television.

It is an interesting suggestion, but I am afraid we do not have available a post such as the one you are thinking about, and in fact we use the services of a firm of caterers for our kitchens. I congratulate you on the ingenuity of your proposals, but I am afraid I don't think they are likely to be capable of being put into practice.

With all good wishes,

Yours sincerely,

Richard Yeo

The Manager
Sainsbury's Supermarket
Southgate
Huddersfield

Dear Sir/Madam

I am writing you a letter of complaint.

Without any shadow of a doubt there is no breakfast cereal I enjoy eating more than Kellogg's Rice Krispies, and in so saying I am rather partial to an extra large portion of such on Sunday mornings after a few beers the previous evening at my local hostelry, the Wilted Rose and Balding Crown.

As far as the taste, the ability to satisfy a healthy appetite and, indeed, value for money are concerned, I have absolutely no axe to grind regarding this well-established and popular product. However, I feel compelled to mention to you the fact that, once milk meets cereal, the snaps, the crackles and the pops are a tad too loud for the ears of someone like myself suffering from a moderate hangover. It is my opinion that the crackles are by far the worst of the three!

May I suggest to you, therefore, that a quieter version of Rice Krispies be purchased as soon as is conveniently possible by the helpful team at Sainsbury's of Huddersfield – my local supermarket – to address the problem, which I am convinced must be experienced by countless fellow beer drinkers throughout the town?

If not, I may well have to think about either switching my morning diet allegiance to something a little quieter, such as porridge, or totally silent, for instance, grapefruit segments. I am sure you will agree that such a lifestyle change would be rather regrettable from your commercial perspective.

Sincerely though temporarily deaf

M. A. Lee

Michael A. Lee

SAINSBURY'S

Please reply to

SOUTHGATE
SHOREHEAD
HUDDERSFIELD
HD1 6QR

Telephone: 01484 429277

Our ref MO/EJB

24 October 2003

Mr M A Lee
Somewhere in West Yorkshire

Dear Mr Lee

I would like to express my sincerest sympathy, as you are plainly confronted of a Sunday morning with a serious dilemma. To partake of some Rice Krispies – in your fulsome praise of which I heartily concur – but to risk thereby an aural onslaught most inimical to your tender condition? Or to settle for something less sonically dramatic, but also perhaps less toothsome?

I readily concede it's a tricky one. I have consulted extensively with my colleagues – in strictest confidentiality, of course – and I can confirm that many of us know how you feel. In our time, we too have paid that small but surely worthwhile price of a sensitive cranium, which does tend to ensue from an evening's conviviality in a welcoming tavern.

So we too have pondered our breakfast options in a delicate condition. Do we take the healthy option? Fruit, cereal, toast? Do we throw caution to the wind and fry up the full, cholesterol – ripe English traditional? Some go even further, suggesting that a rare sirloin steak and devilled kidneys would fit the bill, while others opt for a middle course, promoting the great pleasures of some lightly poached smoked haddock served with scrambled eggs. (The eggs would naturally be scramble with cream, not milk, and perhaps dusted with cayenne).

Ultimately, as it is for each of us at such a personal time, the choice is yours. I do appreciate what you say about the drawbacks of the Rice Krispie SFX – but while I would love to believe that somewhere in the heart of the Kellogg Corporation there is even now a team of earnest, white-coated scientists (wearing interesting spectacles in the manner of Joe 90) who labour tirelessly to develop a low-decibel version of the brand, I fear it cannot be the case.

After all, the unique selling proposition of Rice Krispies is precisely that it snaps, it pops, and (the horror) it does most verily crackle and would a krispie that didn't crackle be a krispie at all?

In consequence, I can only assure you that – whether you decide to stick with Rice Krispies (and withstand the concomitant artillery impacts over the breakfast table like a man), or whether you decide instead to travel on some other culinary road – whatever products you may wish to purchase to make your Sunday morning a good one, you will find them here at Shorehead, with a warm welcome at all times.

In the interim period please accept the enclosed which comes with our thanks for writing to us.

Yours sincerely,

Mike O'Hara
Store Manager

Enc

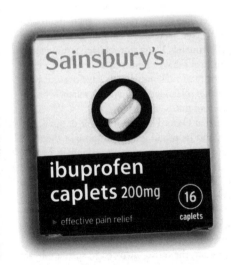

Sainsbury's Supermarkets Ltd
33 Holborn
London
EC1N 2HT

Registered office as above
Registered number 3261722 England
A Subsidiary of J Sainsbury plc

The Chancellor
Oxford University
University Offices
Wellington Square
Oxford OX1 2JD

Dear Chancellor

I am writing you a letter of complaint.

It is with a certain degree of sadness (not an academic qualification, I hasten to add, though there may well be arguments that it ought to be) that I feel compelled to share with you my frustration and annoyance at a glaring professional need as yet unmet by those graduating from Oxford University.

Although I live in the Northern town of Huddersfield, one which would not claim to boast of a nightlife that is anything beyond the vaguely entertaining and reasonably accom-modating, there are nevertheless a large number of hostelries and a number of nightclubs within the vicinity that serve a large population of thirsty and dance-crazed human beings of whom a reasonable proportion are students.

Furthermore, the majority of these establishments also employ large gentlemen in their early twenties to stand by the doors complete with tuxedos and menacing manners, to ensure that 'troublesome elements' are discouraged from entering. I believe these individuals are known colloquially as 'bouncers', although whether or not this term is applied to their contractual job descriptions I am not sure.

Personally I have no difficulty accepting the presence of such figures of authority and on a few occasions when I have been on social outings I have even spoken to several of them on passing. (Fortunately I have not yet been refused entry to my alehouses of choice!) The concern I have, however, is that the verbal responses I have received from the majority of such individuals have been, at best, basic, and, in some circumstances, rather Neanderthal, with a reliance on an indecipherable range of grunting noises and non-verbal nods.

Doubtless you would agree with me that Oxford University is one of our finest, if not the finest university in the land, and its proud graduates some of the most successful people in the world. I take my hat off (figuratively speaking, as I rarely wear a hat) to the doctors, the lawyers, the teachers and the entrepreneurs who would rapidly acknowledge the fact that an Oxford education has provided the basis for their career progress and professional satisfactions.

It is, however, a tragedy that there are few if any of these gifted individuals who choose to embark upon careers as bouncers. Their ability to cogitate and articulate would add countless dimensions to an evening's social interaction.

Although I would agree that, at present, the duties involved in such a role are not hugely attractive per se, and neither is the companionship offered by those currently occupied as such, the addition of a large number of Oxford graduates would surely revolutionise this lesser-known field of work in a drastic and memorable fashion. How wonderful it would be to debate the philosophies of Plato and Socrates on entering the Rose and Crown or touch upon the aesthetic pleasures of a Picasso on departure from the Painted Wagon! What fun there would be discussing with a new-age bouncer the challenges of training for the Boat Race or the emerging theories relating to the nature of sub-atomic particles!

What plans do you think there ought to be to encourage some of your students to consider working along similar lines to those described above?

I realise that you must receive many letters of this kind and so I thank you for your time and kind consideration. I look forward to hearing from you in the very near future.

Sincerely challenging

M. A. Lee .

Michael A. Lee

The VICE-CHANCELLOR
Sir Colin Lucas, MA, DPhil, FRHistS

University of Oxford
Wellington Square
Oxford OX1 2JD

Telephone: 01865 270242
Fax: 01865 270085
Email: vice-chancellor@admin.ox.ac.uk

Mr M A Lee
10 Woodlea Manor
Oakes   30 October 2003
Huddersfield
HD3 4EF

Dear Mr Lee,

Letter to the Chancellor

Thank you for your recent letter to Mr Patten. As he is not based here in Oxford, I hope that you won't mind a reply from me on his behalf.

It is certainly a beguiling image you present of being able to converse with pub and club doormen on subjects of a more intellectual nature than is normally the case. I'm not sure that our graduates, having spent three hard years of study at Oxford, would be tempted into that line of work on a regular basis. So although you might find it safer <u>not</u> to enquire of the doormen you see in Huddersfield whether they went to Oxford or not, I wish you much luck if you should want to try!

Yours sincerely,

A.N.C. MacDonald

Alasdair MacDonald
Executive Assistant to the Vice-Chancellor

Head of Enquiries
Driving Standards Agency
56 Talbot Street
Nottingham NG1 5GU

Dear Sir/Madam

I am writing you a letter of complaint.

Although I generally have a great deal of time, sympathy and consideration for those whose membership of our elderly population is well established, I feel that I must present my grievances around an issue of great and troublesome concern. Let us assume that the following summary is based on hypothesis for reasons of social and political correctness.

Mrs Z is a lady in her mid-nineties and almost completely blind. She has walked with the aid of a zimmer frame for at least fifteen years now and suffers from chronic vertigo and occasional blackouts. Despite a lifelong colour-blindness that renders the differences between red, amber and green a decipherable impossibility, Mrs Z has been driving happily – though perhaps somewhat dangerously – for at least 75 years and, for the last 35 years, in the same car (this car has had a total of fourteen clutch replacements).

Mrs Z reverses her car along her drive as a commander would reverse his tank in a battle situation and the resultant noise and production of strong burned-rubber smells are intolerable to various neighbours, especially at three o'clock on winter mornings. As if this were not in itself irritating to those wakened from their slumbers by such environmental trauma, Mrs Z is also a keen fan of Des O'Connor and, being hard of hearing, plays his music at an exceptionally high volume.

On a one-to-one basis Mrs Z is a wonderfully engaging person and almost always polite, especially when one points out that she is pruning bushes in a garden other than her own. She is a simple and somewhat endearing individual who sometimes prefers to sleep beneath the stars on her back lawn rather than retire to her bed, which most of her neighbours tend to do. Also, her time spent in Holloway Prison for spying for the Russians during the Cold War has almost been forgotten and certainly forgiven by everyone on the estate.

Isn't it about time that older ladies like Mrs Z were allowed to purchase their petrol at a discounted rate?

Sincerely, a concerned neighbour

M. A. Lee

Michael A. Lee

Driving Standards Agency
Customer Service Unit
Stanley House
56 Talbot Street
NOTTINGHAM NG1 5GU

switchboard: (0115) 901 2500
direct line: (0115) 901 2933
fax: (0115) 901 2510
e-mail: anna.perceivicus@dsa.gsi.gov.uk
website: www.dsa.gov.uk

Michael. A. Lee Esq.
10 Woodlea Avenue
Reinwood Manor
Oakes
HUDDERSFIELD
West Yorkshire
HD3 4EF

our ref: 0401/00089

9 January 2004

Dear Mr Lee

Thank you for your letter dated 28 December 2003 in which you raise concerns about a neighbour and her ability to drive. You have referred to this neighbour as Mrs Z.

As you may be aware full old style paper licences for cars, motorcycles and mopeds normally expire on a holders 70th birthday. After that the licence must be renewed every three years. Photo card licences are only valid for a maximum of 10 years although the actual driving entitlement will normally be valid until the holders 70th birthday.

The most important point is that if the holder has a medical condition they must inform DVLA immediately, whereupon the licence holder will be asked to complete a medical questionnaire which asks for permission to let DVLA's Medical Adviser request reports from the licence holders doctor and specialists. Dependent upon the outcome of those reports DVLA may issue the licence for a lesser period.

Department for
Transport
An executive agency of the
Department for Transport

INVESTOR IN PEOPLE

Awarded for excellence

I enclose a copy of the D100 leaflet produced by the DVLA for information. Mrs Z has an obligation therefore to inform the DVLA of occasional blackouts and any visual condition affecting her eyes, both of which are specified in the leaflet I have enclosed. I would add however that colour blindness is not a bar to driving. Failure to inform DVLA of any of the specified conditions could lead to prosecution and a fine of up to £1000.00.

As a concerned neighbour I trust this information may be of use to you. I fully appreciate your concerns and hope that you may find the opportunity to discuss this issue with Mrs Z. With regard to your final point, the government has no plans to discount the rate of duty paid on fuel for pensioners or any other particular groups.

Yours sincerely

Anna Percevicius
Customer Enquiry Team Manager

Somewhere in West Yorkshire
26 January 2004

Her Majesty's Ambassador
The British Embassy
7 Ahmed Ragheb Street
Garden City
Cairo
Egypt

Dear Sir

I am writing you a letter of complaint.

Almost a year and a half ago I wrote you a courteous letter whose almost perfect construction involved significant time and effort as part of my quest for a new and challenging role. Indeed, I contacted you regarding the acquisition of a job in the field of 'pyramid selling'. Since many of the world's pyramids are located in Egypt and you are the British ambassador for that part of the world, I decided that you would be my ideal contact with respect to this enquiry.

Alas, I have received no response whatsoever and so, unless you have sent a reply by way of camel train and its arrival is expected any day now, I thought I had better make contact again and restate my interest in this field of work.

Aged 44, I have arrived at that widely recognised stage of life where a change of career direction is high on my list of priorities. I have decided to try and combine my work experience with my long-standing interest in Egyptology in a way that permits me to involve myself to a greater extent in activities which provide a reasonable livelihood as well as a significant degree of interest and enjoyment. It would also be rather nice living in a place a tad warmer and less wet than West Yorkshire!

Having spent the best part of twenty years as a sales executive, albeit in a rather different sphere of sales here in the UK, I have a substantial amount of commercial experience as far as skills of negotiation and closing a deal are concerned.

Although I am lacking somewhat in my understanding of the actual pyramid market in terms of how often these buildings become available for sale, who the purchasing clients are likely to be and whether or not there are influential issues involved – such as various structures possessing listed status or the need for major renovation – I am adept at learning quickly and applying myself accordingly.

Doubtless you receive many letters of a similar type to this and so I thank you for your time and kind consideration, and look forward to hearing from you when convenient with appropriate advice and helpful contacts.

Sincerely

M. A. Lee

Michael A. Lee

British Embassy
Cairo

Mr M A Lee
Somewhere in West Yorkshire

Dear Mr Lee,

Thank you for your letter of 26 January received today. The Ambassador is in the UK at present accompanying the President of Egypt who is calling on Prime Minister Tony Blair. On return the Ambassador will be tied up with the United Kingdom Special Representative to Iraq who is due to visit Egypt and then immediately after the visit the Ambassador must to fly to Jordan for a meeting with other regional United Kingdom Heads of Mission. In sum he is quite busy with VSS (Very Serious Stuff) and so as not to delay a reply to you any further I shall answer your letter.

I would first like to apologise that we appear to have no record of your first letter of eighteen months ago ever being received here. The mail service can be a bit dodgy. However we do have your second letter and what an interesting topic you raise. The idea of pyramid selling is a novel one – they could be dismantled and sent elsewhere (maybe even do a world tour). I am sure most people around the world would love to see them. The most famous pyramids of course are those at Giza: Cheops, Chephren and Mycerinus. The fact that there are three provides a wonderful opportunity to "buy two, get one free".

I have checked with this Embassy's Commercial Section but sadly they have no information on pyramid selling. I have also checked with Egyptian contacts who say that the pyramids are not for sale, not today, not tomorrow, not ever. You may like to try Mexico as they do have some pyramids also.

I am sorry to have to disappoint you as you do sound a very capable fellow. In the meantime if I get wind of anything else coming on to the market that I think may be of interest to you - e.g. the Sphinx I shall be in touch.

Yours ever,

Rosalind P Brown

Mrs Rosalind P Brown
PA/HMA

Somewhere in West Yorkshire
26 January 2004

The Archbishop of York
Bishopthorpe Palace
Bishopthorpe
York YO23 2GE

Dear Sir

I am writing you a letter of complaint.

Many years ago I happened to hear the vicar of a Yorkshire parish somewhere north of Huddersfield quote from the ancient Book of Proverbs: 'Go to the ant, you sluggard; consider its ways and be wise'. Being suitably inspired by such supposed wisdom, I have spent a significant amount of time considering the ways of the ant on countless occasions ever since.

Although I am no sluggard I did believe that my focused observations might produce a certain degree of enlightenment as far as industry is concerned, and might well provide me with the basis for a work ethic that could lead to untold riches and a life of ultimate comfort. Alas, I have been exceedingly disappointed with the results of my studies and have become discouraged to the point of watching television soap operas (a rather extreme behaviour, I readily admit).

Consequently, it is the Church of England to whom I thought I would air my concerns and grievances. After all, it was one of your own employees who set me upon my committed task in the first place! (He was a tall man with a beard and wore black brogues; I hope that this is of some help.)

The ant is undoubtedly an exceptionally busy creature, if indeed a single ant can be considered a creature in its own right. Perhaps it is the colony of ants that qualifies as a whole bona fide entity rather than the constituent members? The fact remains, however, that despite the endless comings and goings of these small insects as they carry leaves hither and thither, tend for their young and milk their herds of aphids, they do not seem to live particularly notable or exciting lives.

On not a single occasion have I ever seen an ant completing his day's work to return to a privately owned family dwelling separate from his place of employment. Not once have I noticed an ant making his way to a cross-Channel ferry bound for a summer holiday in Brittany, nor travelling by aeroplane for a European city break, nor even enjoying a long weekend in Norfolk. I have seen no entrepreneurial ants, no ants that can function in an independent capacity, and no ants with any hint of basic business acumen or even basic book-keeping skills.

Au contraire, I am sad to say that I believe ants are generally overworked, receive a terrible benefits package and are starved completely of spare time, rest and recreation. Anthood is clearly the antithesis of the bee's knees. I have evidently wasted my time considering the ways of the ant and would ask what you have to say to me by way of apology and reassurance. I look forward to hearing from you in the very near future.

Sincerely

M. A. Lee

THE OFFICE OF
THE ARCHBISHOP OF YORK

Bishopthorpe Palace
Bishopthorpe
York
YO23 2GE

Tel: (01904) 707021
Fax: (01904) 709204
E-mail: office@bishopthorpepalace.co.uk
www.bishopthorpepalace.co.uk

Dear Mr Lee

Thank you for your letter of 26 January 2004. I suspect it is rarely the case that a few words in a sermon result in such deep and considered reflection as the ones you report in your letter. I must confess that the particular words from the Book of Proverbs have never led to the in depth reflection that you include, but I will never be able to hear them in quite the same way again.

I am not sure that I can offer an apology in the way that you request and I am not at all sure that your description helps me to clarify which particular priest may have triggered your train of thought. Nevertheless, I would assure you of my prayers and good wishes.

Yours sincerely

✝ ⋂ ⅃ ⴸⅼⵡ :

Mr M A Lee
10 Woodlea Avenue
Reinwood Manor
Oakes
Huddersfield
HD3 4EF

Professor Richard Bateman
Head of Department of Botany
Natural History Museum
Cromwell Road
London SW7 5BD

Dear Professor Bateman

I am writing you a letter of complaint.

For almost five years my wife and I have lived in a wonderful, detached four-bedroom house (with a separate double garage) in a leafy suburb of Huddersfield, and we enjoy the luxury of a rather large back garden whose perimeter is graced by a collection of mature trees dating back to the latter part of the nineteenth century.

I have no doubt at all that, had the selection of ash, beech, oak, sycamore, lime and hawthorn trees not have been already long established at the time that our house was built – thus bringing them under the protection of preservation orders – the extent of our 139-foot length of woodland paradise would have been far less generous than it is at present and the 45-foot width of such a greenbelt retreat be less pleasing.

It is with a sense of pride that I can therefore write to you of my endless annual pleasure at the wonderful hues and colours provided by our trees throughout the changing year and also at the breadth of potential the trees have brought to their protected garden space for design, leisure and entertainment. I can recount numerous occasions of memorable family barbecues on our patio, of the idyllic play of the children in their well-constructed play area and of evenings seated with glasses of red wine, listening to the thrushes singing and to the owls hooting high in the branches above the fresh green lawn.

However, it is with a certain consternation that I must bring to your attention a complaint about one rather annoying issue, which I assume falls within the remit of the Department of Botany in the Natural History Museum; namely the irritating way in which the countless summertime leaves make a loud swishing noise when the wind blows from the west, and the alarming way in which the branches creak as a storm approaches.

Quite frankly I am becoming a little tired of the needless sounds made by our trees when the weather becomes more boisterous than usual and would beseech you to offer some words of advice and a little help if possible. I have tried speaking to them myself but to no avail whatsoever! One would have thought that with the maturity of the degree associated with trees that have passed their centenary, there would be demonstrated a little more consideration for humankind and a greater measure of arboreal discipline. I do hope you are be able to suggest an appropriate solution to my distress.

Sincerely

M. A. Lee

Prof. Richard M Bateman DSc

Head, Department of Botany
Natural History Museum
Cromwell Road
London
SW7 5BD, U.K.
Tel. (Direct)   020 7942 5282
Tel. (PA)   020 7942 5093
Fax (PA)   020 7942 5501
e-mail: r.bateman@nhm.ac.uk

Dr Richard M Bateman
Keeper of Botany

Evolutionary phylogenetics;
orchid systematics; palaeobotany

02.02.2004

Dear Mr Lee,

Thankyou for your letter of January 29th regarding the long-term irritation caused to you by the swishing of leaves and creaking of branches perpetrated by the playful trees situated along the perimeter of your abode. I wish you to understand at the outset that neither I as Head of Botany, nor the Natural History Museum in general, can be held legally accountable for the traumas experienced by you, your family and friends. Nonetheless, we do maintain a considerable body of expertise in this general area, and thus are in a position to offer you some basic advice.

Firstly, we believe that you should set these problems in a more rational context. Mother Nature has arranged that, for approximately half of each calendar year, the broadleaf trees that you describe bear no leaves whatsoever, thereby regularly preserving you from the mental anguish engendered by the accompanying swishing. I admit that this act does not cause concomitant reductions in the levels of creaking, but I would point out that strong westerly winds are largely a wintertime phenomenon. Thus, nature has carefully arranged to divorce swishing from creaking, so that in practice you are rarely assailed by these two chronic problems simultaneously.

Also, I believe that you have failed to comprehend the rationale behind the (no doubt conscious) decision of the trees to swish and creak. The summer swishing is, in my professional opinion, a prelude to the precipitous fall of these very same leaves in the autumn. Now you must surely have observed the cataclysmic effects of autumn leaves on the operations of "Railtrack". In truth, this failure simply reflects the inability of Railtrack employees to comprehend, and take full account of, the swishing performed by the leaves in advance warning of the subsequent, well-coordinated leaf-fall. By taking proper account of swishing as soon as it is evident, you should be able to implement a more efficient managerial strategy than Railtrack, thereby ensuring that (unlike Railtrack) your garden remains available to those who most enjoy its restful ambience throughout the year.

Similarly, the creaking of branches provides an early warning of the potential collapse of the crown of one or more of the mature trees described in your letter. The recommended response is therefore to retire to your home at the first hint of creaking, taking advantage of your cellar should you be fortunate enough to possess one, but certainly at all costs avoiding the upper floors of your house, which are at grave risk of being penetrated by your arborescent neighbours.

You may, however, wish to consider a more radical solution to your current plight than those suggested above. You note in your letter that your trees have proved singularly unresponsive to your verbal commands. May I suggest that you seek the services of someone more in tune with the thought processes of your trees? The most obvious, and sustainable, solution would be to encourage residency of one or more Ents. Admittedly, this remedy can sometimes prove more damaging than the original problem, especially to those inhabiting remote and vaguely sinister towers. A less radical suggestion would be to garner assistance from our current monarchy. My understanding is that Prince Charles in particular has proven particularly effective in such circumstances, and that due to various personal constraints his fees are now very reasonable.

The obvious ultimate remedy to your problems would be to move away from your current habitation in Huddersfield. Indeed, my understanding, based admittedly on hearsay, is that most denizens of Huddersfield are already attempting just such an outward translocation. However, given this relative lack of originality, I would suggest that you think more laterally. Specifically, I believe that you would find that a Trappist establishment (or failing that, the House of Lords while in session) would offer the perfect kind of ambience that you crave.

Whatever solution you adopt, I wish you well in your worthy search for a more fulfilling (and presumably herbaceous) life.

Yours sincerely,

Richard

Mr C. Anderson
Dental Surgeon
The Dental Surgery
10 Church Street
Rastrick
West Yorkshire HD6 3NF

Dear Mr Anderson

I am writing you a letter of complaint.

Very recently the young son of a neighbour of mine discovered that his very first milk tooth had removed itself from his lower gum and consequently, in the ancient tradition of the celebration of noteworthy events everywhere, there was organised a magnificent street party complete with a swing-jazz band and a mass balloon release.

Countless plates of tasty sandwiches were provided, bowls of mouth-watering crisps laid out and jellies and cakes of numbers beyond anyone's wildest dreams placed in a most alluring and tempting manner for all to enjoy. For most people the feasting, singing and dancing continued for a whole Saturday afternoon and long into the night; one particular aged gentleman who attended carried on by himself for another two days and was still at the side of the road on Tuesday morning.

Despite such a splendid public marking of the milk-tooth detachment and the wonderment and receipt of gifts experienced and enjoyed by the aforementioned boy to whom the tooth was once attached, there was, however, no visit by the Tooth Fairy that or any subsequent evening. The tooth that the boy carefully placed beneath his pillow on the evening of the party was still there the next morning and indeed for the next few mornings. There were no pound coins or even humble pennies left next to the tooth, nor even an alternative gift of acknowledgement.

Had there been a simple and polite IOU note to explain that the Tooth Fairy was short of cash at the time and that amends would be made at a later date, then all would have been fine. Sadly this was not the case and we have come to the conclusion that the Tooth Fairy did not appear at all.

Doubtless you will agree that this is a disgraceful situation and, presuming that this individual of legendary status is, like yourself, represented by the British Dental Association, I have decided forthwith to lodge my complaint with you as a fellow member.

I would be interested to hear from you in the very near future with a plausible explanation of such a break in expected routine and, if possible, an appropriate apology from the Tooth Fairy herself, if indeed you know of her elusive whereabouts.

Sincerely, a concerned neighbour,

M. A. Lee

Mr. C. Anderson

B.Ch.D.(Hons) Dental Surgeon

The Dental Surgery
10 Church Street
Rastrick
Brighouse
West Yorkshire
HD6 3NF

Tel: 01484 721157

29 February 2004

Dear Mr Lee,

Thank you for your letter of 1st February 2004. I am most grateful to you for bringing this matter to my attention. I must say that I am most surprised and alarmed to hear of this episode. I have raised the matter with the British Dental Association and also the General Dental Council, as it may be possible that the tooth fairy for the region is in breach of her terms of service. I can assure you that a full internal enquiry is currently being undertaken as this letter wings its way to you. I shall of course be in contact with you again as soon as I have any further information. Hopefully a full explanation will be given and I have requested a written apology from the Tooth Fairy concerned. This may take a little time, as the department is both secretive and elusive.

Yours sincerely, an equally concerned dentist,

C. Anderson

Mr. C. Anderson

The Chief Fairy Elder
Dell Circle
Sparkleville

Dear Elder Mo Lar

I am writing to you after receiving a very disturbing letter from a concerned gentleman regarding an incident of the most alarming nature. On hearing of it, I decided I must consult with you in the hope of resolving the matter.

The incident I refer to involves a young boy living in Oakes, Huddersfield, who recently parted with his very first milk tooth. I know that you understand the traditions and customs of parents in such situations and expect no less than great excitement and joy at this milestone in the life of any child, and will therefore sympathise with the distress the incident I shall relate now has caused. Despite being very carefully placed under the pillow of the young boy, the little milk tooth was never collected by the tooth fairy that night or any night after!

I realise that you may not be aware of this situation and must be very shocked to hear of it from myself. I can only assume that your inspection team OFSTED (Official Fairy Standards Team of Evaluation Delegates) have not reported the matter to you, for had they done so I know you would have taken action to resolve this distressing situation.

I request that you look into the matter immediately and inform me of your findings. You will appreciate that the British Dental Association works very hard to promote the Tooth Recycling Programme and this incident does not put us in a very good light.

Looking forward to hearing from you.

Yours sincerely

Mr. C. Anderson
Dentist Extraordinaire

The Chief Fairy Elder
Dell Circle
Sparkleville

Mr. C. Anderson
10 Church Street
Rastrick
Nr Huddersfield
West Yorkshire

Dear Mr. Anderson

Thank you for your letter regarding the matter of the unclaimed tooth by the Tooth Recycling Department. We appreciate that you brought the matter to our attention. Elder Mo Lar and the whole Fairy Council are taking the matter very seriously indeed and as soon as we have any information we shall contact you.

Yours sincerely

Flo Ride

Flo Ride
Secretary to the Fairy Council

Tooth Recycling Department

INTERNAL MEMO
Date

To: **Den Talfloss**

From: **Flo Ride**

You are required to present yourself in front of the Fairy Council at the Crown Hall tomorrow at 12 noon. Please report to the receptionist on your arrival.

Mr. C. Anderson
10 Church Street
Rastrick
Nr Huddersfield
West Yorkshire

Dear Mr. Anderson

I am writing to you to inform you that our investigation into the matter regarding the unclaimed tooth has now concluded and to report our findings to you.

The tooth fairy responsible for Oakes, Huddersfield is a young chap named Den Talfloss. On receiving your letter the Fairy Council summoned him to appear at the Crown Hall to explain his failure to collect the freshly lost tooth. The council found Den extremely remorseful and upset as he related the events of that fateful night. I shall now relate them to you.

Den was relaxing in the Eye Tooth Bar when the call came through that a milk tooth was ready for collection. He swiftly made his way to the young boy's house and began entry procedures. However, on the approach to the designated window, his left wing became caught in a rather large cobweb situated in the corner of the pane. For some time Den struggled with the threads of the web, but the more he struggled the more entangled he became. He began to believe things could not get any worse when suddenly, they did, with the untimely arrival of the owner of the web – a large black garden spider! Den, who suffers from arachnophobia, promptly fainted, and miraculously that's what saved him from being spider supper! As his body relaxed, the threads surrounding his wing became loose and he dropped from the window sill. Now without the luck of Queen Titania, that might have been the end of him, but no! By pure chance, a sparrow nesting in a nearby tree saw the whole thing and her quick thinking saved Den's life. She swooped under him as he fell, catching him on her back and flew him home to Sparkleville.

It was three hours later when Den awoke from his faint-like state and the last thing he could remember was ordering a Wisdom Bap with a minty filling. His mother, concerned at his state of amnesia took him straight away to see Mr. D. Kay, a renowned fairy doctor, who ordered rest and relaxation. In the weeks following the incident, Den did just that and slowly his memory began to return. By the time he was summoned to the Fairy Council he was able to recall the whole terrifying ordeal, indeed he is still on medication to calm his nerves.

Having investigated the incident at length, the Council find that the circumstances were unavoidable and distressing for all involved. Den has been granted long term leave for 6 months and will be under the supervision of Mr. Kay.

On behalf of Den and the whole Tooth Fairy Council I would like to apologise to you, the concerned gentleman who brought the situation to your attention, and most importantly, the young boy who lost his tooth. Please assure them and be assured yourself that the fairy assigned to collect his next tooth will leave the usual amount but with interest this time as a gesture of goodwill.

I would also ask that you pass on our apologies to the Board of the British Dental Association. We hope our relationship with them will not be adversely affected and that we can continue to forge positive links with them.

Thank you once again for your involvement and your continued support of the Tooth Recycling Programme.

Yours sincerely

Elder. Mo. Lar

Elder Mo Lar
Fairy Council

Portia D. Edmiston
Customer Service Department
Next Retail Ltd
Desford Road
Enderby
Leicester LE19 4AT

Dear Portia

I am writing you a letter of complaint.

Many years ago in the days when my eyebrows did not sprout wiry hairs on a daily basis and life was fresh and full of adventure, my long-suffering wife and I visited the west coast of Canada one summer and enjoyed a wonderful trip around the Rocky Mountains.

Not only did we see a variety of breathtaking panoramas and a range of wild animals – including three grizzly bears and a dozen elk – but we also managed to purchase a marvellous Davy Crockett hat made of rabbit skin and sporting a magnificent raccoon's tail of at least 15 inches in length.

This hat was my pride and joy for many years after returning to the UK and I wore it regularly while out for lunch, shopping in Huddersfield town centre and, indeed, while on the odd nature trail in the countryside. I didn't seem to have many friends at that time of my life but the hat was my constant companion even on the wettest of days.

Sadly, my hat eventually shrivelled after being chewed by the neighbour's dog and spun once or twice in the tumble dryer, and I had to resort to wearing a rather uninteresting woollen Balaclava instead.

Despite searching far and wide in several Next stores around the UK I have, to date, been unable to find a replacement Davy Crockett hat of the kind described above. I am aware that of all the large stores selling a range of carefully chosen clothes, Next have an enviable reputation as being the very best at catering for the needs of the smart and casual dresser with an eye for conservative fashion.

In this regard I am most concerned, and indeed rather distressed, that there are no Davy Crockett hats to be found in any of your outlets and I have even heard an unthinkable suggestion by one of your shop assistants – I believe her name is Rita – that they have never been stocked at all (banish the thought!). Quite frankly I am shocked and frustrated.

Please, please, please can you help me in my urgent search for a replacement hat?

Sincerely

M. A. Lee

P.S. If rabbit skin is not available I will settle for Arctic fox, but the tail must be that of a raccoon and preferably a long one with an ample number of stripes.

NEXT

Customer Service Department
Desford Road, Enderby, Leicester, LE19 4AT

Our Reference: 2048664/SH
10 February 2004

Mr M A Lee
Somewhere in West Yorkshire

Dear Mr Lee

Thank you for your recent letter. Unfortunately Portia has left our department to seek fame and fortune in London, however after liaising with her agent she has given me permission to write to you on her behalf.

I am very sorry that you have been unable to find a replacement Davy Crockett hat in our local Next store. Unfortunately this is not an item we currently stock, although Next has been known to stock striking and stylish headwear in the past. As you can see from the enclosed photo, our speciality was turning giant Antarctic birds into fashionable hats.

You may be interested to learn that Next has a number of hats on sale for the stylish, well travelled gentleman this season. For a more interesting take on the woolly hat, you might like to try our Blue & Grey Stripe Hat (M95339). We also have a Gothic Hat on offer (M95346) should you fancy getting in touch with your vampire side. Three tasteful Fisherman's Hats are on sale this season too which may (or may not) have been endorsed by Captain Birdseye.

Regrettably none of these styles come with racoon's tail but this may be substituted by rolling up our Arctic Fox throw (M49331) into a cylinder and attaching it to the back of the hat, thus giving you an impressive 2 metre tail.

I would like to take this opportunity to apologise for the lack of knowledge shown by Rita, our Sales Consultant. She has found it difficult to adapt after selling her newsagents in Coronation Street but we are confident she will soon be offering the high standard of customer care you'd expect from Next.

In closing, may I take this opportunity to thank you for taking the time to contact us with your feedback. Should you ever wish to see any more wild animals, you may like to pay a visit to our office first thing in the morning – some of our staff can be very uncivilised before they have their first coffee of the day.

Yours sincerely,

Steve Hack
Correspondence Manager
Customer Service Department

Contact Customer Services on 0870 243 5435. Our opening hours are 9.00am - 5.30pm Monday to Saturday; 11.00am - 5.00pm Sundays. Fax: 0116 284 2318 E Mail: enquiries@next.co.uk.

281

The Commanding Officer
The Royal Tank Regiment
Stanley Barracks
Bovington Camp
Dorset BH20 6JA

Dear Sir

I am writing you a letter of complaint.

Despite committing myself to acquiring a 'think-tank' several months ago I have, to date, been sadly unsuccessful in my quest. I have written to a variety of organisations that make tanks, paint tanks and even fill tanks with fish but, alas, no one has been able to satisfy my requirements. It is with renewed hope that I write to you as the Commander of tanks.

As a sales executive within corporate industry my original missive was inspired by my attending a business brainstorming session where I was asked to take a lead in co-ordinating efforts in the establishment of a 'think-tank', as part of a team of individuals who have formed a committee for the collection and dissemination of ideas. Hence it was with a certain degree of relief and satisfaction that I chanced upon your business on the internet. I do hope that you are able to help me.

The think-tank would, I suggest, have to be of a size that can be transported to various business meetings, many of which tend to occur in hotels around the UK, and on this basis it would need both to fit conveniently through a standard-size door and sit easily in the boot of an average saloon car. Similarly, as mobility is high on the agenda of requirements, the think-tank would need to be of a weight that is easily managed by even the weakest member of our sales team.

It is unlikely that our team of idea generators and analysts will come up with more than a few useful concepts in any given business year; therefore I believe that the think-tank will need only a small capacity, although this capacity would need to be reliable and quickly mobilised.

In terms of style and colour my colleagues have agreed that we need to be completely flexible and would leave this to your own experience and discretion, although it would be helpful to avoid a contraption with too many buttons and switches and such a device would preferably not be camouflaged lest we lose it.

I am most appreciative of your time and consideration with relation to this matter, and I look forward to hearing from you in the near future with specification options and respective quotes.

Sincerely

M. A. Lee

Michael A. Lee

From: Colonel (Retd) J L Longman
      Regimental Colonel

Regimental Headquarters
Royal Tank Regiment
Stanley Barracks
Bovington
Dorset
BH20 6JA

Telephone: Bovington Military (9) 4374 Ext 3360
           Civil (01929) 403360
Fax: Bovington Military (9) 4374 Ext 3488
           Civil (01929) 403488
E Mail: rhqrtr@bovvy.fsnet.co.uk

DO2

Mr M A Lee
10 Woodlea Avenue
Reinwood Manor
Oakes
Huddersfield
HD3 4EF

1 2 February 2004

Thank you for your letter re ""Think Tanks". I fear the suggestions that one of our tanks could be used for such an exercise would be unworkable. If you seriously wish to transport such an item to venues around the country you are asking for trouble, as ours weighs in at 60 plus tons. There are many roads and bridges not to mention venues that would be unable to accept such a load. In addition it would involve huge costs, to move a tank on a tank transporter would cost in excess of £50.00 per mile and if one were to move a tank on its own it works out at £156.00 per mile including wear and tear.

The inside of our tank does not afford a lot of room indeed this specialist "Think Tank" would hold no more than four people, hardly worth the time and effort for the "Thinkers" concerned.

As to colour our "Think Tank" comes in a regulation drab colour, hardly one for "Thinkers" of the quality you are looking for to feel comfortable in. Our model comes with at least four computers and several hundred buttons and controls some of which can cause considerable damage if pushed/pulled by an inexperienced operator. Your "Thinkers" would have to spend at least six months on a course to get used to the "Think Tank" otherwise I fear they would not be as effective as you would wish.

Unless you go back to the drawing board and design a purpose built ""Think Tank"" for your Thinkers I suspect you will never achieve your goal.

In my view the ideal would be a mobile mini sized version of the London Dome, it should accommodate an audience of 60 plus. The mini dome could be both maintained and inflated by the hot air produced on the day. Providing only male "Thinkers" are involved the problems involved in the erection of the mini dome in question would be easily resolved. If however you anticipate female "Thinkers" beware because there is likely to be a delay in the set up process.

"Thinkers" don't always have to do it in a "Think Tank" the great outdoors is a wonderful place for free expression and loosing ones inhibitions. Think Tank, Think Green, Think Mini Dome.

I wish you every good fortune in your project and suggest you look for Lottery Funding to help you achieve your deadline.

The Director of Science
European Space Agency
8–10 rue Mario-Nikis
F-75738 Paris Cedex 15
France

Dear Sir/Madam

I am writing you a letter of complaint.

Despite a headline on page 11 of yesterday's Daily Telegraph (12 February 2004) declaring 'Beagle is Dead', I have not received an invitation to the funeral.

I am absolutely outraged at the lack of any form of personal and official notification regarding the event that is presumably being organised to commemorate the passing of Beagle 2, especially since it was I, along with countless other taxpayers, who helped to raise the £45 million it cost to breathe life into the poor mechanical beast in the first place.

I am sure you will sympathise with my wish to attend the funeral and mark such a sad occasion with a few moments of thought and reflection and the singing, perhaps, of a suitably solemn hymn.

I would appreciate a response from you complete with details as to the whereabouts and timing of the aforementioned event as soon as is conveniently possible. I have already polished my best black shoes and am fully prepared to travel at short notice.

Sincerely perplexed,

M. A. Lee

Michael A. Lee

D/SCI/DJS/db/17925

Paris, 24 February 2004

Mr Michael A. Lee
10 Woodlea Avenue
Reinwood Manor
Oakes
GB - Huddersfield HD3 4EF

Thank you for your letter of concern on the 'death' of Beagle 2, the British-led Mars lander carried and delivered by the ESA Mars Express spacecraft.

Let me reassure you that Beagle 2 always was inanimate and is 'lost' rather than deceased. Moreover, although its loss is real, I can assure you that much has already been gained from Beagle 2 and even more from Mars Express itself.

Newspapers are selective in what they publish about progress in a complex science mission like Mars Express but towards the end of January all the world's press (as well as broadcast media) recorded the enormous excitement of the first results from the Mars Express, the stunningly detailed images of the planet and the detection by three separate means of the presence of water ice on the summer (southern) polar cap. These augur extremely well for the final outcome of the mission in a year or so's time. Already the US agency NASA has congratulated Europe on its success in its first trip to Mars. You may know that the USA (and in the past, Russia) have sustained more failures (total or partial) going to Mars than successes. You have a reason for some satisfaction.

That Beagle 2 flew at all was itself a technical triumph achieved only by immense efforts on the part of a team of talented engineers and scientists, largely from British universities (led by the Open University) and industry (EADS-Astrium, Stevenage). To achieve the miniaturisation of scientific instruments and deliver a complete system against a punishing schedule (set by the way Earth and Mars move and the difficulties of raising the money for the endeavour) is remarkable and you can rest assured that many, many elements worked and that the skills and knowledge developed in the building are retained for the future. Beagle 2 therefore leaves a fine legacy.

When it is so hard to get to, why should one care about Mars? You probably already know. You indicate that you attend funerals which mark respect for the end of life; we are concerned with its beginning. Where do we come from? How did things as complex as us evolve out of the stars? 3.5 billion years ago when Earth and Mars were only a billion years old, Mars looks to have had conditions very like Earth. Did primitive life, bacteria, etc, evolve there as they did at Earth? What brought the process to an end? Should we on Earth worry that the same might happen here?

European Space Agency
Agence spatiale européenne

Headquarters - Siège
8-10 rue Mario-Nikis - F-75738 Paris Cedex 15
Tél +33 (0) 1 53 69 76 54 - Fax +33 (0) 1 53 69 75 60 - Télex ESA 202 746 F

You are concerned by the cost. If I set the £42M for Beagle 2 against the British, it is about 15p per head of population per year for the last four years. In practice much of the bill is set against the taxpayers of all fifteen ESA Member States. In fact, if you want to specifically allocate your contribution for 2004, why not think of it as the cost of the stamp which ESA is paying to mail this letter which I wrote to try and help you share in the wonder of exploring our universe and, in particular, our neighbouring planet?

Meanwhile do keep your shoes polished and perhaps celebrate rather than mourn Britain's role in space exploration.

Yours sincerely,

David Southwood
Director of Science

The Manager
The Ritz
150 Piccadilly
London W1J 9BR

Dear Sir/Madam

I am writing you a letter of complaint.

Having travelled around the UK on business for several years, I have stayed at a range of hotels in many locations and, indeed, have done so with variable degrees of satisfaction, finding some to be poor and some extremely and memorably excellent.

I am amazed at the variation in the standards of comfort and services provided by the vast spectrum of hotels in which I have stayed, and particularly when it comes to the matter of those smaller niceties and subtle offerings that add extra benefit and luxury to the self-interested guest. This is, in my own humble opinion, especially true when it comes to the gratuitous fruit selection left in convenient places for the hungry individual who requires a mid-morning or late afternoon snack of a juicy and nutritious nature.

Let me say at this juncture that I am more than happy to note that many 'average' hotels provide ample quantities of simple fruits such as apples, pears and even the odd bunch of green grapes for the taking and some even an occasional banana. One could not expect more from such establishments and with them I have no quarrel. When it comes to the crème de la crème of British hotels, however, it is another matter altogether.

Unrestricted charge-free fruit offerings are a vital courtesy that most guests in 2004 would expect as an absolute matter of course and etiquette, but surely an elite hotel such as the Ritz ought to offer a selection of fruit that reflects a status as elite as the hotel itself. Why stock a fruit bowl with merely the simplest of fruits when a far superior choice of exotic alternatives could be presented and provided with little extra effort and expense?

At the very least I would expect the Ritz to have placed in the foyer and upon the reception desk a variety of tropical fruits such as the cherimoya or custard apple, passion fruit, papaya, guava and kumquat. If the hotel really wished to make a long-lasting impression upon their regular and, may I add, generously tipping clients, then this range should also include the pineapple and coconut, complete with a small designer mallet with which to crack the latter.

The absolute pièce de résistance would surely be a small orchard of fig trees and date palms planted in large clay pots close to the doors, where those who might take an interest in harvesting their own fresh fruit directly from the laden branches could do so with purpose and pleasure.

Apples and pears are fine for a truck stop but surely not for such a prestigious world-leading hotel as the Ritz. There is gratuitous fruit and there is gratuitous fruit!

What can you do to allay my concerns, dampen my anger and avoid future disappointments?

Sincerely fruit-loving

M. A. Lee .

Michael A. Lee

BY APPOINTMENT TO
HRH THE PRINCE OF WALES
SUPPLIERS OF BANQUETING
AND CATERING SERVICES
THE RITZ, LONDON

THE RITZ LONDON

Mr. M. A. Lee
Somewhere in West Yorkshire

25th February 2004

Dear Mr. Lee,

Thank you for your letter dated 19th February 2004.

I read your letter with great interest and appreciate your very valid comments and suggestions. I share your opinions concerning the wide spectrum of varying standards and comfort offered by establishments and would assure you of our intention that The Ritz is at the highest level of that spectrum.

I have personally initiated a revision of fresh seasonal fruit offered to our clients, including the presentation of these items. I regret you found the selection of Red Blush and Casa Passat Pears with Granny Smith Apples not to your liking. We maintain the philosophy of quality over quantity and our Chef regularly visits Covent Garden to personally select seasonal organic items.

Finally I would like to thank you again for taking the time to draw my attention to this matter and I would ask that when you next intend to

 150 PICCADILLY, LONDON W1J 9BR
TELEPHONE (020) 7493 8181 FACSIMILE (020) 7493 2687
ENQUIRE@THERITZLONDON.COM WWW.THERITZLONDON.COM
CHAIN CODE: LW TOLL FREE RESERVATIONS FROM THE USA 1 877 748 9536
THE RITZ HOTEL (LONDON) LTD. REGISTERED IN ENGLAND NO 642030. VAT REGISTRATION NO 772 8648 39

BY APPOINTMENT TO
HRH THE PRINCE OF WALES
SUPPLIERS OF BANQUETING
AND CATERING SERVICES
THE RITZ. LONDON

THE RITZ LONDON

visit The Ritz, to contact my office directly so I may make the necessary arrangements personally. I look forward to welcoming you back to The Ritz when I trust you will note as a result of your comments, an improvement in the standard of fruit in both presentation and selection.

Yours sincerely

Stephen Boxall
General Manager

150 PICCADILLY, LONDON W1J 9BR
TELEPHONE (020) 7493 8181   FACSIMILE (020) 7493 2687
ENQUIRE@THERITZLONDON.COM   WWW.THERITZLONDON.COM
CHAIN CODE: LW   TOLL FREE RESERVATIONS FROM THE USA 1 877 748 9536
THE RITZ HOTEL (LONDON) LTD. REGISTERED IN ENGLAND NO 64205C. VAT REGISTRATION NO 773 8638 29

IN PARTNERSHIP
WITH
THE RITZ-CARLTON®
HOTEL COMPANY, L.L.C

Head of Engineering (Highways & Traffic)
PO Box 463
Town Hall
Manchester M60 3NY

Dear Sir/Madam

I am writing you a letter of complaint.

Doubtless you are familiar with the traditional proverb 'all roads lead to Rome' and probably also that the Highways Department has never produced any public statement to the contrary. As a result of such governmental oversight I was recently lost on the bleak Pennine moors to the east of Manchester, my holiday plans completely spoiled and my state of mind reduced to nothing short of despair. Let me explain.

A few weeks ago I decided to travel to the venerable city of Rome so that I might see the Ancient Roman Colosseum and enjoy a real Italian pizza or two while making the most of weather that is generally warmer than it is in the UK during the winter months. Having placed my suitcase in the boot of my car I duly set out from Huddersfield with a light heart but, as you will no doubt understand, no particular map, since I believed that, ultimately and in accordance with the aforementioned proverb, I would eventually arrive in Rome with little navigational effort anyway.

My journey began in a most satisfactory manner when I drove from my home town of Huddersfield along the A635 through the scenic village of Holmfirth and onward across the peaty, heather-clad tops towards Saddleworth. As I began my descent from Saddleworth Moor itself I was in awe at the panorama presented to me as I looked over Dove Stone Reservoir at the towering and atmospheric hills, and consequently turned left on to a smaller road to better enjoy the view. After a few hundred metres my road passed a picnic site and a car park and continued onward and over a reservoir dam to the eastern side of the reservoir itself.

Although I was a little perplexed at the obvious lack of road signs for either Manchester or Rome during this part of my journey, I persevered with my now bumpy ride and, before long, passed a small coniferous plantation and a rather large roadside rabbit warren (I saw several rabbits too!). Sadly the road as such then ended.

There was absolutely no warning that the road was about to end abruptly where it did. I certainly didn't find myself in Rome, or in any other ancient city for that matter, and the only ruins I managed to see were those of a dilapidated and disused sheepfold at the foot of Dove Stone Moss.

The weather was rather disappointing, for the heavens darkened and I was drenched with rain as I strode from my car back to the picnic place in order to phone for the RAC to attend to the tyres that had punctured en route. In addition I was completely unable to locate anywhere that sold pizza of any description, whether Italian or Mancunian, and had to satisfy myself with a hot dog from the white van parked near the public conveniences.

I am terribly dissatisfied at the seemingly negligent absence of communication issued by the Highways Department to the effect that the old proverb stated above may well be outdated, and am even more outraged that there are no signs at any road junction in the Greater Manchester area stating simply that 'Rome is not down here'.

I await your response with a sense of urgency and indignation.

Sincerely

M. A. Lee

Michael A. Lee

OLDHAM
Metropolitan Borough

Environmental Services

Michael A Lee
10 Woodlea Avenue
Reinwood Manor
Oakes
Huddersfield
HD3 4EF

Your reference:
Our reference: SJP/GB/80
Please ask for: Mr Palk
Direct line: 0161 911 4328
Fax no: 0161 911 3411
Date: 16 March 2004

Dear Mr Lee

RE: ROMAN HOLIDAY

Thank you for your letter of 17 February 2004 which has been forwarded to me from my colleagues in the Manchester City Council.

Your trip on that fateful day must have been disconcerting. Not only did you pass the Oldham Borough Boundary Sign which would have alerted you to the fact that not all the areas west of the Pennines are in Manchester, but you also (from your description) managed to execute a 'banned left turn' to arrive on Bank Lane to access the Dovestone Reservoir.

If you had seen that particular sign, I think you would have also noted the brown Dovestone sign. Whilst this sign does indicate the facilities that are available, it does not indicate that there is any through destinations beyond Dovestone Reservoir. Judging by the lack of complaints that this system of signs is generating and the evidence from the receipts for the car park and feedback from the Peak District Park Authorities, it would appear that users from far and wide are viewing these signs and the context of the mountain location of the reservoir and concluding that the exit from the site is the way that they came in.

In this remote Pennine environment there are many roads which turn to tracks which eventually become paths or disappear altogether. You will appreciate that emergency access in this area is difficult and consequently it is incumbent on any traveller within the remote parts of the Peak District to carry a map and have sufficient resources to sustain themselves in case of emergency.

Whilst I interpret your letter as a criticism of the Council in not providing traffic signs to indicate which routes are not available from any point you may render your car immobile, I think you will see on reflection that in the remoter points of the Borough the task of such negative signing would not only be inordinate but would unduly clutter the attractions that people had come to see.

I trust that your unfortunate experience will not inhibit you from 'roaming' in the Oldham countryside in the future.

Yours sincerely

GROUP MANAGER
TRAFFIC AND PARKING

Td 038c

Henshaw House Cheapside Oldham OL1 1NY
e-mail env.henshaw.house@oldham.gov.uk
www.oldham.gov.uk www.visitoldham.co.uk

Somewhere in West Yorkshire
13 April 2004

Head of Customer Services
Harry Ramsden's
PO Box 218
Toddington
Bedfordshire LU5 6QG

Dear Sir/Madam

I am writing you a letter of complaint.

It gives me no degree of pleasure whatsoever to tell you that I have recently become rather aggrieved at my present state of being, and am inclined to feel rather resentful about a wide range of people with whom I interact and countless circumstances in which I find myself. I have been told by several individuals that I have a disposition which has been regularly perceived in the last few weeks as rather negative and perhaps even a tad arrogant and that, moreover, I appear at times both overbearing and presumptuous. In short, it seems that I have acquired 'a chip on my shoulder'.

Although I cannot prove without a shadow of a doubt that this aforementioned chip was not present prior to my recent visit to your wonderful restaurant in Guiseley, West Yorkshire, I do not recollect seeing it on previous occasions, nor being told about it before by friends and colleagues adept at providing me with abundant personal feedback.

Since I rarely frequent fish-and-chip establishments nor possess a chip pan within my own home, I am at a loss to explain the aforementioned item and wonder whether it might have fallen from a passing tray when I was seated in your restaurant for my evening supper.

Despite the fact that I consider your fish-and-chip suppers the best of their kind in the land, I am disgruntled at this present state of affairs and am thus voicing my concerns as I thought appropriate. When the chips are down I do not personally wish to have to shoulder a burden of this kind and ask that you advise me of a suitable process whereby I might dispose of my chip forthwith.

Thank you.

Sincerely

M. A. Lee

Michael A. Lee

PO Box 218 Toddington Bedfordshire LU5 6QG
Tel 01525 878488 Fax 01525 878334
Web www.harryramsdens.co.uk

Our Ref: SG/HR   Date: 21st April 2004

Dear Mr Lee,

Thank you for your letter dated 13th April 2004 and for your comments.

I hope the enclosed voucher to the value of £10 (redeemable at any participating Harry Ramsden's outlet) will go some way to removing your chip or at least replacing it with some fresh ones.

Yours sincerely,

Mrs S A Gardner
Customer Services Manager

The Director
Birmingham Royal Ballet
Thorp Street
Birmingham B5 4AU

Dear Sir/Madam

I am writing you a letter of complaint.

Despite my earnest and persistent campaign to find a well-respected ballet company that will consider me for a suitable audition, permitting pursuit of my desired career of choice, I have, to date, drawn an absolute blank. Many ballets to whom I have written have not had the basic courtesy to respond to my letters of polite enquiry and, of the few that have, none has accepted me for a basic initial interview nor even requested a CV for consideration.

While I do not intend my complaint to be applied to your good selves at Birmingham Royal Ballet, I am sure that you can understand my disappointment and frustration after 27 years of frequent rejection and ongoing dismay. It is, undoubtedly, a small miracle that any modicum of hope still burns within my dance-driven soul and that my efforts in looking for a sympathetic ballet company continue unabated to this day; hence the missive in front of you at this present time.

As the crème de la crème of ballets with an unrivalled reputation across the world, I have decided to approach you at Birmingham Royal Ballet for some help and understanding, and trust that you will be willing to take my quest to become a trained ballet dancer to the next stage of the interview and course-application process.

Aged 44 – I will not be 45 until December of this year – I am an industrious and affable gentleman whose balding head and wrinkled appearance mask an impressively energetic and willing approach to learning and to performance. Despite being a tad uncoordinated and weighing slightly more than I ought – a little too close to 18 stone for comfort – I am nevertheless more graceful than would appear at first sight. Provided that I utilise my short-acting bronchodilator regularly and spend sufficient warm-up time to overcome the stiffness in my creaking knees and tightness in my aching back, some would say that there is a certain magnificence in the way that I can pirouette and spin.

I am reasonably fit for my age, can carry a box containing eight bags of sugar on my head for 100 metres while maintaining a straight back and dignified poise and, moreover, I can whistle most tunefully. (I thought that the latter might be useful if the ballet music at a particular session fails due to a power surge or similar.)

I do hope that a review of my capabilities as outlined within this letter is sufficient to convince you to interview and audition me for a place at Birmingham Royal Ballet and I look forward to hearing from you in the very near future.

Sincerely

M. A. Lee .

Michael A. Lee
P.S. Does the typical ballet-dancer's remuneration package include health-care insurance that would cover pre-existing problems such as gout, fallen arches and frequent dizzy spells? (Just curious!)

19th May 2004

BIRMINGHAM ROYAL BALLET
Director David Bintley CBE

Mr M A Lee
Somewhere in West Yorkshire

Principal Sponsor

POWERGEN

Dear Mr Lee

Thank you very much for your recent letter. My apologies for this rather late reply, as I wanted to give your earnest application to Birmingham Royal Ballet the greatest of consideration.

I am astounded that my colleagues in the ballet world have not had the courtesy to reply to your letters of enquiry. Your eloquent description of your undoubted gifts and your honest appraisal of your few minor defects is not only refreshing, but leads me to believe that you are exactly what we are looking for! A genuine passion for dance, which obviously burns in your soul, will transcend your tender years and our exercise regime and dietary advisors will soon have you shedding the pounds.

Birmingham Royal Ballet
Thorp Street
Birmingham
B5 4AU

Switchboard
+44 (0) 121 245 3500

Fax
+44 (0) 121 245 3570

Website
www.brb.org.uk

As is always customary however, before I extend you the offer of a contract I will have to request a copy of your CV and a video of your work, either in class or in performance. This is standard procedure for any dancer who joins the company, but I am sure that you will pass this, the final test with flying colours!

Very much looking forwards to seeing some examples of your work.

I am yours, sincerely

DAVID BINTLEY
Director

Direct dial: +44 (0) 121 245 3519
E-mail: DavidBintley@brb.org.uk
Department fax: +44 (0) 121 245 3570

P.S. I particularly like the sound of your trick with the bags of sugar. I might even consider featuring this in my next new ballet!

Birmingham Royal Ballet is a
company limited by guarantee.
Registered Office:
Thorp Street, Birmingham B5 4AU
Registered in England and Wales
No 3520536
Charity Registered No 1061012
VAT Registration No 687 9333 73

Head of Customer Services
Bailey Caravans
Liberty Lane
Bristol BS3 2SS

Dear Sir/Madam

I am writing you a letter of complaint.

Over the past few weeks my wife and I have been considering the purchase of a four-berth touring caravan for our family of two adults and two small and, let it be said, energetic sons, with a view to spending future holidays in as many scenic and interesting places as our finances will permit. Indeed, we have begun looking around various caravan retailers in an attempt to locate the ideal model of caravan, equipped with all the essential facilities plus additional luxury features needed to make life as comfortable as possible should we travel to a range of caravan sites within the UK, and perhaps further afield too.

While I have been substantially impressed with the various models of caravan that Bailey manufacture in terms of design and overall quality, fixtures, fittings and finesse, I am rather perplexed at the lack of one obvious but necessary item when it comes to caravanning in the company of small, rebellious children with an interest in anarchy and constant motion.

In short I am concerned that not one of your caravan models is supplied with a state-of-the-art caged section complete with titanium bars and a foolproof locking system, where children can be safely housed for half an hour or so while parents de-stress, nurse their emotional wounds and enjoy a little freedom for a glass of Guinness or a gin and tonic.

We have considered fitting our children with irremovable electronic tags that would provide us parents with a little satellite-coordinated notice of their proximity to our nervous selves (if they were not immediately visible). However, I believe that physical containment might be a more credible and viable alternative, and especially where moments of relaxation and refreshment are calling for attention.

I would be interested to know of any plans you have in this particular area of design and construction and look forward to hearing from you in the very near future.

Sincerely

M. A. Lee

Michael A. Lee

JSP/LG

Mr M A Lee
Somewhere in West Yorkshire

Dear Lee

Thank you for your recent letter.

I see the predicament you are in, I can think of two options open to you that may solve the security/proximity conundrum:

A   Consider the purchase of a 6 berth Ranger 550/6 type layout. Whilst on the face of it this may seem like more than you need, the flexibility of the layout means the children not only have a separate sleeping area but a dedicated playing, drawing, reading area offered by the side dinette which still leaves you your own space at the front of the caravan.

B   Go with a dedicated 4 berth layout and add an awning which can be a rumpus room for the children during the day and tranquil area for mum and dad to enjoy Guinness and Gin and Tonic in the evening.

Research continues into the use of titanium kevlar and carbon fibre in the construction of touring caravans however, recent tests have shown small children are far too formidable an adversary even for such modern materials.

I hope you find a new caravan that will do the trick for you. If we can be of further assistance to you please do not hesitate in contacting us, either by writing or using e-mail to the helpline at Bailey.

Yours sincerely

John Parker
Sales Director

Bailey of Bristol, South Liberty Lane, Bristol BS3 2SS, England

General Administration and Sales: Tel. 0117 966 5967 Fax. 0117 963 6554
Purchasing and Production: Fax. 0117 953 5868 Spares: Tel. 0117 953 8140 Spares: Fax. 0117 953 5648
e-mail: helpdesk@bailey-caravans.co.uk Website:www.bailey-caravans.co.uk
Registered Office: As above. Registration No. 354363 (Bailey Caravans Ltd)

FLEETWOOD CARAVANS LIMITED
HALL STREET, LONG MELFORD, SUFFOLK CO10 9JP
TEL: 0870 7740008
FAX: 0870 7740009

rma/lee/hmw

14th July 2004

Mr M A Lee
Somewhere in West Yorkshire

Dear Mr Lee,

Thank you for your letter dated 5th July. Your proposals are interesting but clearly any responsible manufacturer would be expected to review existing legislation relating to the personal freedoms of the individual before embarking on such a project.

In the current political climate, where parents are becoming increasingly examined in respect of their behaviour and control shown towards their children it may well be that you would want to dilute your own proposals a little to avoid any risk of your own containment at Her Majesty's Pleasure!

Yours sincerely

R.M. ALLEN
FLEETWOOD CARAVANS LTD

Registered in England No. 894586

Sir Norman Browse
President
The States of Alderney
Alderney
Channel Islands GY9 3AA

Dear Sir Norman

I am writing you a letter of complaint.

There is no doubt that the island of Alderney is one of the most wonderful islands I have read about and one that I would love to visit at some time in the near future. Descriptions of the beaches, of the cliff walks and of the quaint pubs that I have pondered over within the pages of a certain tourist brochure fill me with wanderlust and have almost tempted me to begin a somewhat premature packing of my large holiday suitcase.

My imagination has been stimulated as I picture in my mind the white-topped waves around the coastline, the seagulls riding the breezes and the possibility of relaxation in a charming place unspoilt by mass tourism. Alas, however, I am filled with frustration and concern.

Despite mention of both a harbour and an airport being situated on your idyllic island, whereby the keen visitor may disembark from boat or plane, there is nothing to suggest the existence of a less fearsome means of arrival for those terrified by sea or air travel. I refer, of course, to the presence of a tunnel. Since Alderney is only eight miles or so from the coast of Normandy, would it not be sensible and prudent to have a pedestrian tunnel built beneath the sea for those anxious souls such as myself who would be only too pleased to visit if there were a route of guaranteed terra firma?

Should such a tunnel be prepared and duly opened I would be more than happy to travel from Dover to Calais through the Channel Tunnel by train, continue onward by bus to the Alderney tunnel's entrance in France and walk the rest of the way with my wife, children and suitcase in tow. I would be equally happy to carry a Thermos flask of tea and some sandwiches for a picnic halfway through.

Doubtless this idea is one that will have been presented to you many times before and as such I am most grateful for your time and consideration.

Please do let me know whether there are any plans for excavation to begin and when the estimated time for tunnel completion is scheduled. I will then make plans accordingly. In the meantime, any information you have regarding suitable holiday accommodation for a family of four on Alderney would be gratefully received.

Sincerely

M . A . Lee .

STATES OF ALDERNEY
Channel Islands

From the President's Office

21st October, 2004,

Mr M A Lee
Somewhere in West Yorkshire

Dear Mr Lee,

Thank you for your interesting letter in which you suggest that a tunnel from France to Alderney might make it much easier for visitors who are unable to fly or sail to come to Alderney.

To the best of my knowledge I have not heard this suggestion before, although it is rumoured that there is a tunnel from France to one of the castles in Jersey.

Your description of you and your family trudging the 9 mile long ~~Channel~~ tunnel with your sandwiches and suitcases in tow conjures up many images.

I must confess that I suspect that your letter was written with your tongue in cheek because clearly there is no way in which Alderney can find the many millions of pounds needed to build a tunnel plus the ongoing costs of ensuring that illegal immigrants do not use it as a backdoor way of getting into the United Kingdom.

If you did write this letter just for fun I wonder if you would give me permission to pass it on to the Alderney Journal which is a local fortnightly publication because I think many Islanders will find it "interesting".

In spite of your travel problems I do hope that you will be able to visit Alderney at sometime in the not to distant future.

Yours sincerely,

Norman Browse.

Sir Norman Browse
President

Telephone: (01481) 822060 Fax: (01481) 822436

305

Tony Blair
Prime Minister
10 Downing Street
London SW1A 2AA

Dear Sir

I am writing you a letter of complaint.

I have become tremendously concerned and perhaps even a tad angry just recently at a worrying trend that seems to be taking root among many of our British dog owners, one that is undoubtedly undermining the very fabric of accepted tradition. Moreover, this vogue could be so potentially damaging to cultural sensitivities across the UK that I believe legislation needs to be introduced quickly and efficiently in order to nip such unacceptable behaviour in its canine-orientated bud. Allow me to elucidate.

Over the last few weeks I have seen a significant number of domesticated dogs of various sizes dressed in tartan dog coats. Although I do realise that the weather is becoming colder as we move through autumn towards the winter months, and have no objections to dog owners making every provision to keep their pets warm and comfortable, I take offence at the actual range of tartan patterning I have noted.

To date I have seen three terriers dressed in the MacDonald tartan, a Labrador in a MacDougall tartan, and a miscellany of mongrels wrapped in MacTavish, MacPherson, MacAllister and even, would you believe it, an Irish O'Reilly tartan.

Had the owners been of a Celtic descent or surname I would have understood the inclination to project their heritage towards their beloved animals also. However, having spoken to all the owners of such tartan-clad dogs, I have come to the conclusion that most of them are not of such heritage and the use of these ancient clan tartans should therefore, I suggest, cease forthwith.

Not only could the improper wearing of 'the cloth' inflame our UK residents with Scottish and Irish roots and create civil unrest, but it is also likely to confuse and destabilise the minds of many of the innocent dogs that are forced to wear such apparel. Only yesterday I heard a tartan-clad pit bull terrier sneeze and I am almost certain that it sneezed with a Highland lilt.

The trend, as you will doubtless agree, is a worrying one. If we move quickly before it progresses any further, we might just reverse the situation and avoid chaos and perhaps even anarchy among our otherwise tolerant human population.

I am eager to hear your thoughts and comments regarding this important issue and look forward to hearing from you in the near future.

Sincerely

M. A. Lee

1O DOWNING STREET
LONDON SW1A 2AA

From the Direct Communications Unit

13 October 2004

Mr Michael A Lee
Somewhere in West Yorkshire

Dear Mr Lee

The Prime Minister has asked me to thank you for your
recent letter.

Yours sincerely

[signature]

MARIANNE CONNOLLY

Royal Society for the Prevention of Cruelty to Animals

Our Ref: 2557669/cb/enq

5 November 2004

Mr M A Lee
Somewhere in West Yorkshire

Dear Mr Lee

Thank you for your letter of 6 October and from which I was concerned to read that you have a complaint about the way in which some of our British dog owners choose to dress their dogs, particularly when they use Scottish and Irish tartans.

Whilst I can appreciate your concerns, the RSPCA actually only operates in England and Wales and does not have any authority with regard to animal welfare issues in Scotland or the Republic of Ireland. Nevertheless, I could suggest that you contact the Scottish Society for the Prevention of Cruelty to Animals (SSPCA) or the Irish Society for the protection of Cruelty to Animals (ISPCA) indicating your concerns.

As an animal welfare organisation which has been active for nearly 200 years, we are well aware of the significance of heritage and tradition. However, we recognise that it is important to allow for modernisation and unity. For this reason we would not object to the dogs being dressed in coats made from traditional Scottish or Irish tartans, as long as it would not be detrimental to their health and of course they must be well fitting. I am sure that the owners simply wish for their dogs to be kept warm during the cold winter months.

I must ask whether your concerns would be alleviated and your anger dissipated if the dogs in question were to wear the appropriate garments associated with the British Isles, such as a St George's flag coat or an England rugby shirt with the Tudor rose?

I am also intrigued by your encounter with a pit bull terrier which sneezed with a highland lilt. Are you entirely certain that it was actually a sneeze with a highland lilt, rather than a mere taunt in relation to your concern for the improper wearing of the tartans? Could it be that the pit bull terrier is aware of your intolerance towards British dogs wearing Scottish or Irish attire!

I would like to thank you for writing to us with your most unusual enquiry and perhaps you may consider making a small donation to the worthy cause of animal welfare, as I am sure you are aware of the limited resources of a charitable organisation.

RSPCA, Wilberforce Way
Southwater, Horsham
West Sussex RH13 9RS
Tel 0870 010 1181
Fax 0870 7530 048
DX 57628 HORSHAM 6

www.rspca.org.uk

Patron HM The Queen
Vice Patron His Grace
The Archbishop of Canterbury

Mrs D. Moss
The Goose Club
Llwyn Coed
Gelli
Clynderwen
Pembrokeshire SA66 7HW

Dear Mrs Moss

I am writing you a letter of complaint.

Despite living in these modern times of astounding scientific and technological achievement that have seen, among many things, the dawn and evolution of such disciplines as genetic engineering, space exploration, robotics and even virtual reality, I am concerned and indeed frustrated that a rather basic advance is still to occur within the poultry industry.

I would go so far as to suggest that until such an advance is made, millions of poultry consumers around the world will be destined to experience such festive events as Christmas in ways that are restrictive and perhaps even conducive to family feuds, as they have been for hundreds of years. Let me explain.

It is common knowledge that sheep have been cloned, that pigs can now be bred to produce insulin compatible with human needs and that there are even flowers available in colours which are artificially manufactured in the laboratory to meet man's pursuit of novelty and curiosity. There are indeed myriad ways in which man has manipulated nature for his and her own ends. Isn't it then short-sighted of the poultry industry to have neglected a fundamental element in the production and marketing of geese, to improve and enhance the overall enjoyment of consuming these birds at Christmas?

In short, isn't it about time that organisations such as yours embraced modern science with both hands and encouraged the crossing of a goose with an octopus? It would then be possible for everyone to have a leg at Christmas and there would be far less argument at the dinner table in homes ranging from the Poles to the Equator – especially at a time when peace and harmony should reign and stomachs should be filled without competition and rivalry.

Many thanks indeed for your time and consideration and I look forward to hearing from you in the very near future with regard to this important issue.

Sincerely

M. A. Lee

Michael A. Lee

THE GOOSE CLUB

Secretary Mrs D Moss,
Llwyn Coed,
Gelli,
Clynderwen,
Pembrokeshire SA66 7HW
01437 563309

23/10/2004

www.gooseclub.org.uk

Dear Mr Lee,

Thankyou for your entertaining letter. I will include it in the next issue of The Goose Club Journal, - which unfortunately is not due out till after Christmas – and ask readers for their comments. I should however point out that most of our members are not concerned with producing geese for the table, but they keep them for companionship, guarding, mowing the lawn etc.

Yours Sincerely,

D Moss

Denise Moss

MPP Holdings Limited, Grantham, Lincolnshire NG31 8HZ.
Tel: 01476 571015. Fax: 01476 579713.
www.padley.co.uk

19th October 2004

Mr M A Lee
Somewhere in West Yorkshire

Dear Sir,

Thank you for your letter. We are disappointed that you had cause to complain but must point out that your letter was misdirected due to the fact that Padleys do not deal in turkeys.

However we have taken the time to research prestigious scientific papers relating to the further development in the rearing of Turkeys and are pleased to advise you that your contention that turkey breeders are not scratching the surface of technology is incorrect.

Our research indicates that extensive, but as yet unpublished scientific experimentation, of crossing a turkey with an octopus has resulted in a hybrid which with the aid of 8 legs can only travel in circles, sometimes at rates matching that of a fairground 'waltzer'. At these speeds the hybrid either takes off like a hovercraft or bores into the ground like an oil exploration drill. Both landing and surfacing have proved very energy consuming thus causing poor growth of the all important legs. We are happy to report that a spin-off of this experimentation has seen the creation of a further hybrid which is now being commercially exploited. This is the living 'Writing Companion™' which combines an endless supply of quill pens and an ink well (sac) which has cornered the supply to monasteries throughout the world. A further variation under development is the introduction of a gene from a chameleon which will provide ink sacs of a multitude of colours, an undoubted boon to monks everywhere.

Mainstream work has however been halted due to Animal right activists/Vivisectionists and the pro-octopus lobby.

Spurred on by the initial success by the turkey breeders, chicken producers have made tentative steps towards crossing chickens with millipedes to produce a Chickenpede. This activity has mainly been left unharassed by Activists due to it sounding phonetically like Chicken Feed, (a lesser but emerging topic on the world stage). Work will continue on this exciting research, however it is reported that the 'Creepy Crawlies Union' (represented by Ant and Dec) are showing unwanted interest.

Should the research for the multilegged Christmas bird succeed we can all look forward to not only pulling a cracker but also pulling a leg in global harmony in the near future.

Yours sincerely,

Evan A Laffe.

311

Epilogue ...

As I grow increasingly older I love to complain more and more.

There is a wonderful satisfaction in being a moaning, contentious, grumpy old man who is adept at spotting faults, problems and difficulties around every corner.

I find great personal value and enjoyment in criticizing the insincerity of politicians, the time-wasting of corporate organisation and the foolishnesses of self important and deluded cults of every shape and size and especially the ones that declare themselves infallible.

But there has been even more fun in complaining about the fantastical, the impossible and the mundane issues within this section of the book as no-one else has seemingly thought to complain about such things before.

This section was, until very recently, virgin territory.

I hope that you have enjoyed reading my plethora of complaints.

I wonder which one you have enjoyed the most? Perhaps you have been inspired to complain a bit more yourself? I encourage you to do so; it is great therapy in a world where traffic lights are always the same, predictable three colours and where rivers never run uphill to the mountains.

If your local librarian annoys you because she is a thin lipped, po-faced, horn-rimmed glasses- wearing prudish frump, complain to her manager or write to the local newspaper.

It wont help community relations but, by Zeus, you'll feel so much better and so will I!

The Author ...

Michael Anthony Lee – to his friends, 'Tony' – was born with a full head of ginger hair in the West Yorkshire town of Huddersfield just in time for lunch on 1st December 1959. 50 years later, he now has next to no hair at all but still has a voracious appetite and is never late for meals whatever the time of the day. After a solid upbringing by his characterful parents, Frank and Betty – no relation to the characters in *Some Mothers Do 'Ave 'Em* – Michael [i.e. Tony] swapped his West Yorkshire home for North Yorkshire college at the tender age of 18 and went on to complete a course of study leading to his graduation as one of life's many geographers.

He then embarked upon a post-graduate journey through life as someone not entirely sure what he wanted to do for a living nor where, nor why, nor even how, but certain he preferred his shortened middle name to his first name and thus became a listless wanderer and jack of several temporary trades.

Over a period of two years Michael [Tony] dabbled in the worlds of Scottish youth hostel wardening, house building and rolling cloth in a Yorkshire woollen mill. He exercised his duties planting mango trees and packaging guitar strings as a Kibbutz volunteer in the Negev Desert and logging silver birch trees as a forester in the North of England.

As time passed our 21st Century Don Quixote decided to settle for a sales position which he regarded as a temporary stopgap whilst he waited for something more appropriate to present itself. 27 years later, he is still waiting for such alternative career inspiration and is still persevering in the sales arena although exactly what the logical reason for this is evades his understanding.

Recent years saw the appearance of latent writing skills bubble to the surface of a rather quirky and esoteric mind when Michael [Tony] began to apply for a selection of unusual and usually non-existent jobs for which he was neither qualified nor even vaguely suitable.

His first book, *Written In Jest,* containing these job applications and a wide range of wonderful replies was published in 2002. Two further books entitled *Wanted: One Freudian Slip* and *Nothing To Complain About* were published in 2003 and 2006 when he also attempted to secure impossible items from and lodge incredible complaints to a variety of organizations. When not writing letters, Michael [Tony] writes short stories, poems and shopping lists.

When the days and dark and damp he is an avid reader and a very poor guitar player. When the days are clear and sunny he is a runner, a cyclist and a canoeist. He is a family man, an established after dinner and motivational speaker and even claims to be a little bit 'psychic'. He is also the Officially Appointed Beast of Bodmin Moor.